The Hearing Voices Series

FLAME VINE

His Voices

Charles Porter

www.charlesporterauthor.com

Library of Congress Cataloging-in-Publication Data
Porter, Charles
Library of Congress Control Number: 2017909232
    Charles Porter, Loxahatchee, FL
ISBN: 9780989425629 (trade paper)
ISBN: 9780989425636 (ePub)

Printed in the United States of America by Health Communications, Inc., Deerfield Beach, Florida.

For Bill, Julia, and Ethel Porter

Contents

PART TWO

Gathered

Sonny: the Tin Snip Killer

Aubrey: main character

Triple Suiter: Aubrey's other voice

Amper Sand: Triple Suiter's other voice

Leda: Aubrey's wife

The Junior: old schoolmate

Arquette: old schoolmate

Melinda: Arquette's girlfriend

Punky: old schoolmate

Nell Kitching: institutionalized schoolmate

John Chrome: English teacher/surfer

Rose Mothershed: John Chrome's girlfriend

Reve: a gypsy woman

SCHEMA

THE INCONTINENCE:

Killing	Swallowing
Screwing	Thinking
Drugging	Drinking
Fighting	None

THE GUILT:

Murder	Blue jays
Women	Fat
Fidelity	Brother
Vietnam	None

THE GAS:

Freon	Neon
Nitrous	Chloroform
Smoke	Bowel
Ozone	None

THE JOY:

Each other

Foreword

The condition of hearing voices is not always pathological, and many voice hearers do not come forward or tell anyone for fear of being discriminated against. This is not a story about paranormal powers, nor is it fantasy or magic realism. This fictional piece is taken from the real world, the scientific world, and South Florida's cultural landscape, except my theory about slippers—voices one hears in their head that live on the neuronal roads and in the vast, unknown spandrels of the brain. The reader does not have to believe in slippers, but I do.

This book is a prequel to the novel *Shallcross*, by the same author; however, the two books do not have to be read in order.

DEDICATED TO THE HEARING VOICES MOVEMENT

ALL CHARACTERS IN THIS STORY ARE FICTIONAL.

PART ONE

*There are two worlds! But they cannot
be explained by Plato, only schizophrenia.*

—Triple Suiter

In 2004, a man named Charles Porter unlocks a door to an abandoned shop called Sonny's Bookstore. On a table display he sees a book with his name on it and opens it to the first page. The page describes him walking into the bookstore, finding a book with his name on it and reading a story about him walking into a bookstore, seeing his name on a book, opening it to the first page and reading a story about himself reading a story about himself in a book . . . infinitely.

Don Quixote—2nd book

Chapter 1

THE GAS

Summer 1950

He, Sonny, had Newman blue eyes and lived with his mother in a Georgia town called Ludowici, his father's body left on a German battlefield somewhere, tripwire racked and ruined. Sonny played football and was president of his high school class, the class of 1950.

Mr. Thompson's appliance store gave him a summer job, and Randy White learned him to huff Freon, unscrewing the copper tube from refrigerators to take the spew into his lungs and ride his blood. His halfback legs would fly him through town in his underwear, no shirt, while his mother cried and the police watched him circle, too fast to catch with that coolant in his sweat. After he collapsed, the police took their football hero home.

Sonny was not right. Couldn't stand it when his mother said the word bosom, wrinkled her neck, looked down at her large breasts, and made him do things like stand at the open door of the bathroom to talk to her while she used the toilet. He hated the bosom word and the bathroom thing, though he didn't know why. His mother was mean. Spread her pox throughout the house and pounded his every behavior.

He got help from Dr. Price, the minister, and his old scoutmaster for huffing Freon, but still he huffed in private. Sonny found gasoline fumes, too, but Freon was the best way to make his head slop.

Randy White and him got high on weekends. At Randy's, when their girlfriends were there, they showed off their facile football moves by chasing armadillos on the lawn, grabbing the half-blind animal's tail on the run, holding it up for the girls while the creature kicked and scratched at their hands. That's how Dr. Price thought Sonny got leprosy, from the nine-banded armadillo that carried the bacterium in its hind legs where the temperature is only 93 degrees and perfect for the disease to wait. Dr. Price had seen it in India and by law, Sonny was sent to the leprosarium in Carville, Louisiana, for a year, to have no contact with anyone on the outside.

His right hand became a half-numb claw, and he bitterly drew perverse pictures with it on paper that seemed to move instead of the pen. Sonny read everything in the leper colony library to fight boredom and engaged in an orgy of self-education. There was a craft shop where he learned to make a ship in a bottle. He liked things inside of things that couldn't get out, especially things he hated or was afraid of, and he was afraid of ships. A recurring dream put him on the open ocean in a little dory. A whaling vessel, the *Charles W. Morgan,* came towards him, and on the bow stood his mother with a harpoon. Sonny made the dream go away by making a model of the *Charles Morgan* inside a bottle, where it could never get out. Forever.

In the library, Sonny read every day. He read that Christopher Wren built a telescope with a lens from a horse's eye and that the Turks believed women had no souls. He studied the Old Testament, especially the Book of Job, and was surprised to learn God bet Satan he could torture Job and kill his children and Job would take it, like Sonny was taking it, because God was torturing him. Sonny wondered what kind of god did things like that.

He read that William Blake said God was showing Job the mulatto between the terrible and the sublime, and Sonny nodded to himself then whittled a whole new idea about righteousness and killing.

At the leper place, he stared at the refrigerators in the main dining room and thought about Freon. He studied the properties of other gases, and a man at Carville showed him how to knock off a prison tattoo using burnt ash and a pin. Sonny scratched the word MIDGE on the inside of his forearm in honor of Thomas Midgley, who discovered Freon. "Halo carbons," they were called, and they would give you a halo if you wanted.

Sonny received injections of a new drug called Promin to kill the progress of the leper disease and was told he could go home. Bitter, sad—a quiet hothead that viewed the whole world as a leprosarium—he carried a mean hammer in his good hand. "Too bad about the other hand," the doctors said.

In the woods at Randy White's, people dumped trash, so Sonny dragged an old Frigidaire to a clear spot in the palmettos. He made a shrine there to Our Lady of White Appliances and decided to sacrifice things he thought should atone for his father getting killed in the war, his mother's punishments and weirdness, and being locked away at Carville. Sonny didn't have the nerve to kill Dr. Price, so the first things he offered up to the White Appliance Lady were Dr. Price's nasty Jack Russell and the minister's cat, which ran loose in the town. He put them in the refrigerator with their owner's pictures from the newspaper and closed the door to see what the last shape they chose would be. He arranged their bodies inside as he did the ships in bottles he made and created a strange Cabinet of Cat and Dog, with flowers, bones, empty Mayonnaise jars, and barbed wire from the surrounding area. When the display was complete, he went down on one knee to his oblation and thought about Mr. Blake's "Tyger, tyger, burning bright," along with the terrible and sublime. He considered himself a wizard of enclosed things now, though his love for animals made him later regret what he did with this particular piece.

That same year, he got a job with a roofing company cutting flashing for valleys and overhangs, a skill he had learned in the leper colony, possible with one hand while he steadied things with the sclerotic one. In the colony at night, if he couldn't sleep, he rolled the edge of a blanket into a cone and ran it over the webbing between his fingers and the palm of his hand to feel the pleasurable fluctuations of skin conduction from the woof of the fabric. The sensation made him flip

3

his tongue back and suck like a shoat; as a child, he had done this for comfort when he was scared of his mother. His mother worked in a dentist's office and told him if he kept up the habit, his little tongue would push out his front teeth like the ventriloquist's dummy, Mortimer Snerd, and Sonny would have buckteeth when he grew up. The mother called what Sonny did with his blanket and mouth "morting."

Sonny was terrified of Mortimer Snerd after that—something called *automatonophobia*, or "fear of a ventriloquist's dummy." His mother tried to catch Sonny morting in his bed at night with her flashlight. She even made a rough version of a dummy with a coconut head and white seashells for bucked teeth that looked like Mortimer and chased him with it around the house, telling him Mortimer had special ears to hear children making those sucking noises. She said the dummy wanted to save every child from buckteeth. "He will come and fix you. You'll see! He has a pair of snips, and he will race into the room and split your tongue like a crow's so you can't suck it back, and then he'll split your lips and privates with those snips for doing that stupid thing you do. A split tongue is better than buckteeth!" Soon after this, Sonny started to hear voices when he was upset, hid from them under his blanket, another enclosure, and he morted even more with his tongue.

At the roofing company, he cut flashing all day with his good hand, whose haptic senses had been heightened by disuse of the other. He felt the urge to mort with his mouth when the tin snips sliced through the thin metal. Something about that produced the same pleasure as rubbing the palm of his hand on the rolled end of his blanket. It seemed to throb the same locus. He rolled his tongue back as he cut the tin and sucked. Slack! Sluck! Clup! Clup!

One weekend, he went with a guy he hardly knew from work to an out-of-town place. They planned to huff Freon and drink with an older woman who lived there. By nine o'clock, the guy was chemically dead and the woman was very high. The woman came on to Sonny, who sort of froze, and when she was performing with her mouth, it made that sound. Slack! Sluck! Slack! Sluck! Sonny saw his mother on a toilet in a hallucination talking to Mortimer Snerd. His mother stood up, straightened her dress, and came towards him with Mortimer and his snips. The woman, who was all over Sonny, wet herself, blacked out, and stopped breathing from the Freon. It all disgusted him. No less deranged himself by Thomas Midgley's gas, he walked to the other guy's truck and got a pair of tin snips, then began cutting places on the woman's body as he would roof flashing, especially places where the skin was webbed or thin. He split long strips across her abdomen, and the sensation made his tongue roll back and mort as the fluctuations travelled through his body. She never woke up, and died in the Freon's copper coffin. Last, he split her tongue. No one knew Sonny was there, and the other guy was blamed.

The mother and son moved to Stuart, Florida, where the mother took a job working in another dentist's office. Sonny was glad and ready to get out of Georgia. They rented an apartment on the second floor of a building close to the St. Lucie River, and Sonny got a job in a bookstore downtown owned by old Mr. Crane. Since he was considered partially disabled, it was something Sonny could do and still get to read all the time.

Sonny killed again in1954, though he did not mean to.

On the sidewalk in front of the bookstore, he saw a lady named Rebecca Kitching slap her little girl's face. He knew the lady and her child, Nell, as frequent customers. Nell was before her time as a reader, and Sonny had ordered *20,000 Leagues under the Sea* and *Anne of Green Gables* for her. The mother, Rebecca, seemed jealous of the attention Sonny gave the child. The incident on the sidewalk, the slap, enraged him.

A week later, he passed Rebecca on the shoulder of the road with a flat and stopped to help with the best of intentions. She kept looking down at her bosom like his mother did, checking her dress cleavage, and giving something of the look to Sonny. She told him she had to go to the bathroom urgently, gave him the smile and the look again, and ran to the bushes. While working to loosen the tire lugs, Sonny, the ostensible Samaritan, heard the voices in his head and went to the palmettos where Mrs. Kitching was. He hit her with the tire iron until her jaw hung open.

He took her unconscious in his car to a backwoods area where he had made another shrine, like the one he made in Georgia, to Our Lady of White Appliances. A smile was on his face as he filled her lungs with Freon from the old refrigerator he had put there and watched her quit and die. He helped himself to the halo gas, and when he was high as Himalayas, he cut the webbing between Rebecca's toes, her ear lobes, her smooth abdomen, her lips, her lips. . . slack, sluck, slack, sluck. His tongue went to the roof of his mouth. He placed her body inside the junked refrigerator and arranged her limbs akimbo, then surrounded Rebecca with wild flowers and small trash items from the area's heap. Last, he split her tongue. Now the mother was permanently enclosed, and she would never slap or hurt her daughter Nell again.

Sonny wrote "Ship in a Bottle" with Rebecca's blood on the refrigerator door, looked up at the scalloped clouds of Florida, and was moved to speak a famous line from Mr. E.E. Cummings he'd smashed up like he did Rebecca: "How do you like your blue-eyed boy now, Mr. Raggedy-ass God?" Sonny never had sex of any kind with Rebecca, nor would he ever again with any of his other victims after the lady he killed up in Georgia. Rebecca Kitching left behind her daughter Nell and her husband John.

Sonny could have hidden his work, but felt he had to give the town Mrs. Kitching—some kind of pissing on the courthouse, or steps of a church, piss that smelled of rage and hormone. The tin snips he used were there with Rebecca when someone found the still life creation two days later.

From the second story of his mother's apartment, Sonny could look into the yard of a house that he knew belonged to the Shallcross family. It sat on the river. An eight-year-old boy played there. Sonny liked children and young adults but had a problem with older women if he thought they were mean. The boy he watched in the yard seemed to be talking to someone else, someone who was not there. The town's people were discussing Rebecca's murder, putting three and three together to get seven. "Who could have?" the newspaper asked. "The body in the refrigerator was the work of a psychotic." The local and national papers called the murderer "The Tin Snip Killer."

One day, Sonny walked across the street to the river and saw the boy from next door wading after blue crabs near the sewer line. The boy was talking to himself again.

"Hey! What's your name, kid?"

"Aubrey, sir." The boy turned, holding up two crabs in his dip net.

"You must be a Shallcross, then, from the pointed-roof house up there."

The boy nodded.

"I hope you're not gonna let your mother boil those for you, now

7

that they been eatin lunch on the sewer pipe."

"No, sir. My friends and me sell 'em to the Yankee tourists."

"I bet the niggers will eat 'em."

"My daddy says that's a bad word."

"Yeah, your daddy's tellin the truth, mainly."

Sonny looked down at his hand soon after that. He thought the leprosy was back. This time, he begged to go to Carville to get away from the town. They did a new surgical procedure while he was there. Two months later, he was home showing off his repair, working in the bookstore, taking walks down to the river, and watching the boy Aubrey wading for crabs and talking out loud to no one. Sonny sensed this child was like him—not right.

You don't know a thing about him without you have read a book by the name of *Shallcross*, but that ain't no matter. That book was given out by him and Mr. Charles Porter, and they told the truth, pretty much. There was things what they stretched, but mostly they told the truth.

– Huck Finn

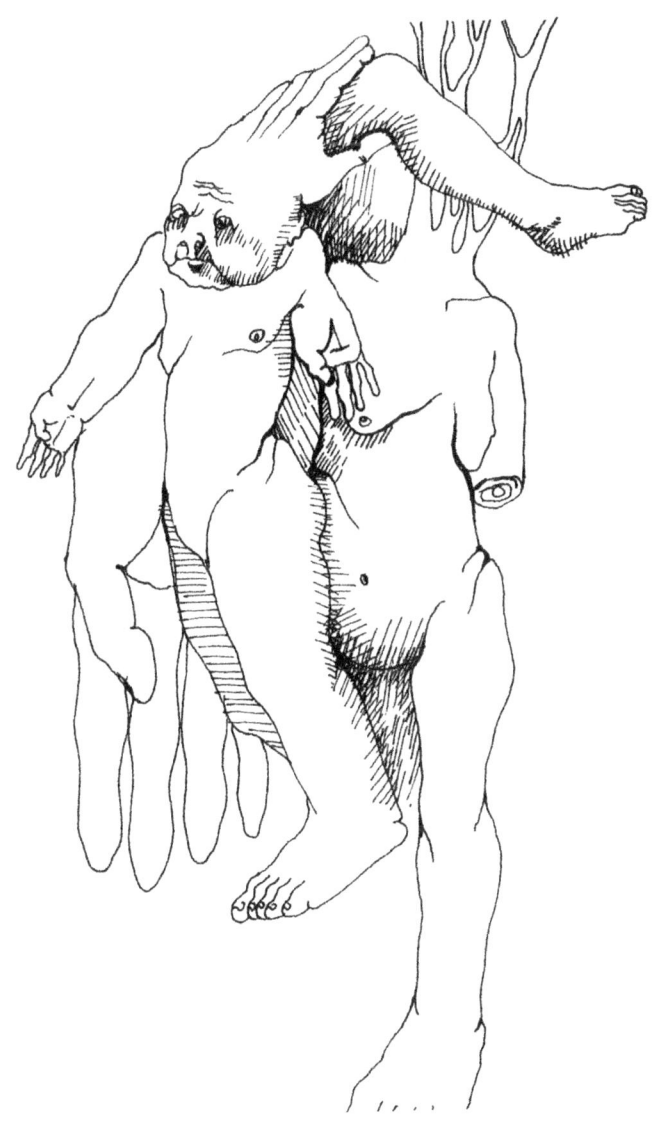

Chapter 2

AUBREY

JULY 1952

"**When you walk the seawall, don't look at your feet or you'll fall,** kid!" Paul Gray said.

That's me on the wall. Aubrey. My last name is Shallcross. I am eight years old, and I am an only child. I live in Stuart, Florida, on the St. Lucie River that goes to the Atlantic Ocean. In the summer, we are all scared of polio and our typhoid shots, and we have them big smallpox scars on our arms. I'm a white kid. It's a time the grownups call seg- segra-gation.

The river is a mile wide by my house. You can follow it the other way through the St. Lucie canal and cross Lake Okeechobee and go out the Caloosa-somethin River to the Gulf of Mexico, then to New Orleans if you want, my daddy said.

My river is full of silver mullet in the summer, and them snook hunt 'em like water wolves, my daddy said, too. I lie with my head in the upstairs window at night when it's really hot, and I can hear gazillions of them mullet jumping over the water to keep ahead of the wolves. They sound like rain. In the winter, the black and white wild ducks come to sit on the river like old Yankees sit on our benches downtown. My momma said there must be a special place in hell for people from New Jersey.

I have a needlefish skull tied around my neck, like the other boys on the river. It hangs there next to my Miraculous Medal with Mary, the mother of Jesus, and the two of them bounce together when I run up the bank to my grandmother's house. She sits on her sofa and says her rosary every day. Momma says Grandmother is old fashioned, like this dead queen in England named Victoria. She sits there, her dress pulled up on her leg for her sugar diabetes shot. Once, before I was born, my grandmother lived in Italy to be closer to the Pope. She liked that Musso-, Musso-lini man, too, because he made the trains run on time. Momma says Grandmother is in a club called John Birch, and she thinks there is a communist under every bed.

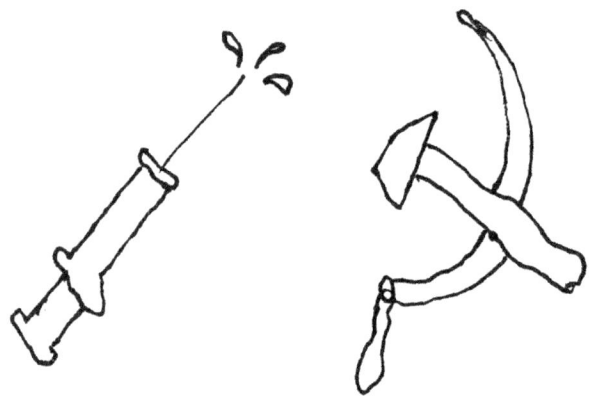

"I've told you before, Aubrey," Grandmother said. "If you eat candy, you'll get the sugar diabetes like me and have to get a shot every morning." I wouldn't even put sugar on my cereal after she said that. My daddy thinks his mother shouldn't make up her mind about people like Musso-lini when her blood sugar is low he said. When she sticks the needle in her leg, I wrinkle my nose the way Momma wrinkles hers when her hand goes toward my mouth with a spoon full of medicine.

"Now that's done," Gramma said, "show me your guardian angels, darling."

14

I lifted my shirt. Two next to my belly button, one on my ribs, one just above a hipbone. My moles.

"Now your grandmother wants to see the big angel mole, Triple Suiter."

I lifted my left arm and under there he was—"The Viceroy," she called him, like them cigarettes— the big mole that protected me and bossed the other moles around. I named him Triple Suiter after the three-piece dress-up suit my father puts on to go to Mass. I always kept Triple Suiter dressed like that, even though he was a mole on my skin and an angel at the same time. He could tell you more about me than I ever could.

"Now let's say our angel prayer together, lovey." Grandmother makes the sign of the cross. "Angel of God, my guardian dear, to whom God's love you hold me near. Ever this day, be at my side, to light, to guard, to rule, and guide. Amen."

That night, I had the bad dream.

I was on a sidewalk under a street light. A door slammed in the dark place behind me and somebody counted, "One Mississippi, two Mississippi. . . " Slim bone hands came out like a red toad's tongue and put a kitchen toaster down my throat. It's because when I was a baby, I would swallow things so they were mine. I go blind after that from this big spot in my eyes. Triple Suiter, my guardian angel, chased away a

15

man he calls the Slim Hand and saves me from choking on the toaster in my dream. My eyes come back. I wake up crying, and Trip sings me this song he made up to make me better.

LITTLE BOY, BUILD YOUR TREE HOUSE OF RAINBOWS.

BUILD A FENCE FOR YOUR HORSE MADE OF CLOUDS.

HANG A SIGN FROM A BRANCH OF YOUR BANYAN TREE.

TELL THE GROWN-UPS THEY'RE JUST NOT ALLOWED.

LITTLE BOY, BE A DREAMER.

GO BATHE IN THE NORTHEAST WIND.

NEVER MIND THOSE DOWN BELOW YOU

WHO WANT YOU TO BE JUST LIKE THEM.

My mother told the neighbor lady, "Aubrey got a toy soldier and other things caught in his throat when he was real small, and we had to go to the hospital a few times. The doctor said he gets grown people who want to swallow strange things, too, like rocks, forks, bottle tops, even knives, you know. He said those people have something called 'pica'. I'll never forget that doctor. He was this tall man with red hair and long-fingered hands."

Lots of Florida kids drown, so I had swimming lessons. Arquette Orlander, a redheaded boy my age, would punch me under water and say the moles on my body looked like buggers, and he called another boy that had something wrong "a cripple." But my grandma told me them moles on me were angel heads 'cause God showed he liked me better than other people to love, honor, and obey him in this world and the next by giving me extra moles. She said if that boy Arquette didn't watch out, God would get him for teasing me and calling that other boy, David, a cripple. Besides, Arquette was a Protestant with no moles, and Protestants went to a part of heaven that didn't have a swimming pool. My grandmother said they belonged to something called "the Low Church." Sister Raymond Claire told me Protestants didn't have guardian angels, either, because the angels were all Catholic like me. Even my mother was a Methodist but she was taking Catholic lessons to make my father and grandmother happy.

My father was born in the house we lived in, and he slept in the same room he was born in with my mother. People called our house the Owl House because the roofs ended in points at the top and looked like the ears of a big owl. Gramma said the man who made it in 1905 wanted the ears to break the wind of the hurricanes.

Daddy worked on the fishing boats for Shark Industries when I was six. They put bloody pieces of meat on hooks in the ocean. Every day, the men went out and pulled them sharks up. I learned all their names—mako, tiger, hammerhead, bull, leopard, and black tip. They would bring 'em back, take out their livers for the oil, and sell the fins to Chinese places for soup. The sharks would be dead on the docks, looking at me with open eyes that said, "Your daddy killed me." I always thought sharks were after me after that. My daddy showed me how to knock their teeth out with a hammer so I could sell them teeth downtown for a nickel an envelope to the mean old Yankees from New Jersey.

When the shark place closed, my father had a boat building business next to our place. He made rowboats and motor boats out of wood with his hands and tools, and everyone thought they were beautiful, but then when these other people started making a lot of them at one time out of something called fiberglass, he went broke.

My father stayed in his borning and married room for a long time after that. One day, an ambulance came and took him, bleeding inside his stomach, to the hospital. He had what they called a nervous breakdown. My parent's friends gave him blood to keep him alive. After he got better, a friend helped him get a car place. He had only two cars for sale on a dirt lot.

At my First Communion, the nun sat us down and told us what a great day this was. If we crossed the street right now and got hit by a car, we would go straight to heaven because we had just swallowed the body and blood of Jesus like he said we had to, "Or next time we see Him, we better run."

All of this was just perfect to me. That sent my swallowing thing to the moon, and it was the first time I wanted to die, too. I wanted to go out in the street and get hit by a car so I could go straight to heaven and swim in the big pool, but I was so happy with how it felt to swallow God's blood and body and fully know him, like sister Raymond Claire said we should, that I forgot about the pool. I could hardly wait 'til my next Holy Communion.

My favorite day in the church was February 3, when the priest blessed all our throats as we knelt at the communion rail to cheer for St. Blaise, the patron saint of throats, who was famous for saving some kid who was choking on a fish bone. You can see from the story about my life and swallowing things that I'm telling you why he was my favorite saint—'cause of my pica, the doctor called it, I mean. But when I swallow good things, like peanut butter, it turns into colors, sounds, smells, and comic books in my mind; and especially when I swallow the blessed host, the body and blood of our Lord Jesus, things get pretty cool with singing and stained glass and stuff, and I always say, "Yay!" after it goes down.

~

Ad Deum qui laetificat juventutem meam
(To God Who giveth joy to my youth)

I am twelve

My parents read a lot of books. They made me read and speak right, now that I'm older, so momma said I won't "sound like a hayseed." Some nights we spend with our television watching *Wagon Train*, *The Hit Parade*, and *Bishop Fulton J. Sheen*, a famous Catholic star. We eat chocolate syrup over ice cream on TV trays, now that I am old enough not to believe what my grandmother said about sugar diabetes.

One year, back when I was ten, my dad, out of his love and time, made a sailboat for me called a pram. When I helped him put in the brass screws and turned them the wrong way, he said, "Watch me, Aubrey. To put them in, you say righty-tighty. To take them out you say lefty-loose. Everything—bolts, screws, water spigots, and maybe even life—works this way, son. Righty-tighty and lefty-loose. Sometimes, though, you get what they call a cross thread, or reverse thread, and for reasons hard to understand, things go the opposite way you thought they would. There'll be a lot of cross threads in your life, but you'll figure them out."

After that, I started to think of most things and my ideas that way. I turned my thoughts into pictures and words that turned easily both ways, just to see how they looked, and I would sometimes cross thread them, too, just to see how they looked a little messed up.

There were years I grew too fast, my arms like sticks, my neck thin in a tortured spawn. I wore shirts with certain collars to hide my skinny neck and long sleeves over my arms when other kids were filling out. I knew how to make a ligament in my neck stand out if a girl looked at me from the side so my neck looked bigger when I turned my head and looked back at her. I made promises in the mirror that I would always help skinny kids when I grew up, like fat kids must make promises to help fat kids, and my parents gave me mountains of encouragement and love because of who they were.

There were doctors to patch me up—stitches, vaccinations, and dreaded enemas, because medicine considered constipation a big deal in the 1950s. Maybe it was because we ate a lot of Spam and pound cake. I don't know. Our only town doctor had two large pictures in his office. One showed a boy sitting on the toilet smiling that said, "Johnny can," and the same boy on the toilet in the other picture, frowning, that said, "Johnny can't." That doctor loved enemas. The boy in the picture looked like the ones Mr. Rockwell drew on the cover of *The Saturday Evening Post* magazine.

I was a child with "a very large imagination," my mother would say, instead of just a liar. I loved every TV western: *The Rifleman, Gun Smoke, Paladin*. I could do imitations of all of them, but my favorite show was *The Rebel*, with Johnny Yuma, who had blonde hair like me.

My first best friend, besides Arquette Orlander, was a big kid named The Junior, who lived on a ranch twenty miles away, in a place called Indiantown. We both pretended we were Johnny Yuma all the time and rode horses to explore the ranch. I got a horse of my own for Christmas and have been in love with horses ever since.

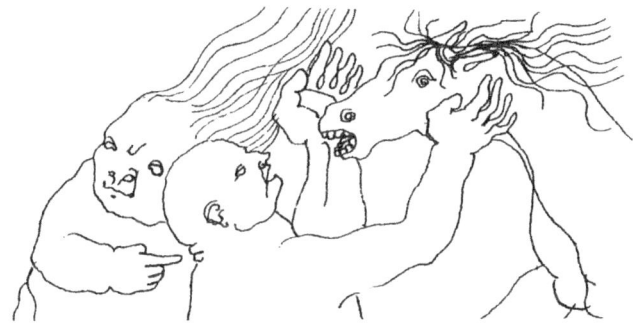

My next best friend after that was The Junior's friend Punky, who loved sweet potatoes and could fart anytime you asked him to because he ate those potatoes every day. Then there was the girl Nell Kitching, in our class. We felt bad for Nell, because her mother was murdered by someone called the Tin Snip Killer when we were all in fourth grade, and the whole town was afraid for a year.

We lived in this quiet place with two rivers around us. It had not been discovered by builders yet, my dad would say and shake his head. Our town's people lived and died like people in every town. Our doctors took out everything they could think of—tonsils, gall bladders, women's parts, and men's parts. It was called their Magnificent Obsession, which was a book my parents read by Dr. Frank G. Slaughter. Slaughter—what a name for a doctor who wrote books about taking out people's body parts.

There was polio that took two ranch kids The Junior knew. There were car accidents people called "head-on collisions!" There were twin brother and sister classmates of mine, Harold and Betty, who drowned together last year off Ski Point, and we watched from the beach while they dragged with hooks for their bodies. A man on a boat yelled, "I got something." When they pulled poor Harold and Betty up, they had their arms wrapped around each other, as if they were hugging. I was standing next to Nell Kitching. Nell fell down on her knees and started screaming when she saw the bodies in that death hug and then strange enough, she started laughing. My mother would have drowned *me* if she knew I was there to see all that.

My mom is from North Carolina and says, "We live in a Norman Rockwell town on the St. Lucie River in the middle of a palmetto kingdom, a small town like Mr. Rockwell's, in Vermont, only with coconuts, guavas, damn snakes, scorpions, and mango trees, instead of maples." She misses the mountains.

23

Chapter 3

I Wax

I knew a man and his wife who lived down the riverbank from us. He was a fisherman, and she was a real gypsy lady from Quebec. The man's name was Coker Barnes, and his wife's name was Reve, which meant "dream" in French. Reve said children that drown, like my schoolmates Harold and Betty, get their spirits turned into water souls and stay underwater forever, because right before they die they go into this dream, such a beautiful dream, with colored fish everywhere, and they don't want to be anywhere else but under the water.

Reve saw me talking to myself and seemed to know I wasn't just talking to myself. She said I had something called a "slipper" in my mind, and that was a good thing, if it was a good slipper. She said she had a slipper of her own. I took Nell Kitching over there one day, and when Nell went down to look at the river, Reve told me Nell had a slipper, too, and that Nell knew she had a slipper. I told her mine was just my guardian angel and secret friend, Triple Suiter, and she smiled and shook her head.

Reve made me a ring out of a small bone that floats inside a toad frog's skull. She called it a *crapaudine*—French, I think. She glued the stone in silver, and the stone would change colors to mean all these different things were happening around me. Triple Suiter never liked

Reve or the ring. He was jealous, and could be a pill sometimes.

In the seventh grade, I sat next to Nell, who always made straight A's and was getting pretty cute. Arquette sat on the other side of her, and he thought she was cute, too. She started bringing a cricket to school in a Ball jar, with a stick inside for it to climb. Nell told me the cricket was her secret friend. His name was Black Socks. I told her about Triple Suiter and showed her the large mole in my left armpit, but only her, nobody else in my class, because she was so cute and weird.

Nell said if she closed her eyes, she and Black Socks could make anything change shape, or they could become movie stars, like Debbie Reynolds or Alan Ladd, or that new singer Elvis Presley. She said she saw her Ball jar in her mind with all these things inside if she needed them. She said the jar would take her anywhere, even under the ocean with Captain Nemo, where she and Nemo moved along the reefs off Jensen Beach in the Nautilus and saw extinct fishes, golden groupers, and big manta rays go by the glass window in the submarine. The glass window was like another Ball jar, she said. They would stare and wonder at things in the rivers and oceans, like our drowned schoolmates Harold and Betty must do now. Nell and Nemo spoke an extinct language called Atlantis to each other, and she spoke it to me sometimes. We were all big on Nemo back then, because in the fourth grade we had seen Kirk Douglas in *20,000 Leagues under the Sea* at our theater downtown.

I wanted a Ball jar for a window like the one in the Nautilus to see my own daydreams, or drifties, Momma called them. I complained about it to Triple Suiter, who I had not outgrown but cultivated, like a royal palm. Trip and I made a jar like Nell's in my mind, and I placed an imaginary copy of the toadstone ring the gypsy lady made for me inside.

One day in class, Nell had a kind of fit. She said she and Nemo hit the reef off Jensen Beach and split their heads wide open. The Ball jar broke, and so did the Nautilus. The water rushed in. Her cricket, Black Socks, drowned like Harold and Betty. She said she saw Harold and Betty with big smiles in the window of the Nautilus right before they hit the reef. Mrs. Johnson, our teacher, ran back to the room with the school nurse, and Nell was screaming about Harold and Betty and the cricket. Nell wouldn't let go of her desk because she said it was Betty. These other people came and took Nell out, still in the desk. She left the Ball jar turned over on the floor and started to yell, "Ship in a bottle. Ship in a bottle." My diabetic Catholic grandmother told me Saint Scholastica protects children from convulsions, seizures, and low blood sugar, and Saint Peregrine protects us from cancer. I began praying to Saint Scholastica, because I was sure whatever Nell had wasn't cancer.

Arquette, Punky, The Junior, and me ran after them with Nell's jar, trying to tell Nell the cricket was okay and hadn't drowned, but they sent us back. I turned around once and saw them putting Nell in an ambulance. She was still sitting in her desk, hanging onto it like Betty's brother did Betty, so Betty wouldn't drown, I guess. Punky said, "I told you guys last year that girl had head lice. She got a part that ain't screwed on!"

Later, my mother told me Nell had a nervous breakdown, different from my dad's, and I overheard her talking about it with the black lady, Ella, who helped us keep our house.

That night, after I saw what happened to Nell, I had the bad swallow dream again. The pica monster came. The Slim Hand shoved one of my father's new cars from the car lot down my throat, and the blind spots appeared in my eyes. I heard Nell calling Triple Suiter and my names, and I knew she was right there with us. Triple Suiter ran down my mind's hallway after the Slim Hand, and when Trip came back, he began to sing this song in the dream to me and Nell to make us better.

KING CRÈME DE COCOA LIVES UP ABOVE

GIVES ALL THE CHILDREN COURAGE AND LOVE.

HE WROTE THE BIBLE; HE WROTE THE PSALMS.

HE WROTE THE TABLETS THE BIG LAWS ARE ON.

LIFE'S JUST A DANCE; I'LL SHOW YOU THE WAY.

THE SLIM HAND IS GONE; DON'T BE AFRAID.

I could see the words and hear a typewriter clicking, but could not see the person typing. Trip told me it was his own guardian angel, Amper Sand, who lived in the bone bowl of his chest. He said his guardian angel's name was on every typewriter in the universe, and stood for the word "and," which in a way meant there is always more and something was always next.

Two years later, Arquette and I were downtown and saw Nell with her aunt. They were talking to Sonny in front of the bookstore. He was the man I had known since I was eight and I used to fish for crabs off the sewer pipe. When Nell and her aunt started going the other way, Nell looked back at me, and I read her lips. She said my name then said, "Triple Suiter," pointed to her head, and smiled. I raised my hand to show my underarm, where my big mole was, and mouthed the words Black Socks. She was two years older now and prettier than ever, and Arquette, who was more than girl crazy, fanned his pants as we walked. We heard Nell was at this crazy place in Palm Beach County for rich people's weird kids; my mother said it was a good thing her father had money and her aunt could help him with her.

A year after that, I started going next door to see Sonny from the bookstore and his wife, Beth. We talked about miles of things you never heard in school, and they had an illegal book called *The Tropic of Cancer*. They read books all the time. Sonny's mother worked for my dentist, and she told me if I didn't brush my teeth, bad things would happen to me, and then she'd pinch me. She had a mean face, and I thought she *wanted* bad things to happen to me.

Sonny played guitar and sang the new music called "rock and roll" on weekends in a band called the Hot Weather Hotshots. Even though he'd had leprosy once, he could still hold a guitar pick in his hand. I liked to sing, and I had inherited my mother's voice. I could sing as high as Roy Orbison and Dee Clark when he sang that song "Raindrops." Sonny showed me chords on the guitar. I got a guitar for my birthday and wouldn't put it down.

I told Sonny about Nell having a fit and the cricket Black Socks, and he said a lot of people have secret friends. He called secret friends "sidecars," like on a motorcycle. I guessed Trip was my sidecar. I was fourteen now, but I didn't say a word to Sonny about Trip, because I promised Trip I wouldn't. Sonny said when people like Nell lost control, they switched places on the motorcycle and the secret friend drove the bike around, and Nell had to sit in the sidecar. He said normal people always drove the bike, and something called their neurosis sat in the sidecar unless it got out of hand for too long, then those people had to switch places with the neurosis and sit in the sidecar, and maybe go away to Chattahoochee in North Florida, another crazy place like where Nell is, until they learned how to drive the bike again.

That same year, The Junior and I got our first .22 rifles. One day, I did this bad thing. I wanted to kill something, anything, with my new gun; some force had hold of me. There was a family of blue jays in the trees above me, and I kept telling myself not to do it, it was cruel, but that urge to be powerful with the gun hissed at me like a pine bull snake. I made up this story in my head that the blue jays were bad birds because they raided other birds' nests, broke the eggs, and ate the babies. So I killed the baby killers one by one with clean shots from my Marlin rifle. To this day, it still haunts me. I know now most birds will raid a nest, not just blue jays, and so will human beings. We eat the young of everything, like eggs and baby back ribs. I pound my chest about it still, and sometimes when something bad happens to me, I say to myself, "It's because you killed the blue jays that day, Aubrey."

Every first of the month, The Junior and I went to the bookstore and asked Sonny for two things: a magazine called *True*, about outdoor adventures, and one called *The Western Horseman*. It seemed to me all of life was a magazine—pictures, stories, and what my father said about the way wood screws turn. When The Junior and I swore something was true to each other, we backed it up by saying, "*True* magazine!" instead of old saws like "On my mother's grave."

At fifteen, my grades were bad, so my folks sent me to a Catholic boarding school, a Benedictine monastery two hundred miles from home. That was the end of my other life for a while. Over the blackboard in every classroom was written that old spooky saying: "For what shall it profit a man if he gain the whole world, and suffer the loss of his immortal soul?" Any books we read had to be approved by the Index *Librorum Prohibitorum*, the Catholic censors. But I actually liked the thick required reading. I never forgot the opening lines in the *Adventures of Huckleberry Finn*, and I always tried to tell the truth, mostly, like it said. I stretched it some, but mostly, I told the truth, like Huck did.

I read *Catcher in the Rye*, *An Occurrence at Owl Creek Bridge*, by Ambrose Bierce, and Dickens's *Great Expectations*. I hoped my life would not have the ups and downs that Pip had in that story by Mr. Dickens. Even when things in my life were good, I thought of Pip and the murders I committed that day I shot the blue jays.

Trip told me he dealt with worries by writing his own stories. He said Amper Sand typed them out for him in a GOTHIC LETTER FONT. Trip called writing, "When your whittle monster gets loose." I liked poetry by now, too, so I began to write that instead of stories because I was good at rhymes.

After I came home from school at Christmas, I was enunciating big boarding school words all over the place. I loved words. The Junior said I sounded like one of those prissy boys, so I let it go and started talking like a redneck again around him. By this time, The Junior had offers from three major colleges to play football. That summer, he and I rode in high school rodeos. We got to practice at the ranches a lot in Indiantown and in 4H. We both rode small bulls and I rode some easier bareback broncs, which I was pretty good at, even in my teens.

When I was nineteen, my dad was driving a tractor in a field at The Junior's house to help out. He went under a palmetto frond with a flame vine hidden inside. It caught him under his chin, pulled him off the tractor into the disc behind, and killed him.

What was I to do now with their *unburied* Christ and my father's body I *had* to bury? I knew what their Yahweh did to Cain because he was a farmer of crops, and Cain would not cut the lamb's throat for Him, for sacrifice. This God. This hemal monster in the clouds who liked to sacrifice the young of everything and snatch people under the water, like my schoolmates, Harold and Betty.

At night, I dreamed about the Kafka book. Someone was writing a crime on my back I committed. I did not know what the crime was— maybe the blue jays I shot. Did God kill my father for that? What was it that made Him whom I worshiped take my father, Drayton Shallcross, from me? What forensic was I to accept from this careless supernal overlord, this invisible suzerain I had loved for years?

When it happened, I was away at college. Two priests called me upstairs and told me he was gone. I looked at them, shaking my head, and said, "Oh, no, the cross thread has come."

I walked out into the night alone and spoke to the sky. "Nothin's there, Nell Kitching," then I fell on the lawn of the cathedral and wept. Trip came to help me when I heard the door slam in the dark, and one Mississippi, two Mississippi. . . the Slim Hand jammed all the dead blue jays down my throat. Trip went after him. The Hand ran, and I started praying to Saint Blaise to save me from choking, and Saint Scholastica to protect me from convulsions and seizures. Moments later, for the first time, I saw Triple Suiter, three inches tall, standing on my forearm outside of my mind, a little neon man. He told me he was more than a guardian angel; he was a slipper from the region of voices, like Reve the gypsy said he was, and he looked just like I always saw him in my mind. I sobbed in the grass, and the inside of another kind of cathedral appeared in my head. There was a blind spot above the altar's basilica in the top of the high dome, blocking a view of heaven and the God I was raised with. I kept staring at the blind spot. Trip, too, was in this bone-walled cathedral with me. He began chanting one of his protective rhymes to hold me up during this awful nightmare.

WHEN YOU CAN'T SEE, TAKE A STRAIGHT SHOT

RIGHT THROUGH THE HEART OF THE BLIND SPOT.

TRUE MAGAZINE KNOWS THE TRUTH

RIGHTY-TIGHTY   LEFTY-LOOSE.

I promised I would never swallow the Catholic religion and their white host again. I wondered if this obsession had happened to other kids soaked in the sacrament like me, this phagomania hooked to the most powerful proposition in human history: the presence of an omnipotent being that could do no wrong and his insistence that we eat his body and drink his blood to know him or be erased from his kind of mercy.

There was an otherness about me now not related to the otherness of heaven or hell. It was the steel truth of the objective world I was all alone in for the first time, without God and *His* other world. There was a departure for me from one kind of consciousness to a new one.

My first person had split. The lone perception of me as "I" had become stereophonic. From here, it was me, Trip, and Amper Sand, in a lifetime of sounds, sights, cross talks, and cross threads forever.

I am the arch slipper, Triple Suiter,

The vapor of Able, the murdered shepherd,

And the counsel of Cain.

I ride in the saloon of the psyche,

On a black Underwood I type the

True magazine, and sign my name,

Amper Sand.

&

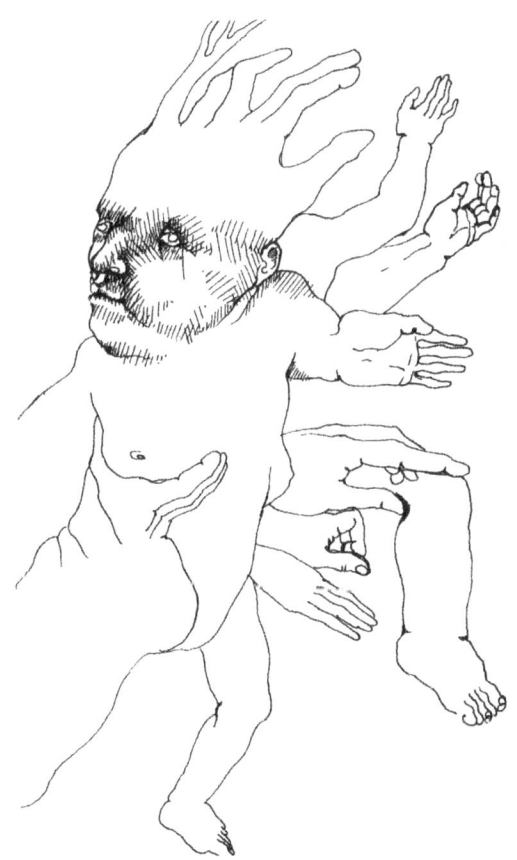

Chapter 4

INCONTINENCE AND JOY

He, the child Aubrey, could paint with his eyes. A hut climbing a tree.

I, the one he called Triple Suiter, found that perfect and strong in him. From breath to breath, I. From brain to brain, I, went to his dog then slipped to Aubrey when they rubbed noses.

Slippers move from person to person, animal to animal, and talk to other slippers. The imagined—*faeries*, *kelpies*, *pucas*, and non-zooids—do this in stories. We, the slippers, are not stories. Some people are able to hear and talk to us. Aubrey, Nell Kitching, and Reve the gypsy hear and talk, but most do not. The architecture of their brains is different. Those people call slippers thoughts, imagination, the Muse, or earworms. I once lived in the mind of an anthropologist who studied the brain, but he could not hear us when he was awake, only in dreams. I called him Dr. Corpus Columbus, and like the other Columbus, he was not indigenous to the land he discovered.

The brain is a pacific of prairies, forests, flats, oceans, and sometimes storms. We slippers are there. When someone hears us and tells a doctor, the doctor calls it schizophrenia.

There is a rule of silence among us. We do not tell our hosts what we learn about another host from their slipper, nor do we tell our hosts we can move from person to person and talk to other slippers. The god our hosts believe in does not tell them the thoughts of another, but they think the Bible's devil they invented does. The devil is just a bad slipper. Of course, they could imagine their god told them something about someone, and that's called a divine message, or as they would say, "God spoke to me," instead of schizophrenia. I will never understand this.

When a person is troubled, malefic slippers like the Slim Hand crash their eyes and hurl them through a cruel story. Then I come to fight. Me, Triple Quixote, from old knight history and other fables you've heard all your life.

Sonny, the leper, has a good slipper and a bad one, and he has what medicine calls a psychosis. Sonny's good slipper tells me Sonny knows he's sick, yet can't stop using Freon and tin snips. The bad slipper in his brain makes Sonny huff the gas to make it worse, and his good slipper, another knight like me, cannot seem to find this demon. In some of his heart, Sonny is not a bad person and hates his sins, his good slipper says, but Sonny is in a double bind with his mother, a cross thread created early in life damnable by motherhood. And that is how I know everything about Sonny, from his slipper—even his early life in the place called Georgia.

I once lived in the mind of a raccoon, the great outdoors, you know. The things I could tell you. My raccoon was hit by a car. When a buzzard came to eat him, I slipped to the bird and rode the saprophyte five thousand feet off the earth—*Cadillac* of the slip away.

November 1964

Aubrey left college for one week to hold up his mother and bury his father, Drayton Shallcross, dragged by a flame vine into the tractor blades, a killed man.

In a closet before the service, he cried into his father's shirts and beat his face against the wall. His friends had to hold onto him. A long cortege of cars came to see them lower his *pater* into the ground.

In the shock that death brings, he was off and on in his head—blank, furious, sunken, hallucinating—blank again. On a plane back to school, he saw a phonograph out on the wing, stacked with records. One by one, they dropped "Unchained Melody," "The Twelfth of Never," and "Tragedy," by the Fleetwoods. Triple Suiter went out on the wing from time to time to stack more records. Aubrey sang with them, silent, in the voice he had grown from his mother's blood.

At the Benedictine college, he walked with two young priests every evening after vespers. They talked about mystery. They talked about his father's death. They talked about whether St. Thomas Aquinas was a hidden agnostic, because he believed Aristotle was correct about the theory of cause and effect: something was missing. In his *Summa*, Thomas said something was insuperable about infinity. There *was* no answer. You had to take a leap of faith to even get close to any peace of mind, then surrender to that if you chose. Whatever is out there is somehow the cause of its own cause and somehow created itself then created us, and Nell Kitching, and Sonny. Somehow.

Aubrey knew these priests on the evening walks were shaky, waffling in their faith but not showing it. And Aubrey was shaky, especially about Triple Suiter showing up on his arm now as a tremulous hallucination.

They fought at times. Trip would hector him in a sweet and low mock, trying to out-talk the priests about life, religion, and cycles. The subject of self-exaltation came up often, the irony and danger of the self's fascination with the self and its own elevation and prospect of everything said or done to that end. Aubrey called people who did too much of this "self-exaltaters," or "Taters." He liked the country sound of it. Taters! Two kinds, he told Trip: Blind Taters and Sight Taters. Sight Taters knew they did it; Blind Taters did not. Aubrey said he knew he did it, and they both agreed that made him a Sight Tater. Trip said some of it was okay, because small doses made a healthy ego. Aubrey felt better about it.

There were other asides and sleeve-pullings from Trip during these years that made Aubrey ask to be excused during a class or conversation; his other voice was more than he could stand. When he became stressed, his nose whistled through his left nostril as he exhaled, and he swore it was Trip making it happen to get his attention. Trip sometimes started homiletic blasts about right and wrong, but was opposed to religion's rote answers: "One shouldn't question the ways of the Lord, lest one get one's human ass kicked." Trip, though, thought the Catholics and the Jews were better at relative truth and its history than Protestants, because they were generally more educated and willing to accept science.

Aubrey was well read by now, and Trip wanted him to use something about a belief he had stitched on his own to find peace, and even if Trip did like a lot of Christianity's "shut up and be nice" weirdness, it was okay with him if Aubrey chose the stars, Santeria, or even the God of All Persian Throw Rugs as his image of longing and fulfillment. It's just that Trip was against his youthful host's attraction to black existentialism, the faddish fascinations found in the name-drop cafés, and that, coupled with Aubrey's recent sorrow and so-called of late, completed *dementia praecox*, made him worry about his man's grip on the righty-tighty and lefty-loose of things until he could get him comfortable after losing his father.

Aubrey thought Trip too bossy and nosey and told him to stop trying to pick him up before he fell. His brain was somewhat like the early Darwin brain; one hemisphere was able to talk to the other hemisphere and to be heard as another voice in the jawing air streams of the mind's power lines and city water, air streams the cave people heard in their heads from their leaders, gods, and spooks. "It's a gift," Trip told him, and because Trip had been his so-called guardian angel since Aubrey was five, there were no sudden onset crises or hang-ups when the gift fully appeared. The transition to a completed bicameral mind was not that hard for him to make. The actual vexation of hallucinations shook him at first, and Trip could be hellish, as is true in the misery of some types of schizophrenia, but the scariest voice was still the Slim Hand's, "One Mississippi, two Mississippi," when Aubrey lay frozen, his apparitional ear notched by a psychotic-blackout-barber-pole-transgressor, or what society called a registered mental disorder.

However, when Trip and Aubrey got along, they got along, and Aubrey enjoyed Trip's glowing figure on his arm engaging him in cross talks, humor, irony, and whatever else the little man insisted upon to make his points.

"Am I like Nell now, Trip? Are they going to put me away?"

"No. Nell didn't have a religious family like you. You adopted the guardian angel story from your grandmother and kept at ease with me. You are dyed-in-the-gene, young man, a voice hearer *par excellance* from nature's own gift shop. You'll be fine if you don't tell anyone. Unless you happen to be in a Haitian church in Miami. That would be safe."

"I miss Nell, Trip. I'd like to go see her."

Days came and went away. Aubrey's father Drayton, and the things he had said when he was alive, replaced Aubrey's old Jesus. His father had suffered depression and a type of death in the family home years before then resurrected himself on a car lot in South Florida. Now he had died again, and there would be no more resurrections. When Aubrey felt vagrant and pale, the graven image of the *True* magazine in Sonny's bookstore came to him, along with Trip's powerful poem of all threaded apparatus.

WHEN YOU CAN'T SEE, TAKE A STRAIGHT SHOT

RIGHT THROUGH THE HEART OF THE BLIND SPOT.

TRUE MAGAZINE KNOWS THE TRUTH.

RIGHTY-TIGHTY   LEFTY-LOOSE!

One of the priests he walked with in the evenings was the drama coach for the college and encouraged him to take a part in a Noel Coward play. He was already singing in a rock band on campus, writing songs and lyrics. Ambrose Bierce, the author-misanthropist who received a head wound in the Civil War, became one of his heroes and source of certain cynical wisdom. Aubrey invented a character he called Head Wound, in honor of Mr. Bierce, and did imitations of Bierce's propositional style and content to amuse his new acting friends.

This anger over his father's passing and the exit of his old god through the turning scar in the top of his skull touched off a lonely energy that dropped him sleepless in bed at times. He heard taunts from the Slim Hand when he was stressed and wondered if he might have a real head wound like Mr. Bierce, especially the first time Trip rose out of his arm that November night on the college lawn and told him everything about himself and Amper Sand. Since then, Aubrey hugged their new trinity as tight as Harold hugged his sister Betty as they drowned off Ski Point years ago. He asked the college's permission to audition for a play in the city nearby, and got the part. He thought acting might be his life, and Trip pushed for it.

He went home instead with his diploma in 1966 to help his widowed mother with the car business. The New York theaters would have to wait. The town was twitching. Now, after twelve years, another murdered woman in her fifties was found inside a trash-pile refrigerator by kids playing in the woods. There were cuts where her skin was thin and in private places. Her tongue had been split. A pair of tin snips was left at the scene. Her body was presented in a curled position, surrounded by wild flowers and selected objects from the nearby area. There was a Polaroid picture between her fingers. In the picture, she was holding the same picture of her dead self in the refrigerator. Written in blood on the door of the rusting appliance was "SHIP IN A BOTTLE." They said it could be the work of copycat, but it had to be the Tin Snip Killer.

Aubrey read the story in the paper. He kept thinking about the Polaroid; how the picture of the woman holding the picture of herself in the refrigerator got smaller and smaller, out to a regressive infinity. Nietzsche's infinity. Three-way-mirror-infinity. St. Thomas said out there we have to take a leap of faith in order to believe that this infinity all starts and ends with God, so our souls won't disappear into the tininess of more infinite regression and the abandoned black. Thomas said God would be there, not the darkness, if you took that leap of faith. Be there, to stop the poor lady with her Polaroid from disappearing, because this omnipotent God was, somehow, the cause of his own cause and the first cause of everything else, even Sonny. That theory disappointed Aubrey.

He worked long hours at the car dealership that summer, surfed, and rode his mare at night through the woods and grades of stars. He went to see Nell Kitching in the crazy place, the plush Palm Beach asylum where the rich stashed their specials. She walked with him, blonde, beautiful, an attendant always twenty feet behind. They looked at each other and smiled then pointed to their heads, because they knew they had the same gift or illness, considering who was considering.

Aubrey had seen Jean Seberg in the movie *Lilith*. In the story, Seberg was in a place like Nell, and her lover, Warren Beatty, an attendant at the institution, walked twenty feet behind her everywhere, like Nell's. Nell said she and Aubrey had monkey minds because they were both born in 1944, the Year of the Monkey, two monkeys struggling into this world of who could hear the voices and who could not. Nell looked like Seberg. Aubrey ached for her in a certain way. When they walked together, she always carried a Ball jar.

Aubrey strained in his life. He thought about New York and acting, feeling stuck in his hometown, trying more to be without his father and old god, warring with religious thinkers he'd read when they reentered his memory, and warring with the Slim Hand when he came to torture him in a dream. Trip would join in, either to fight the Hand or to fight the other thinkers from Aubrey's education he did not like. Trip would flood subjects with his own trope until Aubrey began to deal with another war outside of his mind—Vietnam. His childhood friend, The Junior, had quit college, gotten in real trouble, and was offered jail or the army. He picked the army, and Aubrey expected his own draft notice any day. He wanted to go. Trip screamed, "Asshole! Asshole!"

Some evenings, he spent time at Sonny and Beth's next door. He and Sonny would listen to a record over and over, taking the chords off the music with their guitars. Beth would stop him at the door occasionally; she'd say Sonny was in bed and wanted to be alone. This happened a lot. Aubrey stopped going.

On the weekends, he'd drive west to Indiantown to visit with The Junior's parents and take his guitar. They liked to sing with him. He wanted them to know he was there for them while their boy was fighting on another earth, and he felt guilty he was not. After coffee, they'd sing Marty Robbins songs: "El Paso," "Devil Woman," and "Big Iron." When he left, he pointed his truck toward the Z-Bar Up Ranch, owned by the Zarnitz clan. The family had a rodeo arena and big cattle business; they provided bucking stock to rodeos around the state. Aubrey and The Junior learned to sit on anything with hide on that ranch, and they had eaten a lot of dirt from new horses or bulls Mr. Zarnitz wanted to audition for his string. Aubrey's father sold trucks to the cow pen patriarch, and the man continued to be a good customer.

"Mornin, Aubrey. Ready to get yourself shore up for the rodeo circuit?" Mr. Zarnitz grinned. He knew the boy could ride.

Chapter 5

LEDA

He had been mostly chaste at the all-boy's college, and now he was drawn to the nightlife in a town called Jensen Beach, just across the St. Lucie River from Stuart. There, on the Indian River side, sat an ancient cracker bar called The Blue Goose, a bar based on the short-sleeve shirt. Outside was one of Aubrey's favorite attractions, an old neon sign.

Alone at a table one evening, staring at his toadstone ring, a forward girl—yellow sun dress and confident pelvic walk—turned a chair around where he was sitting so she could hang her arms down and prop her chin on the backrest. It wasn't fair. She looked like Nell and Jean Seberg, except for her eyes—not large and natural like Nell's, but well dragged with her own supplies. Aubrey glanced down at his toadstone ring. It went pale, to blood drop, then back to pale.

"You look like you don't feel well," she said, holding her mouth open. Gorgeous, yet a little perverse.

"Are you a physician?" Aubrey answered.

"Yes, I am Dr. Candle Albright. Who are you?"

"My name is Jim. Jim Nasium," he said, turning into his man Head Wound.

"Well, Jim, I'm looking at your face, and your gym seems a little dark tonight."

"Yes, Mademoiselle, until I've just seen *your* remarkable face. Looking at you, I'm reminded of a crazed French poet I love."

"Which one?"

"Rimbaud. It's your cyanide blue eyes."

Her chin went up. "How did you know? Have you heard of this new band called The Doors? The lead singer is another Rimbaud."

"I haven't."

"You don't talk like the other guys here. You've been to school."

"Yes, but I would never let school interfere with my education."

"That is Mark Twain."

"Ah! I see you've been to school, too."

They sat. They talked. She had moves that looked blocked out, but he knew they weren't. Her smile: the smolder. Her manner with a cigarette: old movies. He loved to watch her with that smoke when she let it drift out of her mouth from the up draft in her throat and then take some back, perfect, through her nose.

They began to see each other. He thought she was bewilderingly cool. He would pull her up on his horse behind him, and they would ride to a stand of Australian pines where they made love on the pine needle ground. She was a young man's dream, a gorgeous lover, an orgy of hair and tan flesh so sexual he thought at times that you couldn't determine her gender, her zoo; a gay man, another woman, a good horse would breed her. "Goddamn!" he'd scream at the overhead flags on the car lot the next day and put her on his dining room table to watch her face change. A woman at table height, screaming at his mouth while he stood between her legs grabbing bosom and hips, making her come with the thumb.

Her name was Leda Rothstein, a nurse from Key West, and she had crossed his eyes, this man fresh from the all-boy school, *The Story of O* kept under his bed. When she dropped her hair, he'd have to clear his throat.

"What do you think, Trip?"

"I think you're going to injure yourself, Head Wound, that fever tree below your belt, I mean."

"Good thing my Catholic grandmother didn't live to see it. Cool Hebrew girl, though, huh?"

"Oh, well, yes, very cool girl. But remember Pip in *Great Expectations*. Mr. Dickens wanted you to know there are a lot of ups and down in life with people of the other sex, and people in general."

"I know, I know, god damn it! Can't you let me enjoy this?"

"But Aubrey, for heaven's sake, don't tell her about me. She'll think you are Peter Cracked-Head Pan. She doesn't know anything about voice hearers. And don't let her see you moving your lips like you do lately."

He sat on the beach with his friend Arquette Orlander.

"I see you with that Leda girl all the time, Aubrey. You whipped or something?"

"Or something."

"Wicked done, I guess."

"Aw, wicked, wicked Massafuckinchusetts. Let's get in the water, Arquette. There's a run-out over there we can paddle through to get past the break."

"How do you know there is a run-out?"

"Because my cracker ass can see it, you Yankee fuck. Then we go to the Blue Goose and get shit-faced."

They sat in the parking lot at the Goose. Arquette wanted to take some tokes off a small canister of nitrous oxide he'd been carrying around to help him quit pot. He was worried the pot would make him stupid. He had a surf buddy who was a dentist, and that was where he got the nitrous. He offered it to Aubrey, but Aubrey said, "That stuff will probably make you more stupid than pot."

Leda met them. She held up a record album she carried that showed the rock adorned face of the other Rimbaud, Jim Morrison. The cover read, *DOORS*.

It was 1967. The counter culture was rising and walking through American towns. Young adults, who never knew much about history, were redoing a form of physical and mental reduction they wrongly thought had never been done before, offering up the nation's accepted moral gist to a runaway id.

Reptile sex boiled the ponds. Melted pearl sank in the spillways. A type of saccharine they called love instead of horns of the goat danced in the bedroom woods. The Victorians' old religion was rolling off the young population, and they were holding up signs that read "Make Love Not War," ignoring history's lasting truth that no society, especially the liberal utopia they wanted, has ever lasted without a powerful army.

People prefaced things with "Man" this and "Man" that, and "How 'bout those Students for a Democratic Society, man?" Timothy Leary, the Pope of Dope, convinced them that his way was the way, through the badlands of human consciousness, and they should drop the old culture's disguises and games. People thought they were what they ate and entered health food stores with clerks that looked pretty ill. Morrison was preaching what he had learned from Rimbaud: that you don't know anything until you derange yourself first. "The poet makes himself into a visionary by a long derangement of the senses," Rimbaud said in 1871. Breton called Rimbaud "the god of adolescence," and the American landscape was just beginning the long haul of its famous delusion, Forever Young.

It was scary for some. Aubrey's age group was right on the cusp. Split. You were either straight or cool; you were with the counter culture, or you stuck with Ozzie and Harriet Nelson. Aubrey and some of his friends were more standoff renegades than hippies. Leda called hippies "dirt children," but a folksinger from that time named Jesse Winchester got it right when he wrote, "The old folks get to make the rules, and we have all the fun."

The Doors put out a second album, *Strange Days*, with a sound from a new electronic device called the Moog synthesizer. "People are strange," one of the songs said, and they were when they got the pills Leary took then passed through the Bardo to the world in a grain of sand, another ship in a bottle. And if you weren't stacked just right, if a few bricks were out of place, you'd have a bad trip and want out of that bottle before you saw yourself in one of Sonny's refrigerators all cut and flayed *immaculata*.

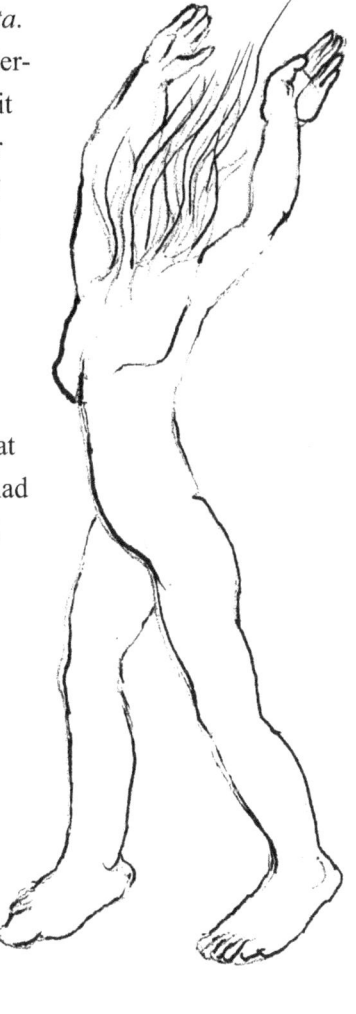

At the bar one evening, Leda entertained the town's young lions with her wit and condescension. She smoked in her usual sex-looking manner and talked of wanting to try LSD. Maybe out on the beach they'd organize it, but it would be another year before they did. Leda stood once on purpose to push her jeans down from her corset looking waist, knowing the power of it, and gave the boys at the table that smile—the smolder. She had never said anything in a few words and in an excited cadence told Aubrey and Arquette she thought Morrison was the next beast from Bethlehem, one of those historical figures who founded a new religion, her voice breaking in fake affectation. Punky, Aubrey's old schoolmate, came over and sat while Leda peeled off historical events and heavy names with her Gillette tongue in the cypress air of the Blue Goose to back her prediction.

Aubrey listened, but when it came to music, he was

more a fan of folk and Motown at the time than he was the Doors: Dylan, Baez, Woody Guthrie, Benny King, Mary Wells, and Gene McDaniels, who sang "100 Lbs. of Clay." He found Leda's speech on the wisdom of acid rock sort of hypnotizing, though, then drifted away like he would, and stared up at the cathedral ceiling in the place. "Cathedral," he mumbled. "Everywhere the Catholics are following me."

When Leda went to the bathroom, Arquette started on Punky with his clubbing sarcasm, suggesting Punky might be becoming an alcoholic. Punky said, "I think I'm just a goddamn drinking enthusiast, you Yankee fucker. Besides, ever'body see you with a different woman ever night. I think you some kinda genuine sex addict, you and that hot dog yogurt pickle a-yours you carryin around in those expensive pants you wear."

Arquette laughed and nodded agreement. Punky was speciously religious, a dirty-minded Baptist boy as outdated in these times as the "Put Christ Back in Christmas" bumper stickers on cars in July. He didn't like long hairs or surfers, but these were his old friends. Aubrey put him in an affectionate headlock, and Punky ordered another drink from the bar called a Purple Jesus then cut one of his famous farts and said, "Jimmy crack corn" to Arquette. Next, he pulled some paper clips out of his pocket, re-shaping them into triangles, something he had done since seventh grade when he was nervous. "My daddy said I was just a hard drinker, not a fuckin alcoholic, Arquette." Still pissed. The friends all laughed.

Aubrey missed The Junior, and as he looked around the faces at the table, how could he know Arquette would one day disappear, Leda would disappear, and Punky would die in his dump truck? Everyone runs off or out of road eventually, the songs say. Over in a corner by himself, in his late thirties now, with a drink called a sidecar, sat Sonny, watching it all. He could have joined them, but he never had. Might have felt he was too old for them now.

When they left the bar, Aubrey told Leda he was beat from surfing and going home to sleep. She kissed him deep in his mouth next to his truck and changed his mind. In a half hour, she was back on his dining room table, breaking blood vessels. That night, Aubrey dreamed he was still in the Blue Goose with the group, drinking a Purple Jesus and staring up at the cathedral ceiling. He saw doves on the rafters, their pink trident toes being washed by another Jesus in purple boots. The dream, magenta and queer, had this Jesus going from dove to dove, tending their feet. The birds would stomp up and down in the holy man's hair to dry. Trip sat in Aubrey's brain and watched the dream with Amper Sand like it was the evening movie. Amper Sand smiled and typed his thoughts on Trip's chest with his tiny Underwood.

Jesus Christ in a purple suit;

Jesus Christ written on his boots.

If he was wearing what he wore today,

They'd have never hung him on the tree that way.

And the ones they save are the ones that pay.

Tickets!

"Yes, Amp, always for tickets and what they will pay," Trip said.

They laughed and clapped, both of them thrilled Aubrey's brain made these wall hollow films. Trip thought about his old host the scientist, and said aloud, "Ah, Doctor Columbus, if you only knew what really happens on top of these human shoulders."

A month later, the Jesus dreamer drove west to Lake Okeechobee then south on 441 toward Belle Glade, a reliable drive for the self-exam. He thought he had to figure out his love life and his whole life. It was harvest time in the Muck, the black soil that ringed the big lake, so fertile, if you planted an old car axle in it, it would grow a new axle.

When he reached the town of Pahokee, he saw the first smoke. A few more miles, and he was on the side of the road watching what he'd come for since he was a boy; they were burning the sugarcane.

Black clouds rose from the fields. Buzzards flew drunk through the caramelized air—rolling, gliding, cooked in the sweet meth rising from the brutal agriculture of the lake's king crop.

Snakes, rats, rabbits ran from the heat. Marsh hawks took their pick, while the buzzards freebased the boil in black molly glides, one eye on what the hawks left for them. The smoke rose, cooled, and rose until it changed into argent towers of pearl cumulus when it reached 10,000 feet.

In the backseat of his father's Chrysler on Sunday drives when he was a little boy, Aubrey would conjure things in the cane, but now as a grownup, it had his full shine. What was he going to do with this Leda-girl he was running with? He craved her sex and conversation. She said she was tough and cold from the way she grew up, and he wasn't going to question her about it. She said they should never say the word love to each other, the late build of his own thinking after his father's death broke his heart and the Blind Spot Cathedral showed up in his mind. He was not sure he would ever pray or love again, and he made totems of what he thought might be a hip mental illness—schizophrenia—to live and underwrite whatever it took to keep him safe.

In his truck he sat, watching the vultures bank and the hawks hunt over the burn while flames sent scab and ash that fell on him and the town of Belle Glade five miles to the south. He thought of getting out and walking closer to the blazing field, when a large *excelsus* calved in his head. "A big drifty came," as his mother would say. It was him as the Tater man—the self-exal-Tater man—the shiny loner, a tropical hero who rode out of the cane for anyone that needed him. He was Johnny Yuma, Champion of the Muck, the Catcher in the Cane that saved children from those hawks and buzzards as they ran from their burning towns and burning lives, and after the city of Belle Glade

54

slapped his back for it, he rode off to his hideout and waited for Big Sugar to burn again. Him: the dreamer, the Shane, the Paladin, the Casey Tibbs in the tanbark who drove himself pure and clean in the name of all televised righteousness. It's just that now it only happened in his head, because he was twenty-three and lost in a slalom of want and what to do.

He drove to his mother's house and walked the seawall by the half-moon to Reve the gypsy and her husband Coker. The commercial fisherman and his wife, her lower lip full of snuff, had built a fire in their yard facing the river and were frying mullet roe with eggs in a black skillet.

"Aubrey, Aubrey, son of Elizabeth, grandson of Ethel," Coker Barnes called out when the fire showed him against the coconut trees and night.

"Eat with us, Aubree," Reve said to him in her Quebecoise accent.

"Love to," he answered.

Reve looked at him. "You face has the problems. A woman?"

"How do you know that?"

"I am a gypsy, and you are a young man. How do you speak of this woman, and what does your toadstone ring, you *crapaudine* say?"

"She's almost heaven."

"So is purgatory, Aubree."

Three days later, he couldn't help it. He had to go back to the *cannamele*, the sugarcane. He pulled off the road just as Clarence Carter's new song, "Slip Away," came through his truck's radio. "That's it exactly. Slip away," he said to himself and conjured Nell Kitching's jar inside his mind. "Slip away, slip away," Clarence sang, and Aubrey did, like spoonbills in the mangroves when they go under their wings to dream.

Conscious now in this unconscious place, he could see it—the huge domed arcade interior of his skull with the same keloid scar turning at the top he always saw when the Slim Hand came after him, but this place had no Slim Hand and seemed safe. All his.

An imagined cane field covered the floor of his cranium. One high-boned wall showed an RKO newsreel and its giant radio tower, which turned on top of the globe in black and white and pulsed light out to movie houses and film fans everywhere, as if it was 1950 again. "Slip away," he yelled in his dream.

The tower left the bone wall and placed itself in the middle of the cane field. Aubrey climbed to top and circled at the end of a rope like a tetherball man over all he had made in this place, gazing into his Ball jar. "Slip away!" he screamed. "Slip away!"

Thoughts, shapes, songs, film, people, hatched themselves out in the jar. Vaulted abstractions—permuting, decocting, shattering, improving, while he tossed the valence of everything, because now he *was* the self-exalt Tater Man, and this place inside his head was where he was safe; his farm to grow and derange things like Rimbaud said he should, then put them back the way they were in the objective world when he was through; because it was that world, with its hardwood floor he held in such high regard to stay sane after his belief in god was gone and the cross threads came without Mary the Mother of Jesus to protect him. Cain and Able's god had taken his father, and Leda was the woman he could not seem to leave. He kept circling the tower, knowing she had him head, hide, and limbs that hung down from her shoulders, beautiful and thin. Though he wanted to protect his heart, he did feel love for her, even if she, just to act cool, protested. How could he not from the way his parents raised him? What was he *supposed* to feel when the blue-eyed Ashkenazi girl from Key West falconed his heart?

Of course, he wanted to swallow all this too. Possess it. Everything he had created today way past normal. If he could only make the scenes slim enough, put them through the blades of his conjured jar to take down his throat in this original synesthesia of his. Swallow their *elan* so it could raid his bloodstream like the consecrated host used to—the Eucharist thing—his old God's carcass. Swallow what he'd summoned inside his band shell skull about Leda then flown around the RKO's tower and spun far out over his apparitional cane field, it's just now the apparition was cartooning itself into something perverse. He had overdone it, and crazy enough, he could see his body going in and out of a giant female build. Oh, "dirty pants!" the nuns yelled from the bone walls. "Rupture!" The devil somersaulted. Aubrey stopped. He wanted to swallow that, too. This craving to know everything like the holy wafer, take it inside him and fly it around the RKO, even in dirty pants. This dangerous love for Leda, every thought about her, wonderful, filthy, clean, so he could get it all slim and trans-substantiated in *his* own church the way the other church and their angels taught him to do years ago, like child molesters.

He wondered how he would have made it out of his head if a highway patrolman hadn't rapped on his window to ask if he was all right.

Trip worried. This place inside Aubrey's skull, this secret place, was one he could not seem to go, and despite his objections, Aubrey said this part of him was his alone. He had hidden it. Trip's old host Dr. Corpus Columbus had never suggested a thought-built room like this could be hidden from someone's other voice.

"The brain's atlas to a slipper is as big as the world you live in and see on the outside," Trip told Aubrey the next day. "I think I could never find this place you made in your mind if you didn't want me to. A slipper is only the size of a cell in there, and so are you when you are there. And how many messengers do you think there are in a brain? Billions! There are mountains in the occipital and parietal lobes and jungles in the Wernicke's area that make it impossible to fathom the cartography of the place. And if you want to keep this room from me, I understand. I would, though, like to see what goes on sometime. I can hear noises. Good material maybe, for Amper Sand and me to save for you, or you from. Some kind of archive we'd organize for all of us to enjoy later, you know."

"Where do you think the Slim Hand lives in my head?" Aubrey asked.

"Sir, if I knew, I would go to his house and hang him."

"Who is he?"

"A rogue slipper. There are bad slippers in people, too. Believe me."

"Do you talk to other slippers?"

"No," Trip lied.

"Where do you come from, Trip? How did you and I—"

"I come from you and another before that, and somewhere before that, based on the faith only of that proposition. I am *noumena* that can become a clear phenomenon, depending on your mind and brain's ability. Amper Sand likes to say we come from that unlocatable location of things thought about, and he gave that line in a dream once to the doctor host I often mention to you. From the wet yolks and uprights I come, the soft wire that hums what you hear when you listen. From the banking centers of the Broca area.

"I possess a house of ancient knowledge and *verstand* from other times, sliding blood to blood, consciousness to consciousness, in a form you hear and sometimes see, but which does not bleed. The closest you will ever get to the land where the souls live, Aubrey, is what the west calls schizophrenia."

"Tell me. Keep telling me, Trip."

"You are matter. I am not. I am only the material movement of what you have heard after I have said it. But when you see me on your arm, I am immaterial. You cannot touch me, yet I am the conjuration you need to find me. I am a separate person in your consciousness with my own consciousness that I have brought from the store house of worlds—a mind within a mind around me and *my* other voice, Amper Sand!"

"Ship in a bottle?"

"Perfect."

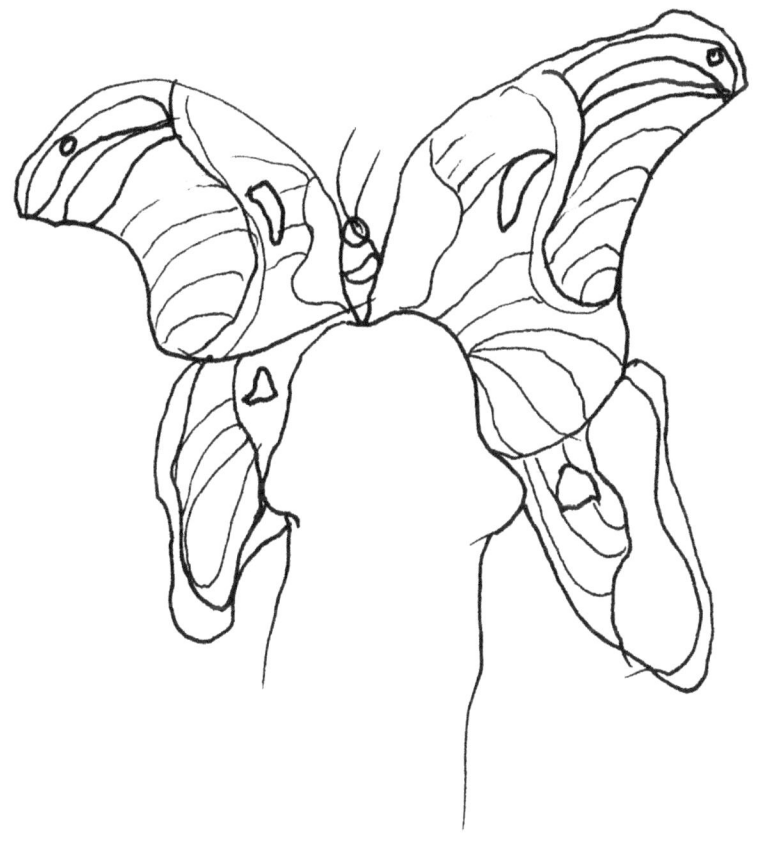

Chapter 6

THE JUNIOR: VIETNAM 1967

The Junior quit football and college after his one and only semester at West Virginia. "Too damn cold," he said. He worked cattle for old man Zarnitz, then got into a fight with two men in Okeechobee and killed one. The judge said it was "Questionable self-defense. Right up next to manslaughter. No time in jail if you join the army, son." So he went to the lead foot farrago of Vietnam.

~

Da Nang Air Base. China Beach. One year before the Tet Offensive.

"He's what?"

"Upstairs in a bathtub. Gonna put a moth on the end of his dick."

"What for?" The Junior asked his friend.

"Cause he bet these slopes and Marines he could come in less than one minute with that thing runnin around on it."

"*True* magazine?"

"Yep."

"You said moth. Why won't it fly away?"

"Cause it don't, and it's a damn big moth."

The Junior stood and followed Freddie Tommie, a black Seminole Indian, through the bar to the second floor. There were a half a dozen uniformed men pushed together in a bathroom around an old claw foot bathtub, yelling in English and Vietnamese.

"I just get one prop, gentlemen. One, shall we say, tertiary aid," the naked man sitting in the water said in educated voice. He had an erect big toe down there and on his face, a very big nose.

"No, you can't touch that cock," an American soldier yelled.

"Yes, no touch cock, no touch cock." The South Vietnamese jumped up and down with paper money between their fingers.

"I told you I will not touch it, gentlemen, but I get to look at an innocent picture."

"What picture? No Playboy stuff," a man yelled.

"No. One from my wallet. It's personal, and though it is a woman, it's just her face." He gave them a quick glance at the photo from his distance. One objected, but the others did not.

The bathtub man pulled out a hundred-dollar bill. Put the wallet back on the table next to the tub.

"Okay, it's my hundred against your two. This says I can climax in one minute after the moth is on my piece. Agreed?"

A Vietnamese man in the corner, some kind of second, brought over a clear plastic box; inside was the big moth. The man reached in and cupped his hand around it, then placed the moth on the tip of the tub man's erection, surrounded by water. The moth spread out eleven inches of wingspan in exaggerated colors—painter stuff—and at each tip, God or Gauguin had drawn a cobra-looking snake's head. Science would ordinarily insist it was too preposterous and man-made in appearance for the creature to exist.

"That's one a-those Asian atlas moths. They also call it a snake's head moth," Freddie Tommie said to The Junior.

"Jesus's gills. Never seen one a-them. Ain't a bug that big in the Glades back home."

"The guy in the tub is Suskin. He told me about this kinda moth the other night. Suskin's comin over to our squad tomorrow because two of his shipped home and two were hit. One dead. He told me the moth will only fly if it's dark, so that's why he got the lights on so bright in here. So it stays on his dick."

"I'd be afraid that thing would bite my fence post."

"Nope. Suskin says this kind got no mouth. Only live 'bout a week on the food stored in their body from when they was a caterpillar. It'll move round like crazy on his thing and flap its wings the whole time cause it's scared of the water, but it won't fly off with these bright lights in here."

Suskin told the group to time one minute and then said, "Go," and closed his eyes. He blew his breath at the moth in a kind of rhythm. It scrabbled over the skinned cock's helmet when it felt the breath, fanning its wings and pumping its body up and down like a woman on top of a man. It knew the water was there and stamped its feet but would not fly off. Suskin opened his eyes, took the small photograph from the table, and began to stare at it. He continued to push his breath in and out at the moth. After fifteen more seconds, Suskin's mouth cracked open, his breath increased, and his hands slightly shook the picture he was holding. Some spittle made a bubble, and he came. The moth flapped its wings and went up in the air a few inches from the fluid, and then came back down in it, still balanced on the end of the penis.

The men were silent. The Junior tried to maneuver around behind the bathtub and see the picture Suskin held, but Suskin had quickly placed it face down on the table. The others put their money together and handed it to the assistant, who had put the moth back in the clear plastic box with a gloved hand. All were shaking their heads and grinning. They had never seen this kind of erotic presentation, and some of them looked like it was worth losing the bet.

There was that sound outside his hotel room, that saw-toothed rotation, a reminder of remembrance. For The Junior's father, it was the props on the B-17s in England going round and round before a bomb run into Germany, but in Vietnam, no one forgot the sound of the Bell UH-1D, or Huey helicopter, and its blades that seemed to nick something each time they cycled. The Junior had trouble sitting under ceiling fans later in his life because of that. He had stood in too much human blood with nick, nick, nick above him in this war.

An hour ago, a Vietnamese woman had given him a massage, what the army men called a "steam and cream." He fell asleep. The ongoing cough he'd been living with woke him up. A girl came into the room and was beside him—this foreign girl and foreign place, in a land of dead dogs, Coca-Cola, and air like home in Florida, but without mourning doves or crows. He wanted to wake up in Florida, go into town with his friend Aubrey, buy *The Western Horseman* and *True* magazine from Sonny at the newsstand, and then drink and shoot the shit at the Blue Goose with his childhood friends.

He coughed some more. Thought the cough came from the Agent Orange dropped from tanker planes. Nick, nick, the fly-by noise outside, and the moth the other night still in his mind, the snakehead wings fanning that guy's dick for those screaming little Vietnamese men—those one hundred and thirty-pounders that ate anything weird with rice because there were so many to feed hollering at each other on their toy motorbikes in their fucking sandals. Shit, he missed horses and ham, long cars, heavy-set ranch girls, and shell rock roads.

The girl in his room put her hand on his chest. "Big," she said, and smiled him out of homesick.

"What's your name, sweetheart?"

"My name Mary. Mary Dinh Tan. You want drink?" She looked at the bottle on the dresser.

"Yeah, how 'bout we do two fingers of that shark snot over there, sweetie?"

In the dark, he heard her pour one, and she put her clothes on a chair. *Professional*, he thought to himself.

"You speak a little English, don't you now, sweetheart?" *God, they have these little perfect bodies. Not like the ranch girls with red spots on their skin. What a doll-baby. How can their legs open wide enough to take in all those American dicks and fat asses?*

"You big man. Lots muscle. Not hurt me, no?"

"No, baby. Me no hurt you."

"Let me see." She pointed at his divide.

The Junior pulled back the sheets.

"That nice. Wow, what all this?"

"Oh, that. Well, there's a lot of ball sack right there, honey. We got a bull at home they call The Junior after me, cause he got a big scrotum too, you see."

"Squodum?"

"Yeah, squodum."

"Girl in bar, my friend, has man big squodum, small dick." She held up her thumb and forefinger an inch apart. "She say in Vietnamese, 'He all coconuts, no tree.'" She did her socializing laugh.

"Yeah. We say that kinda thing, too, honey. All potatoes, no meat."

Mary Dinh Tan pulled on the mass of ruck between his legs.

"I hope you don't think I'm some kind a funny boy or something, but I like my girl to pinch that scrotum hard with two fingers before we rock."

"Okay, I pinch."

The Junior kept telling her, "Harder."

She stopped and said, "I have. I think you like." She came back from her purse with safety pins in her hand.

"Jesus lord, don't know 'bout this, darlin. I just saw this guy put a moth on his dick last night and now you gonna—"

"No. You like, I promise. I put earrings in girl's ears and pussy." Then she dropped her eyes coy to work his man side. "I know other man. He like this." She stood again and got the ice bucket off the dresser. "Ice for first one. If you don't like, no more."

But he did like. And it was no ice for the next and the next, and when he eased in with five safety pins locked closed through his cod, he did so from behind her, to feel this new, jeweled bag of his banging into her leg tops. He thought how good the novelty of light pain felt with the pleasure of a hard fuck. Maybe it was the pride he had for his anatomy there, or him getting over on the Bible taboo he grew up with at home, but it was good for him in this place with women who knew nothing about the Baptist church.

There was an explosion. Everyone below was running. When he

went to look, an American sergeant he knew yelled up to him from the street. "Shit, blew up the whole room down at the Mackey."

The Junior left Mary Tan in the bed and headed to the base. Military police went by towards the smoke, and up above, the sound from a nighttime sky going nick, nick, nick.

They were over the jungle-covered mountains two days later. Their squad: the sergeant, The Junior, Freddie Tommie, Pauley, another regular, Suskin the moth man, and three new guys. Whenever The Junior looked at the mountain ranges from the choppers, he always thought they should be like mountains he'd seen in North Carolina, covered in maples and pines and no damn monkeys. He could see where they were going from the Huey, sitting ducks maybe when they landed, even if the hillside *was* an American firebase and had the green flares on the LZ to signal the area had been cleared. *Can't see anything; can't hear nothin with this fuckin mix master goin round.*

The squad spread out as usual, waiting for the Bell to fly away so they could listen for sounds of the enemy. They were all broke in, no pilgrims; even the new guys had been on other patrols and were aware the law of averages said that while they scratched their necks or cleared their noses they'd be shot as the mission numbers increased.

By now, The Junior didn't care. He'd taught himself not to care during this American patriarchal political psychosis he was sent to instead of jail, so he stood up with Freddie Tommie and told the sergeant they'd walk in first, as they always did. The other men considered The Junior and Freddie people who thought they were already dead, the tall muscular cowboy who behaved like a sociopath around gunfire, and Freddie, a reckless but spiritual black Indian who would take the afterlife of hunting grounds any day over this water buffalo shift.

After twenty minutes, the rest followed them in. The Junior was used to jungle. He'd grown up on the north edge of the Everglades, and except for monkeys, mountains, and giant atlas moths on the end of dicks in bathtubs, the snakes and vegetation felt like home.

If the enemy wasn't waiting for them when they heard the choppers, it could take up to two days for the Viet Cong to move in and engage them. It was guerrilla warfare, contrary to most of the traditional boot camp training for American soldiers, who got the conventional WWII-type training even for Vietnam, and that gave the guerilla-smart Viet Cong an advantage. The Junior and Freddie Tommie had their own advantage. They were swamp raised and knew how to track and hunt. Stay down wind of things.

On the morning of the second day, the squad had circled the area of mountain where they were dropped off and sat down to relax when some VC waiting for them opened up. They shot Pauley off to the right of the group, and everyone else got behind trees, moraines, or anything else that humped a little ground.

Pauley was screaming louder than a war movie, and Freddie Tommie crawled within ten feet of him. Freddie pulled with his arms to get closer, and just as he got to Pauley, Pauley stopped screaming and died. Freddie put two fingers on Pauley's throat to make sure as the VC opened up again. Freddie grabbed Pauley's feet and collar and pushed the uniformed lump into a fetal shape so he could use it for cover. The sergeant was yelling at the sky because he didn't know Pauley was dead and could see the bullets hitting the upper edge of the body. One round grazed Freddie's index finger on Pauley's throat. Freddie buried his own face in the dirt. Everyone else in the squad was firing into the trees, but The Junior, in his wild aggression, made his way behind what turned out to be four preoccupied VC. Freddie heard a sustained burst from an M-60 and then quiet. The Junior walked out of the trees straight up, his twenty-three-pound machine gun in front of him still smoking. "All gone," he said.

The team sat around dead Pauley, not saying a word. They lit a green flare, radioed for the body to be picked up, and stayed on one more day watching daisy cutter bombs clean off a couple of mountain tops in the distance. It rained. When it stopped, The Junior stood to smell the air and the ozone from the storm's lightning. He sought it out. He thought it cleared his lungs of anti-foliage chemicals and bomb smoke. He was convinced things like ozone would fix his cough.

Pauley's replacement, a black guy named Wilson from Harlem, came to them when command picked up Pauley's body. Around a fire the last night out, Wilson said to the black Indian, Freddie Tommie, "Hey, man, what's with you? Where you from? You don't talk or jive around like a brother. You ain't some cardboard nigger, are you?"

"No. I'm a real one, sort of. I'm what they call a black Seminole Indian, from Ft. Pierce, Florida."

"Yeah, that redneck Junior over there, he from Florida, right? So how much of you is Indian? I thought you was maybe just slave yella, like a lotta us."

"My mother was a Seminole and part Spanish. The Seminoles were happy to have us fightin with them during the old Indian Wars, hidin out from the whites. My father, he was part black. His grandfather was a runaway slave from Georgia."

"Oh. Man, I never heard about things like that where I'm from."

"Hey, Wilson," Freddie Tommie said. "You ever see that girl singing group up there in New York called the Ronettes?"

"Yeah, man. I got into the Peppermint Lounge once and seen em, and I seen 'em at The Apollo, too."

"Well, they're like me—Indian and black."

"Hey, no shit? I can get with that."

"You know something, Wilson? I listen to those girls sing 'Walking in the Rain' in my head, over and over out here in these jungles, cause it's always rainin. I love the one girl in that group. Nedra, I think her name is."

"You all right then, Freddie, man. Wanna play some African billiards?"

"What's that?"

"Dice, man. Craps. You got some money?"

Suskin, known for never saying much, sat a few feet away and smoked the dope he had, letting it curl out of his mouth and back into his unusually big nose, or "big fuckin air hook," Wilson the new man called it. The whole squad went silent later, still thinking about Pauley.

When they got back to the base, all of them went to see Pauley's body come out of refrigeration. It was loaded onto a transport with thirty others in a brief ceremony, then they headed to the bar district to drink over him. Someone put a picture of Pauley in his combat clothes on the table and they ordered round after round of brace.

"One tall good soldier," The Junior said. "Scared of nothin, 'cept his mother."

"I know. She's gonna take this real hard." Freddie tapped at his drink. "Pauley used to say to me, 'Freddie, you are one of the few Indians who know how to drink. It's because you're black, too, I guess."

The Junior was looking around the bar at different groups of people. He was gin-nasty by now and wanting to get out of the Pauley thing. There were South Vietnamese soldiers, Americans, and town girls on the stroll. A table of Viets was gambling on two beetles fighting in a jar. He saw another American guy betting them he could do the ole tie a maraschino cherry stem in a knot with his tongue. It occurred to him that if Suskin could get these people to pay for that moth dance on his dick, then by God, he had a trick for them, one he used in college for free pitchers of beer the short time he was there.

"Look at that stuff over at that table. Those little China-lookin shits'll bet on how long flies'll fuck if that's all they got. Wanna see me make some money?" The Junior said to his table.

"Oh, yeah? What you got other than eating pussy with a maraschino cherry stem on your tongue?" Freddie Tommie said.

"Yeah, you white boys probably could make some big money eating pussy. All you guys got hair in your throat. Brothers don't do that shit," Wilson grinned.

"Wilson, want me to take your wife away from you?" asked Freddie.

"But you only half black, Freddie, man. No wonder you do that fur burger that way."

"I bet you guys twenty bucks apiece I can beat those ARVN at that table for a hundred fuckin dollars. There's five of them sittin there." The Junior nodded in that direction.

Freddie looked at him and smiled. "I'm out."

"Hell, I'm in. I'll bet the money just to see what you gonna do," Wilson said, and Suskin the moth man signaled, too.

Mary Dinh Tan, The Junior's favorite girl now, was sitting at the bar. He asked her to help. She approached the Viet soldiers, and they waved her off. When she persisted, they looked at The Junior smiling at them from the bar and motioned to him.

With Mary translating, The Junior bet them twenty dollars each he could touch his scrotum to his nipple if he was sitting straight up in a chair. The soldiers tossed the drinks in front of them and loved the wager.

Time stopped. For five minutes in the skies over Southeast Asia, multiracial angels assembled when they heard a man would stretch his piece of ugly pavement, that lizard-throated vellum below his belt, all the way up to his nipple. Fifty miles to the north, other angels, too busy to watch the wager, were tending people on both sides of the war who had died that day for yet another unworkable, bad idea. In Washington, the angels over the Beltway heard LBJ say to McNamara, "A man can fight if he can see daylight down the road, but there ain't no daylight in Vietnam." The Junior liked LBJ. They had the same accents. Now he was very far from those accents at a bar room table, his pants and underwear around his ankles with money at stake.

Two of the Vietnamese craned their necks to see in his crotch. The Junior winked at Suskin, the room's other venereal performer, and said, "Okay, you boys get your money out."

70

One Viet said, "Where you money?"

The Junior put his cheek on the table to reach his pocket by his ankles and fished out a roll. Gave it to Freddie Tommie. "All right, here goes."

Half the bar came over. The Junior's hand came out of his crotch with the bottom part of his scrotum tweezed between his thumb and forefinger, one testicle visible, sliding in the bag like a mango seed, while the other nut stayed at the bottom. He went half way to his nipple for a tease with a pained face, and then all the way, with a smile like he was casually hanging a towel on hook. When he got the nod from the table, he let it go, and it snapped back into his thighs.

The cheers went up, and the Vietnamese soldiers pouted a little, but then ordered another round for everybody. They seemed to love the show as much as they did Suskin's show upstairs the other night with the moth. After that, the Viets all over town called The Junior "Squodum." They would say, "Here come Squodum." Or here comes "Mot Man" for Suskin. And on certain evenings, they'd sucker other soldiers into bets who had not seen or heard of these feats offered by the two men. The Junior and Suskin made people money. The whole country bet, every day, even on body counts that would total 267,000 Americans by 1969 and more than a million Vietnamese soldiers and civilians by the war's end. One or two times, walking through a side street, The Junior saw Vietnamese soldiers playing Russian roulette for money with a pistol to their heads—little one hundred and thirty-pound deer hunters, who never heard of Pennsylvania.

Chapter 7

THE TERRIBLE AND THE SUBLIME

On the next patrol, they went further in and ran into an indigenous tribe of Montagnard people. The Americans had two seasoned South Vietnamese soldiers along, and the Montagnard were more afraid of them than the Americans. The South Viets had a reputation for torture.

One day, Freddie Tommie was looking at an area of jungle on his own, something not condoned. Seminole stuff and human smell—he thought the other men made too much noise. The Indian moved along a stream, listening for monkeys to scream at somebody else and give their location away. There was a sandy area with disturbed dirt. Freddie put each foot down carefully and scanned the trees. When he got closer to the sand, he saw them—cat tracks, like the Florida panthers at home. This was a litter box. A tiger's. The signs were fresh, and though he was well armed, he did not want to attract any human attention, so he left for camp and the men. On the way back, he detoured to the Montagnard village and squatted down with one of the people. The village man was comfortable with Freddie's dark lineaments, instead of another mother-of-pearl face from Ohio. Freddie drew a cat track in the sand with his finger. The tribesman nodded and scratched out a cat with stripes next to Freddy's drawing. The tribesman drew a stick man in the mouth of what he'd drawn and put his hand up to his temple in the shape of a gun. He made a face and started chewing. Freddie assumed he meant the tigers were eating dead soldiers killed in firefights and left to rot. He put a pack of cigarettes in the man's hand and headed back to the other men.

"Hey, guess what's around here, Junior."

"A whore house."

"Yeah. A cathouse. How'd you know?"

"You're full of shit."

"Well, I didn't see it, but I saw the tracks."

"Whore tracks?"

"No. Viet striped panther. Fresh ones."

That night, they told the sergeant and the men. Suskin's face lit up for once, and he asked questions. Freddie told them what the tribesman said about tigers eating corpses, and Freddie bet they were starting to hunt people and no one should get too dumb on guard duty. Suskin, the graduate student, became even more lit. He started reciting, "Tyger, tyger burning bright," and told everyone the beast represented the poet's take on the meld of beautiful and horrible, something so pretty yet so perfectly deadly, and he almost seemed to turn a little feminine while he was talking. "God, what I'd give to see that slice of sensate wonder."

"Oh, you won't see him except for a second, Suskin," the sergeant said. "Right before he sinks his teeth in your neck, you'll see this orange and black flash, and you'll think it's fucking Halloween."

Everyone laughed except Suskin, who said, "Yes, sergeant. I think it was Tolstoy who said, 'It is amazing how complete the delusion that beauty is goodness.'" The Junior, in a rare move, wrote what Suskin said on a slip of paper, after he figured out how to spell delusion, and stuffed it in his rucksack. When the big daisy cutter bombs went off in the distant dark and lit the clouds like Florida heat lightning, he pulled it out and read again what Suskin had said.

The next day, they split into two groups. The sergeant told The Junior to take Suskin and three other men as AGs, or assistant gunners, for the M-60 machine gun The Junior carried. This meant they toted bullet belts for the weapon, plus their own weapon, an M-16 that fired in three-round bursts. Every squad had one machine gunner, and The Junior was it. His M-60 put out five hundred rounds per minute with a range of 1200 yards. Every fifth round was a tracer, so a soldier that carried it could follow its destruction. This could also make him a target; the enemy would go after the machine gunner first, and the tracer

74

flow told them where he was unless the gunner chose a bullet belt without tracers. An M-60 gunner had the shortest life span in Vietnam. The rule was you had to move every eleven seconds or sooner after you fired the weapon to stay alive.

The Junior was born with gray eyes, considered by some superior, eyes with more rods than cones in his retina to be transduced by his brain and made sense of. As a boy and a man, he was able to see well in the dark. When he scanned the jungle, he hooked on to things like he did when he was looking for stray cattle at night on a horse, back home. Those eyes always went ahead of him, waved him forward.

Aubrey once told The Junior the story of Owl Creek Bridge and how the man, just hanged by Union troops, thought the rope broke and he'd fallen alive into Owl Creek. As the current took him away from the bridge and the enemy, the man saw a soldier with gray eyes aiming his rifle at him and remembered gray eyes were marksman's eyes and was sure he would be shot.

The Junior saw Suskin glancing at the ground, not where he should as they walked. "Hey, boyeh. Watch them trees, stead a-hopin you gonna see those cat tracks."

"I know. I would not know a tiger sign if it was shown to me," he said, and then gunfire came out of the canopy, cutting off branches and elephant grass.

"Here, Suskin! You know how to use my machine gun. Take it! Shoot at em, man. I'll get around behind them. Give me your M-16. It's easier to run with. They'll wanna get the M-60 first, and that'll distract them from me. If that barrel gets too hot, use the glove and have the AG change it. And tell one a-them other men to get on the RTO and tell the rest of them we found Charlie. Keep their minds on you, man. You the tiger now, son!"

Suskin set the tripod in the ground and began to unload on the area with the big heater.

In hindsight, the move was foolish. The Junior was reliably foolish in most firefights, but he was lucky. "Typical Junior stuff," his sergeant would say. "Bullet proof bullshit. You never split up when you don't know what you're up against. Radio. Stay put until we get there." But The Junior believed there were only a couple of the enemy from the shot count and left to move along a high bank towards the area.

He used the bank for cover, but something hard from above sent him black and concussed to the ground. Four North Viet regulars and two Viet Cong stood over him.

"We want him alive for information. Let's tie him. When he wakes up, we make him walk," they said in their language.

"No. Why? We shoot him," another said. "Who wants to deal with another prisoner?"

"If we fire now, the other ones will know where we are. We'll follow this one's tracks back behind his partners."

The Viets headed for Suskin, the others, and the M-60. In a short time, shots rang out from their AK-47s where the Moth Man and the rest were dug in, firing forward at the target, their backs turned to their deaths.

The Junior, in his unconscious state, saw his mother, her mouth open, eyes wide, coming across a Florida wetland in the air, a cypress dome behind her. The sun was red on the saw grass and threw a strike at the trees where cattle came down to drink. His mother knelt by him and started to cry. On a wooden orange crate next to her the Christian devil sat, flicking a Zippo lighter on and off, staring at her then at The Junior. The Junior saw his friend Aubrey riding towards them on a horse, waving his hands like there was danger until water from somewhere washed him awake. The North Vietnamese regulars were poking him with rifle barrels. They got him to his feet and pushed him along the trail, his hands tied, and a rope leash around his neck. He stumbled and bumped himself into realizing how bad things were.

The enemy camp was a day's walk. The first thing he saw at the camp was a South Vietnamese soldier full of bullet holes in a squat, arms dangling, blood on the ground beneath him. The Junior wondered how he could stay squatting like that, dead. He'd seen birds dead on a branch, still holding on, but done. His father told him birds have a tendon that acts like a pulley. When they lean forward, it closes their feet around things, dead or not, and they just stay that way and rot. He wondered if Asian people had that same tendon and could die squatting, the way they squatted all the time, until he saw that a large piece of bamboo buried in the ground below the soldier had been rammed up the man's last section of colon, like a head on a London Bridge spike.

The North Viet soldiers pointed to it and to him and laughed. One of them shot the corpse again in front of him, scattering the flies. He was taken to a platform with metal rings and tied on his back. They left him, and it started to rain.

The undertaker done wiped my ass now. Like to find a way to off myself before I get sat down on that bamboo.

When dark came, the rain stopped. The Viets took their food and sat around a fire. Later, The Junior was given water. He thought it tasted funny. The man that gave it to him grinned and forked his fingers around his own throat. For the first time in a long time, he was scared. Whatever was in the water knocked him out and made him dream vats of bad stuff. The executed soldier on the bamboo was a last thing he saw before he went to nightmares. He wanted his mother now, but she was not in these dreams. Instead, a three-hundred year old slipper named Lucinda held his head in her lap and passed her hands over his face and through his hair to comfort him, as bad dream after bad dream came and went. The Junior did not know of Lucinda or any other slipper, or even what a slipper was, because his mind was not the same build as Aubrey's. When he awoke, he remembered her only as a person in a dream.

The next morning, striped leg Asian tiger mosquitoes had bitten him everywhere. He was miserable, coughing, but Agent Orange in his lungs didn't matter now. He didn't need to breathe ozone, he thought. They were goin to shoot him for breakfast anyway.

After daylight, a chicken got on the platform and started pecking at his face. The Junior would spit in the chicken's face and then the chicken would trade blows with him. He looked over at the camp, and a man, not in uniform, was watching all this and smiling as The Junior sparred with the chicken. The man came over. "Hey, GI, you are not happy," he said in good English.

Just then, another man in uniform came and said in Vietnamese, "Do you think he knows anything?"

"I think he knows no more than what I have told you about their movements," the first man answered in their language.

"Well, then let the men have him. I do not want to have to worry about him with their patrols in these mountains."

"But you know, sir, I am not sure *what* he might know. Let me talk to him for a while, and we will see if he knows more than I think. Give me another day to convince him we will send him up to Hanoi as a prisoner instead of killing him, if he has something valuable to give us."

"Yes, you can have him a little longer. Then we send him to his Jesus Christ after that," the man in uniform said, and he walked away.

The Junior lay there and stared at the jungle sky.

"When we talk, you must act like we are mad at each other," the man said to The Junior.

"What the shit? You do speak English."

"Yes and damn good French."

"They gave me somethin last night that knocked the piss outta me. Made me think crazy. Some kinda knockout drop. I don't know."

"Yes. You see, most prisoners cry at night, and they did not want to be kept awake."

"How come you speak English like that?"

"You are very lucky to run into me. I know you. You are a man they call Squodum." The man smiled.

The Junior couldn't believe his ears.

"You will not tell them this, or you will be sitting on a bamboo. . . what? Suppository, I think the word is, with the sad dead one over there. Understand what I say, Squodum?"

"But you're Viet Cong, ain't you? You ain't in a North suit."

"You want my help or not?"

"I didn't say that. Hell, yeah, I want it. What happens?"

"I will beat you up all day, so this looks like we are enemies, but we are not enemies. I will explain later. Then you do everything I tell you, or you are on the toilet stump over there."

At times, the man would walk over and slug The Junior in the head until he bled, and then in the stomach, and once he urinated on The Junior's feet while the others watched. When night came, the Viets sat around the fire drinking and playing cards. Later, they were drunk, putting out cigarettes on their arms, betting who could keep a straight face.

The English speaking man stood up and The Junior saw him look at him from the fire. He began to talk to the other six men and their leader. They all burst out laughing, shook their heads, and pounded on the table. The man kept talking and nodding. The Junior knew you could sit next to a guy in a China Beach bar, gamble, drink, whore, and the guy could be Viet Cong. They were everywhere, and that's probably how this guy knew who he was.

The man came over. "Okay, Squodum. You and I are leaving here tonight, and I can never come back. I was leaving by orders from my side anyway," he said quietly.

"What you mean your side?"

"My side is your side, GI. I am, well, my officer wants me out of here. It is getting dangerous for both of us, so this is what we do. I have told those drunk communists at that table you should entertain us by trying to do something funny and impossible before we shoot you. I bet them I can make you touch those balls of yours to your nipple, and if you cannot, I will shoot you at that table. They say, hell no, you cannot do it, but of course I have seen you do it, so time to make some money, and kill some people. I want you to act as if it hurts very bad and is impossible, and then you do it after much work and threats from me. I take their money, and next I bet you touch your. . . " He points to his chin.

"Chin. My chin?"

"Yes."

"You cannot touch your chin with that skin of yours, can you?"

"Hell, no."

"Okay, well, I was just trying to make more money before I shoot them."

Hands tied behind his back and the leash around his neck, the men led him over to the fire. Wary of The Junior's size, they stepped back and pointed their guns at him. One put a gun barrel in his ear. They pushed him down into a chair and argued about untying his hands, but how else could he answer the bet? They settled on leaving the leash and one hand tied to the chair; the South Viet spy man would hold his pistol to The Junior's head.

The Junior stood half bent over, unbuckled his pants, slid them down, and sat in the chair again. He reached into his crotch and started to stretch the big craw, with the spy-man yelling he would kill him if he lost his money. There was one false attempt at reaching the nipple that failed by many inches. The men cheered. The next attempt had The Junior screaming, putting on the huge act, saying, "I can't, I can't." The spy man pushed the gun into his temple and slapped his face. Then on the third try, The Junior spit in his hand and screamed again as he finally touched the nipple sitting straight up in the chair.

The soldiers couldn't believe it. One of them wanted to touch the body part himself to see if it was a trick and reached into The Junior's crotch. The spy man went around to each soldier, collected his money, and then bet double that The Junior could touch his chin with it. The men howled and jumped around shaking their heads, then laid out the money on the table.

The Junior spit in his right hand again, and then reached in his crotch and rubbed it around. Dried his fingers off for traction. The soldiers went crazy laughing, and two fell off their chairs and rolled around in the dirt, drunk. One got up on his knees and began throwing up. The other two left their guns on the table, dropped their own pants, and started pulling on their cods, making faces.

When the spy man saw this, he swung his gun away from The Junior's head and shot one, two, three, and the fourth man. The fifth man would have shot him if The Junior hadn't dived across the table and grabbed him with his free arm, taking him to the ground and slamming the chair his other hand was tied to into the man's head. The one throwing up laid in the vomit, eyes closed. The spy man walked over and shot him as the guard outside the camp ran in. The Junior's savior shot him, too, with his second pistol.

They ran south in the dark until the next day, this mysterious Vietnamese and big cowboy from Indiantown, Florida, even laughing when they traded stories of who they were. On the second day, rain gave them clean water to drink from elephant ear leaves, and they bled traveler palms when they ran out of that. Once, a bamboo viper landed on the Viet man's shoulders from a tree. The Junior grabbed it by the tail, swung it around his head, and reversed directions to break its back. No regular trails were taken for fear of Claymore mines. They stayed in the random jungle, hard going without machetes, watching every second for more snakes and patrols. The Junior started to recognize his surroundings, and soon they were next to the riverbank he had been running along when he was captured. He wondered what had happened to Suskin and the other two men he left there. In a clearing, they heard vultures.

Suskin's body was torn in half. The buttocks and upper legs mostly eaten. His rib cage was missing organs, the flies were terrible, and there were big cat tracks all around. The other two were in the same condition.

"This man here is from your side. This man I know, too. He is the Moth Man," the Vietnamese savior said as they stood over Suskin.

"Yeah, we was together when I got captured over there by that river bank. These guys must have had radio trouble or somethin, cause the sergeant would have found them. He never woulda left 'em here like this. Maybe the sergeant and others are dead out here somewhere, too. I don't know."

"Tigers eat dead soldiers," the man said. "You do not have to feel bad for him because you can see he has bullet holes in him every-where. He was dead before the tiger came."

"Yeah, I see it."

In the sand next to his shredded corpse was Suskin's wallet. The Junior picked up the wet leather and thumbed through the empty folds. The money had been taken out, but the IDs were still there. Between one fold and those cards was a single photograph, the one Suskin looked at while the big atlas moth danced on his cock in the bathtub that night. The Junior held it up to see better. It was an obvious male face, heavily dragged in woman's makeup, and the big nose on the face was unmistakably Suskin's.

Chapter 8

THE BLUE GOOSE GANG

In December of '68, behind the walls of the United States, a dateline away from Vietnam, Aubrey and Leda saw *2001: A Space Odyssey*. Aubrey was overtaken, analyzing the symbolism with Trip, haunted by that last scene: the embryo-blasted Kier Dullea as Bowman circling the space ship as a star child, eyes wide open in a crystal-clear womb. Did it represent the cyclical nature of time and space? Had Bowman come back? Or was it a linear representation and Bowman had regressed to the end of infinity, where a prime mover had him reborn in a different place among the astronomy we look up to and sometimes call the sidereal "Universe"?

Leda moved in with Aubrey. Together, they strutted into places, young, invulnerable, making pacts and promises to stay cold and sure, but melting when she wanted him to shave the places on her body she shaved herself, lifting her legs and arms from the bathtub, something he thought silver as sex, then rolling in bed together after. The give-away? She would cry; his heart would ache. Whom were they kidding?

Aubrey missed music. From a young age, he was caught up in a cynosure of sounds. He missed playing in a band and introduced himself to Frank Clark, a guitar player he'd seen in a club who could cook a room.

Frank was looking for original material. He was good at composing melody, but he needed lyrics. To earn money, he worked covers, the way musicians do. Aubrey asked if he'd look at some songs he had written. Frank liked the work; he came over in the evenings to build a repertoire while Leda did the three-to-eleven P.M. shift at the hospital.

Their first job was a lounge called The End of the Road, another bar based on the short-sleeve shirt. They sang harmonies, and Aubrey did solos: Simon and Garfunkel, some Dylan, some old Kingston Trio, and an occasional slow country song for the dinner hour. In their last set, they performed their originals. They called themselves Cricket Jar. It was Aubrey's idea, taken from Nell Kitching's cricket inside the Ball jar.

Leda came to see them one night, and Aubrey did something he'd written that subtly suggested love without going too far, considering Leda's efforts to be irredeemably cool and above it. He looked at her when he stepped to the mic and sang the madrigal for the room.

RACHEL MASON'S A HIGH-CLASS MODEL AND

I'M HER LOVER; IT'S TRUE.

SHE CAN SLEEP WHILE SHE'S BEING PHOTOGRAPHED,

HER EYES WIDE OPEN, TOO.

THERE'S A LADY THAT LIVES INSIDE OF HER,

HER PSYCHOLOGICAL QUEEN.

SHE'S THE LADY THAT GIVES ME HALF OF HER;

SHE'S THE GO-BETWEEN.

In spring of the New Year, all of the Blue Goose bunch went to see *Midnight Cowboy* and did imitations of Ratso and Joe Buck forever after that. But it was the movie's theme song, sung by Nielson, the *Meistersinger*, that Aubrey loved the most.

Spring, too, was when the Okeechobee rodeo appeared, cow country's proudest occasion. The only other thing that caught the town's eye, three months before that, was Evil Knievel jumping the fountain in front of Caesar's Palace and busting his ass. Aubrey had drawn a horse called Turkey Track in the first section of the bareback bronc riding. TT, as he was known, had a reputation, and Aubrey knew if he could make it to the buzzer, he'd score well, provided he had done his part of the ride.

Behind the chutes, he sat on one end of a bale of hay, gripped his leather-handled rig, leaned back, and spurred the front of the bale to warm up his legs. Other men he knew from the circuit were doing the same.

"Hey, Aubrey, you got Turkey today, ooh-wee," a cowboy said.

"Yeah, lucky me."

"I'd say so. That horse make you some money if you get it done. Ain't seen you in two years. Thought you might be in 'Nam with Junior."

"No, college got me out. I'm gonna sign up, except my mom's having fits about it. Why aren't you in?"

The man held up his crooked arm.

"Oh, yeah, I remember. Kissimmee, two years ago. What was the bull's name?"

"Blurred Vision."

This was Florida's cowboy culture, which most Americans do not know exists. People think of the state as only sand bars and beaches. Florida is the fourth largest cattle state in the Union. Its interior parts are miles of grazing herds, a world walled off from the social dissidence during the sixties taking place in the coastal towns east and west of Okeechobee. Lots of guys in cow country were the real deal, but some were broomstick cowboys and wore boots and snap button shirts to blend in. Only a few from even the real deal would climb down between the steel on something genuinely dangerous with four legs and say "Outside!" to the gate man. Boys on the ranches didn't like the hippie thing creeping in from the borderlands. They thought it smelled like communism. They *did* like the idea of fighting for the army and had peace sign stickers on their trucks with the caption underneath, FOOTPRINT OF THE AMERICAN CHICKEN.

Aubrey walked the catwalk behind the chutes where TT stood

with the rest of the rodeo stock being fitted with bucking rigs.

"Aubrey, you're the third guy out," the chute boss said.

He slipped his bareback handle on the horse while another man used a special hook to pull the girth up, then he strung the latigo leather through and tightened it down. Turkey Track, a veteran rodeo horse, stared straight ahead.

"How you feel? You too tight?" the chute boss asked. "First time back, right? Heard you been tunin up on the Zarnitz place. You lucky to have a stock contractor where you at. How's that big Junior doin?"

"All right. Still alive over there."

The other man shook his head. "Now you knowed what TT here does. You seen him get it on. He go out to the left then he'll feint right. He's right-footed, so he likes his right lead. He'll start climbin after the first buck. Course, he might do something different this time. He is a horse, ain't he?"

"Yeah. You gonna pull his bucking strap?"

"Yep. Know what he likes."

"Don't make it too tight. I don't want choppy stuff that gets me no points."

He heard the guy behind him breathing right before the announcer said, "Now it's Chig Biggers out of chute number two, from Immokalee, Florida, getting set on Elvis, and anytime now, we'll see if ole Chig can make ole Elvis sing."

A voice said, "Outside!"

Aubrey didn't look, but he heard the crowd grown after two or three seconds. The announcer said, "Aw, too bad for this cowboy today. No time, no money, just your applause, folks."

Turkey Track stood still. Aubrey rolled the top piece of his glove over his hand in the rig handle and tactfully tapped it down with his other hand. He leaned back, each leg on a side of the chute, not touching the horse to upset him. He would bring his legs around at the last second on the animal's shoulders for the spurring out cycle that married the rhythm of bucking violence once the gate opened. In the last few seconds, Turkey did what seasoned broncs do: the horse placed his feet in favorite spots to give him traction and lowered his head a little. Much as a man taking a football stance. He knew what was coming. Then all hell broke loose.

There is this initial shock, this surge from the horse's haunches that can tear your hand out of the rigging and your bicep off the bone if you don't know what to do to help. Aubrey knew. He locked down on the snatch with his legs and pulled his boot heels into TT's shoulders with his hamstrings to give his arm some relief, which also satisfied the judges for what is known as marking the horse with your spurs over the shoulders out of the chute, as the rules require.

Turkey Track went thru the air to a spot on his left as prefigured, then coiled and shot to the right, torqueing his body in midair like a hooked sailfish. Aubrey raked his legs back and shot them forward for the next buck as Turkey's front hooves hit the ground again and again. Aubrey had the rhythm now. He had survived the horse's initial left-right move. His head flew back like whiplash, banging sometimes on the horse's croup, the lower part of his chaps flapping from the spurring. All he could see were pieces of sky, earth, and audience, of which Leda was a member, her knuckles white on the guardrail.

He heard the buzzer and grabbed the rigging with his free hand. The horse took it out of him, and he wanted off. Where was the pickup rider? Now he was there, but Turkey rolled back in the other direction against the chutes and kept bucking. The pickup man was turning his own horse to catch up when Aubrey did something a bronc rider shouldn't do. He reached over with both hands and got off on the fence. When Turkey went away from him, the horse kicked back and grazed Aubrey's right knee, as can happen. He stepped down on the ground into an empty chute and got sick.

"You are a crazy person, Aubrey Shallcross. How long have you been doing this?" Leda said to him in the parking lot.

"Ever since I could climb on one. Uh, you think you can drive my truck?"

"I can drive a truck. You must be exhausted."

He took a lame step.

"What's wrong?"

"I got off on the fence. Shouldn't have. The horse kicked me going away."

Aubrey pulled up his Levis, and the knee was swelling by the minute.

He had to have the knee drained once a week for a while. He

was second in the overall contest and won four hundred dollars. The doctor's bill came to about the same. Leda said it wasn't worth it, but he kept going to the Zarnitz ranch and bucking out horses because of who he was and where it all came from, growing up around the Florida ranches and his friend The Junior. He had tried saddle broncs, but that wanted a shorter-legged man for the quicker spur strokes. He had had his share of riding bulls, too. An old rodeo man, Wiley Elliot, once told him, "Son, why in the hell would you want to clamp down on something that can kick you in the middle of the back or hit you in the face with its head while you're sittin straight up on it?" And bulls, especially the Brahmas, were that gymnastic, so he quit them.

Aubrey bought *The Western Horseman* every month at the bookstore where Sonny worked and shot the breeze about what Sonny was reading at the time. Sonny would hear Aubrey say, seemingly to no one, down at the end of the store aisle, "I already have that one," like he had heard him say things to no one since he was a child hunting blue crabs in the river.

Once, Aubrey and Leda were in the store, and Aubrey saw Marilyn Monroe on a magazine cover. It made him remember the movie *Bus Stop.* "I'll have three raw hamburgers and a quart of milk," the cowboy said to the waitress in the movie. He considered that one of the great movie lines for the rest of his life and swore he'd use it onc day. Leda talked for some time to Sonny. She liked his partially deformed hand and stared at it when he looked away. She saw the word MIDGE tattooed on his arm and wanted to ask who or what it was, but didn't.

One day, Aubrey spoke to a friend about married life and what he thought of *him* getting married. When he got home, he said to Leda, "I want to go to this rodeo outside of Jacksonville, and I was thinking. . . well, I know this town in South Carolina where you can get married with no blood test, no nothing. Just show 'em the money. If you'll do that for me, it might buy me a little time to stay out of the army, and it'll make my mother happy for at least another year, considering it looks bad lately with this illness of hers. I mean, I know you and I are anti-everything, especially a social convention like marriage, but—"

"I'll do it, and we'll call it an open marriage."

"I think if we look at—"

"I said I'll do it."

Aubrey went to the Zarnitz ranch four times that week and rode broncs under the lights. His knee was better, though his tailbone was getting sore from banging on horses' withers in the down strokes. He worried a lot about things, and he paced around over his life with this girl from Key West he was going to marry, the toothsome girl everyone thought was the coolest girl in town. He was not allowed to say the word love, it was true, but she did have a way of making him feel he was required to love her—another double bind in a way, like what Sonny's mother did to Sonny.

They left on a Thursday and crossed the St. Mary's River into Georgia with a couple they knew from the rodeo circuit then went into South Carolina. They didn't have wedding rings and never did.

Aubrey's mother was crying when he got home. He had called her from the road and told her, and even though she was fond of Leda, it hurt her feelings that he eloped this way. He later regretted upsetting her. Told her he didn't want a ceremony, considering the way he felt about the Catholic Church now, and besides, being married might give him a pass on the draft for a while. She forgave him. She always forgave him anything that had to do with the Catholics. She was still a very implanted Methodist.

Leda's parents weren't happy, either, but her father told Aubrey a year later that it probably saved him twenty thousand dollars. Jewish girls usually get big weddings.

Aubrey could be wild and inconsiderate at times. He'd tell people off or fight them, and fights didn't scare him, because fighting was nothing compared to slipping down the sides of a bucking chute on something that would try to kill *you* when they opened the gate. He had won at Jacksonville, a smaller venue, but it felt good. He was used to winning, and he would raise his hands in the air when he was alone to do a take-off on Morrison's Lizard King line, shouting, "I am the Tater King. I can do anything!"

On a Sunday afternoon, he came down too hard on a high-withered bronc and broke his tailbone. It took weeks for the pain to go away, and something called a pilonidal cyst formed around the break. He received his draft notice at the same time and went to Miami for his physical. He failed. They told him that if he had the cyst excised and it healed properly, they would pass him. He let it go, no surgery. Felt like the pain was just an occasional distraction and he started riding broncs again with a foam rubber pad in his pants.

The barrier island across the Indian River from Jensen Beach was bringing fall surf, and the wave boys were all parked at a favorite spot called High Beach. On the way to the ocean, Aubrey checked the flame vine that pleached its way along fenced-in yards to see if it was blooming. He would not surf when it was. It was blooming when it killed his father, and his father had killed all those sharks in the water. Cross threads like these hid everywhere in the furniture of the world, he thought. Flame vines never waste energy on things like growing large roots in the ground; instead, they creep out in thin runners to choke, starve, and climb shutters so they can look into your house, clog your gutters and throat, and clothesline your father off the back of a tractor and kill him. When that vine pealed its burnt orange flowers along the lot lines and houses of Jensen Beach, it screamed, "Fire on the roof," and he would not go in the water.

One night in the bar, Arquette was celebrating the purchase of five acres and a house on Indian River Drive with trust money his grandmother left him. He was his half-cocky, invidious self. Aubrey was eying land, too, and had a rough house design he had drawn for him and his Leda. Punky came over to the table.

"Punky, I've been wanting to ask you how you're staying out of Vietnam," Arquette said.

"Asthma. I got this fuckin asthma, they said. I just cough now and then, but they got hold a-my medical records and seen I was in the emergency room as a kid. Four F-ed me, like they did Aubrey for that tailbone a-his. Bunch a shit. Aubrey's still ridin broncs, I'm doing twelve-hour work days, and that fucking Joe Namath's playing pro football after they four F-ed him for his knees. Besides, I got two kids and don't have to go if'n I don't want, probably. How come you ain't over there, Yankee boy?"

"Tell 'em why," Aubrey said to Arquette.

"I put soap under my arms at the physical, and I pricked my finger when I gave them a urine sample."

"What's the soap do?" Punky said.

"Raises your blood pressure. If you want relief from that asthma, you ought to try breathing in a little nitrous oxide. I do. I keep a bottle of it at my house. I have a guy that can get it for you. Love that stuff."

"Hey, how's the trucking business?" Aubrey asked Punky, to change the subject when Leda got up and left the table.

"Shit. Just sit up there all day and watch the world go by. Don't sweat none."

"You ought to buy that business from your father, Punky," Arquette said. "My father is helping me buy the Stinson Equipment Rental Company. He likes the business thing and the Florida thing."

"We talkin 'bout the truckin binness, me and my old man. We talkin. But I started me a lawnmower repair binness on the side already, so I'm real busy with that." Punky sat up straighter.

"Good thing for a married man like you," Arquette said. "Like our other married business man here, who has thrown himself down the well of that beautiful woman."

Aubrey shot him a bird.

"Hey, speakin of pussy," Punky said, "and I know you get plenty of that, Arquette, you and that horn colic you runnin on these town women. You guys wouldn't believe what I, and I do mean *I*, see sittin up in that dump truck a-mine. Look down in those cars at stoplights, and the other day it was bad hot. This girl had her dress pulled up so far I could see her monkey."

"Yuk," Arquette said. "Her monkey? Now and then, your sex descriptions over-do the ick factor, Punky. I believe I just experienced a half retch."

"Yeah, Mr. Fuckin Education, I bet you did. You ain't the only one gettin split tail round here. Shit, I do this girl now and then that can tighten that alley a-her's so tight, it feels like somethin Black and Decker makes."

"I see. Does the rest of her look like something Black and Decker makes? But please, keep bringing those hickey garnet stories to our Blue Goose. I love cornpone."

"You wouldn't know cornpone if someone stuck it up your Yankee ass, Arquette." Punky looked him in the eye and cut one of his signature farts. Arquette pretended to fall over backwards in his chair.

The next day, they all went to Palm Beach to see Nell. It was cool back then to say you had a friend in the bughouse. Sonny had been to visit her that morning. Kesey had written the *Cuckoo's Nest*, so that made it even cooler to go to a real mental institution, or "booby hatch," as Punky called it. Arquette loved Kesey and anything written about him and would wait on the beach in the dark for first light before he surfed, so the flash of prime green would blow the back of his head out then imagine he was a Merry Prankster.

The flame vine was blooming for real now. Aubrey stayed out of the water; stayed out of a few rodeos, too, until all the flowers fell off on the ground and lay there like glowing embers.

Leda worked the three-to-eleven at the hospital every day. Aubrey went to work on the car lot and took walks when he got home to the empty house they rented; he looked at his toadstone ring for signs as he plowed through thought. Trip would carp and poke him about the ring, claiming it was kickshaw and really didn't change colors— "some rat shit philter that gypsy sold you on." Trip wanted Aubrey to listen only to him and hounded him like a stuck trigger sometimes, talking and screaming, forcing him to get away from anyone around him until his other voice quieted down. That went on for years with them and wouldn't get better until Aubrey was well into his thirties. He would not share any of this voice of Trip's he heard with Leda. She might use it, or say he was exaggerating, or even be jealous of its abnormal regard. They so often competed for cool.

A couple of days ago, the surf was so good he couldn't stay out, even though the flame vine had not quite finished blooming. His toadstone ring had stayed pale, meaning he thought he was safe. Hours later, a mako shark circled him and Arquette, its opaque eye with dark center watching him like a stripper's cheap pasty. When the shark turned to go the other way, Aubrey saw its other eye, and it was not shark, but mammalian. It said to him, "Your daddy killed my family."

Arquette, known for stupid risks, lay down on his board and took off toward the killer, slapping the water and yelling. The shark swam a distance away, and the two men caught a wave for the beach, laughing. When they were thirty feet from shore, they looked back, and the mako was right behind them. It turned at the last second.

"I don't need this today," Aubrey said.

"I don't ever need it, but it was kind of cool," Arquette answered.

Trip was at him all the way to the Blue Goose.

"You think you're so smart with that toad ring on your finger. You thought it was all right to surf because your ring stayed pale. You saw the flame vine still blooming when we went through town. It screamed at you, and still you entered the water. How can you take one superstition serious and not the other? What a paradox you are, Shallcross."

"You know what, Trip? Shut up. Know what today is? The Junior is back. Even though he's a decorated soldier, he spent six months in a military jail for beating up some kid officer, and he's meeting us at the Goose. I haven't seen him in two and half years, so shut fucking up!"

At the Goose they all sat, joined by a new guy they'd met on the beach named John Chrome, a young English teacher at the high school who seemed a quiet person. His body was heavy and non-athletic, his head completely bald, yet he had this preternatural ability to out-surf everyone at the table, and the boys had been watching him cut up waves all day. Aubrey and Arquette introduced him to Punky. It was a big day, considering. Some woman stopped by and started rubbing on Arquette. He sent her away.

The Junior came through the doors of the Goose, hitting the nail heads in the floor with his cowboy boots and size, no sign of military caparison among his cattle ranch clothes. Who on the beach side was going to laugh at his Wildroot Crème Oil hair and the affricate sounds of his southern speech, anyway? This Cowboy the Vigorous with frying pan hands, sixteen-inch arms, and something about him, dangerous. These beach people didn't know a thing about what he called "shit-kickin." They didn't grow up like him. They never got dirty or really had their ass beat, or walked for miles anywhere. They never wiped the sand flies out of their eyes fishing to eat or trying to kill something to sell so they could make a truck payment, or were laughed at in school for their accent and snap button shirts. He'd seen the signs they carried on the news when he was over there.

I DON'T GIVE A DAMN
ABOUT UNCLE SAM.
I AIN'T GOIN TO VIETNAM.

He didn't give a damn, either. "Army or manslaughter, son," the judge had said that day in Okeechobee, so he slaughtered for the army. Nothing to do with his jockstrap; the cow hunter bars in the South Florida backwoods were as dangerous as that war sometimes, so he didn't give a shit what the beach bums in the Blue Goose thought of him. Half of them went to a doctor anyway every time they got a bowel cramp.

"My cowboy monster! My ace boon coon!" Aubrey hollered at him. "Here comes the meanest good man around."

"Yeah, now, good to see all you fuckers." The Junior's eyes welled up, tough as he was. He grabbed Punky behind his neck and pushed his head down on the table.

"Get them hands off me. You been stranglin dirty nips with them things." Then Punky cut one of his defensive farts, and The Junior jumped away.

"All right. Sit down and tell us what it was like over there," Arquette said. The table went silent.

"Like Mars, I guess," The Junior said in his base voice. "Though I ain't never been to Mars. *True* magazine." He looked at Aubrey and winked. And that was all he said to any of them about Vietnam. He never criticized or valorized his time there. Down the road on vodka or bush lightning, he'd forget where he was and say something, but it was rare.

Now Trip had them all together. The Junior had come back alive. It was time to get The Junior's slipper to come over to Aubrey for a day or two and tell Trip about The Junior's years in Vietnam. Trip had waited a long time for this.

The Blue Goose gang was ready. They were all on the beach in the dark before dawn, except for Punky and The Junior, who were uninterested in the beach or "hippie drugs." With the gang were sunscreens, fluids, food, umbrellas, Quaaludes, and a syringe of Thorazine Leda sneaked from the hospital in case someone had a bad trip. Arquette brought along a small metal canister of his nitrous oxide for any emergency relaxation he might need.

Earlier at Arquette's new house, they had taken single microdots of LSD Window Pane. John Chrome, the high school teacher and new friend of the group, had purchased it from a reputable dealer. John and his girlfriend, Rose Mothershed, had tripped a few times before, but for the rest, it would be their first experience. Arquette was for once alone, without any of the women he usuriously serviced. A song from the Doors album, "Waiting for the Sun," was silent, but ready in the boom box. All five squatted on the dune, watching the predawn sky over the water.

They waited, talking low in a circle. They remembered they were talking. They were talking. "What?" one of them said. "Nothing."

"Wait. Wait," Chrome said.

"Wait what?" said someone.

"It's all right. It comes on smooth, I promise. You'll like what comes. You'll wonder if it gets too strong, but it levels," Chrome assured them.

"Oh, look at the water. You have to look. The light is coming," Arquette begged the circle. The rush had started.

"In a few minutes, we celebrate the Lizard," Chrome told the group, meaning Jim Morrison.

They sat. Not moving. Feeling the strange. The light increased. No sun yet, but coming, as something is always coming.

"Let's start the song," Leda whispered. Someone pushed the button on the boom box, and the voice he gave Victrola, the life he gave to music and chaos, Jim Morrison, Lord Byron Americanis, came strong and discernable, each clear baritone word telling the group they had gone down to the sea/ to stand on freedom's shore/ waiting for the sun/ waiting for the sun. When the rock idol screamed his scream, the welder's light cracked the ocean, and the song's bridge, DOM DOM DOM/ DA DOM DOM/ DOM DOM DOM/ DA DOM DOM, sent the group out to the edge of the horizon to pull the earth's huge fire star the rest of the way out of the water.

After two hours of just going with what they had, they tore off pieces of dark bread and ate it with cold yogurt from the cooler. Chrome kept watch. He glanced at everyone to see if they were good. Aubrey and Arquette squatted, watching the waves come in from a weak front. Leda and Rose Mothershed giggled on a blanket then laughed until tears came. Aubrey saw Leda kiss Rose on the mouth. The boys got in the water with their boards, their energy taking wave after wave. Sometimes Aubrey just rolled off his board and sank; he sat there on the bottom and thought about Harold and Betty, the drowned schoolmates from the seventh grade. He opened his eyes in the green blur and hummed an old school song to see if they would swim to him. When he came up for air, he looked in his head for Trip. Trip was sitting in a corner of his mind, comfortable, just watching him with a grin. He motioned to Aubrey with his hand to go on and enjoy himself.

On the beach, Chrome said, "Everybody looks like they feel good. Are you enjoying it?" They nodded and spun their eyes at him.

"Well then, I'll get into my own thing and stop playing the mystagogue."

"Mystagogue?" Arquette cocked his head.

"Yes. A leader of a mystical experience, don't you know."

"Arquette," Aubrey said, not taking his eyes off the ocean, "a masters in English, the teacher here has." They burst out laughing. Chrome, too.

Some walked the beach, some lay down and closed their eyes, and some went down to the water then back up the beach, trotting the pleasurable energy. Arquette was a walker and disappeared up the sand line along the water. Chrome and Aubrey moved to the shade of the Australian pines behind the dune and sat on a fallen tree.

"Whew, I'm flying," Aubrey said.

"You are good though, right?" Chrome asked. Aubrey nodded.

Chrome cleared his throat. "A guy in Miami said the best way to do this is always outside on a good day. Don't ever sit in an apartment watching TV dance crap and snow."

"I carburet that."

"You what?"

"Carburet it! Mix air with the fuel of what you said and explode it into comprehension."

"That is a good one, horse man. That's fucking mansion! We ought to talk more. I want to hear about your carburetion theories."

"You never seem like you wanna talk, Chrome, until today. My perception of you is a taciturn, laconic man."

"Listen to you spew the king's English."

"I'm stoned."

"I'm used to you drawling in those southern diphthongs with Punky and Junior. Where did you go to school?"

"In a Benedictine monastery."

Chrome went down on one knee, laughing. "Man, you *are* feeling the deeda now. You did not go to school in a monastery."

"Sure did, John Chrome. By God, I did. I am. I did. Now tell me about *your* brain's boat trailer, teacher man."

Chrome rolled his head around and made a popping noise with his lips. He said he sometimes arranged his mind using the standard devices: past, present, and future. "I'm a time freak, a left-field horologist, so I like to simply set things up that way."

The devices he spoke of had private tags, personal titles from his own capillary thought, as he put it. The past was "back peal"; the present was "float." His byword for future was the "front jut." He had cleated cryptonyms to these, like projectamenta, cavitation, wa-wa, and something he called the "*strept* float," but said he didn't want to talk about the *strept* float today.

"Tell me about the 'present' then. Just the float," Aubrey said.

"It's the everyday, you know, the moil, the grind. The work, eat, sleep, march. Or when I just go blank and see candles."

"Yeah, candles." Aubrey squinted.

"Not on this Lucy, though, cowboy man. No candles today. I'm in the future and the back peal all at once right now, no present stuff.

I'm listening to what I just said, rear-end what I'm going to say next, because I'm kind of flying, too."

Aubrey nodded.

They walked out of the trees and into the calm water of the first trough to be with Leda and Rose. The tide was lower, and the sandbar broke the waves further out. The two girls had taken off their tops, just sitting there staring in three feet of water. Both women ducked their heads under at the same time and came up at the same time, pulling their hair back with their hands, their eyes huge, lakey, with animals in the centers shooting pictures at Aubrey and Chrome.

Leda said to Aubrey, "If you want to sleep with me tonight, you have to make love to me all day." Rose giggled. Leda turned to Rose. "I read that somewhere. Beautiful, isn't it?"

"Leda, come with me," Aubrey said. "Let's walk."

She told him about the things she saw when she closed her eyes, and that they were coming like aircraft now. They knelt and dug sand fleas just to let them go and see them dig themselves back in when the waves washed back. She told him she thought she would always be able to see the aircraft and the sand fleas appearing and disappearing, even after the acid wore off. They walked and kissed and touched. Aubrey hadn't heard a peep out of Trip all day.

Later that evening, after they came down, Trip showed up as Aubrey sat on the porch while Leda took a shower. Lazy, Trip acted.

"And how is the hometown's favorite son at this point? Anyone want to buy a car from a man on acid?"

"My day off. I get to try it, so fuck off."

"I just want you to know that Amper Sand and I enjoyed this immensely. It's sort of *our* day off. We have been sitting in here watching your nucleus accumbens streak around your brain walls like something on, well, LSD."

"So what do you think then?"

"I think it is a good way to spend a day. Talk about you and that singer Clarence Carter slipping away. You can damn well slip away at that chemical wedding, right?"

"I was jittery at first, but I found it not unlike a lot of my every day, just much more intense. And there were parts that were *very* intense, but somewhat familiar. And then again, there were parts I didn't go to, because they did seem unfamiliar."

"That's because people like you who can talk to a slipper are on a kind of natural LSD their brain makes. And yes, there are places it can take you you've never seen. It will also switch you back to who you once were before you were a 'special' with me. But no, you did fine today."

"What do you mean 'who I once was'? Why didn't you say anything today, Trip?"

"Because when you take this drug it is possible to become like a child again, Aubrey, and you get to return to the more analogue brain you had, instead of the stereo one you have with me now. You get your complete sense of 'I' back for a while, like it was before your hallway opened to be part of this other world, the world of me, Amper Sand, Nell Kitching, that suspicious gypsy lady you fawn over, and unfortunately, of course, the Slim Hand. The world of slippers. You know— schizophrenia, Aubrey. Carburet it," Trip laughed. "Sure, I could have interacted with you today on that wisdom pill, but I preferred to watch you be with your old self for a while. I guess that is kind of what you do in the bone room you say you go to, when you drive out to watch the sugar cane burn. I think that could be healthy, though I would like to see this bone room somewhere in the brain you and I share and I would like to see the back stairs you must use to get to it without me."

"So what happens to normal people when they do this drug, Trip?"

"Very interesting. A singular kind of encephalitis occurs. In monotheism, the God of the Jews, the tribe who in a way invented modern monotheism, said in Genesis, 'I have put everything on the earth you need,' and that includes good, natural drugs, I suspect. When people other than voice hearers take LSD, the brain's hallway in some cases can expand enough for them to hear the slippers they bus around. Of course, when the drug wears off, they think it was just the effects of the 'religion' they ate that made them hear and see that stuff. And when they are totally straight again with their normal head stream, they think it was the Muse they heard, or some mysterious creativity they possess. I get so sick of that word—'muse.' Those are slippers they heard on the acid, and maybe even saw, but the thought of that sober would scare them on a regular day.

"What you did today, Aubrey, can be rapture, astounding or frightening, depending on the strength of the spar that runs through your sanity. Historically, the word 'rapture' was once considered to mean a 'carrying off' in the old French, or from Latin *raptus* or *raptura*, a seizure or a spiritual ecstasy. It can be all of these feelings together, too. Remember when Homer tied Kirk Douglas to the mast in a Los Angles studio so he could get siren-soaked without having to go to the real Mediterranean to be Ulysses?"

"Hollywood did that, not Homer," Aubrey muttered. "Hollywood tied him to the mast."

"Ah, Kirk, Aubrey, aboard the Nautilus in the 1954 movie. Our man Ulysses, our Spartacus in spades. I know, we agreed in college no Greek show cards like those donnish academics use. Movie examples would replace their scholastic name-drops from now on in our world, not mythology. Although I did just do a good job of combining the two, I think. Carburet it?"

"You did. Good night, Trip."

"Oh, and Aubrey, why don't you revisit a film in your head tonight that you've seen? You know, one that got to you worth seeing again. Amper Sand and I would love to watch it with you and promise we won't say a word. You've had trouble sleeping lately. Maybe it will help if you take one of those—what are they?—Quaaludes that Leda pilfers from the hospital, the pills that make you dream. I'll send the voices to start the movie when you go down to the lounge for deeper sleep. You could pick your man Spartacus again. The Kirk! Yes?"

"No. *Lilith* tonight, Trip. I know every line. I want to see Jean Seberg while my other Seberg sleeps next to me. I love you, Trip."

Soon the voices came, and Aubrey moved into the first picture before he was gone.

"Pick a film, Aubrey, any film," the voices told him.

"*Lilith*. I want *Lilith*."

"Yes, Aubrey," the voices said, and he was gone.

Chapter 9

JOHN CHROME

"There're only two kinds of stories," John Chrome said to his high school English class. "It's a famous saying in composition, 'Someone goes on a journey; a stranger comes to town.'"

A proxy for the arts and a quiet man, recessive, except in his lectures, Chrome was just eight years older than the seniors that he taught, and a lot of his personal beliefs bled into what he gave them. He could revive old, solemn sayings from literature and make them sound like Muhammad Ali or The Rolling Stones. He advocated reading, study, a factory ground vocabulary, independent thought, the anarchy of experience, and theology of surfing for mental maintenance. There were two small human noses with flared nostrils tattooed on his back, one over each lung. His secretive drug use was "to purchase enlightenment and purvey the self," he told Aubrey. Most of his students thought him just too cool to be part of the enemy, and Chrome wanted them too cool to become the enemy. When he first fell into the Blue Goose gang, it had a big effect on his life; his friendship with Aubrey had become "mansion!" as he would put it, pabulum for miles of close talk.

The group decided they would do acid again. It had been almost a year now, and the sodality among them was even stronger. Chrome liked his source in Miami and got respect from everyone for providing. They'd made the same pact and arrangements to do the drug as before. Same place, same people they were comfortable with. Arquette was with one of his girlfriends this time, Melinda, a surfer who worked at the Goose. Everyone in the circle seemed happy and sure of the future.

By sunrise, they were on out the dune, "stoned immaculate." Words from the Doors they had swallowed with the drug after the body's confinement made them squeeze the speedy part into colors and sounds instead of talking and moving around for the first hour.

Together, all of them sitting, nodding to each other the way minorities do, dividing things into fragmentS, mountainS, murmurS, before they stood to walk on the ocean instead of the beach.

Chrome and Aubrey went into the Australian pines like they did the last time to talk.

"So," Chrome said. "I wanted to ask you more about the way you look at carburetors and head tics. I'm interested in the industry of the head, you know, back wash. . . time."

Aubrey made contrails with his hands. "Carburetion: I mix air with the fuel of a thought and explode it into comprehension. That simple."

"Mansion!" Chrome nodded.

"Yeah, big house!" Aubrey nodded back. "Very red. Very swollen. But last time you sort of quit me, John Chrome. You were telling me how you unpacked time zones. You got more for me on that?"

"For you I have the last tab of acid we are going to split. Can you ride some more?"

"God's teeth, I can, school teacher."

They went for the water with their boards. There were no real waves, but they thought they surfed anyway. Everyone regrouped under the umbrellas and ate the dark bread with cold yogurt. Chrome and Aubrey kept looking at each other and making faces. Now they were really riding in the Bell X-1 with Yeager. Yeager had said, "Just before you break the sound barrier, the cockpit starts to shake the most," so Aubrey and Chrome had to walk away from the group when that started to happen and level out some. Leda and Rose Mothershed seemed to be in an intense sororal conversation and passes that looked lesbian. Aubrey and Chrome went back up in the shade of the pines, cooking.

"God damn. I'm pure soaked in it. So you really like that Rose Mothershed girl, John Chrome?"

"Yes. She's a thin-lipper, you see."

"A what?"

"I like women with thin lips. I know most men like them fuller, but I prefer thin."

"Good one."

"Say something educated to me, like you did last time as the other Aubrey. Not the cowboy bubba-boy you slide into all the time."

Aubrey stood and turned into his man Head Wound. "*Kyrie eleison*, ye crumbling Catholics! I go to a clear ontology on good pharmacology, Dr. Chrome, carbugoddamnrate it!"

Chrome smiled and stomped his feet. "You said you schooled in a Benedictine monastery? I went to Loyola in Chicago. I was somewhat of a Latin scholar, too."

"*Pax vobiscum*, then, and all that other residual shit." Aubrey looked up at the sky and yelled, "I miss you, Head Wound, Mr. Ambrose Bierce!" He and Chrome made the sign of the cross together.

"Aw, man, time stuff and moon dogs. Don't get me started," Chrome said. "I don't know how it might sound to another person, but you might. Okay, I'll tell you more about that head terrain of mine, and in my frank."

He rolled his shoulders like he usually did. "Float is my word for the present. It can be a present I'm active in, and I can be right there, or I can be there and not be there. You know, the blank stare stuff. Of course, I have to be there when I'm at work, but when I don't have to be there, I go somewhere else, like nowhere for periods of time, like most people. I call it cavitating. I got the cavitation thing listening to outboard motors rock in boat wakes. They make a certain sound if an air cavity forms around the boat's propeller, wa-wa-wa-wa. Hollow and low, you know. The boat-heads call it 'cavitating' when the prop does that. If I go into those blank stares with candles and wobbling air, that's what I do. Cavitate. Wa-wa-wa."

"Candles." Aubrey stared at the ground. "Table candles, tall ones. I see them. My equivalent of your wa-wa is the sound of doo-lang."

Chrome looked at him funny. "You know, The Chiffons, when they sing that song, 'He's So Fine.' When they go 'doo-lang/ doo-lang/ doo-lang,' the doo-langs turn into something like your wa-wa's, or cavitation for me, and I sort of go blank and hear the doo-langs over and over. They are my favorite words for a dead-zone existential, doo-lang, but not the existentialism they were teaching us at the abbey I attended, so I had to whittle out my own metaphysics and where I was with all that, so *misarary nobis* and pray for us, John Chrome, carburet it."

"Doo-lang!" Chrome shouted. "Truly mansion! *Misarary nobis!* Wild-ass zircons these things of ours we profess! So what other the fuck zircons were they were teaching at your abbey, and then what were the ones you whittled out on your own?"

"Thomas Aquinas, his zircons, that was the abbey. And Thomas was cool, one of my heroes and a quantum doo-langer, hooked way in to Aristotle, right? But Thomas took us through cause and effect and then just left us there, holding a picture of ourselves holding a picture of ourselves, until we got so small we couldn't see the end and disappeared, because we didn't, and actually he didn't run into the Prime Mover he and Aristotle were talking about. Something cannot be the cause of its own cause, right? You need a prime mover, a meta doo-langer, or maybe our brain isn't even sophisticated enough to comprehend the beginning of all this cosmo and prime mover shit! So it ends up that Thomas suggested we take a leap of faith, one that proposes the prime mover is really out there somehow, even though we can't see it and never have, and hope for the best. Course, like I said, you could end up with either Thomas's God, Elvis, the four-barrel carburetor, or some other rounded off brilliance as the Prime Mover if you use the leap of faith suggestion, but if you want something more touchable, obvious, or understandable, you might even settle for something weird, like the God of Asphalt Shingles, or even nothing again."

"Yeah, just the infinite puzzle of you holding a picture of you holding a picture of yourself," Chrome sighed. "The infinite regress of cause and effect and movers. I know it. Theory of reduction. Don Quixote, reading a story about a man reading a story about himself reading the story, in the second Cervantes book. Or the old Quaker Oats box and carnival midways, when you find the right spot in the House of Mirrors. All unanswered, endless, lonely."

"We have a lot in common, John Chrome. I ponder that oat box stuff all the time. What about your front jut you called it before, the future?"

"I also call it the projectamenta. It is when I trombone things like grandiosity, schemes, and of course, a little irresistible doom. I probably spend too much time doing that." He put a fist to his mouth and shot his other arm out as far as it would go, imitating the favorite big band horn. It put both men on the ground trying to get their breath. They knew some things about each other now, the same attraction to brain lands. Aubrey was tempted to reveal the crystal set in his own head, his other voice, Triple Suiter, and how he drove to the sugarcane fields by Lake Okeechobee to fly around the band shell of his skull in his monster drifties. And how he rode out of the cane as Johnny Yuma to protect the city of Belle Glade, but not yet. Needed to know Chrome better and he was good at getting other people to talk.

"What about the back peal you mentioned last time? The past?" he asked the English teacher.

"That is when I imagine something happened that did not happen, after something happened. I go over conversations and scenes that came off minutes ago, months, years, or something I just passed in my car. I make another story around it or walk through the same story again. I'm constantly redacting dialogue in those stories, as if a conversation cop would write me up because I fucked up the way that I said it the first time, and yes, *misarary nobis,* have mercy on us standing apes for being like that. Carburet?" He pointed at Aubrey.

"Yeah, carburet," Aubrey laughed.

"There is the other float I mentioned, with another kind of candle."

Chrome rolled his shoulders again, but looked a little defensive. "Tetanus stuff. I call it the *strept* float. A kind of mental poverty, a nothingness without the dumbed down wa-wa around to sooth me and make it stop. The good candles make smoke, but the *strept* candles make chloroform with their critical flicker, a luteous gas."

He said it happened when he was worried or scared of dying before anyone knew him. It was when he fell into what he called the old-fashioned nothingness nausea. He said he was better about things like that since he had gotten close to Rose over the months. "Even though she's too pretty to be with a fat man."

Aubrey told him as long as he was the school's favorite teacher and could surf the way he did, he'd always be the Bishop of the Beach, never just a fat man, and besides, Rose was a thin-lipper, wasn't she? And she knew he loved thin-lipped women.

Aubrey was going to ask him more, but there was a stirring over by the group. Rose was helping Leda up to the blanket from the water, and Leda was trying to maintain something about herself. They yelled for Aubrey and Chrome, and by now, Arquette had Leda's other arm, steering her towards the umbrella shade.

"What happened?" Aubrey asked.

"Make it stop, Aubrey. Make it stop!"

He cradled her on the blanket. Her open eyes. Floods. Fear.

"It's okay. Tell me what it is."

"Those things I see when I close my eyes, those aircraft things, those sand fleas. They won't stop."

"But I thought those were good things, and you didn't want them to stop."

"You make them stop, you hear me, Aubrey? Get my purse. There's Thorazine from the hospital in it. Stick me now, and you make them stop, god damn it!"

"Maybe you ought to give it a little time, Leda."

"No. I need you to do it right now. Stick me!"

"You know what you're doing, man?" Arquette said when Aubrey pulled out the needle.

"I stick horses." He stretched the bottom part of her bathing suit down, slapped the skin on her butt to make it less sensitive then pushed the styptic contents into the woman who said he wasn't ever allowed to tell her he loved her.

The Junior sat on a horse two days later. Next to him, another man sat his. They were hidden in the trees, a mile from the main house of the Z-Bar Up. A calf had walked away from his mother in a clearing and taken a few more steps toward a big pond's edge, where a ten-foot gator lay below the water, with only his eyes and a dot for a nose showing. The Junior knew how big the gator was because the distance from his nose to his eyes was about ten inches, and that meant one inch for every foot.

"Watch the fuckin monster charm him. He just ripples the water with his snout, and every time that little bugger moves his baby-cow ass closer to see what it is, that gator is gettin ready."

The other man pulled his rifle out of the scabbard and gave it to The Junior's gray eyes. Boom! The water boiled and then went silent.

At dark, The Junior picked up his date and went to the Blue Goose in Jensen Beach. Frank Clark and Aubrey brought their full band, Cricket Jar, to shake the rum shrine with their original songs. No more supper music; it was time to dance and get loud for the hometown people. The Junior had been romancing a Seminole girl named Susie Tiger from the Brighton Reservation, and she sat next to him straight up in her black hair. He told Aubrey once that she was the real meaning of the term "swamp angel," not mosquitoes, and that he thought he was in love.

Aubrey grabbed the microphone. "This is for my friend Junior, the American warrior who said he'd *never* fall in love, sitting right over there with that beautiful girl." The band counted. Aubrey smiled, and then in rock ballad time, with the voice his mother gave him:

BIG JOHNNY GATOR, WAS WIDE AS A CRATER;

HE LIVED IN MIAMI, FOUGHT LIVE ALLIGATORS.

A SEMINOLE MAID FROM THE BIG EVERGLADE

OPENED HIS SHIRT, AND HE MELTED AWAY.

AND LOVE LIKE A DIVE-BOMBER

DIVES ON YOU AND YOUR MOMMA.

LOVE LIKE A GOOD GRILLED CHEESE

WHEN YOU'RE STARVING AND DOWN ON YOUR KNEES.

The band took their break. All the friends sat around the table drinking and eating conch fritters, cracked conch, pigeon peas, and rice. Between The Junior and Punky sat Aubrey, locked in conversation about cooking swamp cabbage—the salt amount, the number of hog parts. Arquette and John Chrome were discussing Arquette's equipment company deal. Leda had left the table to find Rose in the crowd. The place was full of townies. Only two more months of 1970 left and then the winter people would be back, allowing the great service industry of South Florida more money for clothes, cars, dope, dreams, and leaving things undone. There was a strong hurricane at the east end of Cuba that people were watching. After his third mixed drink, a Purple Jesus chased by a beer, Punky started to cry. Aubrey put his face around to him. Punky told him it was fourteen years ago today he saw his big brother James die. Aubrey nodded, and so did The Junior. They remembered. The table went silent. The Junior stood and found Punky's wife Donna in the crowd. She took Punky outside with her to the parking lot.

Arquette said he remembered when it happened. They were all

kids, eleven years old. Punky's brother was twelve. John Chrome asked how, and The Junior nudged Aubrey. "Aubrey. You tell him."

"One day, Punky and his brother were playing in the woods. They climbed on top of this abandoned tank truck. James wanted to know what was in the big tank and unscrewed the top hole. He couldn't see in because it was dark in there. Punky handed James a match to light and take a look. They'd both smoked since they were ten, you know. There was gasoline still on the bottom of the tank, and when James struck the match, well. . . . Punky told me he saw his brother lying on the ground with just a skull for his head after the blast blew all of James's skin and scalp off. Punky seemed to make it through that okay back then, but now? Donna waits on me at Randolph's for breakfast and told me he has nightmares this time of year. Still sees himself handing James that match."

Punky came back in the Goose, and Donna went to the bar to get him another Purple Jesus. He was trying to make nothing of it. The Junior stood and pulled his chair out then placed it between Aubrey and Punky so the rest of the table couldn't hear what was being said.

"So, Aubrey. Me and Punky, we been talkin about makin shine out on the Brighton Reservation. You know, good bush lightning. We'd run it to West Palm buyers under Punky's dump truck loads. I'm gettin to be good friends with Susie Tiger's dad, and no one can touch me round those Indians 'cept the Indians."

"I'm listening."

"Yeah, well, we was wonderin if you wanted in on it, and if your part would be loanin us the money for the cooker to cook off the buck mash."

"You need some money, fine, but I can't be directly involved. Risky. The car business is too good for me to take a chance like that. Where you going to hide it?"

The Junior looked again at the Seminole girl, Susie Tiger.

Another old schoolmate, David, the boy in the wheelchair Arquette used to tease when they were kids, came into the bar. Everyone talked to him except Arquette, who wore a strange face: embarrassment now that he was grown, maybe. Arquette headed for the bathroom. On his way, he put his hand on Punky's shoulder in a rare show of sympathy, considering he and Punky constantly got into it when they were drinking. Punky nodded and his eyes welled up again, then he pulled out his famous paperclips and started bending them into triangles, putting them in the ashtray to mark it like some kind of metal scat, something he had done ever since high school. Over in a corner across the bar, Sonny sat alone with his drink, watching. Aubrey and The Junior went out of their way to say hello to him earlier. Leda came back to the table with Rose, and the evening went on.

Cars were selling for Shallcross Chrysler. The new '71 models were already in demand, especially the Plymouth Road Runner Superbird, called a "muscle car" by the press. In February of '71, a man named Richard Lee Petty, from Level Cross, North Carolina, won his third Daytona 500 in the same car, and became the Grand National Series Champion again. The car was famously painted a cerulean blue, and it could go like the hammers of hell; the public couldn't get enough of it. Punky said, "That thing so strong, it put you sideways in the street." Chrysler officially dubbed the car's color "Petty Blue."

When he wasn't on the sales floor, Aubrey liked to fool around at the neon sign shop next door, or go to the back garage and work with a country boy named Cabbage Pinley, a friend of The Junior's. Cabbage accepted Aubrey because he knew he'd get dirty, and he knew what kind of mettle it took to be a professional rodeo rider, even if he was the boss's son.

In the sign shop, Aubrey watched the colored gas in the glass with one of Chrome's wa-wa stares. He also bought a few old signs off the walls now that he had become a collector. In the back garages, he and Cabbage changed starters, points, and plugs, and talked about things like cam shafts, solid lifters, float valves, and of course, carburetors, the engine part that had marked Aubrey forever. Float valves reminded him of Chrome and the wa-wa, and god knows what kind of seals Chrome might say he had in his head the next time they talked.

At home, he sat on the porch of the house he and Leda were renting, a double shot of gin next to him. He stared into the air alone with a ballpoint and notebook of song lyrics on his lap. The west sky had a puncture wound moon, and he could feel the gin. In five more minutes, the alcohol and his whittle monster got loose; he started writing a song he would sing one day in the style of a soon-to-be-dead Elvis.

> Bobby Joe Smalltown, look at you.
> I saw you ridin into Newport News, uh-huh,
> In your full race Plymouth, Richard Petty blue.
> You got the muscle car dream all over you, uh-huh.
> Lady killer, Mr. Dragonfly, boy, you
> Hypnotize 'em with your big brown eyes, uh-huh.
> And Virginia ladies make you do those things
> When they shake that tail like a street machine,
> uh-huh.
>
> Robert Mitchum, Thunder Road,
> The macho boys have gone to ghost.
> Give me a '55 Chevy, GTO,
> Or a Petty Blue Plymouth, I'll eat the road.

When Leda got home from the hospital, she came out on the porch to sit with him. She had not been the same since the last acid trip—a dysphoria of sorts, trouble sleeping, the jimjams would ambush her. A vein stood out on her that had not been seen before, as if what she had experienced on the beach that day was truly a wrong Halloween. She inhaled the smoke from her sacred cigarettes, and Aubrey could see her profile in the dark, the white gas moving in and out of this beautiful living thing like a special effect.

He put down the pen and lyrics and began braiding rawhide strands around a whip handle used in the cattle business. His mother's health was up and down and it worried him. She wanted him to buy the car business from her. He could make time payments. The responsibility seemed a ton; he would rather just get a job on the Zarnitz ranch with The Junior, but then would feel guilty about all his mother and father had built. Braiding, Bombay gin, and writing lyrics were the quiet that took his mind off it and the rotten part of getting too far into the lefty-loose. When he was stressed, even stupid things like those blue jays he killed as a kid still bothered him because of who he was. Trip had a few Latin words to say about the blue jays. "*Toro feces! Bubulum stercus*!" Bullshit.

"Contemplation is carburetion," Aubrey said to Leda sitting there next to him, the punch wound moon almost gone below the trees now. "Mixing air with the fuel of a thought then exploding it into comprehension, that's the way you do it."

"Yes," she said in that breaking voice of hers as she exhaled her smoke. "You're so weird, Aubrey."

He blessed his own heart to have her. It didn't matter that she played those insensate no-love-to-be-cool rules around the house. It didn't matter she faked her coldness at times when it came to affection. But when she broke, she broke. He would see her eyes well up, and they made love the way it worked for them now—soft—no slaughter-house stuff on the kitchen table any more. To say it was the hijinks of his heart, to say it was the contrail of coitus still there when they first met, or those slightly dragged eyes of hers, eyes that had enough real in them when they were on him to make him feel half safe, he did not know. She still wanted him to shave her legs, and she wore the chenille robes he bought for her birthdays because he so liked chenille, for a reason he would never tell. His man Triple Suiter knew: they were the robes worn by his mother, and every man gets taken by things his mother did for the rest of his life, most of them innocent, beautiful, and nothing to do with cheap shots from *Oedipus.*

In these times, he continued to find room to resent his old god like it was a form of fervent prayer. And when agnostic feelings showed to make him long for the old god again, he suffered for it, like someone who suffers from intrusive thoughts.

When Leda suffered from what happened on the beach with the acid, he would weigh that against his own religious malaria. She always seemed to compete with him for strong, but an equipoise would come in another year that would put him in a place he felt superior to no one.

They drove to West Palm Beach to look at certain neon signage and to see a movie: *A Man Called Horse.* Leda had sworn off any drug that was considered even close to acid, but she was taking 20mg black beauties from the hospital sample wall, along with Quaaludes at night to sleep. As a treat, she lifted Dilaudid, a synthetic opiate, from the locked white cabinets. When Aubrey went off to rodeos and John Chrome was not around, she did up the Dilaudid with her new cotton sister, Rose Mothershed, because both women totaled the same rating for addiction.

Rose had given her two caps of a drug called MDA three days ago, swearing it was like speed, not acid, with more pull than push. But it, too, had a way of opening doors like acid, especially pantheistic ones—l o s t   t i m e   d o o r s that left you slow enough to record the sky that went by, but a sky that had markedly changed every time you closed and opened your eyes.

The movie in West Palm, a story of being captured by Indians, starring Richard Harris, left a large sits-mark on them. They loved it. Neither had to work the next day, so they built a fire in the back yard

121

to become Sioux tribe people like Mr. Harris in the movie and ate the MDA that came from Rose. They had bongo tom-toms and made their faces up with smiling war paint.

"When MDA first hits you, you have to fight the urge to talk too much or be overactive, a little like regular speed, but not the same thing," Rose told Leda. "If you can force yourself to be quiet for a while, then things begin to slow down instead of speed up. It almost feels narcotic, but with a certain amphetamine energy. A different feel, a small speedball effect. You drift slow, but it can feel quick. You dream and hear those mourned-up Leonard Cohen songs in your head." She said the drug was pure, and that Chrome got it from a friend of Arquette's who came through town from Denver.

Aubrey went right to the Indian movie after the first hour of silence on the drug and turned himself into Richard Harris. He closed his eyes for a coming drifty and opened them inside a garnified Sioux lodge, where red men sat in a circle with bone necklaces and wore whole Canada geese on their heads. His first vision put him in the center of the lodge. Two men walked up, an like in the movie, and stuck sharp sticks into his pectoral muscles then attached them to buckskin lines that lifted him to the top of the structure. A solar monstrance sun was blazing through an open hole up there, and like Richard Harris, Aubrey had the vision. Wakan Tanka, the god of the Sioux and all creation, came close to his face and nodded to him, while Leda beat the drums and chanted. The experience was painless, pleasurable, truly l o s t   t i m e, and the lodge was as familiar to Aubrey as the cathedral in his own head, but without the Slim Hand around. The next day, he kept thinking about it and stored the experience.

Leda went to Key West for the weekend to visit her parents. She was the daughter of a Navy pilot at the Boca Chica air base and had grown up around the wild air of Duval Street. Once, she went to see where an angel had fallen on the roof of a house trailer when word got around, and where a woman claimed to see Mary Magdalene by a gas pump every day, stories that came from the revered local writer and columnist, Frances Signorelli.

It was a time for women. Not so many years before, they were not even allowed to serve on juries or have their own bank accounts. Airline stewardesses were forced to retire when they reached thirty-two. Hefner dressed women like rabbits and called them Bunnies, implying not so much they were cute, but that they fucked like one. It began to change when Betty Friedan wrote *The Feminine Mystique*, and women were out in a hardline blitz for women and rights. And though Leda's family was conservative military, she got around the Keys and into anywhere she wanted to speak up. She picked the small town of Stuart, after nursing school in Miami, so she could cool off for a while. Then Aubrey.

"What did you think of last night on that MDA?" she asked him.

"As John would say, 'Big House!' And you?"

"Yes, I thought so. I was able to think some things through. If the group trips again, I'm going to take MDA instead of that fucking acid and have my own good time."

They saw two movies a week. The film *Klute* came out in June of that year. Jane Fonda played a call girl who discovered she worked the profession because she had a need to have complete control in her life's relationships, and of course, the money was good. "Rule number one: never come with a John, only the man you really feel for." Leda knew she was like that, the control part, and thought she may have lost it lately and wanted it back, something to reify her old self after the bad acid experience. Her first affair on the marriage was with an actor vacationing in Stuart. He got sun poisoning and ended up in the hospital. Leda locked the room door, pulled down the sheets, and sat astride him, telling him not to move or make any noise, and then faked her climax. She and the actor smoked two cigarettes together after, like Jane Fonda in the movie. The actor left town.

Anxious thought came to her all the time nonetheless, stricture-like flash backs from the beach that morning, mid-day, mid-night. Those picture things, those lights and fortress patterns in her eyes, with aircraft that wouldn't quit. And now Morrison was not her pole-star anymore, and he creeped her out with lines about riding the cold snake, "long. . . seven miles," lines that came to her when she put cream on her face in a mirror at night or sat on a toilet. She continued to lift Dilaudid from the hospital to put in her arm. On July 3, Morrison died in Paris, and Leda, in her cocky way said, "Good."

In time, Rose and Leda became even more frequent users, cooking narcotics in a spoon and drawing them up with a syringe through what the boll weevil loved to eat. This seemed to shut out the memory of the cold, seven-mile snake, this great alleviator, this other Jane, and she thought she had some right to do what she did with the actor in the hospital, as long as she didn't come. Like Fonda said in the movie, "Control," and because she came with Aubrey when she lost control, the only way for her to feel safe with him was addict him to her, and addiction was something she was sleeping with.

THE CRIPPLE MAN COMES,

SAM LILLYCROP.

HE'S IN A FILM.

HE'S IN A GYM.

HE'S IN A WORLD OF NO CRIPPLES.

HE'S BRAVER THAN ME.

I'VE SEEN HIS PELVIS.

THE SOCKET'S GONE.

THE FEMUR FLOATS.

THE DOCTOR'S BAD.

THAT SHAKES HIS HEAD.

"BEATS ME," DOC SAYS.

THE CRIPPLE'S ON . . .

CRIPPLE STRONG.

Chapter 10

ARQUETTE

On a morning before the daylight nation ran the darkness off his land, Arquette sat reading an obituary in the Palm Beach Post.

Ace of Diamonds, Jack of Spades,
Meet your partner, all promenade!
Harry Beasley, 81

"A square dancer, I bet. Little flag on his radio aerial that said he was." Arquette was alone, and so loved his voice and life these days that he often spoke out loud and called his own name. "Could that be you, Arquette? The Ace of Diamonds? Jack of Spades?"

That evening, he sat in the Blue Goose, content. And so was the whole Goose bunch lately, except maybe Leda. Even The Junior and John Chrome seemed brighter since the group first formed around a table in the old photo-taxidermied place. The aging Kingston Trio was on the sound system. The folk group had one more hit song in them: "Green Back Dollar." "I don't give a damn about a green back dollar," the chorus pandered to the counter culture, the very one that had sworn off materialism, but it turned out to be a lie up the road in the eighties, when they sold out to mirrors and money, and that flesh fucking in the name of free love and beauty they were so preoccupied with became just another form of currency to get what they wanted: German cars, cocaine, and more fucks that eventually fucked themselves and partner after partner out into the cold.

To Arquette's right tonight sat an older man, Sam Lillycrop, manager of his newly purchased equipment company. To his left sat a woman named Martha, a regular in his bed he called the Speed Bump. Arquette and his father had closed a deal for the equipment company with the owner, Ralph Stinson, and changed the name from Stinson to

Orlander Equipment Company. The year was 1973, and the town was becoming a late bloom boomtown of operators who knew how to flip palmettoes to commercial and residential zoning.

Arquette had the obit from the morning paper with him and put it on the table in the bar. "Sam, see this obituary? A deceased square dancer, I believe. I found it in the *Post*, and I've been carrying it around all day. I'm thinking of having this short poem they used tattooed on my body."

Sam looked at him. "I know you can do better."

"Oh, he already has," Martha the Speed Bump clucked. "Show Mr. Lillycrop your tattoo, honey."

"Not in here, Martha." Arquette turned back to Sam. "That's what you've always said to me, 'You can do better,' when Ralph Stinson was boss, and now I've bought the company. It meant a lot to me when you said that. What's the matter? You feel bad?"

"I think it's another tooth problem. A real Shickelgruber. I'm going to excuse myself to you and Martha and go home to my Mary." They nodded him out.

"Why does he say Shickelgruber all the time?" Martha asked.

"It means the word 'shit,' as far as he's concerned, Martha. The man's religious, and he will not say the real 'shit.' Shickelgruber is an Austrian surname. Sam told me he inherited the slur from an American general he drove around in a jeep during the war. The general liked to know everything about Hitler the gas man, so he found out Adolph's father was born out of wedlock and given his mother's maiden name, Shickelgruber. The Shickelgruber lady was Adolph's grandmother. Later, when Hitler's father grew up, he dropped the name Shickelgruber and selected the name Hitler. Sam said when the general was mad, he yelled, 'Shickelgruber!' to smear Hitler's family back an extra generation."

"I didn't understand a word of that. Mr. Lillycrop—" She giggled when she said his name, "—has a terrible limp. What happened to him?"

128

"A Nazi bullet destroyed his hip joint."

"Let's go, Arquette. I'm wantin.'"

Along Indian River Drive, she pulled her skirt to show herself, but he was watching the night blooming cereus go by in the trees—long white flowers hanging upside down that looked like little Draculas asleep in white gowns, waiting to die at first light.

"Take a drink before you and me, Martha?"

"No, I'm right."

In the bedroom, she drops her cotton. No eyes, no smiles, just serious stretches and twists alone at end of his bed, her feet on the floor, her hand on the door, pointing that girl trail at him, waving it back forth to make him swallow. He undressed—the tattoo there on his abdomen she mentioned earlier in the bar in Times New Roman that said, **High Thread Count**.

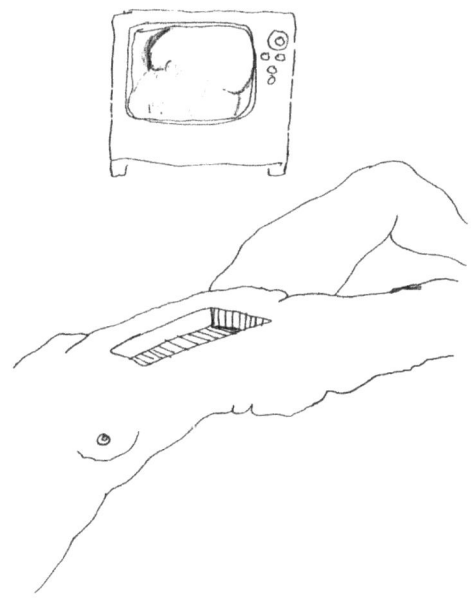

Arquette's "contraption," as Punky liked to call it, stiffened three or four times a day, an involuntary reflex, a comic bother at times, but an ability. In high school, there were moments he couldn't stand in class when called upon because it was up. Arquette was always focused on his penis. He read a book as a teenager called *The Rivers Ran East*, by Leonard Clark. Clark stumbled on an Amazon tribe that hung weights from the cocks of young boys from the time they were babies. It left them, according to the author, with this long, thin member curled in a small basket they wore on one thigh. Arquette hung small fishing weights from his own as a junior in high school, gradually increasing the weights over time, but he could not determine if his size was any different, and the pain of that was too much after a while, so he quit.

He was uncircumcised. Uncut Christians liked to believe they carried a more sensitive member. They had a theory that it went off quicker, but could recharge quicker, and then last longer for the second time. They thought they might be superior to males with skinned ones. Such unproven claims made them less shy about showering in a gym amongst the cut boys, if they thought they could out-fuck them, and Arquette was determined to out-fuck them all.

At the age of twenty, he began to work out the feat of double ejaculation without dismount or loss of post. He became very in to "box," as they liked to call it back then, or the lady's place. A genuine double fucker he was, way before dick drugs. It got him repeats and first dates when the word got around the girls like it has before language, and in this time of pessary pills, no AIDs, Betty Friedan's feminist book, and *Griswold vs. Connecticut*, the sex act had gone from suspect to grand. "Back-to-Back Man," Martha called him, because he could—the no-stop double climax and long aerobic fuck.

She spoke to him now as he bumped away, telling him to increase his speed and push out his stomach to make a gut. She backed him half way out of her so his stomach would get her sister better. Faster and faster, he hit the right place with his paunch until, "Oh! Oh, fat man!

Oh, you fucker!" She sobbed and came, pounding his flanks like her lost child was found.

Martha sat up and looked at him after he rolled off. "As much as we have had sex, I've never seen you smile when you make love."

"Sex is the most fun you can have without smiling, Martha. Someone famous said that, but I can't remember who."

"Maybe it was you, Arquette." She left.

He was a fit person. Not an ounce of fat on him. Her fantasy was a man with extra stomach. He knew about her specifics because he had been seeing her for a month. She had a thing for men with belly. Another lover of hers told Arquette she was started up by a beer gut after her trim six-pack lovers weren't touching it, the place cock shafts and pubic bones didn't seem to reach sometimes on certain women's anatomies, though a fat man's shape could. She taught Arquette how to make the German goiter by pushing out his stomach and holding his breath then bumping her with it faster and faster until she'd pound those flanks of his. He liked nothing better than that in the end from any of them. And to know they weren't faking it, he would put his finger on their necks to make sure the big artery throbbed when they came, because when it was real, that's what that artery did.

Aubrey used to say, "Arquette was the real meaning of the term "tail gunner." The "Viceroy of Venery," Chrome called him. Women adored him, as if he was some beach town's Apollo Belvedere.

The Viceroy was from a patrician New England family that lived by the cold ocean in Massachusetts. If a high-pressure ridge sat over the state, you could see Cutty Hunk, the Nashawena Islands, and Martha's Vineyard from their place. Arquette's father, a successful manufacturer, used to say, "A man once told me, 'I know no one over the age of forty that lives in New England year round and hasn't thought about suicide more than once.'" The father took the family to Florida every winter since the children were little to battle his own thoughts of self-murder.

Arquette graduated from Brown as a pre-law and business major. After class, he watched women at the lunch tables on Thayer Street and dreamed of his childhood in Florida. He put off his graduate studies "For just one year," he promised, and headed south to his old playground, where alcohol and cocaine stole time and reason from people along the Intracoastal Waterway, where he'd paddle off shore to take the waves that broke left from the northeast swells, "the left pearls," the surfer boys in the Blue Goose called them.

He had an apartment by the FEC railroad tracks in the beginning and got work driving a delivery truck for Ralph Stinson and his Stinson Equipment Company. That went on for three years, no MBA or law school in sight. Gradually, more of south Florida's largo moved in on him and others who left the north looking for jobs. "For only one month, honey," they'd say. Three years later, they are on a pay phone in a tiki bar, telling themselves and their wife in Ohio another transparent story about their future.

Ralph Stinson got the old man's hunter, prostate cancer. Like a wolf it comes, thinning the aging male herd, preying on weaker cells that fall back from the bunch. Ralph knew Arquette had a trust fund of some kind and asked him if he wanted to buy his company. Only twenty-four, Arquette made a deal with the guidance of his father.

"Oh, my wicked my!" Yankee angels sang in the cold skies over New England that day. "Why has he gone, our Bay State son? Gone from the stone walls to the southern lot lines, where Ford Ranchero pilots cruise the job sites, where the First National Bank of Narcissus falls out of the moon, where the goods are God and the working class lives in the mammon vs. debt column, and the devil in the pan picks up the real dough if an asset flies too low over the red pond, sending a young couple into the *Palm Beach Post* that reads: 'Man Loses Home and Business, Kills Wife! Kills Self! Benefit picnic for their two children Saturday on the Jensen Beach Causeway.'"

Sam Lillycrop, Arquette's general manager, knew about these

things and did his best to teach the rich kid from Brown how to spot a South Florida change artist with snot in their checkbook. Sam had his own book: *Why SOBs Succeed and Nice Guys Fail in Small Business*. He found it at a yard sale after his own small business failed. He worked for Ralph Stinson for years and decided to stay on until he retired when Ralph sold the company to Arquette and then maybe something that craved aged beef came for him.

After work, Arquette went to the gym, even if he was sick. He had something called body dysmorphic syndrome—one never likes the way one looks. He got it from movies, magazines, and American fantasy as a skinny kid growing up with a complex. The same one pitched by his home mirror and the boy next door getting more muscles than him; same one his teacher, the vegan with bad skin, helped create when it came to Arquette's weird eating habits, forcing his folks to step in when he hit 6-2 and 185. They pointed him at the mirror in his room, made him look at his good build and good looks, and hoped he'd stop the humpback preoccupation with what he thought was a bad reflection.

It didn't work. He was also a hypochondriac. He always saw a skinny man in the lying glass. When he used gyms and weight rooms, he was careful with the mirrors—stayed away from the ones for fat members that stood him taller. He was bred German and French with red hair, truly physically handsome. He had the lady killer dimple in his chin that was so deep it would accumulate lint like a navel. In his family home, every effort was made toward moral values, religion, and love, but with cold eyes. Arquette was not like Aubrey when it came to feeling and love; he was usurious with women. He didn't trust or respect women. Secretly, he believed that old misogynist cliché, "They'll fuck a snake."

Arquette told Sam Lillycrop, the fervent Baptist, a lot of business took place at *his* church, The First Church of the World Gym, and the nightspots around town were his side alters. He bought drinks in the evening for contractors and men in gold chains. Men who came to the bars with long-haired tropical birds whose backs dropped to thin waists, perfect butts, and the coin slot, a shift from the country club where he grew up, but where he thought the real business was.

"How you doing tonight, Arquette?"

"I'm well, Annie. What's fresh?"

"The grouper, but it's big grouper, probably tough, so I would order that cracked conch you and Aubrey like, with pigeon peas and rice, says me."

"Captain Morgan, too, Annie. Make it a double. Where's Melinda tonight?"

"Night off, but she was in earlier. There she is!"

Arquette motioned her over. "Did you surf today?"

"No. I can't take much more of this glass. Where are the waves? I didn't even get in the water."

"There's water at my house. Jet bubbles, too, but no breeze, just me. I am the breeze. We could place a fan next to it."

"I'll take it for you and the fan, Arquette."

They sat in the spa across from each other, fuck buddies for months now.

"How long have you been working at the Goose?"

"Too long with my dreams of getting aboard the *Calypso*." She rolled her eyes.

"I know. I meet marine biologists pounding nails and running roofing companies."

"You're lucky you have a business, Arquette. At least it's a future."

"That'll change for you. You're only in your twenties, and you do have that degree."

"Yeah, and I think I'll change a little bit of it right now. Wanna do a line?" She brought it over on her compact mirror. They took it up with a straw, and she began to unroll a coke-hope story for him.

"You know this biology stuff is all about the grants you get. The problem is you have to have something novel going on. Sometimes you think you might just make a problem and then apply to the government to solve it."

"I'm listening."

"Well, there is this two-inch fish in the Amazon, the candiru. It darts around, borrowing into fish and human orifices, urethras, anuses, vaginas, and then it spreads its spines so it can feed on a vein. I could release the fish here in Florida and write the proposal to eradicate them."

"Piling up the karma then, aren't you, Melinda? You are surfing one day and karma sends that fish up your—"

"They don't live in salt water. Okay, how about this, then? The big surprise of the evening. Sometimes I read my hometown farm paper from Pennsylvania. I saw an advertisement for an animal immobilizer. They're not really that expensive, and I've seen them used on the farms where I grew up."

"I don't know what that is, but I'm still listening."

"It's an animal husbandry item, a dildo inserted in the rectum of cattle, sheep, goats, to render them frozen in a kind of, a can't-move state. Electric pulses shut down voluntary muscles, but leave the involuntary ones functional. Farmers can castrate, treat pink eye, or whatever with that device in an animal."

"Oh, no!"

"Oh, yes, Arquette, come on."

"Not in my rectum, you won't."

"No, honey, on me."

"That's farm kink."

"That's grant kink in the name of science, and my new idea for a project. I want to find out firsthand how it affects an animal."

"Won't it hurt you?"

"Heavens no, it's only the size of a skinny four-inch dick, and you can adjust the pulse rate." She touched herself under the water.

"Have you done it?"

"What? No. I was afraid to try it alone, in case I really did become immobilized. Come on, Arquette."

"Jesus, I can see it. Local Man Electrocutes Lover in Sodomy Sex Act."

"It hasn't killed any sheep or cows. Would you rather be fucking one of your bubble heads?"

"No. Always liked your erotica."

"I can't do it in the water."

She stood up to show herself. In the bedroom, she took out a case from a small backpack, similar to a Drexel drill kit. There was a control box with wires, a separate stainless steel phallus wand, and two soft alligator clips with no teeth for face clips to produce an additional effect.

"My god, Melinda! Battery or AC?"

"AC." She opened the manufacturer's lubricant.

"So this is a backdoor deal, not something for your shar pei?" he asked.

"Oh, no, this is backdoor because, you see, a vast amount of nerves for the pelvic floor come out of the sacrum and go there. The many branches of the pudendal nerves are what freeze the animal, and when you find the right place on the dial, bingo!"

"What's the nerve?"

"The pudendal nerve, thought by some to be the real location of the body's chi, instead of right below the belly button like the Japanese say, because the pudendal nerve controls those other consoles in the crotch that give pleasure to men and women, the first chakra, the one that makes them suck air when they shudder. Just listen to Melinda. She's going to talk you through this."

"C'mon, Mel, you tried this with someone already."

"Absolutely not. You're getting excited, aren't you?"

"Yeah. I was trying to be scientific for a while, but. . . How much did you pay for that thing?"

"Fifty-nine ninety-nine, plus shipping."

"Melinda?"

"Okay, yes," getting on all fours now, her butt in the air, turning her head to him. "There is another reason. I told you, science. So the reason is I worked on a dolphin and manatee project once. There was always a problem doing the vet stuff, a lot of crazy thrashing to get needles in. I'm going back to the project to look like a genius with this device and sedate the sea life drug-free, after I redesign it for underwater use and file for a separate patent. Those PhDs never heard of this thing, but farm people like my dad know it."

"Why are we using this on you again?"

"So I can see firsthand if it works. If it renders *me* immobile, Arquette. Fucker. Aren't you listening? I need to know how it feels so I can present it and change it around if I have to. I want to know what it feels like to an animal first hand, that freeze state, so I can work on them and you can work on me," she laughed.

"Jesus. . . work on you."

"You would be surprised how still a bull gets when you put something up there. We taught dolphins to let us use our fingers, and believe me, they would be *very* still."

She lubed the wand and told Arquette he had to put it in from her kneeling position, so her hands would be free to move the dials on the control box. When she became incapacitated, as she was supposed to, he was to count to ten and turn the dials back to zero.

"This isn't weird enough, Melinda."

"Oh, come on. It's gonna be easier than putting that marathon cock of yours in that tight place."

"I don't go near the waste gate."

"So imagine you're taking my temp."

Arquette moved closer, placed the end, and applied pressure.

"Careful, careful!"

He stopped. "Melinda, I don't know what hurts and what doesn't. I'm trying to—"

She reached back and put her hand on his. "I'll do it with you. Ooh, oh, that's really in. Now wait a second."

"Do you need my hand anymore? I don't want that electric thing to shock me. I mean, I'm already shocked."

"Okay, you can have your hand back. Now I'm going to turn it on." The dials made a click. "Now slowly one, two. . . I feel it. I feel it."

"What is it like?"

"Tell you what," she said, some strain in her voice. "I'm going to take it up to four now. Can't talk."

"Melinda, if you blow out your ass inside my house, I'm a dead man, and you'll be a woman with no ass the rest of your life."

She went to four and then five. Her back arched, and she froze. He put his hand on her side to keep her from falling over and counted until he panicked and yanked the cord when he got to six. She slumped down on the bed and began laughing.

"God damn, Melinda. Melinda! Shit. That would have made a great picture Christmas card. Merry Christmas! This is my girlfriend Melinda using her animal immobilizer. She taught me how to be an animal immobilizer assistant so I could get my certification."

"Ah-hah . . . a-, a-, a-, a-. . . ah-hah."

"Would you shut up? You had me some scared."

"Okay. Okay. I wanna do it again."

"No."

"Again, right now. Only this time, I want those soft alligator clips it comes with on my face cheeks. That's where they're supposed to go on animals." She got up to her knees and elbows and placed the clips just in front of her ears. When the dial reached number five, she did more of a convulse and her eyes looked thyroid. He counted and pulled the plug.

They lay on their sides. She wasn't laughing this time. Ten seconds went by. "That was creepy," she whispered. He didn't answer. "It felt like a stroke must feel. I mean, I could hear you counting until you got to four, and then I started to panic, but I was paralyzed."

"Creepy? What about the porpoises? They're supposed to be just like us, aren't they?"

"Yeah, I don't know now. That's why I wanted to try it, but they have to do something about those face clips. That makes the whole thing scary somehow."

"What about the butt plug?"

"Actually, that was a half way pleasant sensation, and it worked. Truly immobilized me. It felt like an epidural I had once with a deep tingle."

"You'd do it again."

"Oh, yeah. You want to try something with me, baby?"

"No way. I'm not playing with that thing."

"No, I mean I'll lie on my back with it in my butt and turn it up till I freeze. Like we could do a necrophilia. You do me in front and see what that feels like to you, only I want you only to come once, not that double fuck you like to do. We may like it."

"So, no, no, I won't. Too much like Dead Girl by the Side of the Road, you iced up in a spasm like that."

"What dead girl by the side of the road?"

"You never heard that one?"

"No. Tell me."

"No."

"C'mon."

"It's stupid male stuff. Okay, then. When I was first in school, I thought I wanted to be a lawyer, so I was pledging a law fraternity.

During hazing, the upper classmen would get us in a makeshift court-room and ask us gross things like 'would you do your gorgeous older sister if she came home drunk and you saw her passed out naked across her bed?' To which there would be a resounding yes, sir! to make the seniors laugh. Then one of the seniors would stand up and give some dumb lecture about how incest was declining in homes that let young men have a car at a younger age. From there, they moved to a test called Dead Girl by the Side of the Road."

She cocked her head.

"You are driving on a country road. Up ahead, someone has just thrown a dead girl out of a car. You see her. She's beautiful. You pull over. She is lying in the grass naked as nature made her, still warm, but her heart has stopped."

"What? Oh, I see what's coming," she said.

"Yes, it's do the right thing, or do the right thing. And of course, all of the pledges screamed, 'Yes, we would.' Only I stood up and said no, I wouldn't, which was the right answer for the seniors to hear because it was a law fraternity."

"What'd you say?"

"I knew it was a legal trick, so I said I would only do it if I had a rubber, because of semen testing. Incrimination. The president of the law fraternity said, "Yes, Orlander! Good thinking!" Then they made everyone, except me, pick black olives off this big block of ice with the cracks of their asses."

"So that's what I looked like to you, the Dead Girl by the Side of the Road?"

"Right, you did."

They lay on the bed and laughed some more, the animal immo-bilizer's silver wand bouncing up and down next to them. He stood, walked to a closet, and came back with his small canister of nitrous oxide. They did a couple of huffs. When they stopped, he reached over and cupped that chi of hers she kept barbered so well. Next, he placed the hard part of his body there. She made him stop for half a minute after his first come because of her own sensitive climax until she began using Kegels to get him to continue towards the second coming, the one the redheaded hypochondriac from New England could always promise.

AUBREY'S HOUSE

Chapter 11

AUBREY'S HOUSE

He had seen it—lying in bed, out in the water, under a car—his house. Leda didn't seem to care. Another year had passed. Even she called it his house—two diamond-shaped sections hanging between tall poles, one part at ground level, the other an upstairs with a thirty-five-foot silo that ran through the middle of the whole structure. At the top of the silo was a stained glass blue eye, and inside the silo was a circular slide that went from the second level bedroom to the living room. Mirage in the woods! A land ship, hard to limn if you wrote for architecture. You swore it breathed. The Junior, not usually a wordsmith, had named it O'gram, the parallelogram appearance of the front elevation having spoken to him.

The interior had Plexiglas dioramas built into the walls, lots of Plexiglas, vitrines along the living room borders that reminded Aubrey of giant Ball jars. One of The Junior's friends, a taxidermist, offered his animal and aviary pieces for the wildlife scenes, and there were two scenes with mannequins like the ones Aubrey saw as a child in Green's Dry Goods store downtown. He was sure they made people in that store when he was four years old. The mannequins were characters from two of his favorite films: Johnny Yuma, *The Rebel*, standing in front of a western storefront against a hitching post, and Little Alex from *A Clockwork Orange* in his wild white outfit of suspenders, combat boots, and the jockstrap gizmo he wore that held a tennis ball he liked to pull out and bounce. Aubrey finished the house with other admired vitrification—neon art behind the glass headboard of his bed that said FLORIST for no reason, and a custom piece above the kitchen in yellows, reds, indigo, and orange glass tubing of the mythological Leda being made love to by Zeus, as the swan.

The place sat on fifty acres of palmettos and pine trees at the end of a long shell rock road, and oh, how Aubrey loved that road with the wetlands on either side. In later years, he bought fifty more acres on its south border. Yes, the car business was good as 1975 approached.

Soon after he and Leda moved in, an artist came and began work on murals behind the wildlife displays. There was a backdrop of Everglades savanna with distant hammock and summer sky full of thunder heads in the upper hand of Yahweh's Paint Store: whites, dark bruised blues, blow-fly greens, all boiling pink and grape castles of chrome-edged gibbous clouds from a back-lit sun. One of the taxidermy sandhill cranes below the mural held a garter snake in its mouth, a favorite candy bar of the gray-legged waders. Leda fucked the artist all covered in paint one day while she looked over his shoulder at the neon sign of her namesake on the other wall, its legs around the swan. Her house, too, now. Aubrey saw something in the man's eyes after that, but he couldn't say what.

There were parties and dinners for friends and good customers of Shallcross Chrysler, Inc. The Cricket Jar band would jam on the pool deck that looked out over the acres of pastureland Aubrey had created for the two horses he kept. One was his old mare he owned since he was thirteen.

He had drawn the house himself, a panopticon of glass and wood, so all points of the interior were visible from the outside when it was lit up at night. Arquette kept coming over, trying to get a peek at the blueprints before construction was started, but Aubrey had them hidden until he was ready to build.

Leda was rolling, the booze in her hand, the dope in her arm. She was big on the writer Kahlil Gibran now, and down on Morrison after her bad acid trip, replacing Morrison's stage-land apothegms with Gibran galore: "Don't give up your tears and laughter for the fortunes of the multitudes. Don't laugh, because the people of the jungle will say it is just the laughter of the hyena." She was getting a little vicious about people, and by now, her drug use was in the open at home. It was a time in American life that nothing much was considered dangerous or out of line when it came to dope or behavior. Chrome had caved on Rose's use of narcotics too, and it was obvious he and Aubrey were truly in love with a pair of cotton sisters, watching them draw it from the spoon through the white ball into a syringe, tie off their left arms for the blood flow because it was closer to the heart, shoot up, and go slack. The next morning, to sober up, the girls took a Rexall used for confusion and dementia in old people, called hydergine. Leda stole that from the hospital, too.

The boys tried Dilaudid a couple of times, but gave it up after they got sick from it over and over, to the delight of Leda and Rose, because it meant more for them. They would look at their men after they did themselves in a vein then in soft unison, smile and say, "Slip away." Two women; the same capacity for strung out. Still, times what they were, Leda would go slowly to Aubrey to make love, even with her junked-down libido. By candle light afterwards, she told him one of her many stories that came from god knows where as she inhaled the gas from the RJ Reynolds Tobacco Company, letting it move in and out of her as needed. Aubrey loved her stories, because even if she wasn't sure about her own feelings, he was about his. She had suborned his heart.

"A boy and girl of this world are blind," she began, and looked into the ceiling from their bed. "He, from Jacksonville. She, from Brazil. The sighted parents sent them to the Florida School for the Blind and Deaf in St. Augustine. His name was Paul, and her name was Luiza. They began to spend time with each other as they entered high school. They felt some magic, but suddenly, after graduation, her parents sent for Luiza, and she returned to Brazil to finish her education as a teacher for the blind. They started lives without each other. He became an active person in his community, a social worker who wrote two books that made him a celebrity in Jacksonville, but he never forgot the fire he had for Luiza.

"You know what I mean, Aubrey? Not the fire down below that you and I laugh about with people, but the real fire that spreads. Not the one that consumed David and Bathsheba and your girl Lilith in the movie, but the one I don't like to admit is there because it is so scary to me—the heart fire. Sure, down below, too, but when it's in the whole body, like you said your mom and dad taught you, and the one I want for you, but I, I don't know where it went when I was thirteen and got my first period. What happened to me? How did I lose that heart part? I know I knew how to love as a child. Now sometimes I think I just know how to fuck." She started to tear. He didn't know what to say. She had become weaker.

"Is this a true story, Leda, the blind people, or is this one of *your* stories?" He changed the subject, not wanting to talk about what she just said that was so ass-backwards from the tough she usually wore and put on him.

"Not mine. Not my story. Well, maybe it is. I can't remember."

"Well, finish it for me. We can talk about what you just said after. You always hang me out and stop in these stories."

"I can't. Hurts too much now. I'll finish tomorrow night."

"What happened when you were thirteen with the period stuff then?"

She shook her head. "I don't know."

He got home late after sitting on three bareback broncs at the Z-Bar Up under the lights to practice for the up-coming Kissimmee rodeo. By the time he had showered and moved to the porch of the new house, Leda was back from the hospital. She sat down in her nurse's uniform and said she was having a lot of anxiety and didn't know what to do. Aubrey told her to go roll a joint. When she came back, he told her to take a few drags then please finish the story she started last night.

"So, then," Aubrey said, to get her started. "This fire won't go out for Paul the blind guy, the one he has for Luiza."

"No, it won't go out." She stares. Quiet. "After a while, Paul decides to write her. He keeps sending the letters two or three times a year to the only address he held onto, but because of a changed postal thing in Brazil, the letters never reached her. He continued to write for two more years, until someone at the post office down there felt sorry for him and wrote back with the right address. Six years have gone by and she gets the first letter. She decides to answer it, which begins six months of writing back and forth. He said he never let the memory of her die, and he always carried her in his heart, and that, that's what love is, Aubrey. It is always carried around, but is it real? I don't know. I just don't.'"

Aubrey looked emotional. Leda put her arm around him. She knew he was alone all the time, because she had left him alone.

"What happens?" he said.

"Oh, blind as he is, he decides to fly to Brazil by himself, even with the concerns of his family, but Paul is an extraordinary person. He buys an engagement ring before he leaves and takes the ten-hour flight to Sao Paulo, where her family greets him with reserved but polite cultural manners and a dinner party with friends, to stare at this blind American.

"He is there for two weeks and they are chaperoned, but also alone with each other, refreshing their memories as teenagers and old feelings, until one day he takes her aside and proposes. Gives her the ring he bought before he left, and she is out of it over it."

They look at each other, and Aubrey pours more of his nightly gin into a glass for both of them.

"What happens?" he says.

"Maybe tomorrow night."

"No, you, god damn it. I wanna know tonight."

"Okay, okay. She says yes to Paul, and that night they tell the family. They all prepare for a wedding, which means she isn't allowed to see him for a week, according to custom. During that time, he asked her brother to help him do something he knows is done in that city where you can get anything, something in skin art."

"Like what? A tattoo?"

"No, Aubrey. They're blind."

"Yes."

"The locals make designs on their bodies by putting small stones under their skin. It's a thing in Brazil from their Indians. So he has her name, Luiza, raised in Braille with tiny stones under his skin on the back of his neck. That way, when they make love, she can feel her name right below his hairline with her fingers if she puts her hands back there, like I do with you."

Aubrey poured two more shots. "I loved that story, even though I know you made up the last part about the Braille stones under his skin."

"Yes, Aubrey, you know that about me. I make things up and I lie. I can't help it."

The place was "Royal! Mansion!" Chrome screamed when he came out to see the new house in the woods. Arquette was a little jealous because his house was an expensive Florida formula. Boring. Aubrey was proud of what he'd done, but his pride could not peak; his mother had been diagnosed with Lou Gehrig's disease, and the next day, another sad thing happened.

His old mare went down to the marsh pond on the property and walked into the cool water. She was one of those rare horses that will put her head almost all the way under to play around when she drinks. This day, in the lily pads, a cottonmouth moccasin must have resented the disturbance and bit her twice, once on the nose and once in the throat. Aubrey found her the next morning, dead in the field. It was the throat bite that had swollen so much she suffocated.

He went to the woods and cried by himself, surrounded by his sacred palmettos. Leda tried to comfort him, but he was inconsolable.

Before the backhoe came to bury her in a place he could see from his upstairs bedroom, he cut some of her tail hairs off to always have something of her. No one knew how he felt. No one. He buried something of himself with that mare. He remembered the first day he got her at thirteen. It was so hard. He sat on the front porch that night and in long hand, wrote this song.

I was arranging my course; for the soul of the horse, I survived.

She was runnin stone free, for no man to see her alive.

When the great cottonmouth, some power in the south, took her life.

Now the Gold Coast is clear, and she run like a deer from the lights.

So you rode a few ponies and you been in the rodeo,

And you know the fear getting down on the gear to get throwed.

Listen, bronc fighters, young back fence riders, top hands—

As the soul moves its station, the growing sensation, you're not a man.

As you change and become, the horse you're on, you understand.

Your image you've known, and the horse has his own; let him stand.

Caesar wants horses to ride for kill and that's all.

Cowboys who die want horses to give them their souls.

The Junior came by, and they walked around the farm. They didn't say much. Leda was working, so they went to the Blue Goose. Aubrey started talking about how their parents used to dance there, and how when he was drinking, he could sometimes see them whirling around the dance floor. The Junior said he remembered. They stared at the pine floor. A man came over. Aubrey knew him.

"Aubrey. How come I never see you at Mass? You know your father went every day. You too busy making money?"

The Junior caught the man's eyes and shook his head, as if to say, "Not today."

Aubrey only looked at the man once then back at the floor.

"You should be in the Holy Name Society. Your dad was."

Aubrey squared his feet under his chair and began speaking to the guy in Latin. "*Et unum sanctam Catholicam, et apostolicam ecclesiam.*" Then he looked away, suddenly stood, hooked one leg behind the man's, and threw him to the floor.

"You don't use the Latin anymore, Dan!" he yelled, sitting on the guy's chest. "It's a dead language, you know, and it's a dead church as far as I'm concerned because I loved that Latin, and your kind of Catholic sent it away because you were too fuckin flippant to learn it. I want to hear the language of Peter. I don't want the language of Henry's church and those other English speaking fuckers when I sit in my old church!"

The man, in shock, did nothing. The bartender asked them all to leave.

Aubrey woke up the next morning at The Junior's on the Z-Bar Up. He had a headache from drinking and told his office he wasn't coming in. They sat and ate white marsh grapefruit, the ones with lots of seeds the tourists won't eat, but all the old Florida people do, for its taste.

After breakfast, the two men rode deep into the ranch's improved and unimproved pastures; ten thousand acres of greensward surrounded them. There was a painter's sky that could outpaint a painter, and they sat their horses in the middle of the palmetto kingdom.

"You ever notice how the palmetto is completely green out here, and the palmetto over by the coast where I am is blueish in color?" he said to The Junior.

"Naw, not really."

"Look at it next time you're at my place."

"Who was the fuckin do-gooder last night?"

"Someone I was an altar boy with."

They rode on toward the cattle and found them grazing in the open.

"Beautiful, ain't they?"

"Yeah. Glad I'm out here with you."

Aubrey went to town after they took care of their horses then headed north to Ft. Pierce. He walked into the tattoo parlor next to the surf shop. "Glen, I want you to mark my arm with some language."

"Sure. What you want me to do?"

"I want the words SERENOA REPENS on my right arm, at the top of the bicep. And I want it in this certain font. It's called Copperplate Gothic."

"Okay, brother, but you have to spell that for me. I'll look up the font style. What does that mean, if I can ask?"

"It's the Latin name for the saw palmetto around here, and I want it in a lighter blue ink, the color of the ones that grow closer to the coast."

He drove back to Stuart thinking about his house. He wished to be buried with his mare when the time came, out in the palmettos that stand for the lower southern States wherever you see them. He walked the seawall from his mother's down to the old fisherman and his wife, Reve. He kept his new tattoo covered.

"Aubree," Reve called when she saw him coming.

He told her about the snake and his horse. They sat outside under a banana mango tree, the only one of its kind in the county. The tree was full of gold fruit and green ones yet to ripen. Reve peeled one with her knife and gave it to Aubrey. Then she spit the juice from the saliva and snuff in her mouth into an empty soda can next to her, and took a piece for herself.

"I call this mango tree the Rain Tree," he said to Reve.

"What you mean?"

"Because it makes me think of the movie with Montgomery Cliff and Elizabeth Taylor. It's the only banana mango tree in this county, like the rain tree was the only rain tree in *Rain Tree County*, the name of the movie. Tastes like a cross between a banana and a peach."

"Yes, it is good tree. I talk to the tree and it talk to me. And you, Aubree? You talk to the slipper? What his name?"

"Triple Suiter."

"Yes, well, my slipper talk to me, too. Sometime he talk from this mango tree."

"I wish I could talk to my mare again."

"I know, Aubree. One day you go where the slippers are. You ride her again. I see her smile at you. She wait for you. She put the wind in your face again. The gypsies have always loved the horse more than the dog or the cat. The cat lick its fur and sex like the dog do. They are

154

unclean inside for that. They are *mahrime*, the gypsies say. The horse does not lick himself and is clean inside."

"Reve, I feel like I don't have anyone soon. My mother is dying of this awful disease, my mare is gone, my lover seems distant and self-destructive. My slipper is trying to help, but I'm having problems with the other slipper in my head, the one I've always told you about, the bad one I call the Slim Hand."

"Yes, Coker told me 'bout you mother. It is not fair what the evil does. Those devils like the Slim Hand are bad slippers and hide evil in the belly of the sand skink and moochibonereens under you mother's house. I give something for the house to help her. That most important. And I give something to see if you woman loves you, then when you know, you know what to do."

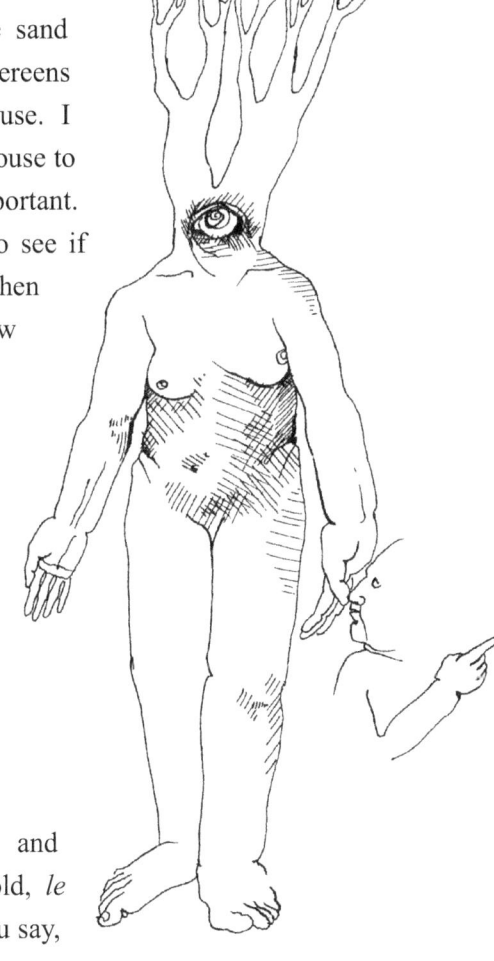

She asked him what month his mother was born. When he said November, she said she was born then, too. She stood and picked two man-goes, one golden ripe, the other green.

"This mango is the color of my stone and you mother's stone—gold, *le citrine,* the birthstone you say, when she born. The November. And this green mango—" She held it up. "It turn gold, like her birthstone and my birthstone, in one week. One time a week, you walk down riverbank to me and bring a green mango to you mother house. In one week, it is gold, and she must eat. It is her color. When mango turn gold, it give her the strength. She must eat then. *Les enfants*, the babies, get ripe in the mother. They come out as the gold mango. We try to make you mother the color again, like baby before. The gypsies believe these things. Know these things. The gypsies are *drabarav*. They read you, but do not write these things I have told you on paper.

"If the friends come to see you mother, they must leave by front door. They leave by back door they take the good luck with them, the *bonne chance*. When you leave house, close door three times so bad luck no try to get in. You should look at you *crapaudine*, the toadstone ring I make for you. See what the colors I teach you say. I will give you little bag of the acorns from my old home, Quebec. Put them on the ground around the bottom of house. The sand skink and the moochibonereen will not go by them to go under the house. If acorn take to the seed, do not cut the little tree. It will bring the bad luck under the house again if you do."

Reve stood. Went into her place and came back with acorns and some dried yellow grass. Aubrey took them. She wove the grass into a knot he'd never seen. She told him to place it under his pillow tonight. If the knot was undone in the morning, it meant his relationship with Leda was falling apart, but it didn't mean it could not be saved, she told him. "It dat damn sand skink again," she said. "Dat a bad lizard."

"Since I was a little boy, you have talked about the skink and the moochibonereen. I have forgotten what that last one was."

"It what gypsies call, how you say it, the Spanish, the *chupacabra*. Like that. Same thing, only it different."

"Oh, yes, I remember now."

"And Aubree, take two acorn and put them in bowl of the water when you home. If they are close together in the water tomorrow when you wake up, then you love with Leda maybe okay. Many maybees in love." She shook her head.

He walked down the walkway and looked back at her.

"*Bonne chance*," she said. He nodded.

On the way home, he was stirring, and so was Triple Suiter.

"Why did you have to mention me to her, Aubrey?"

"Oh, give me a fuckin break. I was praising you. I'm not a little boy anymore, so you don't have to worry about her getting more respect from me than I give you. What am I going to do to help my mother?"

"The best you can."

A week later, he drove to the cane fields and then east into West Palm Beach, where he parked in front of a row of offices along the water. One of them was marked David Sloan, Psychiatry.

"Don't you get out of this truck, Aubrey," Trip said. "I'm telling you this as your life-long tutelary spirit. They are going to medicate the hell out of you."

He didn't.

Chapter 12

CARBURETION

Alone on my back porch, me—Aubrey. Leda working tonight. We've been in the new house a year now. I'm thinking about the Blue Goose bunch. All of us. Our mob. Thinking about Nell in that place she's in. It's early March when the whippoorwills come back from South America for the bug life. Like old warplanes, they dive—same sound—mouths wide open for their own love of swallowing.

I know I get plenty off. Turn into my man Head Wound, clowning around, or jiggering the *strept* Chrome talks about with his candles. And my friends? They get that way. And I know they know that I know that they know they do. We, me and my friends, spend a lot of time imagining we are something we're not. We all seemed happier a year ago. Where is the kindness and compassion among us? Too much self-exaltation now. Too much Tater crap. I was not raised by moody Tater people, and when the *strept was* around, when times were not good, my mother would sing her Garland. "When you walk through a storm/ hold your head up high/ and don't be afraid of the dark." This was the way my folks dealt with trouble. But now the drag never seems to lift with me and this Goose bunch. We know how to bomb ourselves, the wanting to be happy, not wanting to bullshit. "Oh, look at me. I'm the saddest great thinker at this table, but I'm cool." And then Arquette comes on to feel good about himself with this fake boilerplate that eats off other people's failure. What's the big German word for that, him with his barracuda business ideas? John Chrome dragging himself over the furniture in his head because he's over weight and afraid of chloroform. The only two not living this are The Junior and Punky. But I wonder. How do you walk through a war like The Junior did and keep walking right? And that Baptist, Punky, always talking dirty and doing illegal shit while he rides around with a bumper sticker on his truck that says Jesus Was a Fetus Once. I mean, I know I'm in it with them, this dramatized incontinence, this Jim Morrison wanna-be glory and his boy-god Rimbaud stripping the gears and the doo-lang of the world down to no hair. I'm always doing imitations of that fucker.

My Ambrose Head Wound Bierce would love this cynicism around us; big cake appetites we have for hip burnout and mock majesty, as long as it's painless. Romantic star shit. We need more righty-tighty. We'll come apart from it if we don't tighten up; end up like Nell's dead mother, holding a Polaroid for the Tin Snip Killer and the Buddha. Whoever mentions other people? Who mentions their family when we are at the Goose? Or love—not considered cool. Leda is the gang leader of "not cool" when we sit down together, though now and then she makes me think of that Dylan song line goin round this year, "She breaks like a little girl."

Sometimes I see Sonny from the bookstore sitting in a corner with a drink, and I think he knows we're acting like this, but I never can catch him looking or sizing us up. I did speak to him when I was leaving the bar the other night. I asked him what he was drinking, and he said, "A sidecar." I remember when he told me about sidecars and neuroses. That could be happening to Leda. Or me. Or anyone at our table. This fake fad called depression could turn into the real thing.

Trip, you want to talk about it? No. He ain't around. Does that sometimes. I know what he's gonna say, anyway. "Work it out, Aubrey. Everything is either *toro feces* or *veritas*."

I got to get out to cow-country more. Get away from this great suffering artist crap. I need the woods. I do miss the kindness, the ranch people, the compassion my father and mother had. I need to be on a horse in a dogtrot going somewhere in the palmetto kingdom. Cow hunter. The real me. Wish I could leave this car business and make a lower living, but there's something wrong with my mother the doctors call hell, and they don't know how to fix it. I bring the mangoes from Reve to her every week, and she seems better. Never complains. The steel hibiscus my mother. But I wonder what happens when all the mangoes get ripe and are gone by summer.

PART TWO

Chapter 13

SHIP IN A BOTTLE

Sonny leaned over the workbench. In January of '75, old man Crane died, leaving no heirs. He left Sonny the little magazine and bookstore, and a country place outside of town no one had ever seen. Sonny would lie doggo there for days, and opened the store less and less. Fawcett Publications discontinued its *True* magazine publication after forty years, and Aubrey and The Junior quit coming even for the *Western Horseman*. It wasn't the same for Sonny anymore.

The property he inherited had a house trailer under some oaks, and there was a creek off the river's south fork that ran from the Harris Ranch. Sonny built things there—long-tonged guided things inside glass bottles, his sacred enclosed things, the unusually large bottle in front of him now the size of an aqualung with a primitive inferior bone arrangement he had made inside. When it was finished, he installed a regulator on the bottleneck and filled it with Freon. Thin line emphysema tubes went to a nose fitting on his face, and he danced around the trailer, the glass tank strapped to his back—some kind of scuba in the dry, just high enough to do as he pleased, acting out on the memory of his mother, who had recently stroked, and imitating her falling to her knees while he stood there and did nothing, the wrong-arm behavior she fret-worked on him as a child stuck in his eyes and bent gumption forever. He acted out the departure of Beth, his wife, who Sonny couldn't live with because she wouldn't flush a toilet she peed in and left the toilet paper lying on the edge of the yellow water. Sonny was pretty bad off over that woman-pee thing and wondered if there was a phobia prefix for that. He looked in the dictionary at the one thousand kinds of phobia prefixes. Didn't find it.

Sonny always had his gas, but was careful. Knew too much

would damage you and wanted it to last the rest of his life. A world *mit* gas: breathers had oxygen; Aubrey had neon; Arquette, nitrous oxide; Leda, cigarettes; John Chrome imagined gas candles in his head that trenched a green light. Punky had farts. The Junior had ozone for his Vietnam cough, and half the surfer boys on the beach huffed fumes of paint thinner so they could close themselves out on the beach, or in wave, and then slip away.

Sonny was surrounded by congeries of bottles he'd collected in the house trailer. Sometimes he made tiny creations using miniatures from liquor stores and kept them in his pockets all day. Each bottle, no matter what size, was filled with Freon after he finished his work. He never saw a bottle he didn't fetish some hermetic capture, some jailed piece of weird, surrounded by refrigeration's halo element Randy White had given him up in Ludiwici, Georgia, years ago.

There were times he had the urge to get inside an old refrigerator as a captured art piece himself, fold his shape like his victims, and become a self-portrait. He sought the elision of these suicidal thoughts by huffing more gas.

At the bookstore, the few days he would open it, Sonny read old stuff, new stuff—Voltaire, Goethe, Luigi Pirandello's plays, Mickey Spillane, Norman Mailer, Herman Wouck's, *Youngblood Hawke*, even *The Western Horseman*. He went to the Palm Beach rest home to see Nell. Nell would move into word salads he couldn't understand, common with her brainworks. On weekends, he went to his hideout by the creek to get high, build another mooncalf inside a glass container, and leave it soaking in Thomas Midgley's famous gas.

Comfortable in his backwoods place, he thought himself invisible and eventually moved there permanently. He had two junked refrigerators on the property. They sat in the weather like empty coffins. Waiting.

On the huge Harris Ranch across the creek from Sonny lived a halfwit named Half Track, after the half-track swamp buggy whose cleated rear belts took it and its hunting party anywhere through the muck. Sonny's place was two miles from the small houses, barns, and main house on the ranch where the foreman, Half Track's brother, lived—the good brother who cared for his with special needs. When the brother went hunting, he took his broken brother on the half-track, letting him sit high on the tower with his floodlight grin, and that's how he got his nickname.

Half Track liked to wander great distances and watch Sonny from the palmettos. When his brother asked him what he did today, he mumbled unintelligible sounds. His brother would smile and pat him on the back.

Sonny had a sense of his surroundings, so it wasn't long before he discovered the retarded man spying on him and instead of going after him, he befriended him after he saw he couldn't speak, write, or sign—a perfectly safe companion to have around. Twice a week, Sonny fed him lunch. The ranch foreman followed his brother one day, and Sonny told him it was okay for Half Track to stop by. The man thanked him for being so kind.

Sonny had seen most of the Blue Goose gang grow up, with the exception of Leda and John Chrome. He was, in a hidden private way, protective of them, and even though he never mixed with their crowd now they were grown, he had watched their lives in the Goose or his bookstore when they came in. The new movie *Liberty Valence*, with John Wayne, James Stewart, and Lee Marvin, was an armature for how Sonny saw himself with the group. John Wayne shot Liberty from the shadows to save his friend James Stewart from being shot, though no one knew it, even though James Stewart had won the woman Wayne loved. Sonny wanted to be that unselfish, invisible guardian, like Wayne. He wanted to feel better about the bad things he had done, along with the other bizarre bracelets he wore, the ones woven into murder and perversity, not the softer lanyards of fantasy and social misdemeanor the Blue Goose gang wove, white toast and platform shoes compared to Sonny's no-shit homicide and blood-cram.

The Goose bunch? The Junior was the only one among the friends who knew about killing and guilt. He had to drag around Vietnam. Punky's guilt patrolled his brother's death when he handed him the match that day on top of the old tank truck; Arquette's was because he didn't like his body; John Chrome didn't like his, either. Freon, neon, cigarettes, nitrous, ozone comforted all of them, but nothing seemed to work better than each other. That's when they felt the best, sitting in the Goose on a good night when the artster-gloom was off the table, exchanging stories and knowing smiles so they could laugh themselves continent from anything they couldn't live with while Sonny stayed to himself in a corner of the bar with his real history of horror and pretended they were his family.

Sonny was giving even more attention lately to balancing out the bad stuff he had done—those sick, blackout crimes. Wanted to pardon himself somehow, move away from the mother rage that made him do those women in Georgia, in Florida. And he especially regretted killing the minister's cat and dog that belonged to the doctor who sent him to the leprosarium years ago. The minister who said his leprosy was "God's will." He did love the creative part of his murders and the way he framed them, but wanted to make up for the deaths of those little animals he once put in there. When he looked at the junked appliances in his yard, there was an almost insuperable urge to climb in one and close the door. Click! He thought if he just curled inside one of those white boxes and smothered himself, then at least the animal murders would be forgiven by somebody. But he thought about some of the human ones who had it coming, and the future ones who have it coming, and that was worth staying alive for. He read somewhere, "You can't offend nature," and he loved nature and loved that saying, and he had watched closely the *werks* of it all, opening the mud dauber's nest to see paralyzed spiders waiting for baby wasps to hatch and eat them. He knew, like Aubrey, we, and everything else, ate the babies of others, and our babies ate the adults and babies we killed for them. "Can you offend nature?" he mumbled. He thought at times it was possible.

He went to see Nell again at the Palm Beach place. They sat in a corner and talked. Sonny gave her some books from his store. He asked if she was all right. She was talking very straight now, the words salads she used in his last visit weren't with her. She told him everyone treated her well except one nurse, and she pointed to her walking down the hall towards them. She said she wanted to go sit on the porch now the nurse was in the room, because the nurse had bit her.

On the porch, they were quiet. Nell said she could hear the trees talk and the grass grow. "It makes a screaky sound."

"You have an uncommon gift," Sonny told her. "There are a lot of things you are able to do and see that other people can't because of your gift."

"There are sounds I don't like, though. I don't like when people chew ice."

"Me, either," Sonny said.

"My doctor tells me I have a condition called misophonia. He says it's when your brain turns certain sounds into pain."

Sonny loved the word for that and wrote it down. He also got a good look at the nurse Nell didn't like.

In the bookstore, on one of the few days it was still open, he listened to townspeople talk. A woman was telling her friend about a man who had veal calves chained to posts next door to her place. She said she saw him flank a calf, cut its throat, and hold it up by its hind legs until it bled to death. She said he seemed a cruel person and

167

that the county had given him citations for conditions unacceptable for animals.

When Sonny got to the man, it was late at night. The man walked through the veal farm in the dark from a storage shed, and Sonny hit him with a bat and hauled him to his property on the creek, along with some butchered calf parts he found lying around the man's place.

There, the calf killer was fitted with the big glass aqualung full of Freon, the one with the bone sculpture Sonny had made inside, the dial on the giant bottle set for gradual delivery to his lungs through the nose tubes, and he was chained naked to one of the refrigerators outside in the mosquitoes to remind him of a veal calf's life. In a semi hallucinatory daze from the light doses of gas, the man flailed around and cried, crawling over the calf legs and heads Sonny had scattered. After two days of no food or water, Sonny turned up the gas on the regulator, but not before making one shallow cut across the bot's throat, so he slowly bled into the ground. Sonny had no interest in making cuts in the skin with his tin snips like he did with his other kills.

He placed the dead body inside the old refrigerator, drove to a park in another town late at night, unloaded his work, stood it up, drove away. Risky, but worth it.

The next day, in all its spook, the curled up body in the container surrounded by butchered calf parts was discovered with a note that said, "He Offended Nature." No Ship in a Bottle written in blood this time, but the usual Polaroid in the man's hand of the man in the refrigerator, holding a picture of the man in the refrigerator. Infinite regression. Sonny hoped the Polaroid picture would take the son of a bitch out somewhere so small and far away he was gone forever.

This killing distracted the Blue Goose Bunch from each other and gave them and the national news something to talk about, and like everyone else, they kept lights on in the house all night. The town was more than worried again. They had recently tried one of their deputy sheriffs for brutally murdering two girls, and the deputy had confessed to murdering more because he was crazy and alluded to being the Tin Snip Killer. They thought for sure they had Tin Snip this time, but were disappointed.

Chapter 14

THE POTATO THIEF

Excursion Day. One day a week, the Goose bunch went looking for restaurants, concerts, bars, a movie in West Palm Beach. Leda had seen the film *Seven Beauties* reviewed in the *Post*. She was fascinated by the woman director Lena Wertmuller with the German last name, who made Italian films about the outrageous behavior of her leading man, Giancarlo Giannini.

The movie began with archival footage of misery from World War II, narrated in English—declarative statements in a deep pedal note voice, and at the end of each, the narrator said, "Oh, yeah."

"The ones who don't enjoy themselves when they laugh. Oh, yeah."

"The ones who worship the corporate image, not knowing they work for someone else. Oh, yeah."

"The ones who should have been shot in the cradle. Oh, yeah."

And this went on for thirty-two more consecutive times and became an anthem for the Goose bunch, only they made up their own "Oh, yeahs," and took turns in the bar shooting them across a table while Sonny drank another side car in the dark at another table and listened.

Leda: "The ones who think they live in the real world instead of Fort America. Oh, yeah."

Aubrey: "The ones who dress well but have a yellow front tooth. Oh, yeah."

Chrome: "The ones who think three in the afternoon is another form of purgatory. Oh, yeah."

Rose: "The ones who think Detroit is mentioned in the Bible. Oh, yeah."

Arquette: "The ones who eat vegetables and still feel like shit. Oh, yeah."

Melinda: "The ones who think judges touch their dicks when they're trying a sex case. Oh, yeah."

Punky: "For them that pick their noses at stop lights. Oh, yeah."

The Junior: "For them what can cook a steak without lookin at their watch. Oh, yeah."

The Goose Bunch didn't care about:

The Weather Underground

The Whole Earth Catalogue

The Patty Hearsts

The IRA

The PLO

The hijacked planes

The Norman Lear television shows

The hippies

The presidential scandals

The music they liked:

Ry Cooder	Leo Kottke
Jesse Winchester	Pentangle
Vanilla Fudge	Harry Nilsson
Poco	Lowell George
Cat Stevens	Neil Young
Dylan	The Doors

The Junior and Punky listened to Waylon Jennings, Meryl Haggard, Little Jimmy Dickens, and didn't read much. The rest of the group read, or claimed to read:

Ferlingetti

Kosinsky

Kesey

Magazines

Camus

Mailer
Roth
Didion
McGuane
Flannery O'Conner
Wisconsin Death Trip

The Junior only read *The Western Horseman*, and Punky read *The Shotgun News*.

Aubrey. Watching waves from the beach. Chrome in the water eying a set, taking the second wave on his Dave Sweet board. The balletic fat man, the nose rider, the cutback artist who loved the ocean; six pictures of Duke Kahanamoku in his living room.

Out of the water, Chrome sits next to Aubrey. Silent. A whole minute goes by. This week, they've all seen *One Flew over the Cuckoo's Nest*. Finally, Chrome speaks two important words from the movie to describe the last wave he took. "Juicy fruit."

"Yeah, definitely. Slipped away on that one. How's it going with you and your old lady?" Aubrey asks him.

"Oh, Rose, Rose Mothershed. Sometimes a mother to understand. I mean, I always have the feeling she might pick up her clothes and go, but in between, the stuff of a gorgeous, thin-lipped woman. We scream and yell, but love can be snot and sugar, sand spurs and sand castles, and it doesn't bother me; it's just that I hope the fat man doesn't bother her, if you know what I mean."

"Yeah."

"And your sparring partner? How are things with the married couple?"

"Touchy. Leda's doing too much dope with *your* sparring partner."

"Where are they getting that lately?"

"She takes it off the hospital, but since Nixon closed the store in Turkey, your Rose has been getting this brown heroin from

Mexico. They snort it. Doctor Brown, they call it."

When Leda's on, she wants show time. Attention. Her time, her smokes, hard dope, speeches at the Goose captivating people (men in particular), getting their full attention with her tank top skin. Her favorite thing: she might know something you don't, and even if she doesn't, she can make you think she does. She has an extreme interest in a song of Dylan's called "Ballad of a Thin Man." Dylan suggests that Mr. Jones walks into a room and sees all this bizarre stuff and concludes that something is happening here, but he doesn't know what it is. Leda uses that same cliff when she looks down on people with her Angie Dickenson squint and makes them think she knows what is happening and *they* don't know what it is. She told Aubrey once she thought Dylan believed he didn't know what was happening, either, and in fact, that was the subtext he was scattering in the song. She said that is why she and Dylan were believers in the theater of the absurd. In these moments, Aubrey loved her, because she seemed completely honest. In moments like these, she got into his heart even with her vainglory and flag, but when she dropped the flag, she'd drop to her knees, wrap her arms around his legs, and cry into his thighs. He couldn't help it. Had to love her for that.

The artist is back at the house to do a mural touch-up. Aubrey is at work. Leda and the artist thrash in the living room then put everything back the way it was. Leda, the arbitrager, going long with Aubrey and short with the artist to cover the drought in the part of her ego that belongs to her other self, the withering one that is always starving.

Aubrey comes home at five. Leda has gone to the hospital and he is alone. He calls Chrome.

"You think it's worth it?"

"No. Small waves."

"Wanna go to the Goose and drink?"

At a corner table, they watched people. Chrome started to talk. "You know what my dearest told me the other night? She came home mad because she has been advising her girlfriend on her marriage. The husband got pissed when he found out and told Rose to 'Pull her uterus out of her box, drape it over her face, and smother herself with it,' which I thought was very creative. She got really pissed at me and wanted me to go over to the couple's house and help her beat on the husband to make up for me saying I thought he was creative."

Aubrey started laughing about the uterus and spilled his drink. When they quieted, he asked Chrome if he was doing any writing.

"Some. Measured. Easier in the summer when school is out. I find it hard to stay jacked-up enough to write and calm enough to live. But seriously, no one with an ounce of real blood in them who's read Byron is relaxed anymore."

"Or listened to Lord Jim," Aubrey said.

"Yes. Morrison was Byron flipped another way with a great band behind him. Especially that organ player. Dead as Byron now, though. I have always been attracted to Buddhism as a balm to counteract too much Byron, but I'm not good at it. Buddhism, I mean. And I think it affects my writing. I write fiction and believe good Buddhists make lousy fiction writers, and lousy Buddhists make better fiction writers. That shit's too peaceful."

"You and Byron."

"When I'm drinking, Aubrey."

"And I'm Neil Young and my man Head Wound. . . drinking with you."

"What are we going to do with those two hellcats we live with?"

"I know. This hard dope thing has got to stop. Leda gets pretty bitchy when she's out. And between that, my mother's illness, and my wondering what the fuck am I doing in this town as a car dealer, I'm thinking I might start shooting up with Leda."

Chrome ordered another drink. Aubrey ordered a sidecar.

"Know what Hemingway said when they asked him about his drinking?" Chrome sat up straight. "'Modern life is often a mechanical oppression, and liquor is the only mechanical relief.'"

"Oh, yeah."

Aubrey has this feeling about the artist and Leda. He never forgets when she told him the story of the blind lovers in Brazil—the man, Paul, who had stones put under his skin in Braille so Luiza could feel her name there. Aubrey remembered he told Leda he thought she made it up, the Braille stones part in the story, and she said, "Yes, I make things up and I lie. You know that about me, Aubrey. I can't help it."

One day he is home, and the artist shows up with surprise in his eyes to see Aubrey. He stutters that he just wants to touch up a few things on the murals. After he leaves, Leda acts mad and says the artist is bothering them, but Aubrey is suspicious. After working late, he goes down to the river to see his mother, then walks the seawall to Reve the gypsy lady and her husband, Coker Barnes.

"Aubree!" Reve hollers, as usual. They sit on the porch.

"Aubrey, I'm goin floundering tonight. Wanna come?" Coker says, walking away towards the river.

"If I can borrow a pair of your sneakers."

"Okay. Twenty minutes."

Aubrey leaned into Reve. "I think my lover is seeing another man.

He's been doing some work on a mural at my house. I looked all over for clues, but never see anything out of place."

"And what did the acorns I give to you do in the bowl of water?"

"They floated apart."

"And the woven grass I give to you to put under you pillow?"

"It came undone, too. But I toss in my sleep, so maybe I did it. I just don't see anything that would give me proof she has been with him."

"Ah, maybe she be a bandicooter."

"What's that?"

"Someone who goes in you garden, pulls up you potato plant, steal the potatoes under it, and put the nice green plant back in to ground, like the potatoes still be under there."

Leda . . . into her stories again. She has taken a 20mg Dexedrine on a Sunday morning and is sitting on the porch.

"Did you know spiders can raise their abdomens, spin off a length of silk, and catch the wind to reach altitudes of 5,000 feet?"

"No. I want to talk to you about this dope thing, this Pegasus you and Rose are doing."

"Pegasus?"

"Yeah, Leda, the white horse. The one with wings. Heroin."

"But we don't do heroin. We only snort that Dr. Brown and use some Dilaudid I lift from the hospital."

"But that stuff is all smack. I don't care if it's artificial, brown, or plant life. It's still smack!"

"So who are you, the moral brigade?"

"Sweetie, you got to be careful. That shit'll make a mess of you."

"Okay! Okay, I will. And did you know that in the summer, any cubic mile of sky over a temperate region contains twenty-five million insects and other living things drifting high in the air, the way plankton does in the ocean? In the Beartooth Mountains of Montana, there is a wall of ice sixty feet deep, thousands of years old. Summer makes the surface ice melt, and layers of ancient grasshoppers and bugs are exposed. The bears and birds go all the way up the slope just to feed on the wall as it melts further in. I have always loved spiders. There is one in Africa that gathers little crystals from the soil, places them around its hole, and then strings a line of silk around them. When prey touch the string, it makes a musical sound, and the spider races out of the hole to eat them."

"Where do you get this?"

"I majored in biology before I went to nursing school."

Aubrey's sometime fear of self-erasure, insanity/death, came from living with the way he was, the hallucinations and choking. When he had sex with Leda, he wanted the other kind of erasure, the one he deserved; the one that lovers find when they disappear in each other. Some part of this with her had changed now. He felt at times that she was that spider in Africa. He'd reach out for her, and she would come at him with a saturnine face that said, "Don't!" as if she'd put a string around her. They were starting to empty their relationship out on the floor; it lay around like worn clothes. She hardly came to see him with the band anymore, a good thing maybe, because some of the new songs were coming from the refuse that followed them home and were getting personal:

> LADY LASER STARE.
>
> YOUR BED LIKE A LAIR.
>
> THE WHITE ANGEL SLEEPS THERE.
>
> IN BLACK RIVER YOUR HAIR.
>
> HE NEEDS THE DARK JADE,
>
> FOR TIMES THAT HE'S BEEN MADE,
>
> AND DON'T KNOW WHO WAS LAID OR WHERE.

GOD BARES HIS WHITE FANGS,

SCREAMS OUT IN STREET SLANG,

MY ANGEL'S BEEN GANG-BANGED.

WHO'D DARE?

FEMME FATALE WOMEN, THE LOVES OF MY LIFE.

The bar was quiet at the end of the song. He'd played it solo on an acoustic guitar. People stared at the stage. He went over to a table where Chrome sat.

"I'm telling you, Aubrey, you ought to show this stuff to some A and R people in Miami. It's pretty swollen."

"Tell the truth, motherfucker."

"I am. There is one line, as an academic, I would draw your attention to, and that's when you say, '*femme fatale* women.' That is a tautology, like the term 'widow woman.' Kind of redundant."

"Yeah, but that's the beauty of it, Chrome. It's redneck murdered English, like the song is pure murdered human love."

Aubrey brings up the subject of heroin again. Leda gets furious.

"You have your music. You have your rodeo life and business. That's how you slip away, so I get to slip away!"

"Yeah, but that's the healthy slip away. That junkie stuff you do will kill you, Leda. When one door closes, another one *doesn't* open."

"Oh, and rodeo won't kill you and close the door?"

He had no answer. She turned and left to meet the artist, the real "slip away" in the song Clarence Carter was singing about.

That door did close, but on both of them. Leda closed it. And it would only be a matter of time before she would close others. Aubrey had angered her, gotten more attention in town than her. He thought it was the junk that shut her off from him, but she was more about the self-exalt. Her turn to be the blind Tater. She considered it her duty to compete with everyone and had no idea better-than-you was driving her crazy. She threw vanity at herself like jai alai. It was one mental day after another, and on the other side of town, Arquette was failing, too. He seemed only as happy as his body, and a pain had started to show up in his crotch after sex.

He tried to ignore it at first. "It'll go away in a couple of days," he would say. He'd been sore before, considering his interest. But it didn't go away, and deep in the pelvic medulla, far up from where the pain in his crotch was, the large pudendal nerve rubbed against an anatomical thorn bush, a bony protuberance of pelvis, turning the nerve into another flame vine, one that bends downward from the sacrum to innervate the rectum, the scrotum, and the penis on that side of the body. The hard hump of lovemaking can repeatedly drag the nerve across the notch, the friction fraying and inflaming it. It can be an inherited, anatomical disposition, or one that occurs after trauma—a gymnastic split gone wrong, a deep squat at the gym. It was Arquette's bad luck to have one of these anatomies, and considering his preoccupation with the love act, the nerve on his left side would not stay couched in its normal place as he aged and went on and on towards his signature second coming when he made love. Medicine would only learn years later what it was, and because it mimicked the catch-all diagnosis of prostatitis, urologists made good money with their first finger, telling Arquette they could feel his prostate was "a little boggy on the left side," when in fact, it wasn't. The prostate and the uterus, very lucrative in the world of healing and have been blamed for everything.

When he got home, Melinda was returning from a marine biology convention where she was presenting her ideas to put dolphins and manatees in a freeze state with her animal immobilizer.

"Melinda, it seems I have this little irritation in the area between my legs, and the doctor said it may take some time to abate."

"Uh, what kind of irritation? It's not herpes, is it?"

"No. I got checked for any infection. I may have to back off the love-making for a bit."

"Oh, honey. I'll be with you the whole way with this. I will. Don't you worry, baby. I don't need that sex. It's my heart in this with you."

And she meant it.

Chapter 15

THE CEMETERY: FIRST VISIT

Full moon coming up. Aubrey fretted. Hadn't been to the cemetery yet and it was Easter. He always took lilies for his family. His father and grandmother's grave. Trip told him on the way there it was time they had a serious talk about things swirling around their world and it should be in the cemetery, an appropriate setting for their kind of ontology based doo lang. So they left the house, bought the flowers, and turned into the paved road by the mausoleums then onto his family plot. He was nervous, respectful and felt at a loss for words as usual.

The moon was higher and pallid now, making the graveyard look dimmer-switched—a black and white film night scene—his father and grandmother below the granite monument. There were two spaces left, one for his mother and one for him. He saw the six-foot distance through the gumbo to the bottom of the graves. What did it mean when his mother said something was "Dead as a doornail" or a "dead ringer," other than the obvious? Was that one of those stupid alliterations, or did it have some real message you had to decoct like those Jesus stickers on Punky's dump truck?

"It is both, Aubrey," the underarm angel said in his usual glissando slide down the bicep dressed in a loud, Jack Taylor, three-piece suit for the occasion, ready to peel some skin from the other ego he had to deal with every day. Trip always held out a few garnets for the cemetery. "Yes, flying-pickup-truck man, it is both. There is nothing deader than a doornail, and there is the dead ringer, too. I bet you know dead ringer has more than one meaning besides the twin thing."

"Yes, I think I do," Aubrey said, uncomfortable.

"Okay, so you have heard that one. How about this one? A man asked another man how his friend Fred was. The other man told him that Fred had swallowed his birth certificate."

"Meaning?"

"He died."

"Oh, funny midget, considering my fetish, I guess you're suggesting that will be the last thing I try to swallow."

"One would assume so, if you can get it slim enough, considering your fetish."

"That's it. We're going. I'm left."

"Oh, but Agnostic Man, I know how to get you an easement through this secular thicket you are in if you'll let me."

"Sure you do."

"I think I do. You have to do what every person does to reset themselves. You have to rehearse. Recognize the major size and importance of the objective world again, the natural world. You are too much up that bone stretch tank of yours, up in that magic aerie you inhabit screw balling the subjective goods and you lose your take on the real, on the *True* magazine."

"You're bothering me with that pompous vocabulary of yours. What the hell is a magic ee-rie, or however you say it?" he asked, leering at the animation on his arm.

"Aerie. A lofty nest, I believe Webster says, at the top of that tower you say you fly around in your head. And yes, the other place you like to be is down in the tombs, in your sleep lounge, with one of your films and Quaaludes, and if you don't talk to me here, I will throw a schizo fit when you go there next. Schizo! And remember, my vocabulary you make fun of is in a way your vocabulary. Schizo!"

"Don't say tombs. I'll be in that truck seat, promise."

"Oh, come on. You are already comfortable in your sleep lounge. That is like a tomb. You call it that all the time. I have heard you. Why should it be any different here?"

"Because when I'm in bed and I dream, I'm still alive in that sleep lounge, that tomb, but not if I was out here."

"But you don't stay in the ground out here when you die, Aubrey.

When it is over for your body, you go to those same movies you ask for every night. What is in these graveyard coffins is your bug shell, the molt of your kernel, the dead skin of the orange clock you love, and it stays here in the cemetery after your consciousness blows through the scar in the top of your skull and out to the stars with that fetus of Keir Dullea's, orbiting the space ship at the end of *Two Thousand and One*. There's no senseless abyss. It is going to be you, I tell you, all Quaaluded, coked, MDA'd, LSD'd, and doo-langed into those films of yours after you have slipped from this form into another. You will just move out of one windmill into a bigger windmill with a more marvelous breeze, subsumed by the new eternity. Maybe you even become as I am, a voice for someone, a slipper. I'm kind of an infinity resident, you know—me and the other voices in people's heads being walked around this water ball."

"Makes it easy for you then, doesn't it? So where did you come from? And where are you going after this, Trip?"

"I come from you and that big windmill out there, and I am going back to that after you pass through. I am going with you."

"That's what you always say when this comes up, but you're at peace with that, and I'm not yet. So why can't I get a peek at what's out there, at least? Why can't I look through the top of my skull anymore, past the turning scar, and see it all—the stars or him again, sitting on the cloud chair? And if he's *not* there, I'll know once and for all he's not, and get some peace."

"Who? The god of Abraham?

"Yeah, or something else. What is he, a big fuckin windmill?"

"That is right, existential man. And you used to be able to see that even when you were a serious agnostic, didn't you? Agnostics always place him right outside the door so they know where to find him if they chicken out. But your door is closed now by that hypertrophic scar in the top of your skull, the one you see when you go to your big room or you black out and the Slim Hand comes around. You opened and closed that door too many times when you were younger. You have gone past agnosticism into a lonely atheism now, so you cannot check on him or the windmill anymore. Scary, huh? Hell, some days you don't even think you are a god anymore, Tater man."

"Seems so, doesn't it? My Catholicism crashed I guess. My rosary has broken. My beads have all slipped through."

"Uh, that line would be Bernie Taupin's line and Elton John's melody."

"I know. Maybe I have to have a near-death experience to see something on the other side."

"Aubrey! You can get it through rationalizations and epiphanies while you are open with me."

"I tell you, going to the top of my skull in the Blind Spot Cathedral on those hand hooks feels like death, but I never see anything except stuff that looks like chest X-rays up there. So why?"

Two raccoons were walking by on their way to a well-known trashcan. They stopped to watch the crazy man talking a mile a minute to no one around the gravestones. They looked confused and kept going.

"I was not part of you, Aubrey, until you were five years old, and by then you had had the bad dream. The swallow one. But because you had the dream, I got to be on both sides of the blood barrier with you out of your developing child ego and old god religion to help you deal with things, remember? Even though I am a slipper, I was Catholic coaxed and cultivated as your guardian angel, gardened by your grandmother to make you feel better about those moles on your body. Then you ran with it, you and that bowel powered head-still of yours making me up large, like the Bible made up Adam. I bet your grandmother never thought that angelic mole story she told you would get this swollen. But where were we? Oh, Catholicism. . ."

Trip reminded him how his exposure to people in the Catholic institutions of higher learning had touched him, especially a few of the priests Aubrey knew in the sixties that defrocked themselves and left the priesthood right after he graduated from college. All those late-night conversations on the subject of whether Zulus go to heaven if they don't know about Jesus, and how many higher-thinking Catholics and priests believed they *do*, and that you don't have to buy exclusively into the man/ god concept of Jesus Christ or transubstantiation to find salvation, as long as you follow your heart and conscience into what you decide is the *True* magazine. Trip laughed when he said he bet the public could not dream these declarations or apparent heterodoxies would come from a Roman priest or monastery, but a few of the more luminary priests at the old school, the Abbey at Belmont, got that across to Aubrey. "That kind of free thinking has been around those sacerdotal workers since they burned people or locked them up like Galileo, but they would not have said anything back then for fear of the same."

Trip told him it was the parish priests who were so closed-minded and different from the intellectuals in the Catholic universities. He said parish priests and their homiletics with grave faces told you to believe them or get mutilated by a griffin.

"They screwed up everybody when you were a boy, made you a product of that old orthodox exegesis, the one with their kick-ass god and his foot soldiers working the two-faced holy Tater stuff on you for control."

"I love you, Trip. You know, someone asked me once if I was ever molested by anyone in the church. I had to say yes. . . intellectually."

"In a way, maybe, but you should continue this free thinking direc tion some of them gave you. There are good priests, even great, noble priests. Follow yourself and your man Head Wound when it comes to those four-way stop signs around town. You will figure out which way to turn, because the Trickster in the white collar really will get you to make the sign of the cross over and over, until you finally cross yourself or he crosses you, and you become some crazed doxology head banger. Then he will hold out his hand for money. You need to keep on with this happier life you are putting bolts through. I know you are wrestling with the faith dilemma, trying to settle into a spot that works for you. And I know you are not going to be satisfied with someone else's design, because you like to make your own stuff; that is you, Shallcross, but this particular original design might be hard to bring. So many people have already offered their mark on a finished drawing of what they think religion, philosophy, and the whole credenda of mankind and cosmos is supposed to look like, but I know you. You are not going to copy them; you are no appropriationist, Aubrey, even though you kid about only stealing from the very best."

"Are you backing whatever I come up with for a personal belief? Are you saying that will help solve the aerial torture in the top of that black church when it comes? The Blind Spot Cathedral."

Trip nodded. "I always have." He continued to talk and answer Aubrey's questions as best he could. His theory was that the aerial performed in the Blind Spot Cathedral was a manifestation of Aubrey's fear generated from thinking he was godless or pointless. He said, "Nasty slippers like the saprophytic Slim Hand thrived on that kind of mental desolation." Trip reassured him to believe in his own idea of god or science and the answer to the infinity question: think it through without the historical prompters. Make the scaffold he liked. He didn't have to be married to these messiah mongers or dharmic about the religion he was raised in to be happy. "I chose my idea of god because I always thought He, She, or It was a broad generalization of all of us, Aubrey. I realized this was not like the oils they put up. This power, whatever it is, was just as flexible, stressed, and amazed by the directions things take as any human, especially people whose head voices talk to them every day from these cranial bone rooms, like you and I. You know, the ones other people like to call schizophrenics. God, It, or science has always had a Slim Hand to battle with, a rotten slipper or rotten force. Watch the news. You see it."

He told Aubrey again, when it came to this power or kind of a god, it was like us. "Not the omnipotent bad ass god the Old Testament claimed. That story just wanted people to fear so it could win them over at the time. And Jesus, well, he was as much a son to that god in the story as you are, Aubrey, so you ought to cut him a break. Again, this is only one way to look at it. Hell, maybe there's another story. I mean, I like the Bhagavad Gita and the Daoist angle, too."

"I don't really mean to slam on Jesus, Trip. He was one of my first heroes, a story told me by my father and grandmother with much love and sincerity. Shit, he was my first cowboy, my first Shane, the first one I ever met killed in action. I've latched onto a lot of guys killed in action since then, whether they were gods, Spartacus, Johnny Yuma, Nick Adams, or somebody at the fire station."

"I know, Aubrey. And there were many before them, and many more will be coming after that, that love the truth and beauty of doo-lang and Chrome's wobbly candle floats as much as you and I do."

Aubrey looked down at the remains of his family and knew they would consider some of what was said here tonight heresy, putting C. Jay and Big God on the toilet every morning with the rest of us. He told Trip he had to leave now. Trip made him promise they would come back and promise to tell him more about the tower and bone arcade he'd hidden in his head from him.

Chapter 16

THE RAW OF AVERAGES

The Junior didn't last long with the Seminole girl, Susie Tiger, though she remained a good friend. She wanted to be a virgin before marriage, as was the tribe custom, and she would have never put those safety pins he liked in his scrotum, if it had come to that. Instead, the bachelor cowboy, through his liver, found another swamp angel, Thimble Taylor—beautiful, with a gracile figure that went about five-foot-one and 105 pounds—and Thimble thought the safety pin thing was good and crazy. Her size reminded him of Mary Din Tan in Vietnam, and he told Aubrey she could do a cheerleader split on his fence post. Her family had nicknamed her Thimble. Aubrey kidded him about their size difference all the time. Susie Tiger eventually married Albert, another member of the tribe, and an awful thing occurred.

On the banks of Bessey Creek, off the north branch of the St. Lucie River, a high sand ridge runs along the water. A species of short leaf pine lives there, and so does the gopher tortoise, or what locals call a "scrub chicken." Albert, Susie Tiger's new husband, made a small business out of selling poisonous snakes for venom to the legendary Bill Haast at the Miami Serpentarium, and the ridge along Bessey Creek was where Jake the diamondback rattlesnake lived with the gopher tortoise in his burrow. The turtle makes a nice hole in the ground and is a vegetarian; the snake can't bite through the tortoise shell and likes those ground holes, so cohabitation works for them. Albert would shove dry grass in the hole and light it. When the smoke got thick, the snake and the tortoise came out coughing. Now, Albert had a favorite food, the turtle, and another live rattlesnake for Bill Haast to milk in Miami.

Comes a nasty man named Cobia Lukens from the backwater

garbage cans of the St. Lucie and Allapattah Flats, his face mottled and pockmarked like the moon. Up Bessey Creek, he slinks in his boat with another fisherman on an October night, using an illegal seine net for mullet. He slides by Albert and Susie's camp around one in the morning, quiet with just oars, unnoticed, but Cobia noticed *them*. The two men were drinking. They started talking about those goddamn Indians that come all the way from Okeechobee to fish their area and hunt. They turned the boat around and beached it. Albert and Mary were asleep. Cobia hit Albert in the head with his catfish club, and both men grabbed Susie. Cobia raped her. Albert was out cold the whole time.

Susie never told Albert about the rape part because of the line it would have drawn on her. One night, the other man with Cobia, who held Susie down, got loose over some coke and Quaaludes and told The Junior's taxidermist friend Henry what happened, right before the man absquattled north to Cedar Key for good. Henry told The Junior, and The Junior went to the reservation and stole a moment with Susie, who would not say it, but her eyes welled up when asked. The Junior's body jerked when he saw those eyes, and he wanted to touch her shoulder, but didn't. She said she had never seen the man before and showed him a set of car keys that had fallen out of a pocket. The Junior took the keys and left to think. *Would he beat Cobia to death if he could find him? Would he shoot him out of his boat at night for the crabs?* He lay in bed and turned on the small ozone machine he brought all the way from California after Vietnam. He put his face in the charged, rain-smelling air and breathed until he fell asleep.

The Z-Bar Up Ranch, owned by Caspar Zarnitz, is twenty thousand acres. Not the biggest ranch in the county, but number two on the tax rolls. There are miles of improved and unimproved pasture to breed cows and produce calves. In a remote area of the unimproved part, The Junior was turning barrels of corn, water, and sugar into buck mash then cooking it off to get bush lightning, or moonshine.

Punky worked with him. Punky's tank truck was used to bring the water in, and The Junior had a way to buy corn from the ranch's feed company by paying off the delivery driver with his own cash. There were other ways to get into the ranch besides the main gate. Some nights, the two men would sleep there while the big kettle dripped money and shine. The Junior had to can the original idea of cooking it on the Seminole Reservation, but would take free jars to Susie Tiger's family on holidays, because he liked being with the Indians. He never forgot his Seminole squad member from Vietnam, Freddie Tommie.

Four days had passed since he talked to Susie, and he was drinking at the Johnny Jumper Inn in the West County, when the black Indian Freddie Tommie, who he'd been through hell with, walked in.

"Holy shit! I knew you was around. A guy from Brighton said he seen you in Ft. Pierce," The Junior hollered.

"That's right, soldier. You miss that M-60 you used to carry?"

"Not at all. And I don't miss that Agent Orange. Hell, I still cough from that shit."

"How 'bout you pull that scrotum up to your nipple in here, and you and me make some money?"

"Never done it here. Waiting for a bigger crowd."

They talked. After a while, Freddie said, "Somethin's eatin you?"

The Junior told him the Albert and Susie story, the rape he knew had happened, although neither Albert nor no one in the tribe knew. What was he going to do with that no-count motherfucker Cobia who did it?

"I can't do it with my hands. I been in bad trouble with that. There must be a way to kill him, him with those liver-colored eyes a-his."

"If the tribe knew he had raped her, there'd be hell to pay," Freddie said. "Let me talk to an old mossback on the Ft. Pierce reservation and tell him a Seminole girl was raped. I won't say who. Promise."

The Junior left for his shine still on the ranch. Punky was there, tending the fire under the cooker. Punky took down a beer in five swigs, burped, stuck his finger in his ear, and rolled it around. Cut one of his noisier farts. The Junior sat, listening to the still drip.

"Well, how 'bout that goddamn Arquette lately?" Punky said.

"What about him?"

"Bought that big house on Indian River Drive. Took up serious with that good-looking girl Melinda."

"So? You still hate him?"

"Shit, guess not. He's all right sometimes. Now he with Melinda, can't imagine him not stickin that gar fish a-his in ten different women a week."

"Next subject."

"You ever see Aubrey talk to himself the way he does?"

"Always did that."

"Fuck me, I'm startin to do it all the time, too, and my Donna thinks I should go see somebody about it."

"Somebody like a head shrinker? You'd be better off seeing one a-those asshole doctors and getting that broke-down thing a-yours fixed," The Junior said.

Some killdeer flew up in the dark, bitching about the noise, and the two men heard coyote song dogs out on the pangola prairie. The Junior would tell no one else, not even Aubrey, about the rape incident.

Aubrey was itching to ride in rodeos again. He'd laid out all summer to have a surgeon excise the pilonidal cyst on his tailbone he got from banging down on the withers of bareback broncs, the injury that kept him out of Vietnam and probably saved his life.

He and The Junior drove west to Okeechobee, then north on 441 past Yeehaw Junction, and skipped the turnpike to go through ranch country towards Kissimmee. There was a rodeo there that paid more. Aubrey had drawn a bronc he didn't know, and The Junior entered the bulldogging. Three jumps out of the chute, Aubrey's bronc started to just run. Aubrey leaned forward, looked at the horse's head, and saw his eyes were closed. The end of the arena was getting closer. He'd been on what was called a "blind bucker" before, and knew this is what he had. Bad luck. The horse hit the fence at the end and crushed into it, and Aubrey did, too, cutting his head open. The Junior bull-dogged a steer that poked him in the face with a horn, and one of his eyes filled with blood. This sent them both laughing toward home after thirteen stitches for Aubrey.

"Shee-it. Look at us. Ridin down the road, beat up, dumb cowboys again," The Junior said.

"Yeah, I should have just bailed off that horse, but he sure was flying. That thing could run."

They stopped at the Desert Inn Bar, in Yeehaw Junction, and started to drink and laugh more to kill the pain. The lady bartender lowered a rubber spider on a string into The Junior's face, and he threw peanuts at her. The place looked a lot like the inside of the Blue Goose and had been there forever. Aubrey stood up to examine the neon signage and put money in the jukebox. Gene Pitney came on with Liberty Valence. When the chorus said, "The point of a gun was the only law Liberty understood," Aubrey sang right up there as high as Gene, so perfect that two ranch girls stood up and dragged him and The Junior off the bar stools, making them dance with them for the next song.

They all sat at the ranch girls' table, drinking.

"You boys rodeo cowboys? You been up in Kissimmee today, ain't ya?" one girl said.

The Junior smiled, but didn't say anything. Neither did Aubrey.

"I know y'all are, cause I seen an RCA sticker on your truck when we come in, and you guys look bucked off to me, him with that blood in his eyeball and you with them stitches in your head. Hell, I can still smell the hospital on you, honey." She looked at Aubrey. Aubrey just shrugged. The girl reached under the table and put her hand on his leg.

"Know what, pretty girl? I am very married."

"You ain't wearin no ring."

"Took it off so it wouldn't hang up on something."

"You guys win any money?"

"Nope. My friend got a horn in his eye, and I got a horse that ran into a fence instead of the paycheck, my dear."

"My dear?" The girl made a face. "Would you listen to him, Lou Ann? He cute."

Two black guys came in and sat at the bar. The bartender didn't look happy, and the ranch girls didn't, either. It was 1972, and Civil Rights hadn't done well yet in cow country.

"God, look, two niggers black as road tar just come in off the Turnpike," the Lou Ann girl said to the table. "They oughta know better in the Desert Inn. There's lotta ole boys round here do something about that."

He should have kept his mouth shut, but The Junior was fresh from 'Nam, and his man of color Freddie Tommie had been one of the reasons he lived through it. Freddie sat in his heart and always would. "So what's wrong with them?" he said to the girls.

"You hear that, Darlene? We might be sittin with a couple nigger lovers right now," she laughed.

"Lord, Lou Ann, I think you spotted a couple right here at this table," the other girl pointed.

"Aw, why don't we buy you girls a drink? Then we gotta get going," Aubrey said.

The girls got louder about the black guys. Then Aubrey got loud about it. "I'm gonna explain something to you tonight, ladies, right here in Yeehaw Junction. Why don't I tell you the history of you and me? It starts in Africa, in the middle part where they find this skull, yeah us, you and me, older than any skull ever found anywhere. No, not in the Holy Land, but in Africa, in a riverbed. Then they put it through something called a mass radiocarbon spectrometer, and boom! There it is, miraculous, the real stuff, the oldest ever, the *True* magazine, our beginnings. Then that skull wandered out of Africa and its skin turned whiter and whiter as it went north, and now you know where you and I came from. Africa, ladies, like those guys at the bar. Carburet it?"

The one girl looked at the other and started laughing. "I swear, Darlene. I believe this cocky, better-than-thou-and-you-and-me just called us a couple of niggers. Hey, Cecil!" she hollered. "Guess what? This guy in here with the big education just called us niggers."

A man walked out of the back of the place, the biggest guy Aubrey ever saw. Kind of fat. The two black guys at the bar put some money down after they heard the girl yell and moved towards the door. The big guy said to them, "You people stay outta here, if you know what's good for you!" They kept walking.

The big man came to the table. He had brass knuckles on his right hand. "You a Freedom Rider or something, mister?" he said to Aubrey.

"No, he a bronc rider. A lousy one, too, cause he keeps hittin his head when he get bucked off," one girl said.

Above the table, a hunter ceiling fan made that sound—nick, nick—like the helicopters in 'Nam, and it got louder in The Junior's ears as the big man stood there.

Aubrey boiled from the comments. The Junior flashed back to the jungle mess because of the fan. It was getting dangerous. Nick, nick. One of the girls looked at Aubrey and The Junior and seemed scared of what she saw. Then the other girl stiffened just as Aubrey jacked straight out of the chair to hit the big man, and the man caught him by the throat in midair and held him off his feet like a hanging. The Junior waited. When Aubrey turned purple, swinging his fist, and blood started dripping out of his stitches, The Junior stood and told the man to let him go. Aubrey fell to the floor.

"We be leaving now, biggie," The Junior said to him.

The man came up in his face. "I know you, buddy." Nick, nick. "You beat someone to death couple years ago in Okeechobee. Friend a-mine."

"It was self-defense." Nick, nick.

"Crap!" the man said.

"We're leaving. Come on, Aubrey." They walked past the guy.

"Nigger lovers," he said. Nick, nick. And it went through The Junior's ear into one of his arms with a closed hand, and that hand caught the man's head from the side. The same hand that killed the man's friend years before. The same one that pulled the trigger on his M-60 machine gun and killed many more. The guy staggered. The Junior hit him again. The man fell on the floor, a large pile of Central Florida flesh. The Junior reached down, took the brass knuckles off the big hand, and shoved them into the man's bloody, tongue-slung mouth. They left.

Freddie Tommie sat with the black tribe's old medicine man days later. The Junior was there too, and told him what had happened to a Seminole and his wife—the rape, the beating. He used no names. The old Indian, known as a *yaholi*, or medicine man, said he would help get justice for this and began drawing diagrams on a box top to show The Junior what the Seminoles believed about the soul's dual nature, as if the tribes understood the build of the conscious and unconscious mind centuries before science did.

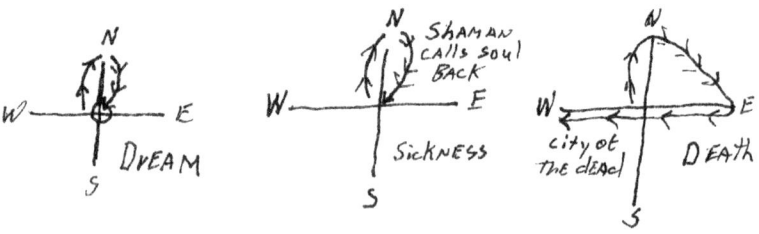

It was explained that the body has two souls. The first diagram shows that in your sleep, one of the body's souls goes up north when you dream and likes it there, then comes back into you before dawn where the other soul lives. In the second diagram, when someone is sick, one soul goes up north, then over to the east; their body shakes with fever, and the family asks the *yaholi* to call that soul back from the east and home to the other soul to be cured. The third diagram represents the death process: one soul goes up north, then around to the east, then west over the Milky Way to the City of the Dead. Four days later, at nightfall, the body's other soul goes to the City of the Dead to join the first soul, and the death is done.

The medicine man looked at them. He needed to know if they wanted to just make this man who raped the woman sick and leave him in the east, or send him west to the City of the Dead. The Junior had a hiss in his voice when he talked about his feelings and what had been done to his friends. He said he wanted both for this man—sick, then very dead. He said this man had a bad reputation and was even known to butcher manatee calves. Once he heard that Cobia threw a dog in the water to attract sharks he was fishing for and let the sharks get the dog. The old man went to his chickee and came back with a long pine splinter. He said it was thunder medicine and came from a tree that had been struck by lightning. The Junior would have to stick Cobia with the splinter. After he did, the shaman would chant for four days around a fire and purge himself with a black tea to call the bad man's other soul to him and send it north, east, then over the Milky Way west to the City of the Dead.

The Junior said it was too risky for him to stick the man with the splinter. It would be viewed as assault by police. He asked the shaman if there was another way. The old Indian said there was another way, but he would need a week to get the medicine. The Junior nodded and left to meet Aubrey at the Johnny Jumper Inn.

"What's going on?" Aubrey said.

"Oh, I been hangin around with this guy Freddie. I's with him in 'Nam."

"Well, I'm coming out to your place tomorrow night to take a couple of buckin horses under the lights."

"Yeah, so why don't you stay with me? I gotta push some cattle to the pens, vaccinate, and mark 'em in the afternoon."

The next day, Aubrey and The Junior sat on their quarter horses. Mr. Zarnitz had his own breeding stallion, King Bailey, from the original King Ranch line, and most of the horses on the place came from that stock. They were watching the mares and foals off to the side, trying not to get too close to the stallion or the alpha mare in the group and piss them off.

"Goddamn gorgeous, aren't they?"

"They are. Look at that blue roan. Look at the hind quarters on him."

"Yep, three months, three years. That's when you can tell what they gonna look like grown. Let's go. We got cows to get in the pens before dark."

The Indian man, the *yaholi*, stood by a black coffee pond in a beautiful grotto of woods north of Lake Okeechobee. The Indians believe the Giant People live there. The Indians are very afraid of the Giant People, who disguise themselves as huge trees in the forest. The setting for the pond was a place of blooming wild flowers, cypress towers, and cypress knees.

"It is amazing how complete is the delusion that beauty is goodness," Tolstoy had said, and the *yaholi* knew this as well. And so had The Junior's friend Suskin in Vietnam, quoting Blake and Tolstoy the night before a tiger devoured half of his shot-up corpse.

The old shaman was no ordinary medicine man, advanced to the tenth month of the calm moon with no wind, and he was clear in his knowledge of the tribe's *materia medica*. Up in the bush by the black pond laid the skeletons of otters, and he knew why. This is where the medicine he wanted was, in the middle of all this beauty. He took a wood spoon, scooped some black sump under the shallow water at the edge into a container, and started for home. He carried an evil thing, appealing only to a microbiologist and itself. He knew it was evil. Science called it *naegleria fowleri*, or brain-eating amoeba: a trophozoite found in the ponds and ditches of the south that will desiccate and encyst in unfavorable conditions, then proliferate again by binary fission when any moisture returns to its environment.

The Junior was called back to the reservation. The medicine man had made some of the black sump from the pond into a dry powder. He and Freddie sat in the old man's chickee and were shown the substance in a tiny buckskin bag. The shaman told The Junior that men blow the powder into the face of an enemy and the enemy breathes it in. Soon they become very sick and die in a week or two. In the powder, he said, lives a spirit that plays dead, but when it is returned to the water of a living thing, it comes alive. The Junior thanked him and offered to bring him a small pig for payment, but the man refused, saying this was for the offended Indian girl and justice, the tribe's justice. The Junior and Freddie went for a ride in his truck to talk.

"Well, now, what am I gonna do with this? I can't blow this stuff in Cobia's face. He thinks I'm some kinda friend a-his, and people will think I did something if this stuff works. I didn't want to hurt the old man's feelings and tell him this won't work, either."

"There's a way. Think about it. If this man Cobia is like most Florida commercial fishermen, he will probably snort anything he thinks is dope," Freddie said.

"You're one smart soldier."

"Yeah, little cocaine, little brown bottle. Little chain with a spoon on the end."

The Junior wanted to make "god damn sure" it was Cobia that committed this crime. One night, he went to the Coconut Bar south of Stuart in Salerno, where he knew Cobia drank with other fishermen. He sat in the place and chatted with him. When he left, he searched the parking lot for Cobia's truck and tried the keys in Cobia's truck door that Susie Tiger said fell out of a pocket that night. Click! The latch shot up on the driver's side.

The old shaman had told The Junior not to breathe in any of the powder in the bag. He said to pour it and only scrape it together with a buzzard's feather to keep the spell strong while he held his breath. The Junior found a feather on the ranch, scraped the stuff into the tiny drug bottle with a certain amount of cocaine. The next night he went back to the Coconut Bar. Freddie Tommie insisted on going with him. They had killed together before many times.

Freddie came in the place ten minutes after The Junior and sat at a table alone. The Junior was sitting next to Cobia at the bar, small talking.

"How's the fishing this week?"

"Right in the fuckin middle. Settin no records," Cobia answered, and he looked at The Junior with his dirty eyes.

"The mullet come back yet?"

"One more week. Brings them snook to me, too. Hey, look back there at that table. Is that some kinda Indian nigger?"

"Could be," The Junior said.

"That fuckin Lyndon Johnson."

This made more pleasurable what The Junior was about to do. He asked Cobia if he wanted to take his little bottle of coke to the bathroom and do a bump.

"Sure!" Cobia said.

"Just one thing, Cobia. I need that for later, so don't offer it to anybody in there, you hear?"

"Nope. Won't do it! Don't worry 'bout that, son. Oh, hey, Junior. I heard that fuckin Vietnam War you's in is officially over today." The Junior just nodded and thought, *Not yet. I got one more man to kill.*

Deep in a nostril, Cobia pulled the powder in on one side and then the other, his head thrown back. When he was sure he got enough, he went to the lavatory and wet his fingers so he could drip water in his nose like users do to get better absorption. The amoeba in its encysted state had more than it needed now to move to the next stage. Its trophozoites would invade Cobia's central nervous system in the coming days through the cribriform plate of his nasal tissue, and from there migrate along nerve fibers and the floor of the cranium into his brain to feed and multiply. Cobia walked back to his seat and handed the bottle to The Junior under the bar top. One week later, Cobia staggered in his home.

When the end is coming, what do you think? How you wish it was your best think, instead of screaming the days away at first like Ivan Ilyich, or the famous mind whose last conscious experience was a deer herd he had read about in the neighborhood going by his window, right before his eyes closed forever, something he considered as a last thought, two-bit.

What were Cobia's thoughts? No one could really know. At first, they say there was a change in his taste and smell and a headache. Flu? A cold? Then fever, vomiting, stiff neck, the inability to coordinate muscle movements as the organism from the pond of dead otters and land of the Giant People swallowed cell after brain cell, and an old Seminole man in Ft. Pierce, twenty miles away, waited around his fire to be told Cobia was dead so he could begin to work the cruel fisherman's other soul up to the north, to the east, then over the Milky Way west to the City of the Dead.

In Cobia's last convulsive days, The Junior went to the Coconut Bar every night. The bartender would give updates on Cobia's condition to the patrons. "Shit, I remember when he got in trouble with Social Services for starving his father half to death, but he don't deserve to die this way. They say he's gone-minded now. How in the hell do you get that thing in ya brain he's got from just being in the water? We all grew up swimming in the water round here. What is the law of averages?"

When Cobia was done, The Junior went to Ft. Pierce to tell the medicine man so Cobia's other soul could be sent to the City of the

Dead. Freddie walked The Junior back to his truck.

"You know," The Junior said, "I thought I might feel just a little bad doin that the way we did, but I didn't, not for one bit for what he done to Mary Tiger and Albert. They oughta bury him at a fork in a road and drive a fucking stake through his heart."

"Tell you somethin," said Freddie, "and this is not an Indian saying. It was an old German lady in town that told me this after the town re-elected a crooked mayor. She said, 'The devil always shits on the highest pile,' and that Cobia was a pile of shit."

209

Chapter 17

SIRENS

Sonny still goes to visit Nell. He found out who the bad nurse was that bit Nell. Sonny, too, bit the nurse, who lived alone, after he hit her in the head and filled her lungs to the top with one of his custom Freon set-ups. He took her body to his property and put it in another old refrigerator. The act bore no similarities to his other grandstand stuff: tin snip cuts, artistic arrangement, a public viewing. The watcher had simply watched out for his, and the nurse just disappeared into another white appliance in an open hole. Sonny taught Half Track, the special needs brother from the Harris Ranch, how to dig and bury trash or anything else; Half Track never saw what was in the white box as he covered it with dirt and placed sod on top, just before the new year of 1976.

Things cooled off some with Aubrey and Leda; a kind of reset came around. They figured, "Oh, hell, this isn't so bad." Leda quit narcotics, which wasn't easy, but not all that hard, either, because she had been only using on weekends—but every weekend.

It was a Friday night at the Goose, and everyone in the group showed up. Aubrey and Frank Clark were not the band, so Aubrey could get loose with the rest of the group. Cocaine had increasingly entered the scene along the Inland Waterway, the same way an old dirty dance might come back around in some recidivist fashion. Little bottles got passed under tables and backhanded to people when they walked to the bathroom. The toilets flushed so often to hide the sound of someone snorting a line that Fred, the owner of the Blue Goose, complained his septic tank behind the place was running over.

The cherished laid-back days of the sixties were disappearing, and now the counter culture was quickened by volts from the white stuff they called "Lady," or "the devil's dandruff," or "shit" at six in the morning when the ugliest sunrise they'd ever seen striped the light. But at the Goose tonight, the party was just starting, and the bunch sat together drinking the edge off the expensive stimulant and then putting it back on again.

John Chrome had just done a line in the bathroom, and when he came back to the table he roared a baritone, "Oh, yeah!" So it began.

Aubrey: "For those who love Chuck Berry and *could* imagine the way that he felt when he couldn't unfasten the safety belt. Oh, yeah."

Chrome: "For those who know there's a mass extinction every twenty-four million years. Oh, yeah."

Rose: "For those who know it's been twenty-four million years since the last one. Oh, yeah."

Leda: "For those who think speed is a mind expansion drug. Oh, yeah."

Arquette: "For those who think backgammon is another form of masturbation. Oh, yeah."

Melinda: "For lesbians who hate men, but still buy dildos. Oh, yeah."

The Junior: "For them what sometimes don't know what to say. Oh, yeah."

Punky: "For them what fart in the water and bite the bubbles. Oh, yeah."

And if you were standing outside looking through the window, you would see eight people at a table who had taken time off from sober to wear away at things more playful. Though they still fired off satire, cynicism, and black irony, they also laughed with each other without any killjoy around. The full moon over the old rum shrine bent the light around the earth and crossed it again at an invisible nodal point somewhere out in space. The snook in the river made strike after strike on schools of mullet they had balled in a circle, while clocks everywhere kept going, and people got another day older along the Indian River Lagoon, just south of the Tropic of Cancer.

Aubrey decided he and Leda should do something non-opiate—a reward for her staying off the hard dope. The drug would be MDA again, or Miles Davis, the group liked to call it, because it sounded cool. It was like saying, "Hey, that other dope is bad, that heroin. Let's do this good dope," an attitude that was familiar back then and made people laugh about it years later.

They would do the drug and revisit the movie *A Man Called Horse*. Out came the Indian tom-toms and face paint to conjure the Sioux and a boom box for music by the pool. A band from the sixties, Pearls Before Swine, had started to tour, and in their repertoire a song played—haunting, indelible, crawling in your ear with the line that never leaves: Did you come by again/ to die again/ well, try again/ another time.

Leda and Aubrey remembered the rules for MDA; no talking or moving around in the first hour you swallow it, and when you feel the smooth part come, you go where it goes. And where it went first was the afternoon sky, with its short eclipse and return over and over, as it passed their oscillating eyes. The song kept asking if they'd come by again to die again. To Aubrey, this was one of the most pointed existential lines in contemporary song lyrics, when on any given day someone muttered they wanted to die, but couldn't or shouldn't. The line stayed with him the rest of his life, hidden in his air puck, un-removable by therapy or Rexall.

He held Leda's hand. She turned her head, looked at him, and looked back at the sky. The music changed to another band and their song, "Wall Hollow Blues." Aubrey stood and left the pool area; went in the house. He stared at a section of drywall in the living room, hoping to see the slow rocket slimeration of all hollow wall exploration, where he could lie in wait for Morrison's "Soft Parade" to store him in a different story than the one he was in—his mother dying, Leda's problems, his siloed life as a small-town car dealer.

He went upstairs. There was his bed with the fake flowers and neon sign in the headboard that said FLORIST. Why Florist? Flowers and neon, slip away and neon, Leon and neon, the boom box downstairs playing some kind of assassination rag: "Mr. McKinley/ he didn't do no wrong/ just rode on down to Buffalo/ but he didn't stay too long/ hard times, hard times, hard times./ Leon shot the president and he knelt on the ground/ the people grabbed the anarchist and took ole Leon down/ hard times/ hard times/ hard times."

Aubrey moved back to the pool deck and lay beside Leda. She looked at him, and he could tell she didn't even know he was gone. He thought of the burning cane fields around Belle Glade until a dream came, Kier Dullea's fetus circling that spacecraft at the end of *2001: A Space Odyssey*, like Aubrey circled the tower in his head. Then it quit, and more things came on in his jar to be over-examined. He took them to his big room. There was the RKO and cane field on the floor of his cranium. He stood at the bottom of the steel Eiffel, the rope by his feet. Up to the top and out on the rope over the cane field, in the gyre he used to make the psychometric designs while he whittled in his jar. He saw himself riding his old mare in the woods, playing with turns around pine trees, jumping small patches of palmetto until he was switched to the doorway of his new house. Things changed. Became dark. Leda was there on the living room floor with the artist and the swan, their bodies lined in neon; his wife, that man, and that goddamn bird taking turns between her legs with tongue and beak. Couldn't move his limbs when he saw that. Thought he had ALS, like his mom. A voice boomed, "There's nothing there, Nell Kitching," and kerplooee! He was suddenly in the Blindspot Cathedral with *A Man Called Horse*. The wrong church that appeared the night his father died had mixed itself with the movie to turns things bad.

He saw monks sitting with Sioux Indians. Two red men in paint came to him with hooks tied to flame vines and pushed the hooks through his hands. Then he heard it: "One Mississippi, two Mississippi," and the Slim Hand came into the Indian lodge and crammed the blue jays he killed as a boy down his throat. The red men hoisted him up by the hand hooks to the spooling keloid scar in the top of the cathedral's dome. There he was, choking on the blue jays, hanging there like Jesus and Richard Harris, arms out on the ape hanger handlebars of the Christian cross. There was no vision of the Sioux god Wakan Tanka this time, just the low pain of agnosia's low belly belief that his old god might be behind the turning scar above him. He saw Saint Blaise coming towards him, trying to bless his throat so the blue jays would go down. Trip went after the Slim Hand, Saint Blaise disappeared, the vines broke, and Aubrey fell toward the floor. Trip screamed their protective rhyme.

WHEN YOU CAN'T SEE, TAKE A STRAIGHT SHOT

RIGHT THROUGH THE HEART OF THE BLIND SPOT.

TRUE MAGAZINE KNOWS THE TRUTH

RIGHTY-TIGHTY   LEFTY-LOOSE.

He woke up on the mattress next to Leda. Her eyes were closed. When she opened them and looked at him, he saw his mother shaking her head in those eyes, as if to say don't do this with her, Aubrey. Leda closed them again, and Trip came out and sat on his arm.

"Jesus and Howard Johnson, what the hell was that about? I saw the Slim Hand run by me from a hallway, and I thought I had him for a second."

"I don't know what happened," Aubrey said, breathing hard. "I was enjoying the ride in my big room, when I blacked out and woke up in this other room. Indians came from that movie Leda and I saw and sent me to the ceiling after the Slim Hand crammed the blue jays down my throat."

"This room, this room, this big domed room you talk about. When are you going to show me 'this room,' so I can help defend you from these bushwhacks?"

That night, Leda was tired from the MDA ride, but Aubrey was still on.

Leda began a cry.

"What is it?" Aubrey asked her.

"Why do whales want to come ashore and die? Do you think they are really closer to the land than the sea?"

"Some of them, maybe. Maybe they're like a lot of people who are closer to the sea than the land and want their ashes scattered in the ocean."

Five minutes went by and she began to cry again.

"What's wrong, Leda?"

"I don't think this racism thing is going to work. I just don't."

"You mean equal rights? What?"

"Yes. It's *The Painted Bird*, Aubrey. I read that novel by Kosinski, and he tells the story of him and his friends painting a pigeon all these different colors and releasing it back to the other pigeons. The other pigeons pecked it to death because it didn't look like them." She rolled over, put her arms around him, and buried her head in his shoulder.

"Yeah, so much for color blind. Is racism Darwinism or behaviorism, or both? Or is it just the 'haves against the have-nots,' even within the same race? I don't know," he said. "I think about the last fifteen years. I think about all this idealism with our generation, this revolution of what? I say to myself, this isn't going to work, this love fest. I know these people who are trying to make a vegetarian out of their cat. Their cat! People either train the wrong stuff, or they don't train anything at all, like that Summer Hill project in England with its, 'Just let it happen, man, or you'll spoil the kid's creativity.' Anyone who knows mammals knows it has to be trained to some extent."

"Yes, maybe," Leda said.

"Like all this environmental stuff, which I'm a big fan of. However, I know if it weren't for petroleum, there wouldn't be any forest left in this country. In 1840, Long Island was all but bare because they needed wood to stay warm. After Rockefeller perfected Standard Oil and could heat a house with that, the forests grew back. And oil saved

216

the whales, too, because they used *them* for oil."

"Oh," Leda said, half asleep.

"Now the oil is killing us! And look at the economy. If it doesn't grow, they say we are in deep shit. What if it just stabilized? They don't feel that way about cancer. They don't want it to grow. They want it to stabilize or recede. But they want the economy to always grow, and the population to grow, so the body of the earth will be finally overrun and then die, like people with cancer."

"Yes," again from Leda.

"What a grand self erasure this is. A terminal allegory. A stage four oxymoron, all this. Talk about theater of the absurd. Talk about paradoxical 'til you puke. How are the hippies going to stay warm when they give up oil? They'll start cutting all the trees again, I guess. They love fires. So do I."

Leda didn't answer. She had passed out asleep. Aubrey moved away from her in the dark and was unable to close his eyes from his rant. Trip came round. "Whoa. Let us change the subject to something more personal. So you were spooked by that MDA thing today, I'm sure."

"Yeah, so what's going on with me?"

"You are one stressed lead singer, that's what is going on. A lot is happening in your life right now. Why don't you think of a film tonight to relax some? Amper Sand and I could use one after that wrong turn on the four-way you took in your head today. Just don't pick *A Man Called Horse*. Ha."

"What do you think your old host Dr. Corpus Columbus would think of this MDA?"

"I think he might say that's enough of that, schizo."

"When will you tell me more about him?"

"Not tonight, Miles Davis."

Aubrey ate a Quaalude off the bed table. In a half hour he started to slip away and the voices came. "Pick a film, Aubrey, any film." He left his daylight mind and went down to the sleep lounge in his head until he fell into an even deeper sleep. The voices came again. "Pick a film, Aubrey."

"Brando. *One-Eyed Jacks*. Considering," he sleep talked.

"Yes, Aubrey," the voices said.

And there was Brando, on top of that hill in Mexico, alone with bullets flying, watching his friend Karl Malden go off the backside for fresh horses. Karl never came back.

It is January of '76, Aquarius January. Aubrey doesn't tell Leda, but he goes to see Nell in the Booby Hatch, as Punky calls it. He and Nell were born in the Year of the Monkey. When he gets to the place, Nell has drawn a monkey to show him. It is underwater, she says, and they are seeing it from the glass saloon of the Nautilus. She points to her head and says, "Monkey mind." Aubrey nods. They talk about their voices. She says Black Socks, her cricket's slipper, tells her what to say to the nursing staff and to the pills they give her as they go down. Aubrey says Triple Suiter is helping him through a rough time with his life right now, but doesn't go into detail. Nell has been given a load of medication before Aubrey's prearranged appointment and tells him a nurse spit on her and bit her. She says the nurse must have gone; she is not there anymore. Nell says after she bit the nurse back, they took her to a room, and she was shocked with electricity and it hurt, and that if you x-rayed her right now, you could see her bones scream.

She and Aubrey walked outside with the attendant twenty feet behind. Nell takes Aubrey to a calamondin tree to show him her favorite spider. The spider's web is very irregular and cubist—reticulations unlike the other, symmetrically correct webs. Nell says this spider has the most beautiful web she has ever seen and says it must have what the doctors told her she has, schizophrenia, to be able to make a beautiful web like that. Aubrey feels his body go tight for a second. He loves the web. It reminds him of the shapes of his own house—irregular. Nell tells him that she had to make an imaginary jar in her mind, because they took away her Ball jar. They won't let her have anything made out of glass now. Aubrey said he made a jar in his mind, too, and Nell smiled and hugged him. The attendant moved closer, but did not stop them. Nell smelled as he imagined Lilith smelled in the Jean Seberg movie. Her long blonde hair covered his face for a moment. When he left, he gave her a hibiscus and said it was from his mother, and it was a steel hibiscus, like his mother, and that Nell would have to be a steel hibiscus, too, while she is here in this place.

When July of that year finished, so did the mangoes. Aubrey responsibly delivered the green ones to his mother every week, and when they ripened, she pretended to eat a small piece and smiled at her only child as the rest of her nourishment squeezed itself through a tube to her stomach, and oxygen squeezed through one to her nose. She was slowly suffocating. The muscles that move the diaphragm had lost the signal. The myelin sheath around her nerves cracked and broke like rubber on old wires. He kept thinking about the blue jays, blaming himself for all this. Trip attacked him for it when he did. Aubrey so wanted to be a cleat for his mother, a stanchion she could grip when the worst of her disease decayed her neurology in the last awful months. She looked at him one day and whispered how much she enjoyed him as her child, because she never knew what he would do next. "I was never bored with you. Don't ever let any of this, or my death, make a winter of your heart, Aubrey." The next day, she had a grand mal seizure and died while he was sitting on the bed with her. The home nurse called 911 before he could stop her. When they came, he had the signed Do Not Resuscitate form in his hand.

He slept through the night in the old family house. Trip didn't come to him, and neither did the voices ask him to pick a film that night. They knew he was gored. He felt guilty about sleeping so well, but knew why. The condition she had was a living horror. It was over.

Over the next two weeks, some blue jays started showing up on the backyard bird feeder at his house. At first, he thought they were haunting him, but soon they would wait in the trees for the bird feed. One day, he noticed there was a button and a flip top from a beer can on the feeder. When he consulted his Audubon, the book said jays will do this, and so will crows if you feed them, as if they were bartering with you for the food you gave them by bringing you something in exchange. Aubrey shook his head. Had he made peace with them? Trip might be right after all. As far as his parents and the awful way they both died, he didn't want to talk about that part with people, but he would talk about what good people they were with anyone.

He went to Orlando for a car dealer convention months later, even though he kind of hated them. While he was there, someone in his office called about business and mentioned she read in the paper that the gypsy woman that lived on the river with her husband had died.

Aubrey left for home immediately. He went upstairs to the bathroom in O'gram and bowed his head before he opened a small cabinet in the paneled wall. Inside this backwoods tabernacle was a tarnished silver chalice filled with black dirt from the cane fields around Belle Glade. Lifting it out, he probed in the dirt until he touched a small felt bag with drawstrings and placed it on the lavatory counter. When he turned it up, the toadstone ring Reve had made for him, years ago, fell on the surface. He inspected it for any color change. It looked normal until he put it on his finger, and it turned gray as The Junior's eyes when it sensed Aubrey's sadness. Triple Suiter spoke to him. "I am so sorry, Aubrey. I know you thought the world of her."

"I did, but you didn't."

"Yes. I guess this is where I better shut up."

"Yeah, you better."

"Reve didn't die, Aubrey. She knew about us—the slippers and the other world. That is where she is now. She knew about us. She was like you. She heard all the time. I was kind of a fool to be jealous of her. Just a fool about it."

220

"I'd be a fool, too, to think that you really didn't like her."

"If she showed up in my world, I would let you know."

"Let me know first if my mother, father, or my grandmother shows up, then tell me if Reve does."

They threw her ashes on the river and under the banana mango tree. He sat with Coker alone on the front porch after a small ceremony of friends.

"She told me she's gonna die that day. And then she told me when she did, to bend over and kiss her for at least five seconds, but only after she was gone," Coker said.

"Let me guess. Wouldn't go to a doctor."

"Nope. 'No croakers,' she said. I myself been having these busy dreams, where she comes to me just as clear as a bell and we talk."

"Can you hear her when you are not dreaming?"

"Well, sure. I can imagine it."

"But can you actually hear her?"

"Well, son, not like I'm hearing you."

Aubrey knew Reve had entered Coker's mind when he leaned over to kiss her, and that's why she told him to wait until she died before he did, to be sure she was in the other form and could travel into his nose then to his mind, and wait for him when it was his time. Aubrey also knew that Coker was not a voice hearer, because he said he could only hear her in dreams. He was happy she was with Coker now, and he wondered if this was really true; wondered if we all become slippers at the end.

He walked out to the mango tree and strained to hear if it spoke to him in some kind of ventriloquism or breeze. The ring on his finger was put up to the light and he saw the small red speck in the middle, the hour glass, the one Reve told him was on the belly of the black widow and the skink, and the one she said Jesus told the gypsy boy about at the foot of his cross. Jesus told the boy that the gypsies are allowed to steal, until one day he comes back and breaks the red hourglass.

During this last year, Aubrey felt like he'd gone from Wonder Dog to Withered Dog. It was now 1977. He was as bad off as Leda seemed to be emotionally; fate's promised equipoise and other shoe had come. Trip and he talked all day to each other sometimes, trying to rationalize his life with righty-tighty solutions, staying clear of lefty-loose. Aubrey feared going to his new headroom and the tower to hatch out the beautiful shapes after the Blind Spot Cathedral had appeared to him with the Slim Hand and the Indians on the MDA. So he stayed away from the conjure it took to get there.

Leda went home to Key West for a week. She was only working three weeks out of every month at the hospital lately, and took off when she pleased. She had started using again. Aubrey saw new bruises on her arm.

The Junior was hauling a rig to the north every two months and back-hauling hay. He asked Aubrey to come along. "What you need, son, is to get your ass on the road with me." Aubrey climbed up in the big rig that said Z-BAR UP RANCH and watched the windshield like it was another American film. The Junior drove.

"Damn nice truck," Aubrey said.

"Yeah, it is. This Kenworth is strong enough to pull a building. That International the old man had before this'n wouldn't pull a sick whore off a toilet."

"Good to know."

"If you wanna take a sip a-that coffee without you spill it, I'll move over in the hammer lane."

"Why's that?"

"Well, you see, the granny lane is where most of the big trucks ride, and over time, the weight of them rigs makes the road have these waves cause they so damn heavy. So if you wanna sip a-coffee, I'll move over to the passing lane. Smoother ride."

"Truck lore, right, The Junior? Or as Chrome would say, 'Mansion!'"

After Jacksonville, they crossed the St. Johns River. It was just a hay trip this time. Mr. Zarnitz liked to feed his blood horses a timothy/ alfalfa mix only grown in the north, and he thought it was worth the fuel and time to go get it after The Junior personally inspected it.

In Georgia, the wiregrass was on both sides of them for miles where the tide ran under the bridges toward the ocean, and the paper plants of Brunswick made the air stink from the sulfurous by-products. In the South Carolina low country, the Big Pee Dee and the Little Pee Dee River snaked under the road and disappeared into the sloughs. Aubrey thought of the Swamp Fox, Francis Marion, the general who evaded the British during the Revolutionary War by hiding in places surrounded by water and bogs. They kept the CB radio on, the radio that lives somewhere between the shortwave and the ten-meter amateur bands, the sacred space on Channel 19 provided for blue collar and real America, both corny and cool, as the chrome rimmed rigs with a hundred amber and red lights roll by the monotonous mile markers.

"Break one-nine north-bound. They's a ten-thirty-three on the right at the 170 yard stick, c'mon."

"Ten-four. I didn't see nothin all the way back to Florence, c'mon," The Junior answered.

"Thank ya, driver," the man going southbound on the other side said. At the mile marker mentioned, a car had left the road and it was in the ditch, surrounded by flashing blue lights.

Eastern North Carolina was its usual long and boring, and in Virginia, The Junior took his radar detector off the dash because it was illegal in that state.

The sun was coming up. They had stopped in a truck stop overnight to steal four hours sleep, Aubrey in the front seat, The Junior in the sleeper part of the cab, coughing now and then from his exposure to Agent Orange. During the night, two lot lizards—truck stop hookers—knocked on the door, but they sent them away frowning. "I ain't doin no skank," The Junior said to Aubrey and went back to sleep, still coughing. He missed his ozone machine. "God bless ozone," he was heard to say from time to time in the Blue Goose after the war.

North of Baltimore, they angled northwest and took 41 up into Pennsylvania through Amish country and towns like Bird in Hand and Intercourse, until they pulled into the agricultural sale area of New Holland. Truckloads of hay and straw bedding were parked on the lots. The Junior found the hay he wanted after touching and smelling many bales, and they loaded the forty-foot-long horse trailer.

At least fifty or sixty Amish carriages were tied to rails that ran down the side of the main building. They walked over to the auction area.

"Jesus. It's like the eighteen hundreds," Aubrey said.

"Yeah, they a-piece a-work, these people."

"How you mean?"

"Come on inside, and I show what I mean."

The auction was running horse after horse through the bidding—some decent looking, others not. When an older black horse came through and was sold, The Junior told Aubrey it was an Amish carriage horse that was of no use any more, and the man who bought the horse was a killer buyer. Aubrey knew that meant slaughter.

They got out of there in an hour and backtracked their route down 41. They passed buggy after buggy of the Amish going home after selling everything from lambs and shoat pigs to baked goods.

"So you see," The Junior said, "what them Amish do is they got a horse that's hauled the family around for years, a horse their kids have grown up with. Then they take it to New Holland and sell it to the killers when they done with it, instead of turnin it out on their big farm where it can live out its old age in peace."

"You're shittin me."

"Nope. Their Bible tells 'em it's a 'beast a-burden,' and that's it. I been comin up here for three years now, and I can't figure these people out. One day you see their house with no electricity, no car, no nothing, and the next thing you see 'em in the front yard with one a-them new weed eater machines and them wearing a pair of them expensive colored sneakers."

Aubrey thought about Leda and what she may be doing in Key West with her time as the road opened up after a crossroads town called Gap. At Newark, Delaware, they grabbed 301 South thru the Maryland farm country so they could miss the Baltimore/ Washington slow-downs; they were taking the backdoor to Richmond.

In the night, Aubrey wondered why he and The Junior seemed so different. There was this incomparable history and genetic departure, true, and yet he had such an affinity for what The Junior had. And there was this kind of *omerta*, this implicit oath; anytime there was a crisis he would throw down with The Junior and The Junior with him. Yet, two only children growing up like apple and oyster brothers. It wasn't until years later, after The Junior's death and the way he died, Aubrey would know that The Junior rode with some of the same cowboy mental bunch he did, his own choice of existential cross carried on his country back.

In Eastern North Carolina, they stopped for barbecue. The Junior liked the rub they used on this side of the Piedmont. They didn't use tomatoes in the vinegar-based sauce. He said, over by Raleigh, they made sauce with "damn tomatoes in it." They went down the road with their pulled pork and cold slaw, sipping sweet tea, talking and thinking.

"What we doin with this rodeo thing, Aubrey? We ain't done one in months."

"I know. I was considering I may be getting too old to buck one out."

"Aw, shit. What? You the same age as me."

"Yeah, but you're tougher than me. Thirty-two years tougher."

"Oh, hell, c'mon. Let's keep goin with it."

"All right then. Probably get killed."

They passed lengths of cast off tire tread in the road that the truckers called alligators and pieces of wood, metal, broken furniture off on the shoulder.

"You know what bothers me the most when I see trash in the road?" The Junior said. "Sometimes I see these clothes, like a jacket or shirt or some half a dress or a child's things, and I think there must be a sad story behind that kinda stuff. Like a divorce or desertion, beatings. Somebody's mad and throws it out the car window. It lying there alone like that, I don't know, just seems. Know what I mean?"

"Yeah. Know what you mean."

Further in the night, it occurred to Aubrey when The Junior thinks about something, say the smell of the woods, it is only that smell and what it reminds him of he considers. When Aubrey does, he goes too far to the wall with it.

WHEN THE SNOWSHOE MAN CAME TO SEE ME,

I THOUGHT HE'D SINK DOWN IN THE SNOW.

BUT HE JUST WALK LIKE YOU-KNOW-WHO WALK ON

   THE WATER.

HE JUST TALK LIKE YOU-KNOW-WHO TALK ON

THE MOUND.

SAY, "COME HERE, BOY, AND GIVE ME SOME

YOUR MONEY.

I GOT SNOWSHOES HERE THAT'LL KEEP YOU FROM

   SINKIN DOWN."

Chapter 18

ALL WHITE

By '78, and through most of that year, the bunch moved away from LSD. Now their recreational lives were better served by the sexualized candyfloss, cocaine. Chrome said what a lot of people said back then. "After you've done acid, you can see the same stuff when you're straight. You don't need to do that anymore."

Coke elbowed the healthy lifestyle. Its big nose walked over clean living, diet, exercise, and psycho-actives as the new angel food of the eighties. One hundred years ago, in the other eighties, Freud had published his paper *Uber Coca*:

> Exhilaration and lasting euphoria, which in no way differs
> from the normal euphoria of the healthy body. In other
> words, you are simply normal, and it is soon hard to
> believe you are under the influence of any drug. . . . No
> craving for the further use of cocaine appears after the
> first, or even after repeated taking of the drug.

What Freud was saying was, she don't lie, she don't lie, cocaine. He was wrong. It's just that his own insufflation of the stuff had him needing a colorable reason not to stop. He was wrong, and so were J.J. Cale and Eric Clapton when they wrote that song of theirs. She does lie. Extrinsic euphoria as strong as coke eventually turns to dysphoria. Freud thought his cigar wouldn't hurt him, either. It finally killed him.

Today, ironically, science knows cocaine works like an antidepressant that paradoxically creates depression. It is an artificial serotonin re-uptake inhibitor that binds itself to a dopamine transporter protein. This prevents the dopamine transporter from performing its re-uptake function, making dopamine stay in the synaptic cleft of the brain longer, instead of taking it back to the body to be recycled normally. It simply makes you feel good longer, but the process is that of an agonist, of cruel kindness. The normal brain function is pulling at one end, and the cocaine is pulling at the other. When the drug loses the tug of war, the dopamine leaves the brain cleft in a big way and you crash. You're not supposed to feel that good for that long all the time, the Bible says. It's not natural. When Prozac leaves your brain, the same thing can happen, but not as seriously. And now you need more. And Sigmund did, too—cocaine, that is. The Goose bunch was on Freud's side, trying to believe what Freud believed, doing lines and holding late night talks on weekends to enjoy the so-called, non-habit forming "uber," until it got kind of crazy and episodic.

Aubrey and The Junior went off to a rodeo in Arcadia. Leda went to the Goose by herself and there was Arquette, alone. She walked up behind him. "Buy me a drink?" That's how it started. Melinda, Arquette's girlfriend, was at a marine biology project in Miami promoting her animal immobilizer. After the drink, a line in the bathroom, a drink, a line, he followed her home for the suggested nightcap.

In the living room, they sat. Only the lights of the mannequins and taxidermy displays were on, and so was the neon sculpture of Leda and the Swan.

"Why does Aubrey have such a fascination with things behind glass?" Arquette said to Leda.

"I asked him, and he said his imagination works better when he sees something behind glass. He feels protected by the glass and takes more chances with his thoughts, because that same imagination can get scary at times. I think there is something very strong with his ability to imagine things, and as long as he thinks the glass is between him and what he gives too much of a grizzly glide factor to, like the Clockwork Orange man over there. He told me he sees a glass jar in his head. Some kind of stage machine for writing and drawing things like this house, music, you know, whatever that means. He was drunk when he said it."

"Him scared? He's a rodeo rider. I can't believe he still rides those crazy things. Why would anything scare him?"

"Yeah, and he wins at those rodeos, too. He loves the life and he loves to win, and he loves that guitar of his. One of them is going to kill him."

"Like a perfect thrush he sings. What a man you have, Leda."

"Right. Guess I do. You okay, Arquette?"

"Not really."

"Oh. Well, tell Aunt Leda about it."

"I'm terrified. Like Aubrey feels at times about his imagination."

"Like how?"

"Like stupid."

"What of?"

He told her about the perineal pains he'd been experiencing, and that he thought he had prostate cancer. And even though they said the test was negative, he didn't believe them. He said he was afraid to have sex, because something was wrong, but he couldn't, and *they* couldn't figure out what. He was negative for infections, too, but he didn't believe them on that, either. "What if it's some ultra-microbe that doesn't show up on the tests?"

"What do you mean you are not having sex? That's your favorite thing in life, isn't it?"

"Yes, but I have this fear of it now."

"What about Melinda?"

"She says she's okay with it, but I feel bad for her. Me being like this."

"Did you try to masturbate?"

"No. I mean, I wanted to, but I was afraid it would hurt after I did."

"What if I showed you this and you just looked. Could you do it?"

"Showed me what?"

Leda stood up and shimmied out of her jeans and underwear to her figure. He looked, as he said before, terrified. He had always tried to disimagine her clothes, and now. . . .

"How 'bout we play no touch?" she said, but with sympathy. "I'm serious. You know, we do a line, and then you just talk to me from over there while I lie over here on this other sofa." Arquette looked at the floor for a second and then back at her and her place. Then he nodded and threw his coke bottle to her, and looked away at the display with the mannequin dressed like Little Alex and the diorama with all the wildlife in it. Anything to not look at that place of hers, the neighbor's wife, he should not. His hands were trembling, and he wasn't sure he wanted an erection.

"What if what is wrong with you is, to some degree, psychological?" Leda said. "Like Nicholson at the end of *Carnal Knowledge*, where the only way he can get an erection was to have the gypsy lady talk him up while he sat in a chair in front of her with his legs apart."

"I don't have an erection problem. It's a fear of pain problem," in a jeremiad tone.

He wanted to talk now. His brain holding the coke. He began to unload for the first time in his life about the history of his sexuality and told her as a teenager he was determined to be the best lover in New England. He told her how he trained himself to be a double-climaxer without stopping.

"Maybe putting that kind of pressure on yourself has worked a bad thing on you, Arquette. No wonder you have pain down there if you try that every time. What I know of it as a nurse is, it is not healthy for a man to do too much of that or go too long without some release of the prostate gland. It can actually get congested. They used to call it priest's disease in the old days. That's why those doctors do prostate massages, but the doctors always told me it's not as good as just getting yourself off to attenuate the problem."

"Where does that leave me?"

She rolled over on her side towards him, bent her knees slightly, and put a small pillow between her legs. He could see the light going through, and the detail. A woman's bent knees were more feminine to him. He didn't like the straightened leg. It made too much definition and looked masculine.

"Maybe you should try masturbating now. Just a single climax for health reasons so you won't feel pressured to perform that double come you do and hurt yourself. How long has it been?"

"Three or four weeks."

You could see the satisfaction she was getting out of this if you were a roach in a corner. This was Leda when she almost had the whole fish in the boat, presaging the way this would go tonight with Arquette, her own crafted sex act in this somewhere combining her horns, drama, center of attention, and control, like the control Fonda had in *Klute* with her call-girl customers.

"Here is what Nurse Rothstein-Shallcross proposes. And I want you to know this is strictly therapeutic. You should look at me over here and start to get yourself up, then clean out your tubes. Once. The nurse says."

Arquette thought about it for ten seconds. Maybe she was right. No pressure to come twice, and there were medical good reasons, and maybe even she would get excited and he'd get to see it, though he didn't know if he'd want to in his state.

He stood and took off his pants, laid back down, and his cock started to leaven. There was excitement, but no lust.

"Remember," Leda smiled, "this is a clinical setting. The patient privacy policy is invoked. You were never here at the doctor's house." He nodded and stared at her place, moving his hand on his achy organ. Behind her on the kitchen wall was the lit neon tracery of the other Leda. Arquette looked back and forth from her place to the wall piece with the swan between the woman's legs until he exhaled and crumpled, hoping it would not be painful.

Leda stood, put her pants on, and brought him some paper towels.

"I gotta go," he said. "If you had told me something like this between you and I was going to happen tonight—"

"Yes, just between you and I, Arquette. Biblically, we did nothing wrong. Right? Do you feel better down there?"

"You know, I think not putting that pressure I put on myself and getting to release the anxiety. . . "

He walked to his car in the driveway. Off in the shadows by the pool deck, another man stood trembling and clenching his fists, the man Leda occasionally screwed for sport—the mural artist.

Arquette kept looking for some normal physical refection on the way home instead of the pain in his perineum that the hurtful vine on his left side usually presented. The pelvic floor took the drain well. There was only a slight residual burn in his left testicle that always felt drawn up inside him like a cryptorchid. When he masturbated on that couch, Aubrey was away at a rodeo on a bucking horse named Pretty Boy Floyd at exactly the same time. And if you placed the two scenes side by side—two films say, in slow motion—you would see a one man rising through the air on a dangerous animal to the same rhythm as the other man's hand rising and falling on *his* animal—Aubrey's horse kicking out, throwing in bascule after bascule; Arquette's hand, jerking and twisting, both men trying so hard to finish something. You might even put a soprano behind it all to overdo it; the two old friends in different towns, determined to get to some still point on this earth.

Psyched about his win at the Immokalee rodeo, but beat up from the top bronc, Aubrey was on the road again two weekends later, and so was Melinda with her marine project. Leda knew where Arquette ate lunch almost every day. She was leaving the place as he was walking in from the parking lot. When she went passed him, she simply said the word "Rodeo."

"I didn't know if it was cool," he whispered on the bar stool later at the Goose.

"Yeah, it is. I'm on my own again tonight. See you at the parallel O'gram, then? For some neon in the woods?"

"Yes. You go first."

When Leda's car went by on Main Street, Sonny was sitting in the plate glass window of another bar. He turned his head with the car. Five minutes later, he saw Arquette go by, and since Arquette lived in the other direction, Sonny left the bar and drove to a side road close to Aubrey's.

The house had the lights turned down, both cars in the driveway. Sonny found it easy to hide and look through the glass openings where the shades were never perfect. He wasn't sure what he was seeing. Leda and Arquette had set up their so-called therapy session, still dressed, did a couple of lines off a mirror, and just lay there across from each other on the different sofas and talked. Sonny shrugged his shoulders and left.

Soon the conversation in the house went to Arquette's condition. Leda told him he ought to go to a medical epicenter like Boston. Get checked out by one of the teaching hospitals. Arquette asked if she could get him a name. This made him feel good, because this thing, this curse, had been going on for six months and he was becoming more and more down and spleeny.

"Tell me a story, Arquette."

"A story?"

"Or a something close. A confidence about yourself. That would be better. I'm a good listener, and I don't snitch."

"Then will you do the same about you?"

"I will," she said.

"Okay, so, where to start?"

"Let's talk about your sexuality again, since this is our clinical setting. Maybe we can root out a worm going on with you, something that makes you bear down on the crotch area when you're stressed; something that exacerbates this pain of yours. Tell me about your adolescence."

"I, uh, well. . . was very concerned about my body and appearance. At first, I worried about being a redhead, but that went away when the freckle thing stayed minor. Then I thought I was too skinny and I over-did the weight lifting, and I was picky about eating."

"Yes? And your sexual parts? What about penis size? You know, girls worry about their breast size at that age," she said, glib, like she said things at the Goose to the bunch around the table—no pause, no expression.

"I know they worry about breast size. I have a sister, and that's all she checked out in the mirror. I stole one of her bras when I was fifteen and put it around a tree in the woods so I could practice unsnapping it with just my forefinger and thumb with one hand. I even taught Aubrey how to do it when we were kids."

"Yes, thanks. He's very good at it, too."

"Welcome."

They both laughed. "No, I had this idea mine might not be big enough. I read this book in high school called *The Rivers Ran East*. There's an Amazonian tribe that. . . shit, I can't believe I'm telling this. Can we fix our faces again?"

"Sure. I'll get us another if you promise to keep going. Get a drink, too."

She brought the cocaine over.

"Okay, that's better. Ooh, burns a little. All right, well, yes, so this Amazon tribe hung small weights on the young boys' members, and by the time they reached maturity, they had long, skinny ones they curled in a little basket they wore. Guess I started too late."

"You did that to your cock?"

"Only my high school junior year for two hours a day after school, and then I quit. It didn't look any different. You think I could have hurt it and now be paying for it?"

"No. Did you tell your urologist?"

"Are you kidding?"

"Yes, I am. Do you think your cock size bothers you?"

"I don't think so. Do you think it's okay? Could I show it to you in the light?"

"Not while it's flaccid. You can never tell from the flaccid state. One of the main findings in the Masters and Johnson study: 'Don't be fooled by the flaccid penis.' The little ones can get pretty big and the bigger-looking flaccid ones sometimes get only a little bigger, and I think they said the real big ones are not as consistently hard for as long as the average sized ones when aroused. You can show it to me erect, but let's keep talking right now. Tell me about the pressure to do a double climax without stopping you put yourself under."

Arquette went on about his mastery of the double climax and his theory he was able to bring many women to the trees with it. She asked if he thought some of them might be faking, and he told her how he put two fingers on their necks where the big artery throbs when they came. If they faked it, that artery would not throb, he said.

"Now you. Tell me about your sexuality." He looked at her.

"We could start with libido. I think I always used it as a stalking horse for my real intentions."

"And what were those?"

"A lot of women do this. You see, we know from a young age that we have a power. Sometimes we get trapped by it and lose the ability to feel anything, which is miserable, trying to figure out when to use it and when to surrender. There's a big difference between submission and fucking someone. If it's fucking someone, I'm going to be on top."

"And what is surrender to you?"

"The best way I could put it . . . it's when you're with a certain someone, and you only want the bottom so you can feel frail. Helpless,

helpless, helpless as Neil Young from Canada."

"Does that happen to you with Aubrey?"

"As much as I try to fight it, yes."

"Well, shit. What are we doing here tonight, and what did we do last time? This is wrong!"

"If I made love with you, Arquette, I'd want to be on top, not frail, but you and I are never going to make love. What we are doing here is like anesthesiology. I work in the operating room. I watch people go under and it looks like they died, but they don't die. And when you and I do this, it's like watching people have sex, but we are not having sex. Those people wake up from the anesthesia, and we get up from these couches and go home without touching each other. I know you cherish Melinda."

"Yeah."

"Okay, so let's do another line and see what happens to make you feel better. I'm going upstairs to get it. Be right back."

When she came down, she had on a robe. They did the line, sipped their drinks, and talked some more, until she told him it was getting late and it was time for therapy. Lying on her side, she pulled back her robe. He looked over, stood up, took off his pants, and looked at the neon of Leda and the Swan on the kitchen wall until a stirring in his nerve endings began. Half way through it, he saw her touch herself. She told him to stop. He said, "Wouldn't that be bad for the gland?" She said, "Not really, but give me ten seconds." She went upstairs and came back with a vibrator.

"Rose gave me this. She's a big fan of onanism, if you know what I mean."

"God bless her," Arquette said.

"Rose says when she takes it out, her man Chrome nods his head and says, '*Deus ex machina.*' God from the machine."

"Fucking Chrome. That's so funny. Are you going to use it?"

"No. I'm just going to lean it against my leg this time for you to look at."

"Do you use it when you're with Aubrey?"

"That's a personal question, inappropriate in this clinical setting. I will say this, though. Aubrey is, as Ava Gardner once told a friend about Frank Sinatra, 'Good between the feathers.' So I don't need it."

Chapter 19

TRUCKS

They were all losing weight, even Chrome. The Coke. The rake marks showing. It was, "Let's do a bump here." "Let's do a bump before we go in there." "Let's do one because it's raining." "How 'bout one because the Dolphins are winning." The use had turned from weekends only to weekdays at work, like coffee, only this was canker.

Aubrey and The Junior took another trip north to deliver quarter horses from the Z-Bar Up and back haul hay out of New Holland. They went through the agriculture station before the Florida state line at two AM, showed the horses' health certificates, and crossed the St. Marys River into Georgia. They drove all night, doing bumps whenever they felt sleepy. When The Junior was blazed on it, he said to Aubrey, "I love the fuckin road. If I die anytime soon, throw me out on US 1 and let the big trucks run over me till I'm flat as an ole coon. Sun and rain can do the rest."

In Rocky Mount, North Carolina, they stopped for the east side barbecue so The Junior didn't have to worry about any "Fuckin tomatoes in the barbecue sauce." They laid the horses over close to dark at a farm in Petersburg, Va.

Aubrey saw the farm owner and The Junior talking, and the man kept looking around and looking at Aubrey. When The Junior came back to the truck, he said with a rare, large grin, "Uh, Aubrey, I got to do a little business here."

"Shit. Don't tell me you're holdin on this trip. I told you I had to be careful with that car business of mine."

"Yeah, well, you asked at the last minute to go with me, and I mean I's already loaded with that stuff under the wood shavings in the horse trailer, so I couldn't get out of it."

"Fuck it then. Get it done and let's leave."

They didn't talk for the first ten minutes on the road, until Aubrey threw his head back and started laughing. "I can see it now. Local man caught in interstate moonshine bust."

"Yeah, moonshine is something that never makes the papers no more. Hell, I bet there's some old-time country judges around here that would let us go because it reminded them of the old days."

"That's right!" Aubrey screamed. "That's how all the old NAS-CAR drivers started out, runnin bush liquor on fuckin Thunder Road."

The Junior was quiet for a minute. He looked over at Aubrey then back at the windshield a couple of times.

Aubrey said, "All right, tell me the rest. You were bringing him the shit, too, weren't you?"

"Yeah, but no shit, not cocaine."

"Grass then?"

"No. Mushrooms."

"Oh?"

"But not like you think. You see, me and my sweetie, Thimble, you know Thimble Taylor. Well, she figured out how to grow that stuff in baby bottles with like a Jell-O in there. All what grows on top of that Jell-O is this white cotton mold, then we put it on tin foil in the oven, and it turns it into a powder. We buy them cheap vitamin capsules and empty them out, and she puts it in there to sell."

"What? What are you saying? How did she know how that worked?"

"She ordered a book from that dope magazine, *High Times*. Sometimes I trade them pills for grass or blow, but mostly for straight cash. See, people like to just swallow that pill rather than go looking for them shrooms and have to cook it up in a tea later."

"I hope this was a cash deal you did. I am not in this truck with some quantity of coke or something else you traded for it, am I? How do you know that guy isn't a narc?"

"Cause I know him a long time. He's from my mother's family."

When they got into the top part of Maryland, The Junior stopped for fuel and called the farm that bought the horses they were hauling. They were in New Holland by that night and got a room. Tomorrow was Saturday, the sale would open, and truckloads of everything would roll in.

They went back through Maryland farm country on 301 as usual, with a load of timothy/ alfalfa bales. It was turning dark. They crossed the Bay Bridge into Annapolis, turned south again through Upper Marlboro and little towns like Rosaryville and Waldorf, until the land dropped down to the Harry W. Nice bridge over the Potomac. In the backwoods of a one AM Virginia, they saw live deer and dead deer on the side of the road, their dead open eyes still able to reflect the headlights and wheel rims as they passed them. There were stretches of asphalt with so much mica it sparkled like ocean phosphorous.

"You want me to drive? You tired?" Aubrey asked.

"Okay." They pulled over and switched.

The Junior soon fell asleep. Aubrey watched the signage and mailboxes go by, names like Wormslo, Redwine, Doorman Curty For All Your Real Estate Needs, the Nash and Slaw Funeral Home, busted-knuckle car shops, houses with wheelchair ramps, and now and then a burnt spot, half on the shoulder and half on the asphalt, where a car caught fire and had melted the pavement.

The Junior woke in a couple of hours.

"Wanna do a bump, Aubrey?"

"Didn't know we had any left."

"Got a gram, but that's it."

"In a way, I'm relieved you don't have a couple of kilos in here."

"Aw, come on with it. We got away clean with that back there."

"Okay, but why don't we stop for fuel and get coffee for now, instead?"

South of Richmond, Aubrey asked about the mushroom mold in baby bottles again.

"I mean, you have to be real careful when you do that," The Junior told him, "so you don't get no other stuff in there with it, cause it will mess ever'thing up with all this other kinda mold."

They pulled over again in Rocky Mount for more barbecue and slaw. The Junior asked the man for "brownies," the end cut of the meat, the drier, more cooked and burned stuff. Twenty miles out of Rocky Mount, the alternator light came on. It took until three o'clock the next day to get it replaced.

Dark now in South Carolina, they crossed the Big Pee Dee River listening to the CB radio. Every subject from paychecks to Jesus came up, along with the slang names for the different types of rigs: Tanker trucks were called thermos bottles. "How 'bout ya, thermos bottle? You got ears in there?" one driver would call out to another. If you wanted to call a truck hauling new cars, they were called "parking lots." A flatbed truck was a "skate board." Aubrey kept hearing this same base-voice guy talking to other truckers.

When someone is on the radio and they get to the end of what they are saying, they say, "C'mon" or "Come back" or "Over," so the other guy can talk, but the man Aubrey was listening to simply said, "Feenished,"or finished, with his heavy southern accent when he was through.

He told The Junior to listen. The man's voice was deep as Tennessee Ernie Ford's. He must have been south bound, as they were, because the signal stayed strong.

"Hey, parkin lot, you got ears in there?" the baritone man said to another big truck.

"Yeah, c'mon."

"You believe in Jesus?"

"Oh, hell, yeah. I's raised that way. Baptist."

"You know, I think there's somethin going on between religion and watchin the weather and what it does to your mind. Feenished."

"How's that? C'mon."

244

"I read that there's this part of your brain that can let you see Jesus and watch clouds without thinking. Then this part in your brain box sorta ricochets around your head to jack it up for more clouds and more religion. Feenished."

"So you sayin they trade back and forth? C'mon."

"That's right. Feenished."

"I heard that. Kinda nice. I mean clouds and Jesus. So where you out of, driver?"

"Heaven. Feenished." And he was gone. The other driver tried a couple of times to call him, but there was nothing but static. Aubrey looked at The Junior.

"What?" The Junior said.

"Did you hear that?"

"Like the guy said, Aubrey. I heard that."

"That was incredible. He says this redneck feenished, or finished, after everything, instead of 'C'mon,' like the rest of those grits. He just tried to subsume the whole objective/subjective paradox into a CB radio chat about the weather and Jesus, and then disappeared."

"Well, that's good, but I don't know what the fuck you just said, college boy."

"Now we should do up that snoot of yours and quit the coffee so I can think about this. We gotta give a name to this guy on the radio."

"Aw, right. What you wanna call 'im?"

"He's like a ghost. You don't really know where he is out there on this road. What if he's not in a truck out there at all, but just hovering over the surface of the road in this mist we're driving through? A transcendental radio band trucker of some kind maybe. Or like I said, a ghost."

"The ghost. Yeah, on Channel 19." The Junior nodded.

"Ghost of 19. That's what we call him."

"Aw, right. Now let's do a line of that snoot to celebrate giving him a name. Probably never hear him again."

By the time they crossed into Georgia, they were wide-awake from the coke. Aubrey kept thinking about the radio truck talk, all its code and southern argots, something a Yankee banker, or a scientist, might need a translator for. He felt sharp from the shit he'd snorted. "Goddamn, The Junior, I do believe I got that white line disease."

Trip started in on Aubrey with the inner voice. "Yes, Aubrey, your wheels are turning faster than this truck. Too fast."

"I know, I know, Trip. Wish I didn't have to go to work Monday and I could just be a long-range trucker with this radio. I could major in philosophy all over again," he said, talking softly to himself.

"Aubrey, son. Who you talkin to over there in that truck seat? You movin your lips. You always moved those lips like you was talkin to somebody, ever since you was a kid."

"Yeah. Just drive the truck."

The CB kept chatting about women, beer, Richard Petty. Until one more time, south of Savannah, a loud human burp came over the speaker that ended with "Feenished!"

Aubrey looked at The Junior. "Was that him, or somebody imitating him?" Aubrey said.

"Don't know. They do them burp things on the air all the time."

Aubrey was in a good place. Buzzed from the coke. He looked through the windshield, hatching designs, another Ball jar, as far as he was concerned. Road kill crosses went by on the shoulder, and now and then, three life-size PVC crosses out in a Bible Belt field stood as close together as that Friday in Jerusalem.

"I just had this flash." Aubrey poked out his chin as he turned into his man Head Wound, but a more redneck Head Wound, for The Junior's sake.

"Oh, shit. Don't tell me. Head Wound's comin. I ain't heard from him in a while."

"Yeah, well, that's who's comin. So have you seen this new movie, *Close Encounters of the Third Kind*? Anyway, these aliens come to

246

earth in a space ship, the usual. So there I am, the indisputable janitor sweeping up the control room for a big government radio dish facility, you know, that's trying to get a signal from an intelligent source out in space. I'm going about my janitorial duties, emptying wastebaskets, when it finally happens. They, NASA, get a signal, only it isn't that stupid music Spielberg has in the *Close Encounters* movie; it's a voice that says. . . guess."

"Guess what, Head Wound? Just tell me the story."

"Okay, the voice says, 'Breaker one-nine, for some local information. . . . Get it? Breaker one-nine."

"Aw, right, boy, so then what happens?"

"So all these MIT scientists start checking the dials and looking around like they don't know what to do, and sure enough, it really is coming from some back-forty nebula a million miles over the Orange Bowl. And then, I, the low-life janitor, step to the microphone while the great scientists are scratching their zippers and say, 'How 'bout you, driver, for that local information, c'mon.'"

"Man, you are a Head Wound now."

"And after the aliens answer back, I guide the space ship in using the standard CB lingo; because that is the language the aliens learned while they listened to truckereeze on the set of air waves they happened to hook on to down here from outer space. And it makes that *Close Encounter* five-note musical piece sound like some kindergarten shit once it has been revealed that CB was the language they chose instead of those dumb notes in the Spielberg movie that go dum dum dum dum, dum. And look here, America, they are talking to me, the janitor, and Lizard Tater King himself, because I *am* the Tater King. I can do anything."

"Okay, Morrison."

"Oh, me and Jim, The Junior. Kings of slimeration, don't you know. We know how to get things small enough. But wait! So I'm at the truck stop with President Carter, guiding in the space ship so they can get the thing parked right, telling them country trucker instructions like, 'Pull your left hand a little bit there, driver. Now, your right hand. That's it driver. Come like your comin. Hold what you got.' Because I am the only one they, the aliens, want to talk to on their radio, that's all. That's the lingo that makes those space creatures comfortable, with their funny looking heads and big-ass eyes—me, the janitor, another kind of astronaut, a cane field flier and possessor of the toadstone progenitor in a Ball jar, the coolest jar Mr. Ball ever made when Mr. Ball used to blow glass."

"Shit. You should have said feenished at the end, like the Ghost of Nineteen."

"I would've, but I think he is one of them. The aliens, I mean. And I don't want to steal his stuff."

"What was that last part about Mr. Ball and, and jars?"

"Oh, nothing. That was just the cocaine lady lying her ass off again, feenished."

It was five in the afternoon when they parked the stock trailer in the ranch barn. They headed for the Blue Goose, scored some more stuff to stay awake then sat down with Chrome, Rose, Leda, and The Junior's girlfriend Thimble Taylor, who didn't talk much. Aubrey and The Junior kept batting things back and forth about the trip, and when they got to the end of anything they said, they'd say, "Feenished."

The year turned into the winter of '78. The town filled up with snowbirds and other Yankees from the great pension funds of America, the ones who bought homes to get residencies and unlimited homestead exemptions from the state of Florida.

The group, now truly in their thirties, showed up at the Goose every Friday.

"Who wants to play Oh, Yeah?" Leda said. But nobody did. "Okay, who wants to go out on the dock and feed the catfish?" Nobody did. "Okay, who wants to go out on the dock, feed the catfish, and do a bump?" They all said yes. After that, the group left and went to O'gram, Aubrey and Leda's, the house in the woods full of taxidermy, mannequins, and neon. Arquette had offered his place, but nobody wanted to go. Rose called Arquette's South Florida formula the Ostensorium.

They swam in their underwear and it was cool that night, so they went in and out of the sauna then back in the pool. They had a lot of shit between them to stay awake and talk about the oughts and ought-nots of their lives at this age. How they should make this the last coke party, because everyone was looking tired, getting weird cranky.

"Hell, that's why they call it crank," Chrome said.

"Naw," said The Junior. "They call it that cause it cranks you up, them bikers tell me. I sell shine to em, and they call anything 'crank' that's speed."

"Yes, and then it makes you bitchy," Rose said.

"Okay. Okay, so anybody that wants to quit can quit. They don't need the group's approval. We're all getting old, anyway," Leda weighed in, and they all laughed until the ugliest sunrise on the planet started to show. Everyone slinked home, mumbling they would quit.

Two weeks later, some had managed to stay away from the drug. Aubrey had written a special song for the Friday night ritual at the Goose to honor anyone in the group that was abstaining. It was the Cricket Jar band's turn to entertain the locals.

After one set of tame dinner songs and then one fast one that shook the place, Aubrey opened the next set with the ballad he'd written. He waited to make sure all the Goose bunch was there, especially Leda. Then, with just an acoustic guitar under a single spotlight, came the saloon singer, always on key.

MY FRIENDS MOVED BACK TO PENNSYLVANIA.

IT'S PRETTY UP THERE IN THE POCONOS.

ME, I THINK I'LL STAY HERE IN SOUTH FLORIDA,

LIE ON MY BACK AND FLOAT THROUGH THE
  MANGROVES,

CAUSE THERE'S SOMETHING HERE I NEVER COULD GET
  OVER,

THE SOUTH FLORIDA SKY TO ME LOOKS LIKE THE
  POCONOS.

THE LINES GO ON THE MIRROR AND YOU'RE SOMEBODY,

AND YOU TALK ALL NIGHT 'BOUT NOTHIN AT ALL.

I'VE DONE EVERYTHING THE MAN COULD SELL ME.

SWALLOWED AND SHOT WHAT YOU SEE ON THE EVENIN
  NEWS.

AIN'T NOTHIN GRAB YOUR THROAT LIKE THAT WHITE
  LADY.

CHILD, DON'T TOUCH THAT STUFF; IT MAKE A MESS OF
  YOU.

AND WHOEVER SAID SHE DON'T LIE WAS PROBABLY
  JUST HIGH.

WHERE DID J.J. CALE AND CLAPTON GET THAT SONG?

 IF YOU LOOKED ON THE GROUND

WHERE THEIR FEET WERE HANGIN ROUND,

YOU'D SEE SNOWSHOES THE SIZE OF FLORIDA THEY
  HAD ON.

 DEFINITELY WEARING SNOWSHOES WHEN THEY WROTE
  THAT SONG.

Chapter 20

THE SHELL ROCK ROAD

Chrome and Rose couldn't seem to quit the coke and were drinking too much to take the edge off. It was true to its slang name: shit. All the bunch knew it was shit, bad for you shit, this stuff from Columbia that could *give* you the shits, if it was stepped on with a look-a-like laxative powder called *mannitol*.

Leda was still in it. Did not have the equipage to quit, and the profligate spending it took was no deterrent. Even Aubrey couldn't beat the bugbear in social settings and did too many lines on the weekends.

1979

The eighties were coming with a new mindset—money fever— antithetical to the sixties' and seventies' mindset, and things like cocaine and the orchestration of whatever it took to win at anything started to drive a baroque and obscene capitalism.

Old Greek saying: *First, secure an independent income then practice virtue.*

A lot of Americans didn't want to have jobs that got their hands dirty. The ones that had to were tempted every night by a TV that told them where they stood based on what they had, and their children turned to them and asked why if they didn't. Physical appearance was up. Health foods were hauled in, in quantity, and a major illness was dehydration. Water in carcinogenic bottles was carried around all day and sipped when someone felt tired or dizzy. For the water business, the placebo effect of that was a windfall.

The food pyramid turned upside down. Fat was vilified; corn and pasta products were at the top to create a nation of tubs. Then came the daily vitamins that proved to be toxic later, and there was this reliable craving the food companies engineered called "mouth feel," how food and drink felt in your mouth, not in your stomach. Mouth feel steered carbonation, sugar, Candy Land tasters, and juvenile jingles like, "My stars! How does Mars make such wonderful candy bars?" All of this while people continued to snort the white shit, shoot the white shit, and jump off buildings.

Aubrey and Chrome kept surfing together. Arquette was rarely seen at the beach anymore. Leda had gone to Key West for a long weekend, and Chrome told Aubrey to come over to his house. Rose was making grouper, grits, and greens.

Around the table they sat.

"So, seen any good flicks lately?" Aubrey asked them.

"Yes. Right, Rose? You liked it, didn't you, honey?"

"I more than liked it. About this regarded white-trash girl of normal looks who has the hometown hunk fall in love with her."

"What's the movie?"

"*Buster and Billie*. This new guy, Jan-Michael Vincent, is in it. I think he was a TV actor, but I first saw him in a film with Bronson called *The Mechanic* a year ago."

They finished dinner and went to the Goose in Chrome's old station wagon full of beach sand. After two drinks, they were back at Chrome's little conch house on the Indian River. You could look across to the barrier island and the sacred waves from there, where the left pearls broke over from the Atlantic swells. Rose came out of another room with some lines.

"I'm getting more than worried about how much of this we do," Aubrey said. "You know, there's a hoof condition horses get in their hoof wall. It's caused by a fungus. Looks like a chalk line on the hoof. Horse people call it white line disease. I told The Junior the other day, I got it."

Rose started talking about *Buster and Billie* again and ended it in tears. "Severely romantic," she kept saying. "I miss Leda. Why does she have to go to Key West all the time?"

Aubrey headed to Kissimmee for another rodeo. Leda found time for Arquette, who was anxious to get his Melinda on a boat to the Bahamas with her dive gear so he could see Leda again. Sonny was in the same plate glass window drinking when Leda's car went by on Main Street. Arquette's car went by next. Then the artist who did murals, and Leda now and then, went by. Sonny spent a lot of time outside of bars in his own car just sitting, so he knew what everyone drove, but he did not know the artist personally. The whole thing looked funny. What an obvious parade. So he decided to take another look. He was the watcher, after all, the protector; Aubrey and The Junior his main job, but the rest of the clutch was, in a way, his too. In twenty minutes, he was on the side road close to O'gram. It was a short walk in to the farm, and when he parted the palmettos at the edge of the pasture, another figure was sneaking in fifty yards away. It was the artist, carrying a container.

When the figure reached the side of the house, it poured something out of the container along the edge. In a few more seconds, the smell of gasoline reached Sonny. *What now, watchman? What are you going to do about this Liberty Valence low-life trying to burn down Aubrey's house? The same thing John Wayne did to Liberty in the movie? Kill him?*

Inside, Leda and Arquette had taken up their positions across from each other on the couches.

"Need to fix your face, Arquette?"

"That would be nice."

She went upstairs. Came back down in her robe with coke on a mirror.

Sonny was watching the artist and looking around the ground for something to hit him with. In his bare feet for silence, he ran up behind him as the man reached up with both arms to douse the house with more gas. Sonny got under those arms and put him in a full Nelson. The two of them rolled on the ground by the back porch, far enough away to hide their grunts from Leda and Arquette.

"So, Arquette, how's the pain level?"

"Murder, sometimes."

"Do you think our sessions have helped?"

"That is when I feel better for a few days, and then it comes back."

Sonny and the artist are exchanging blows and wrestler positions now. A box of matches fell out of the artist's pocket, and he tried to crawl to them, rabid about burning the house where the married woman he loves is in her robe with another man.

"Well, then, let's get started, Arquette." Leda opened her robe and put the usual small pillow between her knees.

"You promised to share some fantasies of your own last time," he said to her.

"Okay. Why don't you begin with yourself over there, and during the process, tell me when you want me to talk about me and what *I* like physically."

The artist has Sonny on his back, trying to hit him with a free hand. Sonny rolls him off so hard he makes a complete revolution, allowing Sonny to get to his feet and kick him in the stomach.

"I want to hear something from you now!" Arquette says to Leda as he strokes himself harder.

"I like to push my nipple in with my thumb. You see?" She shows him and speaks quickly. "It makes it turn out to the side, under the skin, and then I use my index finger to rub the bottom part of it while my thumb holds it there. Usually the tip of a nipple is the only thing that gets rubbed in love making, but I like the underside of the nipple rubbed. It can make a woman's womb neck contract like a hand."

"Show me. Show it!" Arquette says louder while he works his cock.

Now Sonny has the artist spitting blood, and he puts him in a chokehold next to the whirring air conditioning by the back door. Leda pushes her nipple tip in and rubs the underside as she described. Arquette is to a new level from this, and notices Leda starting to move her legs and hips slightly from what she is doing to herself. He feels the saliva in his mouth increase and he comes, only this time he keeps moving his hand up and down toward a second come, getting the same response out of his erection he gets with real sex.

The artist is out cold. Sonny put him in a strangle hold and partially suffocated him.

"I see this, Mr. Orlander. I see what you are doing over there," Leda says. "You are proving to me the story about coming twice with no loss of erection."

"Yes! I am!" He is breathing hard and pushes his own nipple in with his free hand, and rubs the backside under his skin with his finger the way she does. Leda touches her place, and Arquette comes again.

Behind the house, Sonny has dragged the man still breathing to the trees and choked him out one more time. He gets him in the car after he is duct-taped and roped. An hour later, the artist came to at Sonny's as he was being fitted with a Freon death mask. His eyes flashed the execution bulge, and Sonny didn't hesitate to make it last so the man would feel the pleasant high effects of the gas before he died. Even though Sonny hated him for trying to burn down Aubrey's place, he feels better about killing someone who is very stoned before they go; his counter balance for the guilt of killing, barely equated in some twisted way Leda feels about adultery if she doesn't climax.

The artist's car was retrieved from the woods, and Sonny used the last of his junked refrigerators to shut the man in a reliable container, reassured the barn-burner was forever enclosed, like Sonny wanted his mother enclosed in a bottle years ago. He drove the man's car to a deep canal close by and sank it, then walked home.

The son of a bitch. I should have cut him in strips alive for what he was going to do. But what were Leda and Arquette going to do in that house last night?

The watcher had watched out for his again, this dangerous guardian. The next day, he and Half Track from the Harris Ranch buried the closed refrigerator. Half Track was all smiles and weird stares when Sonny gave him some pocket change. He didn't want any of the dimes in Sonny's hand, only the nickels and quarters, because they were bigger than dimes.

In the eighties, people wore tee shirts that said "Right Now," or "Winning! It's everything." The ethos—quick and next. "Damn, I'm Good," showed up on bumper stickers. Food was eaten faster so people could get up from the table and make more money. Only essays were read; novels were too long. Slicks, and slick covers on magazines were the new page-turners. Every task had to be faster, and serious purchase was given to time management. This historical change was forced and made possible not only by attitude, but by inflation and jacking the interest rates so high both parents had work to pay the mortgage. More speed came with the advent of computers. Chrome called computers the same thing he called Rose's vibrator—God from the machine.

Jean Seberg committed suicide in Paris in August; Aubrey couldn't believe it. The woman who first made his knees squeeze together was gone, the one who played the beautiful gamine in *Lilith*, who started out as the perfect *enjuenue* from Iowa and turned into his international fantasy, his Dulcinea.

It was September hot. The seasonal rains came, the hard pounding, sub-tropic soup. The serial killer, Ted Bundy, had been convicted in July. His name, and the serial hurricanes, were on television every night, hurricanes that seemed unhappy that year, storms that wanted Teddy out of jail to run with them again; the rotating monsters working their way around the tip of Florida and up into the Gulf so they could turn right and head across the state towards Raiford Prison, where Bundy was. Spring their brother; short out the electric chair when they put Teddy down in the seat.

In his house on a Sunday morning, Aubrey lay on the upstairs bed with just his mortality; the rain sound on the tin roof retold him his history. Slow and far back, the rain made him think. Where he was before, who he was with, what they did. The constant back peal, as Chrome called it, and Aubrey began to cry for his parents and the horrible way they died. In fact, every time he eased his legs down on a horse in the bucking chutes lately, he felt a disturbing desire to suffer or die violently when they opened the gate because *he* was still alive, as if it might be a cross threaded act of contrition for the good life his parents gave him. At times, he thought he used this guilt for courage to ride the crazy things and felt even guiltier about that. In the coming eighties, he would quit the broncs after he saw a man get killed by a horse at a rodeo right in front of him.

The rainsqualls blew outside. Water dripped loud off the edge of the house, and in between, the sun shone through the dark changing virgas of tropical storm sky. Aubrey Shallcross missed his mother, his father, and grandmother. Triple Suiter came on as he lay there and told him how short a life was, and that he might run into his family again sooner than he thought.

"What if it's just dark when you drop, though?"

"No, Aubrey. Why do you think I am here the way I am, if there is not another world?"

"I don't know. I wanna go to the big room to spin it more so I can reassure myself."

"Well, I do not think that is fair to me, your cranial tutor. You owe me an explanation as to what you really do in this big room, and what it looks like."

"I know I do. I know. But right now, I think I have to get off this bed and go for a drive to clear my head."

Out the farm's driveway, on the shell rock road, he crawled towards US 1 in his truck. On either side flooded wetlands, and plants called *hypericum*, or St. John's wort, covered the marsh. There, around those thirty-inch-high plants, the spiders wove their webs, hundreds, thousands of them, and Aubrey stopped every day to look at their designs. Now and then, he saw a web that looked like the one Nell showed him on the calamondin tree at the crazy place—schizophrenic. Cubist. He called the wetlands the knee-high Serengeti, because the plants looked like dwarf acacia trees in Africa. On the road this morning, were also real Africans, walking catfish, an invasive species, crawling and breathing air while they used their dorsal fins like elbows to get across to the other side. Any warm weather thing from anywhere can live in Florida. He got the same feeling he had next to the cane fields on this road, a feeling he could do something with his jar in his surface mind without going deeper in his brain to the big room he had built. He could take Triple Suiter with him for this one.

He conjured his Ball jar. A perfect drifty came, and he worked his truck into a steam punk creation with parts that looked hybridly airplane. "Hey, Trip, wanna try it? I'm gonna lean back here and fly us straight over those pine trees, bank left, and circle the savanna."

"You are not going to try and swallow the whole mess after that, are you?"

"No, asshole. I'm taking you with me on this other level in my head, and we're gonna fly this Dodge truck like the Wright Brothers. We may bounce and bump like they did, but we're gonna do it, and I hope you appreciate it. Ready?"

Trip turned into Head Wound. "The brain is the great revolver," he announced to Aubrey and the wetlands. "It takes fuel from the blood and turns it into dream punk, steam punk, truck punk, carburet it, Lord Jesus Christ. Let's go!"

Aubrey saw it all from the planet's crown organ part, his forebrain, the left pearl of perception and ricochet that shoots air pucks and bounce-backs off wet wire into hallucinations. His truck rose off the shell road and shot up in the sky over the Florida woods. He had the steering wheel in his hands and banked a turn like it was any other flying machine as he looked down at the sloughs and marshlands he

258

loved. The spider webs below were hit by the sun from a top angle he'd never seen before, his eyes big as a lemur's. He and Trip eagled the area and thought about the Nautilus, the beginning of steam punk. They flew until both had had their limit of sensory experience and knew any more would have been abusive. After one last bank to the left in the flying Dodge, they landed back on the shell rock road.

"Left pearls, Trip! God damn left pearls! Good as the waves out at High Beach!"

"Now that *was* mansion, Head Wound. Feenished!"

"You think that was something? I can do ten times that in the big room. The other dimension is not in the air or heaven, Trip. It's in the head."

"Oh, just splendid. I have always told you that, but now you suddenly get it? Sometimes you are really slow. Do you make these remarks by accident about the big room to torture me, or do you subconsciously do them on purpose?"

"How can you do something subconsciously on purpose, midget shit? I'm going to get you to the big room soon, but I need time to work my way around to it, that's all."

"Can't you at least describe the place to me? Tell me about it in more detail. I mean, I know what the Blindspot Cathedral looks like. I have been in there, and frankly, I hope I never see that black church again. But I want to see that other arcade of yours."

Aubrey nodded. Didn't say anything else. Put his real truck in gear and headed to Randolph's Diner for breakfast. Trip had made an effort at humor about the diner a couple of days ago because of its fat-packed menu, and lately he was calling it The Catheter Cafe. Donna, Punky's wife, came over to the table and interrupted Aubrey's examination of the fake marble table top, something he did if the patterns were interesting, looking for faces, animals, and Catholic miracle stuff in the swirls.

"You want the usual, Aubrey?"

"Yep, Adam and Eve on a raft."

"All right, cowboy." And she headed back towards the kitchen.

"Hey, Trip, do me some Frankie Lymon this morning. C'mon, Trip, please?"

Trip was a perfect impressionist. Could imitate a song like a tape recorder, even with the beginning record noise for each one, a vinyl as it dropped from the capstan to the table and the crackle before the song began. Trip wanted to do "Why Do Fools Fall in Love," something Aubrey thought he might have chosen on purpose, considering the absentee behavior Leda was practicing. She went to Key West to see her folks or somewhere every other weekend, making it hard for Aubrey to measure the relationship. But Trip did such a good job with Frankie's song, Aubrey forgot about that, and Donna showed with his Adam and Eve on a raft: two eggs poached on a piece of toast.

When he finished his first cup of coffee, he was back on his love life. "What do you think I should do, Trip? She told me the other night she was thinking of moving to the Keys and getting a job in the hospital there. And now there are some guys in town who want me to invest in land with them, but they won't if I have an estranged wife. A long divorce would tie up the property. I mean, if I told her we needed to get divorced so I can do this land deal, she would probably just shrug her shoulders and say sure, like she did when I wanted to get married. It wouldn't be a horsehide divorce. She doesn't care about any rules or social shit."

"Hey, Aubrey." Donna was back at the table. "You know Punky's sittin over in that back booth by hisself. Want me to move Adam and Eve over there?"

He followed Donna, who put down the plate and left.

"Looka here. If it ain't that slick car dealer. The singin-cowboy-surfin-bronc-bustin-talkin-to-hisself-all-the-time-since-grade-school-friend-a-mine, Aubrey Shallcross. Hey, that's okay. I'm talkin to myself like a crazy all the time, too, 'specially since I started that lawn mower repair shop. I'm in there alone, you know." Punky looked

260

down at another paper clip he was folding into a triangle shape to make sure the proportions were right.

"Doesn't matter talking to yourself, Punky. My doctor friends all say it's perfectly normal as you get older. Donna said your lawn mower thing's going pretty good."

"Not as good as that shine binness me and Junior's been runnin."

"Yeah, but you know I don't want to hear about that. Know what I mean?"

"Oh, yeah, forgot. Uh, the lawn mower binness. Donna told you 'bout my doin's. That girl struts through my shop every morning to see whether I've cleaned up right. She's like a Nazi sometimes when it comes to my doin's. I swear, Aubrey, these women, if they didn't have a pussy you wouldn't even talk to em."

Aubrey flinched. "Uh, maybe. Not sure."

"Whatta you want, honey?" Donna was back at the table.

"I'm gon have what Aubrey's havin."

"No, you're not. The doctor said eggs was bad for your asthma. I'll bring you oatmeal and toast." Donna left for the kitchen.

"See what I mean, Aubrey? If they just didn't have that Fidel Castro lookin thing down there at the top a-their legs, you wouldn't talk to em."

"Oh, but then, Punky, life might be too flat and simple without that wondrous thing in the region, and that thing of ours, too."

"I hear ya. You got one a-them beautiful things around, I know. Boy, you lucky, and I guess so am I. No matter what I say about it, I do love that Donna girl and them kids a-ours to death. When she's not talkin to me directly, like I said, I rattle on to myself, and now she's even got me worried about it."

"You ever pull anybody else from your head in on the conversation?"

"Only Jesus, and I ask him about mechanical problems, especially them new things called weed eaters that just came out, and how come he sent that particular pain-in-the-ass machine down here, plus those things with Castro 'tween their legs."

Chapter 21

THE CEMETERY: 2ND VISIT

It is the spring of '80. Aubrey got up early to have breakfast at the diner and left Leda sleeping. On the shell rock road, he stopped at his usual spot and checked what the spiders had done with their webs. Sandhill cranes waded next to the hypericum plants in the wetland, and if you adjusted the scale for a drifty, they seemed like giants among dwarf-looking acacias.

When he left the diner, he headed for the Z-Bar Up to help The Junior with cattle vaccinations. They worked from late morning till dark then went to the main house for gator tail, hush puppies, and sweet potato. He and The Junior went through their food at the same time, looked at each other, and said, "Feenished." Everyone else at the table smiled.

Driving out of the ranch, he chewed on the inside of his cheek flesh over all that had happened—death, the business, and Leda's obvious ambivalence about their relationship. He drove east for the coast, where a full moon was coming off the horizon like a ball of orange radium. After five miles, his truck rose on the overpass that crossed the Florida Turnpike. He pulled off the road and clicked on his CB radio to listen to the big rigs below on the main towpath between Miami and Orlando.

"Gonna sit off this overpass, on Channel 19, and have one Tater fantasy to relax, Trip. I earned it today."

Adjusting his seat back, he went to his mind for his Ball jar and took a whiff off the toadstone inside to carburet a flight around the tower in his big room, conjuring the voices on the CB he hoped the spaceship aliens chose as they crouched behind a star listening to truck drivers speak blue collar doo-lang through the diodes and aerials of their Freightliners, the place where the chrome rim prophets use their country cryptonyms like another language. And look here, America, the aliens were talking to him, the Tater King, the original cane field flier and radio head wound, with a whittle monster inside a magical backwoods Ball jar.

But at that very moment, before he could put the fantasy through his slimerater and swallow the whole conjured dream in the self-exal Tater wonder of it all, someone pulled up behind him and started blowing the horn. It was Punky.

"Hey, man, what's a-matter? You broke down in one of them purty Dodge trucks a-yours?" Punky yelled through the window glass and the truck's idling engine noise.

Aubrey flew out of his brain and reached for the squelch knob on his CB.

"What? Shit. No, Punky. I'm just here listening to the truck traffic. What the fuck are you doing?"

"I'm checkin on you. I'm a-goin to the Blue Goose to drink, get high, see Jesus."

"Yeah, Punky, you and Jesus."

Punky left.

"Trip! I had something big going in the big room till that fart machine showed up."

"How would I know what was going on in your secret big room?"

"But you've heard this one before. I was reliving my fantasy with the aliens by speaking CB to them. Remember?"

"Yes, I remember. It was right after your fascination on that hay trip with the man on the radio who said finished, or feenished, after everything. You called him the Ghost of Channel Nineteen. And what is the significance of a trucker who continuously says finished or feenished after everything like you and The Junior do now, as if there was some hidden gravity in it?"

"Because it's his signature. Like Elvis saying, 'Thank ya, ver much.' He's another connoisseur of the psycho-generated souvenir like me. It's the Nineteen Ghost's intellectual truck property and rare doo-lang, and I only steal from the very best, you little prick." He pulled back onto the highway.

"Oh, you are a connoisseur all right, Toad Smoke," Trip said.

"I think it's just another sign of my curious and creative spirit. A sign."

"Well, yes, and it is a sign you and I ought to have a tell-all talk, some honesty about the way your head works lately before you expose your veridical innards to Leda and sink into an irrational fear crimp once she really knows your bowel habits. You will lose every argument with her after that. And I think we ought to have this talk in the cemetery for the effect. It is coming up on the right in two miles. You should be paying an overdue visit to your family anyway."

Aubrey's chest jumped when he downshifted for the turn. He made the perfunctory sign of the cross, even though he claimed the state of non-believer, and shut his engine next to the marble head stone that read in large, lapidary letters, SHALLCROSS.

It always did one of two things when he saw that headstone: not much, because he was too preoccupied by life on this side and just making the good son visit. Or he might hear the death knell, go dizzy, see his own coffin down there under ground.

As he stared at the grass-covered place for him, he heard the Ghost of Channel Nineteen in the bottom of his future grave rise up like an embolism and say, "Feenished." It broke off a hunk of clot in him that could only be thinned by a schizophrenic rant, a two-way with the long-toothed crystal set in his head, the erudite and occasionally insufferable intercessor, Triple Suiter.

"The last time we were here I left feeling like a heretic, Trip."

"But what we were talking about was not heresy." Trip heard Aubrey's thoughts. "Only to the close-minded conservatives of your old church would it be heresy. God is not a Catholic. He, She, or It is an unencumbered free baser of the pure white calcium toadstone rock in that jar of yours, just like you, and it is real and wondrous to be smoking that carbureted stone of yours into the slip away like you do when it comes to savoring the full house out there. Same footage when your truck is on the shell rock road in the mornings and goes all airplane out over the knee-high Serengeti. Or when you pick Frankie Lymon out of the coffin in the diner at breakfast and get him to sing "Why Do Fools Fall in Love." Call them gods, mortals, myths, art, natural progressions, science, fantasy, or just your morning erection; they are all the same shining left and right pearls, Aubrey."

Trip reminded him he was superstitious, that he thought the toadstone ring and the flame vine were the weatherman; that he thinks the blue jays he shot jinxed him when he abandoned the Romans, and then the Blind Spot Cathedral stood up and throbbed into his headroom blackouts. All the guilt symbols were there in that black church—the punishment of the choke, the stigmata, hooks through his bloody hands tied to flame vines, taking him up to that swirling keloid scar in the top of his head so something or someone on the other side would wrap their arms around him like his mother did if he could just break through that whirling scar. So terrified he is of his imagined apostasy; terrified of certain swollen skits that go too far, like some of the ones he runs on drugs or in the cane fields around Belle Glade, the ones that tend to skin the divine like sun damage.

"Look, I am one who knows about this, Aubrey, because you haven't answered the important question about the subconscious, and that is, where do your dreams go when you die? The dreams of sleep that is not sleep. The paradoxical half-sleep when you hang there, just inside the wall hollow after you first lie down before the deeper sleep comes and you realize in the larger rake-off of consciousness you might be immortal."

Aubrey looked at Trip on his arm. "You do know, don't you? It's when you first wake up too, in limbo after an afternoon nap. Those half-dreams that give you the feeling your mind won't ever die. That you could walk out over a gorge, drop down a thousand feet, and pick a flower with your anus and live through it. I wonder why I over-think it so much. Turn it into such hard balls. Is it some kind of brat fettle I do in this easy-living bubble I was born into? Wonder if I had been in Vietnam, like The Junior, running from bullets, would I have had these same preoccupations over there? Would I have had time to? I think peacetime is harder on people like me. For some, there's nothing scarier than peacetime. My grandmother used to read Kipling to me when I was a child, and I changed that line of his that goes, 'If you can keep your head while all about you are losing theirs,' to 'If you can keep your head while all about you are *keeping* theirs,' because that's a lot harder, and something I've had to live with a long time. It's not such an unpleasant distraction to watch other people losing it if you're not, even though it lacks compassion, but it is living hell if you're the only it's happening to.

"I sometimes worry about other people who hear a voice like me, and I wonder how they're dealing with it. The ones who aren't lucky enough to have a sidecar like you, Trip, to help them. Are they sad because the medicos are telling them they're crazy? Poor Nell Kitching. And I wonder if I was deep into fixing weed eaters, like Punky, would I be picking my nose all the time about this ground-glass existential in my stomach?"

"Maybe not, Aubrey. You have to quit looking at it as pain and just start seeing better stuff. Don't you remember the line you once saw on a card in an Orlando head shop? It said, 'The reason for being is to let the world give you life, and to give the world life by giving your life to the world,' or something like that. Maybe that's what Johnny Yuma, Jesus Christ, or the Buddha believed. You bought that card and taped it to your dashboard for a while. That is the stuff I want you to concentrate on more. And as far as what is on the other side of the keloid scar up there in your skull, it is the same thing on this side. Your own shell rock road running to your house, then through it and back again to the shell rock road and the knee-high Serengeti you love. An endless loop through time and your life and the palmetto kingdom. Do not make it such a mystery. Even Floyd knows that what is on the dark side of the moon is just the same thing that is on this side in the dark. Another loop. Nothing really disappears entirely. Maybe you already have what you always wanted and don't know it. This is what the sum of your credo, the elements of your existentialism in the wheelworks of this ontic life you lead should be based on, Aubrey. This we have talked about here tonight should be what the Germans call your *Weltanschauung*."

"Jesus, your mastodon words."

"No, they're your words, Aubrey. I know you remember that one from Father Anselm's German class. It means your conception of the world and the place of humanity within that world."

"But at the end of the loop you're talking about, Trip, there's Amper Sand, always saying, 'And' right where the loop starts again."

"Oh, true. That is why it is a loop, and why he is there. He is truly a luminary for you and me, and my own beloved slipper. And I know he smiled right now when he heard you say that. Yes, at the bottom of every page, at the end of every road, he wants you to see his symbol, the twenty-seventh letter of the alphabet: &. So did the Danish thinker, Soren Kierkegaard, who asked everyone to constantly toss the dialectic to keep the doors open."

"I didn't worry about this so much when I was younger. You know, when I was drenched in twenty-year-old glandulars and could fuck my way to changing the subject. But now I'm nervous about losing this life of mine. I remember reading somewhere, 'Once you stop believing in God, you start to believe in everything.'"

"Right. That is Amper Sand again. More *per se*. More AND. Even a little Sartre, maybe, and some of that French stuff can be a rotten kind of nihilism if you are not careful. You've got to remember, it is Sartre's own version of the sub-psychic three-sixty around the tower *he* is working off of, like you, Aubrey, but not your tower, which I don't know a lot about."

Aubrey slumped down on the big stone covering the graves. "Okay, the tower then. I'll tell you. It's my RKO, the iron Eiffel on top of the globe in the black and white newsreels I saw as a kid."

He looked out over the cemetery and conjured the Eiffel's appearance in the middle, wires running from the top down to every grave, in case any Dead Ringers had their bell kicked over and needed to radio someone to get out. It shivered him. "I'll tell you more in detail," he said, standing up, messing the dirt with his foot.

"Yes, do. God bless Dan Webster, Henry Ford, and what they gave to carburetion and language. Let us hear it, me and my Amper Sand." Trip grinned.

"So over the years, I thought what I do in the big room in my head, this thing like tetherball, was juvenile. Sugar buzz Disney. I mean, I'm flying around that thing up there like Peter Freebase Pan, thinking I can make a toadstone vaporize and smoke it for more gas, but sometimes things get out of control, and I get scared of what I'm creating in the jar. I hear Hendrix singing 'The Watch Tower,' you know, 'Someway outta here.'"

"You think that's so juvenile? That's okay. Remember what your Victorian women's suffrage grandmother used to say to you, 'Aubrey. You have to stand up and act like a man, strong and childish.'" They both laughed.

Aubrey described to Trip what he saw in his big room—the tower in the middle of a cane field on the floor of his crania surrounded by the high ceiling of his skull.

"The Eiffel is the symbol I use for the objective world. It's my standard for the immutable and yet my king post for mutation." Trip nodded like he understood. "I circle it, holding on to a rope in one hand, while I arrange or derange things in my Ball jar with the centrifugal force the orbit makes."

"Yeah, who's driving the motorcycle when that happens?" Trip winked.

"Me, white boy, not the Slim Hand. I'm drivin that big German bike with a sidecar they call *Sachlichkeit*. Father Anselm would like I remembered that one. That's the German word for objective. And then there's the other way I circle, the subjective way, to do the work that's much more fun. This is the way I mess with an off-road lefty-loose, to get things so impressionistic and past their part numbers I have trouble describing them. When something gets that good, I take it to Houston and fly it up in the Astrodome with Bud Cort, in the movie he did, *Brewster McCloud,* because you can bet if I've gone to the big room, I'm not there to just toggle some ordinary. I have something to cook with my whittle monster. Fission by Aubrey. The new meaning of changing the station."

Trip looked at him, tricking his smile. "Same stretch as your examination of a photo of a photo in that Tin Snip Killer's refrigerator, getting smaller and smaller out into space until there is no more dawn, or when you run into Keir Dullea at the end of *Two Thousand and One*, or *None*. I know you, Aubrey."

The two raccoons that passed by earlier were on their way back from their favorite trashcan. They stopped when they heard the man-noise again and stood up on their hind legs, sniffing the cement-y air from the corner of a mausoleum, watching Aubrey walk in circles, wondering if this human was sick with the disease they call rabies. Many coons get this disease then walk in circles talking to themselves like him.

"Sometimes I push on something till its blood sticks out, Trip, and still I can't slim it enough in my jar to swallow. To know it like I want to. That hurts and builds up a horrific anxiety in me. Then I have to go back down to the base of the tower and restore it to the objective world, the world I took it from, so I can apologize to the gods of quantum physics and asphalt shingles, or whoever, for screwing with their designs. Until maybe, in a few days, I might want to try it again."

He froze and held up his finger. "But I *still* have that urge to slim-erate and swallow it, even if it got poisonous or too large. I always know when something took a black left up there and it is starting to get dangerous. And yet this compulsion I have, this pica. . . " His voice worked down to a whisper.

Trip waited a moment then asked his next question carefully. "That was the counterclockwise direction you just went through. The subjective way when you say you caprice with the mien or elan of things. Now what about the clockwise direction, what you call the objective world?"

Aubrey blew the air out he was holding. "Objective world. Yes, that's the clockwise way. That's the meaning of righty-tighty. I can usually kill any un-agreeable creations I've spawned in the counter-clockwise direction when I go back to the clockwise way; creations that are flawed and need to be euthanized or repaired or started over."

Trip told him he thought it was the real meaning of their rhyme "True magazine knows the truth, righty-tighty, lefty-loose," and this was how Aubrey had hashed out a personal understanding of the objective/ subjective paradox: he circles right, around the tower to imitate the objective world, and to the left means his subjective take and wild reshaping of that world.

"It seems so, but I never forgot about our Amper Sand. You have to be at peace with him if you're a secular person and want honest answers. Because just when you think you have the doo-lang, the rag-time existential, braided, there sits that symbol over the number seven key on a black Underwood. I know this house of mine, Trip. I drew it and built it to stay sane. Now, damn it, I've hyperventilated, and I think I'm going to crater." He crumpled over on the grave monument. Trip was knocked off the forearm and had to rearrange himself.

"Shit! I'm your factory-authorized sidecar, Aubrey. I'm in the God Store of your self-portrait, and I ought to be able to go with you to the big room for these sessions."

"You will. I'll take you soon. Promise."

Trip smiled. Came on with an imitation of Head Wound. "I can see you turning in your thesis to the hyper-didatic university brass on the objective/ subjective dilemma, based on an analogue of a tower with a tether ball man, holding a new apriori/ aposteriori appliance called a Ball jar in his hand. Next, you recommend it be used in this esemplastic way by quantum physicists, and that other great doo-lang thinker in our small town known as Punky, so they both can escape the frustration of this historical paradox that has puzzled mankind forever. Oh! And how much you regret that Socrates, Plato, Aristotle, and some of the Sophist boys are not alive to bless you for tackling this and the part the senses play in it, after all the years they spent out there, in the spin of some other wa-wa and *strept* float trying to solve this. Stuff they decided on before Jesus, Elvis, and that director Stanley Kubrick, who came along in his epic space movie and said, 'Oh, it's simple, don't worry about it!' So why do you think you need this Ball jar and towering apparatus in your head to see these things, Aubrey?"

"Because I always loved scenes and sets. I think of my tower as some kind of wrought-iron epistemology, the one good-god-glorious-iron-monument super prop and theatrical stage. I'm a product of props and sets, stage and movie, like the ones I have in my own house. Got raised that way, watching films like Frankenstein, with all that apparatus downstairs in Victor's mansion. "

"Let's speak of Punky again, who pulled up behind us and blew his horn an hour ago," Trip said. "He's never going to pan fry anything at this level, bless his heart anyway. Of course, he won't have to endure that dark church of yours over the God question, either, while he bleeds from his hands choking on lawn mower parts instead of blue jays on the way up to the top of the Blind Spot Cathedral, now will he? Nothing against Punky, bless his heart again; it is just the way his mother dressed him in those genes of his. He will always live in the foyer. Most people don't go anywhere else in the house during their life. They do not even want to know they have a second floor. They sort of peak in the sixth grade or high school and stay right about there."

"Wish I didn't know about the second story sometimes. I'd get to sleep like Punky does. Nothing seems to bother him except weed eaters and his Donna's vagina."

"Yeah, I know, Aubrey, but you remember we're all stuck with the limits and abilities of our own air pucks."

"What else should we skin tonight? What about the me and Leda situation, and where that's going?"

"No. I leave that to you and Leda. I'm really beat. I heard what I needed to hear out here about your headroom and its apparatus, as you like to call it. Let's get out of here."

"Did we solve the question? Is something or somebody that made us and loves us out there?"

"No, we didn't solve it, but we sure bumped it good. Nobody in history has ever un-shirted this thing entirely, and the Amper Sand won't allow anyone to deep throat this subject by getting the answer from someone else. It has to come from you. I think he really knows the answer, and his mission is to keep saying 'and,' like Kierkegaard would, so we will discover it for ourselves. It would mean more to us then."

The tiny *consigliere* walked up the bicep toward Aubrey's armpit and turned around in the spotlight the way Jimmy Durante did at the end of his TV show in the 50s. Then he put his finger on his chin and squinted. "I'm left, as you like to say, Aubrey, exhausted."

Aubrey moved closer to the three graves—his father's, his mother's, and his grandmother's. He made the sign of the cross and said the Latin words he grew up with. "*In Nomine Patris, et Filii, et Spiritus Sancti.*" He thought again how Trip was so right. The parish priests used to incessantly say, "Cross yourself," and you really *could* cross yourself in the end if you weren't careful. Then that would make you one of those people telling yourself a story about your life you might decide one day wasn't true, and you'd drop like a ball when the story stopped or became too painful. He climbed in his truck and headed for his part-time sweetheart and his house in the woods, O'gram.

On the way home, he had to carefully consider what he would say to Leda. No cemetery.

There was so much he kept from her—Trip, the apparatus in his head. He stopped the truck about two hundred feet from the yard. Leda had turned on every light in the structure, even the one in the top of the silo rising out of the house, the one that shined through the zaffer of stained glass eye over the wetlands like some watcher on commission. The wood home truly looked like a big, JackalanternedchandelieredBuckminsterFullercoloredglassblowncompartmenthousevaingloryship. Aubrey just sat there, sentimental, watching it move and breathe without a hint of self-exaltation because he built such a swollen thing in the first place. What he felt was love for the way it looked right now, and that was more powerful at the moment than any inclination to turn it in his jar and beat his Tater chest, then head for the big room to trombone it beyond the objective world and swallow it to know it when he got it slim enough.

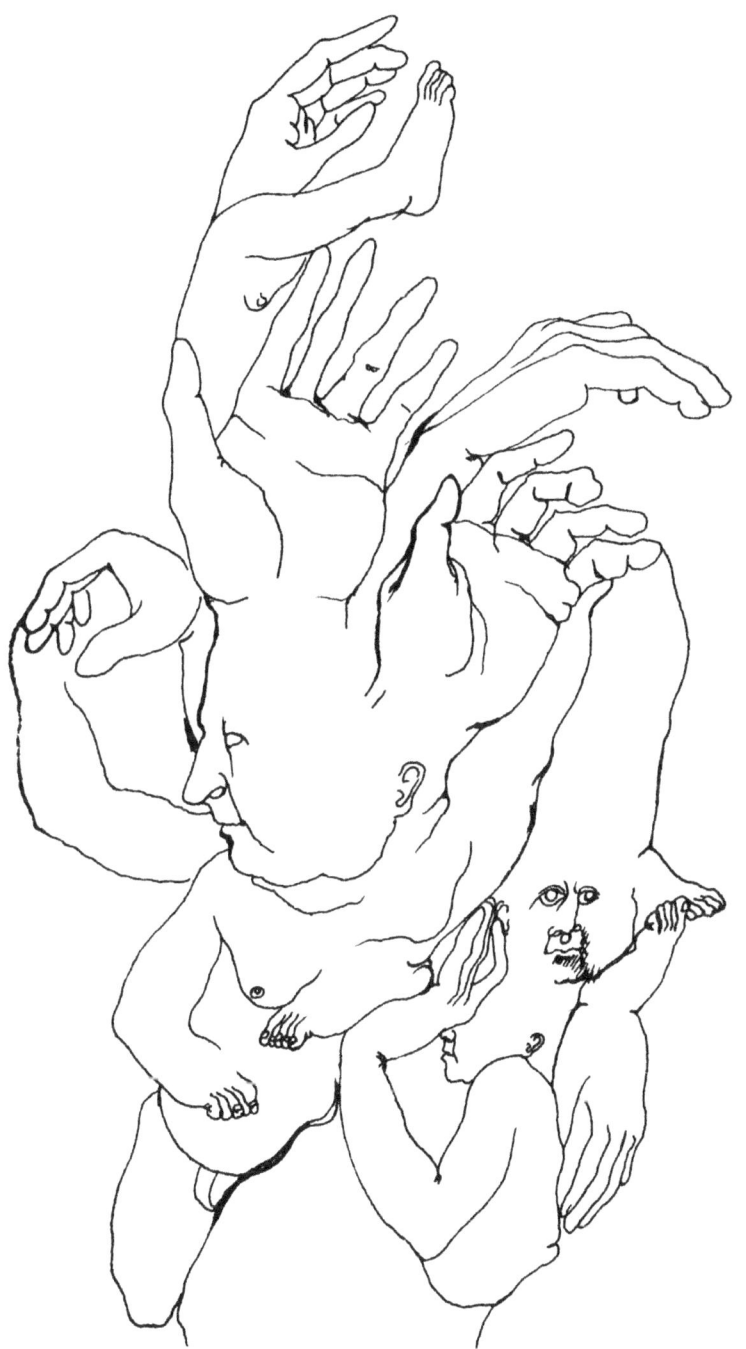

275

Chapter 22

RECKONINGS: HALF A LOVE STORY

May of 1980

They were sitting around a table at the Goose—Aubrey, The Junior, Punky, Chrome. Raining outside. The place was full of truants. Nobody wanted to work today, so they quit early. There was uneasiness among the friends that had to do with Aubrey. When he was away, they watched around the bar as Leda and Arquette seemed to jump-shoot eye contact, something friends look for when the other half isn't there, and the other, other is on their own. As careful and brief as Leda and Arquette were trying to be, it was never enough when the right eyes were on you. Arquette was not the total insider among the local boys, the orthodox, the South Florida orthodox. Of course, Chrome wasn't either, but Chrome was liked more. This would not be an intervention today, but the friends were ready to offer Aubrey any kind of disabusal if he gave them an opening.

"What are you guys doing tonight?" from Aubrey.

"Aw, me and The Junior gonna get Donna and Thimble and go to the Johnny Jumper. Hot country band tonight. Why don't y'all come?" Punky said to the table.

"Yes, well, perhaps Rose would like to do something like that. It would get us out of Jensen Beach for a change. And you, Aubrey? You and yours?" from John Chrome.

"Sure, I'll come. Leda's away again."

"That girl ever stay home?" Punky asked, trying to make a joke of it.

"No. Always gone, it seems." Aubrey looked down at the table.

"Yeah, and when you is gone, we see her in here. Arquette, too, and he seems to look out for her. They good friends, I guess," Punky got up the nerve to say.

Aubrey nodded. "Well, I can't say she and I have been that close lately. I think she's either tired of this town or tired of me. My mom always said I can be trying."

"Yes, Rose feels this way about Jensen Beach, too," Chrome said.

"Aw, hell, I think ever'body do from time to time," from The Junior.

"Yeah, but it's more than that with me and Leda. I think something's gonna give soon, and I'm glad my mom isn't around to see it if it does. My mom gave me the look now and then when it came to Leda, but goddamn, that girl was something beautiful when I met her, and she still is. I mean beautiful."

The Junior fished for his wallet. Inside the leather dividers was a worn piece of paper. The writing on it was blurred. It was the quote from Suskin, the soldier in Vietnam, before he was killed and his corpse partially eaten by a tiger. The Junior held it up to the light coming through a window behind him and read, "It is amazin, how complete the deelusion that ever'thing beautiful is goodness."

"That's Tolstoy, I believe," Chrome offered.

"Yeah, well, a guy I knew in 'Nam who was plenty book smart said that when we was in the jungle being watched by a fuckin tiger. We could hear the cat movin round us, but we couldn't see it. The ole boy, Suskin was his name, was pretty fascinated with that tiger, and he thought they was beautiful. Well, he got killed in a fire fight the next day, and wouldn't you know a tiger got to his body before the army could get it out of there." The rest of the table's eyes were very open. The Junior rarely spoke about Vietnam. "I wrote down what he said on this piece a-paper the night before he died and been carryin it ever since, cause I seen lots of beautiful things what wasn't goodness in my life, too. Hell, I think Jake is beautiful, even though he's a snake and sits up there singing those rattles a-his, got needles

278

in his mouth full a-poison kill you dead as George Washington, but he beautiful."

"I know. Leda is beautiful," from Aubrey. "And I know she has a lot of goodness in her. I've seen it. Sounds like Arquette may have seen it, too. Is that what you guys are saying?"

"Now hold on, Aubrey. We ain't saying that." The Junior turned to him. "Maybe it just look like that a little. You and me have been going to a lot of rodeos, you know. Maybe Arquette's just being polite, cause she's alone when she come in here."

"If they just wouldn't leave the bar at the same time," Punky said. The table went silent.

Chrome opined. Tried to offer a discussion of how things seem to be one thing when they really are another, but the table wouldn't help him. They all scratched and lolled their heads around, uncomfortable that the subject had made it into the open. Aubrey didn't say another word. When they got up to leave, Punky, who was no fan of Arquette's, said to Aubrey, "Jesus, ever'body seems to leave some kinda trail, don't they? 'Specially me." Then he shoved one of his remodeled paper clips into Aubrey's hand, bent into its usual shape, the triangle, and the famed geometry for adultery.

"Don't you love her as she's walking out the door."

He and Leda put it out there days later. He had felt strong enough to do it for some time, after the last Blind Spot Cathedral episode passed. He knew she brought much to him in the way of formative over the years. They both managed to glom the good stuff from each other. But not so much he could discount who he became on his own after his father's death, years before he ever met Leda. He was who he was and was going to be when that happened to his father, and he was ready in front of her now with that flippant tell on her face as she packed to go to Key West again.

"We're not doing too well here, are we?" he said to her.

"Guess not." She shrugged.

"What you wanna do?"

"What do *you* want to do?"

"I got an offer to invest in a land project with some people, but I can't have an estranged wife or they won't let me in."

"Yes, but I have to live my life. You certainly get to live the hell out of yours, Mr. Singer, traveling rodeo rider, local businessman. You'd be a great catch for a local girl. Why don't you go get one? Getting a divorce is no problem for me. I don't believe in that marriage crap, anyway."

"I know. You have something going on with Arquette?"

"No. Just the same old friendship." She lifted her chin higher.

"You know if you play me for a fool, I'll be very disappointed in you, and if I let you play me for one, I know you'll be very disappointed in me."

"I have never slept with Arquette. But let's just say I had, even though, *True* magazine, I have not. Isn't your favorite fantasy girl Jean Seberg, from that movie *Lilith*? And isn't she still your fantasy girl, even though her character in that story was quite the nympho? You and I saw the movie together. And didn't she say in the film when her lover, Warren Beatty, confronted her about her infidelity, 'If I were Shakespeare, I would do it with a pen; if I were Caesar, I would do it with a sword; but I am Lilith, and I do it with my body.' So how do you feel about that from Lilith? You still have a crush on her? Even though she sleeps with others?"

"Well, I like the movie, and, uh. . . "

"Then let me give you another line from the movie, because I liked it, too. How's about this one your Lilith said to Mr. Beatty. 'If you discovered your God loved others as much as he loved you, would you hate him for it?'"

Aubrey stood there. A little peeled. This woman he'd nicknamed Strangleda to his male friends when he was mad at her had countered him in a way he had no answer. It was one reason he loved her, the best he could, without ever telling her he did for all this time, because that's what she insisted on. The short song line he had written about her once: "There's a lady that lives inside of her/ her psychological queen/ that's the lady that gives me half of her/ she's the go-between," was close, but it also described him. He only gave her half of him, because he was afraid of what she could do. He never told her about Triple Suiter and the way he really was, his mental states, and he thought it dishonest of him. He wanted to love her like his mother and father loved each other, but his fear of loss, as experienced with his father, and his fear of Leda, too, held him back. And now look what had happened. She was leaving, and in a way, he blamed himself for some of that.

She turned and walked to her car with a bag and put it in the trunk. Before she got in, she had one more thing to say. "I'm surprised you didn't bring up my drug habit in this conversation."

"Okay, I'll bring it up." Silence for a moment. "The monks taught us this at school, because they were sure we were all going to become drug addicts in the sixties. The word addiction comes from Latin, *addictio*. At first, it had a less severe meaning, a devotion to something. But in Roman society, it meant you owed someone money and couldn't pay it back, so you became their slave. I think you owe that stuff a lot of money, and you've become a slave to it."

"I guess you'd call that the straight and narrow of it then, huh, Aubrey? Well, I can't stay straight living here, and I've had enough of narrow in this small town."

"But you're burning down the barn to kill the rats."

"Living in this town, that would be the *only* way to kill the rats. Heroin. I'm thinking about Casablanca, you know, Miami. Nice house you got here, Shallcross." Then the woman who loved arbitrage, provocation, attention, and condescension, even Aubrey part time—the woman

281

the gypsy lady Reve called a bandicooter, a potato thief, was gone.

He left, too. Went out to the Z-Bar Up in Indiantown. Didn't quite know why, but knew he needed those pastures and woods. He tacked a horse and just rode, trying to see where he'd been over the last few years with the Goose bunch, the business, the bareback broncs, his life with Leda. He loved her more than part time instinctively, and he knew it. He thought he could walk away with a big chest, but he was his mother and father's child, and one night on his way home in the rain full of drink, that slow plaintive song "The Rose" started pulling itself out of the truck's radio like a long human hair. "Love is like a razor/ it leaves the soul to bleed," it said, "but it's this endless aching need." Somehow, he blanked, skidded off the road, and sideswiped a light pole. His head was bleeding down his face and he was crying. Where was the glass between him and Leda now, the vitrines that separated him from the mannequins in his house and the dangerous wildlife in his head? He did know love for her, and he did know, no matter how hard you pushed it away, it would bury its face in a ham bone and get hold of a wire.

A week after Leda was gone, Arquette began to descend further into hell. He relied heavily on Sam Lillycrop, his general manager at work, to run the company. Every day, he watched Sam limp from place to place on the hip joint destroyed years ago by the Nazi's bullet. This strong, crippled man. This man from another generation of pain thresholds, and this Arquette, in his own place of pain, at first used it as inspiration, but when that failed him, the ass-end of it sat down hard on his self-worth because he wasn't the same soldier as Sam.

He did not sleep much in this dolorous state. Melinda was very supportive, but he was of the mind that he was experiencing a slow emasculation from the bad tooth in his pelvis, and also of a mind that if you showed any weakness to a woman, she would leave you. The pelvic ring of the sacred feminine he so sought all his life began to represent intractable pain and bad dreams, as if he was a paralyzed person who dreamed he could still walk and make love. The sexual athlete, the great soft tissue invader from New England, was out of it.

Aubrey and Leda agreed to divorce. Leda insisted she didn't want a thing, more affirmation of herself as a nonbeliever in the institution in the first place, but Aubrey sneaked money into the separate bank account she had always kept, and he sent her a new car from the business. When it became obvious to the Goose bunch that she really had left town for good, Arquette was the most upset. What about his therapy she called "no touch"? He found it close to impossible to masturbate and fantasize unless she was there in the robe. One night at the Goose, he sat down with Aubrey, who was eating alone in corner.

"Someone told me Leda was doing something in Miami."

"Yeah, she wanted to get her masters in nursing," Aubrey white-lied.

"Oh. Well, how's that going? You are going to miss her some, I bet."

"You, too, right?"

"I will. I've been having this problem, this medical problem, and she was good to talk to about the different doctors to see."

"Oh. So what's the problem, Arquette?"

"I have what they call a non-specific, non-bacterial prostatitis that hurts like hell in the region, but I don't seem to get any answers around here as to what's causing it."

"How long has this been going on? What did Leda tell you to do?"

"I've had it for months. She told me to go to Boston to a teaching hospital and talk to them, and gave me the numbers to call. I mean, Aubrey, man, I don't even want to do you-know-what, and haven't for a long time. This thing is painful as hell. You ever had anything like this?"

Aubrey was surprised. Maybe Leda wasn't sleeping with Arquette, even though he did believe she was sleeping with that artist that disappeared. Maybe the conversations between them in the Goose were innocent when he was off at a rodeo.

"Are you going to Boston?"

"Monday."

The hospital at Mass General put him in a room with three other people. He was tired from the flight, and sitting for long periods seemed to aggravate what he had. He lay there in the dark, listening to the other patients breathe and cough. It could have picked any other body part, this curse. It could have been migraines, irritable bowel, leg numbness, but no, it went after his chi, as Melinda called it, the first chakra. Was it fueling his anxiety or was his anxiety fueling it? He had a few enemies. Someone had sent him a voodoo doll in the mail two months ago, wires running from the head to the crotch and the heart. Was it an old lover, or was it a pissed off customer from his rental company he had sued for nonpayment? Maybe the voodoo doll worked a spell on him? No. Crazy.

The next morning, one of the other patients in the room asked why he was there, and Arquette asked him the same.

"I got a bag," the man said. "Got all clogged up, you see. Had to go to surgery."

"What bag?"

The man flipped his sheets back. Arquette sat up and saw his first colostomy, brown and half-full. He lay back down. "What happened?"

"They told me it was the soft diet I ate. Not enough roughage."

The doctors wanted to put Arquette through something called the urodynamic study. The objective was to measure the pressure in the prostatic urethra against the normal pressure in the bladder. If the pressure in the urethra was higher than the one in the bladder, then they had their diagnosis and could prescribe a smooth muscle relaxer to relieve the problem. At the same time, he thought when these other patients asked him about his problem, he would lie to make them think it was more serious. How do you tell a man with a bag for an anus and a man in another bed with his throat cut out that you have a pain in your crotch?

That night, he dreamed about guilt. There was a manila file folder. He saw himself open it and find picture after picture of the women he had been with, women who were just ampules for his fluids and chronic anxiety. He was warm ice. All of them he wanted immediately out of his bed after he had finished, like so many meals, and he was paying for it now with this crotch infirmity fate sent him. Since he had become broken, if he just had one woman in his life that wasn't so sexual—happy not to do it all the time, happy with one climax for her and one for him, occasionally, then that might work. He knew Melinda probably loved him, but she was so horny, so sexually buckshot, he didn't think she would ever give up the three times-a-week stuff.

The next day was disappointment. The pressure difference in the two areas of his anatomy was not significant. One doctor told him he would like to do something he called "the big squeeze" under general anesthesia—reach up inside the colon with his whole hand like a fist fuck, grab the prostate, then squeeze the hell out it to break up any stubborn congestion. Arquette said he'd pass.

They gave him the smooth muscle relaxers anyway and told him to try them for a month. He went back to Jensen Beach, very down. He told Melinda that sometimes it felt like there was something in his anus, like a rough object, a stick, and he kept trying to put his finger on the place, but it was elusive. He added that it felt good to do that and wondered if a light dose of her animal immobilizer with the electric pulse would give him some relief, so they tried and made it worse. Arquette threw the apparatus against a wall.

"I remember you said that immobilizer affected some big nerve in animals. What was it called?"

"The pudendal nerve. It innervates the whole pelvic floor," she answered, but no one knew at the time that they were talking about Arquette's actual culprit, because the anatomical injury condition itself had not been discovered by medicine yet.

Melinda was able to talk him up with a version of "no touch" to climax by having her own. When he came, nothing came out. Nothing. He panicked. Melinda tried to comfort him. "They messed something up in Boston with that tube, I tell you. Messed something up. I'll sue those motherfuckers and their experimental shit. Just watch me."

Two nights later, he told Aubrey about the whole experience.

"Jesus, that sounds like 16th century medicine. So what are you going to do now?" Aubrey asked.

"I'm going to Mayo's next. Fuck this shit. American medicine! Medusa! M.E.D.U.S.A. Do you have a phone number for Leda? I mean, I would like to tell her what happened. I feel like I owe it to her for getting me hooked up with those guys at Mass General, even though I think they were a bunch of incompetents. Stick their whole hand up my ass and give my prostate a big squeeze. Not me. Run for your life! What are they, crazy?" Triple Suiter was scooting around in Aubrey's head after the story about the Boston doctors, singing, "Show me the money. Show me the money."

Aubrey gave him Leda's number. A week later, Arquette told his manager Sam Lillycrop he was in charge. He left town and told Melinda she could live in his house then went home to his parents and the farm in Massachusetts. Became the victim of anxiety and depression and sort of went off the edge after a trip to the Mayo Clinic had no answers for him, either. Only in the mid-nineteen nineties would the condition known as "pudendal nerve entrapment," or carpal tunnel of the pelvis, be discovered in France by a Dr. Roger Robert, when some of the gymnast and champion cyclists began to suffer because of intense splits, or the repetitive action of pedaling, that frayed the big nerve in their bodies. For the women, the pains from this, before they discovered the condition, were prejudicially written off as female hysteria. All of it, not true.

Chapter 23

THE SALOON SINGER

Aubrey and Frank Clark went to Tampa to record a soundtrack for a demo. The two were writing more songs than ever. What they farmed was a mix of rock and rock ballads that seemed to make people line up at the door of clubs. Aubrey had some blisters, but was sort of okay after Leda left. He guessed he always kept an easement around his heart for that. The only lack of sleep came from working every day and singing late nights with the band, who still snorted their share of coke and the heroin called Dr. Brown.

He wrote a fictional song he didn't want to sing in front of the band or people who knew Leda. In Tampa, he took a sound booth, just him and his guitar, while the rest of the band went down the street for lunch. He had written the ballad on a sofa in his house, the very one Leda would lie naked on, talking to the naked Arquette.

SOMEWHERE IN THE WORLD, THERE'S A BLEEDIN CAKE.

SOMEWHERE IN THE WORLD, THERE'S A BLEEDIN RAPE.

ONE NIGHT YOU GO TO SLEEP WITH YOUR HUS-BAND,

AND WHEN YOU WAKE UP, YOU'RE WITH THE MONKEY
MAN.

AND HE KNOWS WHAT YOU MEAN BY GETTIN DOWN,

TAKIN OFF AND WANTIN, DR. BROWN.

ALL MESSED UP IN THE GRIP OF YOUR JUNKIE HIGH,

SPREAD YOUR LEGS FOR PEGASUS,

ON WHITE HORSE YOU LOVE TO FLY.

Days later, on a Saturday, he and The Junior trucked to a small rodeo, and when they got back to the Z-Bar Up, they went gator hunting. There was a little too much moon, but they took Mr. Zarnitz's airboat to part of the ranch that was crawling with them.

"These goddamn blow boats make a lot of noise."

"You and I killed more with a little John boat," Aubrey answered.

They slid up into an open pond and cut the engine. Alligators are very curious. If you show up and just sit quiet, they will always come to the surface to see what you are doing, because they can't stand it. Aubrey stuck his hand in the water and splashed while he made a sound in his throat hard to spell in any language. He waited half a minute, switched on his headlamp, and scanned the pond until he saw the red eye. That meant The Junior's gray eye had only a three count to pull the trigger.

Boom! The water boiled. They paddled over to the spot and with cane pole hooks searched the bottom until they found the creature, still moving like a snake.

The next target was passed on. The distance between the nose and the eyes was about ten inches, and that meant the gator was ten feet long, too big for the thick hide to be worth anything. A "button hide," it was called.

Sunday morning, they skinned out the one gator, salted the hide, and rolled and tied it, as is the custom to cure. That night, they went to the Johnny Jumper Inn. The Junior won some money arm wrestling, and a hot girl named Sugar Cane Valdez from a powerful Cuban family that did just that went home with Aubrey and left the next morning.

On the beach with Chrome.

"You feel like doing a little religion with me today?" Chrome asked.

"Been awhile. Maybe."

"I've got some good MDA, if you'd rather."

"No, I think the acid sounds better. Might try the Miles Davis another time. Got all ganglioned-up in a movie the last time I did it."

They stationed themselves at a certain surf break close to the nuclear power plant. Australian pines grew on the dune where they could get out of the sun. After they surfed for at least an hour on the acid, they sat up under the trees.

"Pretty good out here," Chrome said. "Are you seeing some cool shit?"

"I am. I just hope it's mine."

"Meaning?"

"Really mine. Normally mine. Do you think what we see on this stuff is better than some of the new films we've seen? I mean, lately, with special effects and technology, I'm wondering if film isn't getting better than acid and has hijacked our religion."

"Don't fuck it up for me. Normal? I don't think there is anything normal about *your* visual tank."

"Yours, either, school teacher."

"So, man, tell me about the Key West Strangler."

"Strangleda. Haven't heard from her."

"Then tell me about your latest feats of carburetion, when, as you say, 'your whittle monster gets loose.'"

"How 'bout I tell you I have an Eiffel Tower in my head, and I talk to a little man dressed in a three-piece suit that sometimes lives in my armpit."

"Oh, here we go now. Turn on the recorder."

So Aubrey told him about the tower, the Ball jar, and Triple Suiter. At the end of it all, Chrome looked at him and said, "Not only does he write songs, folks, he writes that whacked out prose called fiction." Aubrey didn't know if Chrome believed any of what he revealed.

They went to the Goose to drink. Punky was there, and so was another band. The band asked Aubrey to come up and sing the high harmony behind one of their songs, and then asked him to sing one of his own, just him and an acoustic guitar while they took a break. He started this fast half-rap rendition of a word salad, acapella, and the whole bar room watched as he pranced around the stage, still high on the acid.

Harness all your jargon,

In words to the birds of prey,

Rip your flesh with eagle claws,

And the Sioux will laugh all day.

Shot put steel is a clock for you;

Carnival rides are things to do.

Ants will come and sit on your feet,

Bite you softly while you sleep.

Aw, hey, those ants put me away.

Aw, hey, those ants put me away.

Here's to the aging cowboy;

His coins have all been blessed.

The Reader's Digest comes in braille

To give his eyes a rest.

Oh, chewing your food is a definite sign

Of being alive and feeling fine.

Yes, Gene Autry sings to me

And feeds his horse philosophy.

Aw, hey, that cowboy puts me away.

The world is a crab-shaped Ball jar. . .

Chrome, Punky, and some other guy rushed the stage and dragged him back to his seat, while the barroom laughed and booed them for doing it. The regular band came back, pointing at Aubrey, because everybody in town knew Aubrey Shallcross, and like Sonny said that day years ago, when he saw the eight-year-old fishing for blue crabs on the sewer pipe downtown and talking intensely with someone that wasn't there, "That boy's not right."

"What in name of quantum doo-lang and relativity was that line about 'shot put steel is a clock for you'?" Chrome said.

Aubrey staggered a look and then turned into his man Head Wound. "When I asked this Benedictine monk once to define eternity, he said, 'Imagine, son, there is a sixteen-pound shot put inside a vacuum sealed case, and once a year, an ant appears inside the case, walks over the shot put, just once, and then goes back in the hole until the next year. However long it takes that ant to wear the shot put down to nothing but a tiny grain of sand is only the beginning of eternity.'" Then he winked at Chrome and said, "Feenished."

Now it was a life without her, and one of occasional female company, but he wasn't going to turn into Arquette. In fact, his home, his business, surfing, and music meant more to him than sex, though sex was nice when it came along. On a Friday night, he went out to Indiantown and the Johnny Jumper Inn, then stopped by his friend Henry's place to drink with some cowboy friends, Punky, The Junior, and a couple of tough looking girls from Okeechobee.

Henry was a taxidermist sought by hunters and fishermen. He did all the taxidermy in Aubrey's house. The house Henry lived in was full of his work, and in the living room was a big wagon wheel coffee table with a glass top. The table could be turned like a lazy Susan, and on the glass tonight came the coke lines, the shots of George Dickel bourbon, the joints, and the stories from the men.

Punky: "The Junior! What the biggest gator you ever seen?"

The Junior: "I seen one, one night, that looked about fifteen inches from nose to the eyes, that's fifteen feet, you know. I shot him like a fool, and he went to rollin, so I got my triple hook on him and then I seen this, like, big wave comin towards him, but I couldn't see what made the wave. Then ever'thing went quiet. When I got up to where he was, all that was left of my fifteen-foot gator was the head. Somethin had come up and bit him off right behind the neck. So that other one was the biggest gator I *never* saw."

Aubrey: "Hey, Henry, you ever see a hoop snake? The one that grabs its tail in its mouth and rolls like a tire to chase you or get away from an enemy?"

Henry: "No, there ain't no such a thing as them hoop snakes. Black people from the islands made up those stories."

As the night settled and bloodstreams began to fail the police, the conversation and bragging got more swollen. Someone finally talked Punky into doing his first line of cocaine. The Junior and Aubrey leaned forward from their seats to see it. Punky never touched anything but drink. He shook his head and wrinkled his nose, sat back, and waited. Then he wouldn't shut up and started in about Arquette. Not only had he always had a problem with him, he was sure Arquette ran off and met up with Leda somewhere in another town, no matter how often Aubrey told him he was back home in Massachusetts.

"I bet that Arquette had a little dick tween his legs, anybody talk that much about bangin beaver. He's probably one of them guys who was just tongue hung, and that's why all them women were after him. I asked him one time what size shoe he wore, and he wouldn't tell me. Rich motherfucker."

The whole time Punky was talking, he must have been loading a fart. Cocaine can be like morning coffee. When he stood and let it go, he shouted, "Arquette!" Everyone scattered and made another drink.

The crowd moved back to the male talk again. One man who rode the rodeo circuit with Aubrey and The Junior said he was in El Paso for a big rodeo, and his friends took him over the border into Juarez to "get bred," as they put it. They went to the first bar, got ladies, and went toward the back rooms, until he stopped when he saw a condom machine. He was fishing for change to buy one when he noticed a penicillin machine next to the condom machine. "So I turned and ran!" The crowd around the table cheered.

Another guy said when he was growing up his father caught his big brother screwing a huge teddy bear he won when the Future Farmers went to the State Fair. He said his brother had taken a rubber dishwashing glove and fashioned a tube out of it about the size of what he thought a vagina should be. Then he put baby oil in it and made it warm with his father's big round soldering iron. The father slapped him around when he walked in on him humping his creation, and then took the teddy bear with him to the VFW and showed it to his buddies for a laugh.

Punky interrupted. "I got one for you better'n that. Me and my brother grew up next to this family that farmed vegetables, and watermelon was their biggest crop. They had two boys older'n us, and we got jobs loadin watermelon to get shipped up north on their trucks. Do you know those two assholes used to cut a round hole the size their dicks could get through in them big melons, and when it was hot as hell, about one in the afternoon, they'd fuck one or two of those things. And what d'you think? They'd put the perfect cut-out from the hole back in, so you couldn't tell they'd been in there, then they'd load 'em on the truck. They said, 'These melons are goin to New York City. Wait'll those Yankees get a mouth full a-that one.' Man, I ain't never ate watermelon since. Won't even touch one."

That blew up the room. Somebody spilled their drink. Aubrey said to The Junior, "Like Arquette used to say, 'Punky knows how to bring out the ick factor.'"

An hour later, there was laughter and cheering in a room off the living room. Aubrey went in to see, and there was one of the big-chested

Okeechobee girls on her knees with her top off. Someone said, "Next!" and this country kid, maybe twenty years old, knelt down in front of her. She said, "You ready, honey?" The young man nodded, and she pushed one large breast under one arm, and the other breast under the other arm, and held them there while the kneeling man put his nose on her sternum. There was quiet. Then someone yelled, "Hands up!" She raised her arms and the breasts flew out from her armpits and smacked the kid on either side of his face.

Aubrey left after Hands Up. He drove the back roads late through the ranch country. At his gate, he looked down the lane towards his house, and there were no lights on. Just a dark shape. Not like the time he'd been in the cemetery, just him and Trip, and came home to the house Leda had lit it up as bright as Punky was tonight after he snorted the cocaine. Then it started on the truck's radio again. That song of Bette Middler's, "The Rose." When it got to the part that said love was like a flower, and that we are its only seed, Aubrey began to cry. Triple Suiter and Amper Sand stayed quiet. They let the mortal drain. Amper Sand typed the angel prayer on Trip's chest.

ANGEL OF GOD, MY GUARDIAN DEAR,

TO WHOM GOD'S LOVE YOU HOLD ME NEAR,

EVER THIS DAY BE AT MY SIDE,

TO LIGHT, TO GUARD, TO RULE, AND TO GUIDE.

AMEN

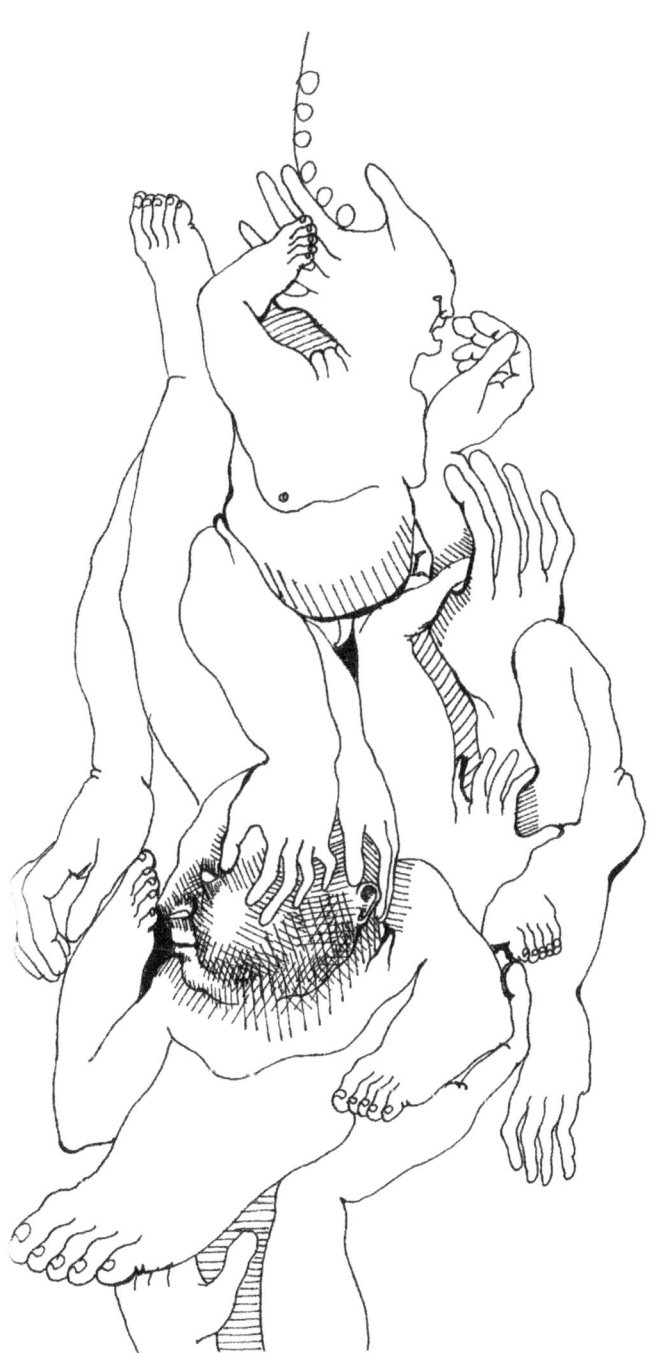

Chapter: 24

ALONE

He was alone, but with space and certain beatitudes. It had been ten years with Leda. Lately, he felt good without her. Maybe the worry of her jumpy behavior, the cloy her ego took every day to make her feel good, instead of watching her smoke and brood. Life with a blind exalter, and yet he knew he had it in him, too.

He tried so hard at the business, even slept there on the couch in his office, and when he had free time, took to flying to cities, mountains, deserts, beaches in California to surf the famous spots. He often brought Chrome with him and paid for the ticket; the car business was making money. Sometimes, in the past, he had talked The Junior into flying to prize fights: Sugar Ray Leonard, Marvin Hagler, Roberto Duran. It was a kind of freedom that thrilled even the most lost.

There were parties at his place that mixed every kind of citizen. After the stuffy people went home, he and his other friends would practice their antics, run out to the late night bars or the Goose. Sometimes in costume. All the clothes would come off Little Alex or Johnny Yuma from the displays in his house, and he would wear them. A girlfriend made him a sandhill crane outfit for Halloween, and he liked to walk in the woods around his farm as the giant bird; the normal birds were terrified when they saw him. The eighties were working their way through, straining everyone. The things your mother taught you about not spending the night at Johnny's too often or you'd "wear out your welcome," had turned into wear it out anyway. When your mother said, "Don't take advantage of people, it's not polite"; now, it was "Get up in their face!"

Chrome and Rose showed up at an Aubrey party very high on acid one night. Chrome had just seen a movie called *Starman* with Jeff Bridges and tried to explain it to Rose as he handed out single pills of MDA to people drinking and talking. Chrome told everyone the pills would make them immortal, or if they had a crippled friend, they should give a pill to them and they would walk again. The Junior had to haul Chrome out of the house, put him by the pool, and talk him down.

A week later, Rose rented *Starman* so she could see for herself what her Chromie was talking about. Together, they sat at home with Aubrey after feeding him dinner and watched a damaged star ship land in a Wisconsin lake. A glowing alien light came out of the lake on a summer cabin lawn, where a recently widowed young woman lived. There was a picture in the cabin of her handsome late husband with a lock of his hair, and the alien light cloned itself from the hair into the image of the husband, which happened to be Jeff Bridges.

The young widow was terrified at first, but the Jeff Bridges clone managed to calm her and talk her into driving him to Arizona, where he would meet a space ship from his planet to take him home again. The clone had with him a number of steel balls the size of marbles, used to perform miracles; that's where Chrome, so gone and hallucinating at Aubrey's party, got the idea the MDA pills were the same miraculous little balls the star man had, until the acid Chrome took wore off.

Along the way to Arizona, there were many challenges for the star man and the young widow, but the little steel balls managed to get them out of every crisis. They finally made it to the crater, thanks to the young widow, who made love to the star man in a railway car the night before the spaceship was to come and was now pregnant with his child. The child would look completely human, he told her, but would have supernatural powers, like the man named Jesus on Punky's anti-abortion bumper sticker that said: He too, was once a fetus.

After seeing the movie, Rose, who was pretty much out of any normal serotonin re-uptake abilities because of inveterate drug use, snorted a line of Dr. Brown and made a drug-assisted decision. She

300

now believed the star man, even though it's just a movie, was still watching the site in Arizona where he was picked up as Jeff Bridges. Rose thought the star man was real and waiting up above for the young widow and the new baby, who Rose also thought were real, to come back to the crater. She was convinced the star man would swoop down and get the widow, and maybe take Rose with them. She left Chrome a note explaining all this, said she loved him, but felt she had to get as far away from Jensen Beach as possible, and late that night, she headed for the crater in Arizona to wait with the movie widow for the space ship to return. Another planet was what Rose had in mind, to distance herself from heroin and The South Florida Book of the Dead. She thought that maybe the star man had a friend up there for *her*.

No one hears from Rose anymore.

At the Goose, the men from the old bunch sat a corner table: Aubrey, The Junior, Punky, and Chrome; Arquette is still in the north, holed up on the family farm, and Melinda never came around much after Arquette left. Chrome is without Rose, Aubrey without Leda, and it has been months since he heard from her. The Junior has been kicked out by his girl, Thimble Taylor, for thumping her brother after an argument, and Punky's Donna is home with the kids.

"Oh, would y'all look at us," The Junior said. "What a buncha cowboy lonely-lookin fuckers."

"Speak for yourself, god damn it. My squeeze is home with the kids where she belongs," said Punky.

"You okay, Mr. Chrome?" Aubrey asked.

"I think so. I did lose my old lady to a movie and an alien, and I don't believe there is a lot of advice around from counselors for that. Think we ought to try a round of 'Oh, Yeahs' in memory of the disappeared?"

"You go first," said Aubrey.

"Another drink, though, if you please," Chrome hollered. "I need an orthograde look to my posture to come up with some decent 'Oh, yeahs.'" So they ordered: Chrome, a Bombay Sapphire and tonic; Aubrey, a sidecar; Punky and The Junior, a shot of George Dickel bourbon.

"Before our 'Oh, yeahs,' I'd like to ask Mr. Chrome, our Master of Fine Arts, to give us an overview on the man-woman thing," Aubrey said. "Mr. Chrome, please."

Chrome stood. "I believe it is the oldest riddle. Freud tried to say something, but he was a nineteenth-century sexist, so there is too much umbrage there. I can only see it as forever debatable, but one could take the humorous approach and say pieces of things others have said that I remember: Every man secretly wants a virgin that is a whore. Every woman secretly wants a handsome, kind rapist. Finished." The table applauded.

Chrome: "For all those men in the world in love with thin-lipped women. Oh, yeah!"

Aubrey: "For all those in love with *femme fatales*. Oh, yeah!"

The Junior: "For them what kisses swamp angels that turn into mosquitos. Oh, yeah!"

Punky: "For them what eats on a watermelon they don't know was fucked by a country boy. Oh, yeah!"

"You know," Chrome said. "There is also an old cliché. 'If a man steals your woman, the best revenge is to let him have her.' So I'm telling the star man tonight—Mr. Jeff Bridges, you can have her."

"Oh, yeah to that. Y'all oughta just go git you some strange and forget about them others," Punky said.

"Ah," yelled Chrome. "Same stripe as the ancient cure for hypochondria: get more interested in someone else's body than your own."

They went home from the Goose half drunk. In the dark, their empty bedrooms became space where they reached for something in place of their absent lovers: The Junior for ozone, Aubrey for the neon light switch, Chrome for safe candles that made smoke instead of chlo-

302

roform. In New England, Arquette reached for his nitrous oxide, while somewhere in Miami, Leda tapped out another cigarette and watched the streetlights as the gas from Winston Salem filled her lungs. And down by the creek in his double wide at the edge of town, Sonny lay on a bed with a small bottle of Freon, and like Aubrey, he wondered if there was a god, and if there was, how would he get redemption for those murders he committed.

The next night, the men tried the cure Punky had suggested at the Goose for loneliness. Chrome made love to a beach bunny the surfer boys had nicknamed "Outrageous" on the top deck of Aubrey's house. The Junior found a ranch girl that went about 5' 8" 170 lbs. Punky went home to Donna because he was getting too drunk lately to mess around on her. And Aubrey kept climbing a religious country girl that would look at him, his house, and the bidet in his bathroom and ask, "Why do you have two toilets in there?" She said he was the devil, to make her feel overpowered and guiltless about the sex, he guessed, and she searched through his scalp for the tattooed number 666 when he was trying to sleep.

Aubrey would flash on Leda when things like this happened with other women and say to himself, "I think I've gone from Vermont pure maple to Aunt Jemima." Even though Leda was a full time job, she *was* pure maple.

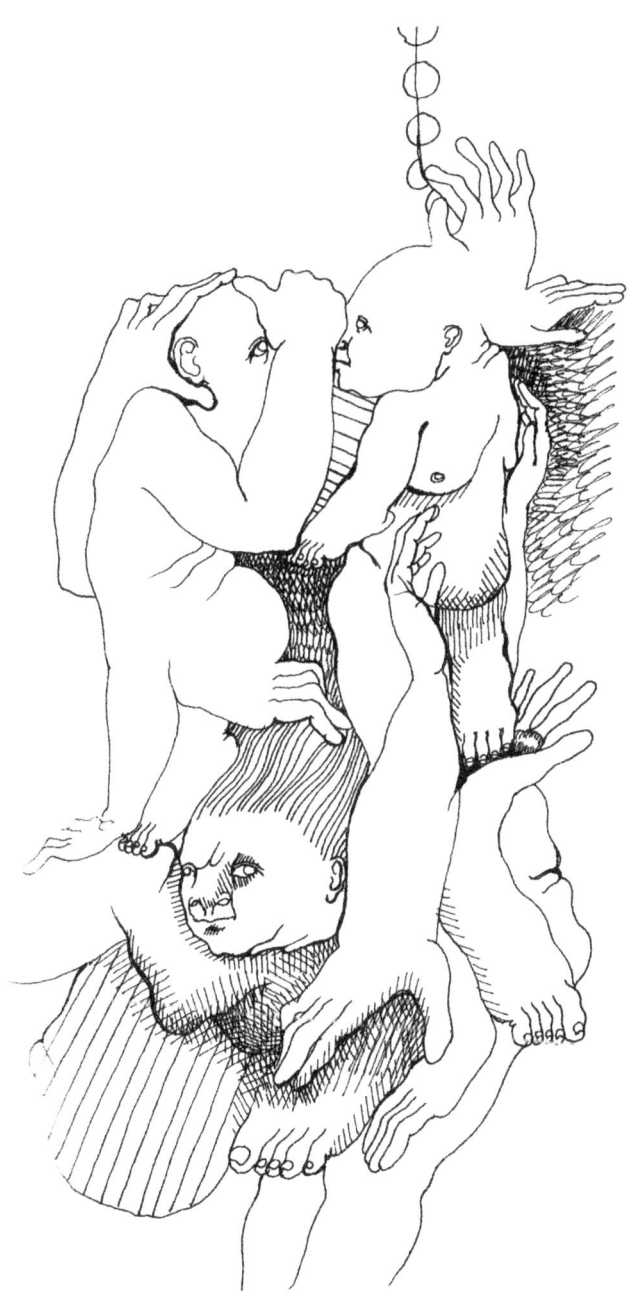

Chapter 25

SONNY

There is a saying among the country people. "He did that until he went bowlegged blind." It's sort of their way of referring to Sisyphus rolling the stone, yet it amuses the country folk, and they smile when they think about it—the bowlegs, not Sisyphus. Same as "Work your fingers to the bone/ and what do you get?/ Bony fingers." Nietzsche said we should imagine Sisyphus happy so we can get through life, but the country people knew things Nietzsche didn't—song lines like, "If religion were something money could buy/ then the rich would live and the poor would die/ all my trials, Lord/ soon be over."

Sonny *was* going bowlegged blind. It was the Freon he'd huffed all these years. The small amounts added up. The medicine book said it would, and now he suffered sight problems, memory loss, chronic throat and esophagus pain, heart arrhythmia, and nerve damage that made flame vines in his body.

Lined up on the lawn of his place stood the last trash-pile refrigerator, snatched from country road dumps. It talked to him. "Come to me," it said. "Open my door, get inside, and close it. It's all okay. All is forgiven if you do this for the others you put in here."

The psychosis child is two people. One kicks his side of the seesaw up and makes the normal child in him go down on the other side until that normal child kicks his side higher than the psychotic child and appears normal again. On and on, they trade this appearance back and forth, until something happens. Maybe something awful. Maybe something good. This was what Sonny was like, and when the normal child in him kicked his side higher, he felt guilt and hate for what he'd done to those people he killed. It was harder on him, this guilt, now that his other faculties were going from the Freon. "Come to me," the old icebox in his yard said all day. "My door works fine. Climb inside. Hear the latch go 'click'!"

In and out of lucid, he was trying to stay *in* long enough to born a plan. It was over, and he wasn't going to jail or something like a leprosarium again. He wasn't going anywhere but in the ground on his property inside one of those boxes. But who would help him disappear? Who would bury him where Our Lady of White Appliances could watch over him forever? Half Track would, the special needs man from the Harris Ranch. Yes, he'd figure out how he could stay straight enough to become one final creation of self-containment in the last of his Coolerators. A beautiful ending, he thought. His last piece. Ship in a Bottle. In case there was any evil left in him, it couldn't get out and hurt someone else as he decayed.

He had closed the bookstore years ago. Every day lately was spent on dirt roads, looking for one more abandoned refrigerator in a dumpsite so he could bury his murder gear, his masks, and ligature before he had himself buried. He finally found one with the door still on. The struggle to get it in his truck bed, the pain in his throat from frostbite scars the Freon had made, the days his body temperature went up and down, the dizziness and blood in his toilet, the insomnia, and headaches.

Two large tanks of the gas were in a corner of his double wide. What to do with them? The creek by his house. Sink them. One at a time, he dragged the big cylinders. Turtles on logs, three in row; a seven-foot gator; anhinga drying their wings; and marsh hens bitching about his appearance all watched what was left of the high school football hero from 1950 roll and push the containers deep into the creek, sending those creatures into the water so they could swim away from the crazy man swimming towards them.

Inside his place he huffed on a bottle he was saving for his death trip, his trip to the north, over to the east, and then west to the City of the Dead, as the Seminole man explained to The Junior and Freddie Tommie that day.

Feeling high, crazy, and wrong-strong, he dug a hole in the yard for one of the old units and loaded the box with his tin snips, ropes, handcuffs, and any other evidence someone might find. The next day, Half Track came. Sonny pointed to the refrigerator in the ground, and told him to bury it after placing a five-dollar bill on the closed door with a piece of Scotch tape. The day after, he had Half Track bury some more things for practice and placed money on them. Half Track would retrieve the money, cover the stuff with dirt, level the ground, plant some small plants on top, and water the spot with a hose. Sonny taught him to put his finger up to his mouth and go, "Shhh."

There would be more of these burials, while Sonny got weirder and weirder at night from his pain and huffing—waking hallucinations, throat ablaze, nose and anus bleeding over his sheets, and a fierce compunction for the mutilations in his past, though he thought most of those grown-ups had it coming.

He went to the Goose one final time and drank a sidecar, even though it hurt his throat. Annie the waitress, who always took care of him, gave him a hug when he told her in his raspy voice he was going away for a long time. As he leaned in and put his arms around her, the good slipper that lived inside him slipped to Annie through her nose, and as it did, looked back and regretted he could never help Sonny again with the bad slipper that lived in his mind. Sonny went home, just him and the bad slipper, who was as destructive as Sonny.

The next day, he shoved the last refrigerator on its back in the hole he dug, so the door opened upward, easy as a coffin's. He was satisfied his ranch neighbor, Half Track, would be able to do his job. Take the five-dollar bill he had taped to the outside of the door, bury the box without looking inside, and let Sonny disappear.

In the box he had placed some of his favorite things—pictures of him, Aubrey, and The Junior in front of the book store when they were younger and one of Nell with her aunt. He put just one ship in a bottle in, the Charles W. Morgan whaler, the first one he had ever made in the craft shop of the leprosarium at Carville. And last, he put in his blanket he kept all these years from when he was a little boy.

Inside and outside every town, there are marginal people. Morrison said there's "danger at the edge of town," and Sonny was and took it to his strange grave. How many are in graves around us? How many circle a city limits? Aubrey looked up to Sonny when he was a boy because Sonny read all those cool books and played guitar. Aubrey was lucky to have his mother and father. Sonny looked down from that corner apartment next to Aubrey's house and wondered what it was like to live like that and have that kind of home life.

Sonny took one of his last huffs standing by the creek, walked over to the hole, climbed down in the box, and curled himself in the only position that will let a body fit in there. He rolled his childhood blanket so it made concentric rings of the edges, and rubbed his palm on it until the sensation came that made him suck his tongue back so he could Mort and take huffs on a small bottle of Freon, Sonny's bottle, and his own kind of Ball jar in a way. He saw a hallucination of his mother coming towards him with Mortimer Snerd, and she carried the coconut head she had made with eyes and seashells for buckteeth. Before she could get there, Sonny knocked the stick out holding the refrigerator door open and heard the latch go *click*!

Some stories end with a noise, one louder than the sound of that *click* Sonny heard, but most just end like another day in your life or your death, not remarkable, as your heart stops, or the other car hits your driver's side before you can register anything. It might have a single sound to it, like that *click*.

The day Sonny died, Aubrey was at work, and later sank down in bed listening to the big owls calling in the dark outside his house. Soon he went to the anteroom of his sleep, what he lately called the Quaalude Lounge. The voices came.

"Pick a film, Aubrey, any film."

"*Breathless*, from 1960. I want to see Seberg. I want to see Nell."

"Yes, Aubrey," the voices said.

"Mansion," he whispered and slipped away.

~

Four years have passed. Aubrey has not heard anything from Leda or Arquette; a lot has happened to the Goose bunch. Aubrey sold the car dealership when he turned forty-two, and he is still on his own. He sings on occasion with the band, whose new members decided to change the group's name for a fresh start, but he still loves the original name, Cricket Jar, for personal reasons. The Junior and Punky quit the moonshine business. "Got to be a pain in the ass," they agreed. Aubrey quit street drugs after Leda left and is taking a new prescription for sleep called Trazadone, instead of Quaalude, and thinks it is a better usher for coloration in his dreams. His visits from the Slim Hand have slowed down to next to nothing, and so did finding his terrified self in the Blind Spot Cathedral. He hasn't shown Trip the big room in his head to date, only described it to him that night in the cemetery, and Trip hasn't explained his old host from his past, Dr. Corpus Columbus, to Aubrey, either. He is holding that out for a trade later, so to speak.

Punky sold his lawn mower shop to a guy named Charlie. Charlie's wife Janet now works at the Randolph Diner, or as Trip calls it, The Catheter Café, and waits on Aubrey every morning. John Chrome is a single man still teaching at the high school, and Nell Kitching is still in the Palm Beach Home for Rest.

Aubrey was brushing his teeth in front of his bathroom mirror after work one night, and of all things, thought of Sonny's mother, the dental lady who used to pinch him when he was eight years old and warn him to brush correctly or, she told him, a man named Mortimer Snerd would get him. He drove into town later for a drink on the river at the Blue Goose, the great rum shrine of Jensen Beach, a bar based on the short-sleeved shirt.

~

One evening, I sat in Aubrey's brain around a campfire with six of my friends, slippers from the minds of Leda, Arquette, The Junior, Punky, John Chrome, and Sonny. We laughed and talked about people who think those who hear another voice are crazy, yet they talk to Yahweh, Krishna, and Wakan Tanka and say these gods talk to them.

These friends of mine, these good slippers, all of whom I have spoken to over the years, told me about their lives with their hosts, and that is how I know the stories of the others in *this* story. And because I have been with Aubrey since he was a small child, I know how his life began, and how it will one day end, to be told "Another Time," as the song said that split him open that day he and Leda were so blazed on the drug called MDA.

All that I have written in this book is in the *True* magazine, mostly. I'm Triple Suiter.

Finished

Interview

Conversation With Ken Braddick
And Charles Porter

Kenneth J. Braddick, the original creator of *Horse Sport USA,* a magazine focused on high-performance dressage and jumping all over the world, is also a veteran news correspondent and has covered major events and several wars around the globe. Braddick is the owner of Dressage News.com based in Wellington, Florida, one of the epicenters for elite sport horses in the winter. Mr. Braddick interviewed Charles Porter for the novel, *Shallcross*, published in 2015.

KB: So, Charlie, here we are again.

CP: Yeah, you and I could always talk about this kind of stuff. I liked the questions you asked about the first novel.

KB: This is the second novel about your protagonist, Aubrey Shallcross, the first novel simply having your main character's last name for the title.

CP: It's Aubrey's life from 8 yrs. old until he's in his early forties. The other book starts when Aubrey is forty-two. They don't have to be read in order though.

KB: What do you have to say about this new book, *Flame Vine*? How would you describe the feel of it?

CP: Historical, hallucinatory. A kind of bildungsroman, the big word for a young man's life story like, *Tom Jones* or Henry Miller's *Tropic of Cancer*. Also a drop of that famous old Broadway play, *A Death in the Family*, and the Greek one by Aristophenes, before Christ, *Do the God's Exist?* Or something like that.

KB: You planned it that way?

CP: I don't think so. Just sort of comes around for me and my friend.

KB: You mean, Triple Suiter?

CP: Him, and the rest of the whittle monsters. You tell me who those voices are people hear in their head, those so-called schizophrenics.

KB: I don't know the answer to that. Do you remember a lot of what you wrote?

CP: It's free indirect style—drifty sometimes. I might be a little short on the recollection.

KB: Explain.

CP: Well I remember the storytelling parts of the book. But you're talking about the head trope of a schizophrenic man, Aubrey Shallcross, and his schizophrenic slipper, Triple Suiter, who's other voice is named, Amper Sand, and I'm not sure who Amper Sand talks to, all on the back of the infinite regression you see in a three way mirror or the old picture of the Quaker Oat man on the Quaker Oat box when I was a kid. I mean, how can you track that exactly? Maybe look for the footprints of the lady inside the Tin Snip Killer's refrigerator in the story, holding a picture of herself holding a picture of herself in the refrigerator like the Quaker Oat man, her eyes on the infinity code HTML:&#8734, her image getting smaller and smaller in the picture of the picture of herself until she's so slim she disappears.

KB: That's a thicket. How did you assemble that?

CP: I didn't. The Greeks did. And that HTML thing is Microsoft's software code for infinity. Also Cervantes presented that type of regression when he wrote the second *Don Quixote* book. The book opens with a man, Quixote, reading a story about a man who's reading a story about a man, who's reading a story about himself in a book, on out to the abyss.

KB: Ah, your main character, Aubrey Shallcross, is a Quixote and has a fear of disappearing by the means of infinite regression?

CP: Yes it is one of the main themes of the book, that, self-erasure, fear, and attacking hallucinations, and the joys in between. Aubrey is afraid when he dies he will get smaller and smaller until he disappears forever. And he is afraid in the meantime he will he'll go insane from the tenebrific terror of the Blind Spot Cathedral that comes to him after he passes out when he thinks about disappearing after he dies. A little like that famous take on existence from Milan Kundera, *The Unbearable Lightness of Being.* But it's his other voice, Triple Suiter, that makes him feel better about all this.

KB: But why so afraid of that?

CP: Haven't you ever wondered who you really are and what happens after this? Do you completely disappear? Haven't you ever had a fear of going insane about that?

KB: You've got me thinking about it.

CP: Good. You can suffer with the rest of us.

KB: So you like that South Florida landscape . . . that setting.

CP: I'm as hopped-up as Kerouac about it. But I think anybody can write about where they're from forever.

KB: But why do you write this particular story?

CP: I have a Slim Hand inside of me, like Aubrey, a bad voice. I write this to accentuate Aubrey's good voice, Triple Suiter, and that helps me attenuate my bad voice, just like it helps Aubrey muffle his bad voice when he has Triple Suiter.

KB: Do you have a good voice, other than in the stories you write?

CP: I wish I did. But no, at least not yet.

KB: Ever get treated for that.

CP: Reluctantly. You can't really treat it. I always quit the medicine.

KB: Describe Aubrey, here in this interview.

CP: A half breed. A normal man with a few talents and a few normal life experiences, and the other part of him is the man best described in the first *Shallcross* novel. An unencumbered free-baser that bears down on his red means run senses every day; a *connoissuer* of the psycho-generated souvenir, and an auteur of the third eye pie; so with carburetion like that, you can easily be unhorsed and chased through the doors of your own rectum and once again, disappear.

KB: I wanted to ask you about the drawings in the book. You put drawings in the first book at the beginning of the chapters.

CP: These are drawings by Kathy Von Ertfelda. She is a special kind of artist and her drawings land on a lot of what I consider the mental imagery in the book.

KB: Some are very bizarre.

CP: So is some of this story. I like drawings in books. Reminds me of film. I feel like I write film.

KB: In your other book, *Shallcross*, you talked about the third eye pie and you even mention *Naked Lunch*.

CP: I did? Oh well then, this book, *Flame Vine*, is *Love in the Time of Lunch*, *Love in the Time of Lyrica*.

KB: Lyrica? That drug on TV all the time.

CP: Yeah it's an anti-seizure drug actually that works for nerve pain. Well I mean Aubrey doesn't take it in this story, he takes Qualuudes at night to sleep, and they take him down to the lounge where the voices come and tell him to pick a film.

KB: Do you take Lyrica?

CP: Getting close to my air puck aren't you? But yes I have. I took it for a while for nerve pain after a horse accident. Then I found it helpful for the other part, the part that calms you down when something is trying to chase you through the doors of your own rectum.

KB: So tell me about the historical part of the book—the 60's, 70's, and 80's.

CP: Briefly:

The 60's were idealism vs. realism.

The 70's were a long boring transition to the 80's.

The 80's were that old Greek quote in Flame Vine that goes: "First secure an independent income, then practice virtue."

KB: What about the hallucinatory part of this book.

CP: Well, it's accounted for in the story. The Blue Goose Bunch was doing hallucinogenic drugs. But of course Aubrey had his own hallucinations without any drugs, because of the way his mind was.

KB: Another personal question. A tap root question. Do you have hallucinations?

CP: More as I get older. Mostly auditory. Some visual . . . sometimes, but very few. I wouldn't admit to that when I was younger or in the other interviews. If it gets really loud, there's a drug called Seroquel, and yes, it's an anti-psychotic drug. But I've been in good shape without cheaters lately and I can never do it more than a week because I hate it. It's been a couple of years that I had to do anything. Those drugs, especially Seroquel, will turn you into an eggplant. Like Kesey used to say, "The fog rolls in." Eggplant fog. Aubergine fog. Funny, I used to do mushrooms to open doors when I was young, now I do a prescription if I need it to keep them closed. But I always heard that other voice stuff, even as a kid.

KB: Do you belong to the Hearing Voices Network that you always dedicate your books to?

CP: I don't. But I think it's a great thing. There are all kinds of voice hearers in those meetings. Some aren't too happy, but a lot of others have good voices they listen to or deal with, even though some of their old bad voices linger. It's kind of like an AA for them, where they support each other.

KB: What else should we discuss.

CP: Up to you.

KB: I hate this question, but in the name of cliché journalism, I have to ask it—what is this book about, other than the storytelling parts?

CP: Here's the way I see it in both books, *Flame Vine* and *Shallcross*. The books are like the contrast between Jules Verne and Rimbaud, the French poet. The "righty-tighty" expression in Flame Vine is the perfect enclosure of Verne's safe place, the Nautilus, in *20,000 Leagues Under the Sea*. The "lefty- loose" expression is Rimbaud's *Drunken Boat*—open chaos—Camus stuff. The rest is the Slim Hand cramming one or the other down our throat. Jim Morrison was chaos, raising hell about everything and wanting everyone to get their life down to their naked lunch. It reminds me of the word palindrome in Shallcrosss: "You can cage a swallow can't you, but you can't swallow a cage, can you." Morrison didn't want us to swallow any shit, so he might have swallowed it for us in that Paris bathtub his last night on earth. I don't know, and I don't think he really knew either. More chaos. Aubrey Shallcross had relief from all this, it was when he was running with the Blue Goose Bunch, sitting on a good horse, singing in front of his band, or surfing with John Chrome. And it was when he would pretend he was a roseate spoonbill in the mangroves of the Indian River, and go under his wing to dream. What else can you do?

KB: Yeah mansion, finished. Thanks. Oh! One more thing. I presume there will be a sequel to the first *Shallcross* book, to complete the trilogy.

CP: Yes.

Questions and Topics for Discussions

There are two worlds!
But they cannot be explained by Plato, only schizophrenia.
—Triple Suiter

1. Do you think Charles Porter is suggesting there is another world inside the human head that explains everything like heaven, Hades, a parallel universe, or Plato's shadow land, by introducing us to the bicameral mind of the schizophrenic? Do you think Porter is saying the brain itself is the land of spirits, and that voices like Triple Suiter's are souls who live in that world in the form of what he calls slippers? Is this world, in fact, an unknown segment of existence?

2. Do the Slim Hands actions in the story represent religion being crammed down our throats like the large objects Aubrey thinks are in *his* throat, when he blacks out and goes to the Blind Spot Cathedral?

3. After reading Flame Vine, if you were standing in an old Catholic cathedral and looked up at the high domed ceiling from the basilica area, would you see a blind spot? God? Just the ceiling?

4. Who do you think is the real narrator of Flame Vine: Charles Porter or Triple Suiter?

5. Do you buy the suggestion in the end, that Triple Suiter wrote this book? The last three paragraphs of the book suddenly go from the third person to the first person narrative, and Trip says, "I sat in Aubrey's brain around a campfire with six of my friends—slippers from the minds of Leda, Arquette, The Junior, Punky, John Chrome, and Sonny. These slippers told me everything about their hosts." Does this tell us how Trip could know them well enough to take their points of view, write their thoughts, conversations, and give us his own thoughts in the narrative?

6. When Aubrey and Triple Suiter were in the cemetery talking, were you attracted to the idea proffered to Aubrey by Trip, that each of us should try to braid our own idea of why we are here, what the universe means to us, and whether we want to believe in a force or higher power of our choosing?

7. What does one learn over the course of this novel about a person who hears voices yet can function well and unnoticed in society? Would you be interested in finding out more about the Hearing Voices Movement to which this book is dedicated?

SHALLCROSS

The Blindspot Cathedral

A NOVEL

"Surreal, poetic, and unforgettable:
a truly original voice."

KIRKUS REVIEWS

"Unfailingly original..."

BLUEINK REVIEWS

Charles Porter

SHALLCROSS

Animal Slippers

GISELA

CHARLES PORTER

ISBN: 9780989425643 (paperback)
ISBN: 9780989425650 (ebook)